also by
JESSICA PETERSON

LUCKY RIVER RANCH
Cash
Wyatt
Sawyer
Duke

JESSICA PETERSON

Bloom books

Copyright © 2026 by Jessica Peterson
Cover and internal design © 2026 by Sourcebooks
Cover art © Jenny Richardson

Sourcebooks, Bloom Books, and the colophon are
registered trademarks of Sourcebooks.

All rights reserved. No part of this book may be reproduced in any form or by
any electronic or mechanical means including information storage and retrieval
systems—except in the case of brief quotations embodied in critical articles or
reviews—without permission in writing from its publisher, Sourcebooks.

No part of this book may be used or reproduced in any manner for the
purpose of training artificial intelligence technologies or systems.

The characters and events portrayed in this book are fictitious or
are used fictitiously. Any similarity to real persons, living or dead,
is purely coincidental and not intended by the author.

Published by Bloom Books, an imprint of Sourcebooks
1935 Brookdale RD, Naperville, IL 60563–2773
(630) 961-3900
sourcebooks.com

Library of Congress Cataloging-in-Publication Data

Names: Peterson, Jessica (Jessica L.)
Title: Duke / Jessica Peterson.
Description: Naperville, IL : Bloom Books, 2025. | Series: Lucky River
 Ranch ; 4
Identifiers: LCCN 2025030900 | trade paperback
Subjects: LCGFT: Romance fiction | Novels | Fiction
Classification: LCC PS3616.E842865 D85 2025
LC record available at https://lccn.loc.gov/2025030900

Printed and bound in the United States of America.
KP 10 9 8 7 6 5 4 3 2 1

For all the cowgirls and cowboys playing the long game: Your perseverance will pay off. Patience is everything! And so are honky-tonk hotties in jeans that fit just right.

CHAPTER 1
Bull's-eye
Wheeler

NOVEMBER

That's my cowboy.

I know it three heartbeats into the extended eye contact I make with the tall, broad-shouldered blond who greets me with a smile as I walk into the ranch's enormous kitchen. He's the kind of handsome in his faded button-up and baseball hat that makes my stomach do several backflips.

It's my first time visiting Lucky Ranch, so I have no idea if cowboys in general are this friendly and gorgeous or if this guy is special. Whatever the case, I don't hate it.

"I'm Duke." He extends a hand. "Pleasure to finally meet the gal Mollie's always talking to about boots on the phone. And about banging—"

"Can you not be gross for five fucking seconds?" Cash rolls his eyes. He's my best friend and business partner Mollie's boyfriend. He's also Duke's older brother.

Cash can be gruff, but as evidenced by his smile, he's a secret softie. That smile probably has something to do with the fact that Mollie is tucked into his side, her eyes sated and happy as she looks up at him. They've been dating for all of two months, but it's obvious they're smitten.

"Banging *business ideas*." Duke's lips twitch. He looks a lot like Cash. Blue eyes. Square, Superman-like jaw. "Just showing respect where respect is due. As co-CEO of her own damn company, Miss Wheeler Rankin here knows what I'm talking about. Ain't that right?"

I laugh as I take his hand. Mollie told me cowboys are a different breed, but I didn't believe her until now.

The guy already knows my last name. Does that mean something?

That has *to mean something*. Mollie must've really talked up my arrival, and Duke must've really been paying attention. The idea makes a shiver of excitement dart up my spine.

The kitchen is full of people, their voices rising and falling in a happy kind of chaos. The space is clearly built to accommodate a crowd, with a huge island and a farm table with room for at least twenty.

Warmth blooms in my center. Feels good to laugh and be around people. Get out of my head for a minute.

Duke holds my hand—holds my gaze—with warm, intense confidence. His grip is firm.

"Nice to finally meet you too," I reply.

Be careful, a voice inside my head warns as I stare into his eyes for a beat too long.

But then I remember my stay here on the ranch is temporary. Stumbling into any kind of real emotional intimacy is impossible when you're literally and figuratively all over the place. Which is why I'm only looking for some no-strings-attached fun right now. Considering cowboys have a reputation for never resting their heads on the same pillow twice, I figured they'd be a perfect fit.

There are five Rivers brothers, all of them part of a long line of ranchers going back generations. Is being charming and gorgeous and so damn…big in every aspect part of their DNA?

Dallas may only be two hundred miles northeast of here, but you'd think the ranch was on a whole other planet for how different these cowboys are from the guys back home. Men there will approach you, but their friendliness is all pretense. All a show of swagger. But Duke here? His friendly energy feels genuine, like this is who he is all the time.

I also adore how he drops compliments that actually land.

Guys back in Dallas definitely don't have hands this calloused. A hot, lovely drip of awareness works its way through my center at the feel of Duke's palm pressed to mine. It's dry, smooth in the center but rough at the base of his fingers and thumb.

Mollie was absolutely right about cowboys being a different breed. She discovered this fact after recently inheriting Lucky Ranch, her wildly wealthy late father's two-hundred-thousand-acre property in the small town of Hartsville, Texas. After butting heads with the ranch's foreman, Cash, the two of them promptly fell in love.

Now, Mollie has decided to split her time between Hartsville and Dallas, where our company is based. As her business partner, that means I get to regularly visit

Lucky Ranch. Which is, well, lucky for me, because I'm interested in this cowboy.

Very, *very* interested in having some of that meaningless fun with him.

Judging by his expertise in flirting, there's a good chance Duke just might want the same thing. *The twins—babies of the family—are wild cards*, Mollie told me, referring to Duke and his brother Ryder. *You never know where they are or who they go home with*.

Perfect.

"You know a lot about Bellamy Brooks," I reply to Duke, referring to the cowboy boot company Mollie and I started in our dorm room eight years ago at the University of Texas.

"Big fan. Just waitin' for y'all to start making men's boots."

"So you can model them?"

Duke's smile touches his eyes, making them glimmer. "I've been told I'm very photogenic. Just keep me in mind, yeah? I'm cheap—"

"And easy," one of the other brothers says with a smirk. It has to be Ryder, Duke's twin. They look almost exactly alike, save for Duke's slightly shorter hair and the barely visible scar on Ryder's bottom lip.

"My fee is just a pair of your beautiful boots," Duke says.

I realize we're still shaking hands. The warmth of his, the viselike sensation of his grip, has me feeling giddy. "I'll have my people reach out to your people."

"Ma'am, when I have 'people,' you and I are gonna finish this conversation on a yacht somewhere in the Caribbean."

Ryder groans. "Keep dreaming."

Another brother, this one with shaggy, dark blond hair, rolls his eyes.

But me? I grin. What a freaking delight, meeting a cowboy who thinks outside the box. Ranch. Whatever.

"I like to travel. Visiting new places is one of the biggest perks of owning a business." Dropping his hand, I fold my arms over my chest. "Let's save the date."

"I like to travel too. Hope to do more of it." His eyes, so blue they seem to glow in the soft light of the kitchen, bore into mine. "And yes, it's a date."

It's hard to look away. But then a ponytailed woman bearing two bottles of wine approaches, introducing herself as Patsy, Lucky Ranch's chef.

Cash and his four brothers, along with Mollie, Patsy, her husband, John B, and their daughter, Sally, all crowd around the farm table. Mollie's attorney, Goody Gershwin, and her wife, Tallulah, also join us. We tuck into a homemade meal that's absolutely delicious: pork tenderloin roasted with apples, along with mashed sweet potatoes and sautéed greens.

I can't remember the last time I sat down to supper. Growing up, my family ate together almost every night until my brothers and I got so busy with school and activities that the ritual happened less and less. My parents abandoned it altogether when they *really* started to not get along around the time I was entering high school.

I miss those suppers.

Really, I miss the time when our family was (relatively) happy. Because we were at one point. Dad wasn't quite so angry. Mom wasn't depressed.

Preston wasn't a jerk. Then slowly, bit by bit, everything—everyone—changed.

My stomach flips for an entirely different reason when Mollie pulls out her laptop after we're done eating. She and I have been working on a big proposal for days now. I'm excited for her.

I'm also a little wistful. A few times, I found myself wishing that someone could love me the way Cash loves Mollie. The two of them have chemistry out the wazoo, sure, but they're also friends. He's got her back, and he cares about how she feels. What she needs. Wants. Thinks.

I've never seen anything like it.

As usual, Mollie slays the delivery of her proposal. Cash and his brothers were raised on their family's neighboring property, Rivers Ranch. They've struggled with its upkeep since their parents' passing in a car accident twelve years ago. Mollie told me Cash has always dreamed of saving his pennies and restoring his family's land.

Mollie gives him the plans to do exactly that. She proposes combining Rivers Ranch with Lucky Ranch, creating Lucky River Ranch. Mollie and the Rivers brothers would split revenue equally. She and I even designed a logo for the new property, a turquoise horseshoe flanked by stars and the ranch's name.

Cash cries.

Mollie cries.

We all cry. And then we all burst into a fresh round of tears when Cash proposes, and Mollie accepts with a *hell yes*.

We pop champagne and toast to the newly engaged couple.

One of the cowboys—the one with the shaggy hair who I *think* is named Wyatt—slams down his drink and says, "Let's celebrate! To the Rattler!"

I glance at Duke to find him looking at me. My stomach dips for the hundredth time.

"Best dive bar on the planet," he explains. "You in?"

I shrug. "It's not a yacht in the Caribbean."

"All good things, Wheeler."

Why is it so damn sexy when a guy says your name? Really, when *this* guy says it.

I'm smiling like an idiot. I like how easy this feels. How light and fun, the opposite of how I felt when I woke up this morning.

"I'm in."

We pile into a convoy of mud-splattered pickup trucks and head into town. Hartsville has all of one thousand residents, but Main Street is hopping tonight.

It's love at first sight when I lay eyes on the Rattler. It's tucked into a row of weathered buildings with big, old-fashioned windows whose hand-blown panes waver in the gleam of passing headlights. The sidewalk is lit up with every shade of neon, thanks to the beer signs that hang inside the bar.

Duke holds the door open for me. Like his brothers, he's put on a broken-in denim jacket. I'm glad he's still wearing the baseball hat. Add in his smile and the way his eyes crinkle at the edges, and you have one very tall glass of water.

Ryder catches me ogling his brother. "You sure that's the twin you want?"

Duke scoffs, rolling his eyes. "Trust the lady. She's making the right call."

"Ain't my style to step on any toes." Ryder holds up his hands. "But you change your mind, Wheeler, just know that I'm available."

He disappears into the bar. Duke waits for me, still smiling.

"Such a gentleman." I cross my arms.

"My brother's not. Just so you know."

"So you're different, but I'm guessing you're also identical? As in y'all are identical twins?"

Duke's barrel of a chest rises on an inhale. "Unfortunately, yes."

"But fortunately, you're the better-looking one."

His lips twitch. "You tell it like it is, Wheeler Rankin. I like that about you."

"I like that about you too." I step inside the Rattler and inhale a lungful of stale-beer smell. "But wow, I *love* this."

"Just wait 'til the music starts. Whatcha drinking?" Duke nods at the U-shaped bar that dominates the high-ceilinged space.

"I like Shiner. Here, I'll get the first round—"

"You're cute." Duke grins down at me. "When you come to my dive bar in my town, I'm buying. Shiner it is."

I follow him to the bar, where he tells the bartender to put the pair of longnecks he orders on his tab.

This man couldn't be more classic small-town cowboy if he tried.

Then again, he did talk about that yacht. And he kept bringing up Bellamy Brooks, which made me think he's interested to know more about the business.

Maybe Duke has dreams that are bigger than Hartsville. The idea makes my chest feel funny, maybe because I also have dreams that are bigger—different at least—than the dreams my parents have for me.

Ignoring that, I focus on the tug of heat I feel low in my center as I shamelessly check out his ass. It looks *cute* in those Wranglers.

"Hearts or darts?" He turns around, beers in hand.

I furrow my brow. "Is that cowboy for 'hello, here's your beer'?"

"Nah. We usually just hand you the beer." He passes one of the longnecks to me. "What I'm asking is do you play games with hearts or with darts?"

"Ah." I take the beer, our fingers brushing, and grin. "Can I say both?"

"You can say whatever you want." He flashes me a wide, white smile. "I like a challenge."

"You're gonna be disappointed, then." I follow him to the far corner of the room. A pool table is tucked underneath a stained-glass Budweiser light fixture. Beside it, a dartboard that's seen better days hangs on the wall underneath a pair of antlers mounted on a license plate from Alaska. "I suck at games."

He narrows his eyes at me. "Why do I get the feeling you're already playing?"

Damn, he's good.

The heat of his gaze follows me as I pluck the darts off the board. "You ask a lot of questions."

"Just trying to get to know you." He tips back his beer, throat bobbing on a swallow. "A friend of Mollie's is a friend of mine. Haven't seen my brother this happy in…well. Forever."

So casual. Like he has real conversations with strangers on the regular and talks about his family with no trace whatsoever of awkwardness or trauma.

I envy him.

"They're cute together, aren't they? Mollie and Cash." Darts in one hand, I tip back my own beer with the other. It's all I can do not to groan. The Shiner Bock is ice cold, its earthy flavor refreshingly delicious. Didn't realize I was so thirsty until I take one long sip, then another.

"It's sickening." Duke sets down his beer on the nearby whiskey barrel that's been repurposed as a drinks table. "What's your game? 501? 301?"

He's referring to the different games we can play with the darts. Players start with either 501 or 301 points, subtracting the number they hit on the board during every turn. Whoever gets to zero first wins.

I'm smiling again as I flatten my palm, offering him the darts. "This is your bar, so it's your call."

He shakes his head and grins. "Nah, sweetheart." Stepping closer, he curls his hand over mine and rolls the darts back into my palm. "You're my guest, so you get to make the call. Although I know that call is gonna be 501."

My pulse skips. My skin ignites at the casual, confident way he touches me. "I'm Mollie's guest too."

"I don't share. 501 is your jam because you play the long game. You're a steady Eddie chiseling away at those points, making your opponent think you're not all that good. But then—bit by bit—you crush them, and then you finally go in for the kill."

I lick my lips, pulse racing, even as that voice in my head sounds a warning. *Careful.* This guy is good.

Really, really good at reading people. Reading *me*.

We're just flirting, though. This is harmless fun. Nothing more.

I deserve to blow off a little steam, don't I? After years of struggling to get Bellamy Brooks out of the red, Mollie and I are getting *so* close to hitting it big. Just this week, we heard from *Elle* about a feature they're doing on Western wear for the spring. They want to possibly feature our Jocelyn boots, a pair of midcalf, almond-toed beauties available in coral and turquoise full-grain leather.

There's no guarantee the feature will run or that our boots will end up in it. But it's still a big deal the editors noticed us. We've only been knocking on their door for, oh, close to five years now.

Everyone thought I was stupid to pour my time and my life savings into a cowboy boot company. I'm ashamed to admit that on bad days, I think I really must be stupid to bet so big on myself. Who am I to believe I know what I'm doing? I've had to borrow way more money than I'm comfortable admitting from my parents and grandparents to keep the company afloat. I've only been able to pay back some of it, which is reason number one thousand why Mom and Dad don't approve of the career path I've chosen.

But even though no one in my family really believes in me, I can't quit. Not yet. Deep down, there's a voice that keeps telling me we can make Bellamy Brooks work.

"I hope you're not in a rush." I set down my beer and assume the position: weight balanced evenly on both feet, shoulders relaxed, grip on the dart delicate. "You're right—501 is my game."

One side of Duke's mouth quirks upward. "I got all night."

"It won't take me that long to kick your ass."

"You talk a big game."

"I'm not afraid to make big bets."

"Awful risky when the margin for error is so small." He nods at the board. The areas with the highest scores are placed directly beside areas with the lowest scores, so when you aim for twenty points, you could easily—very, very easily—end up with a measly one point.

"You gotta learn to be okay with losing." I flex my wrist, muscle memory taking over as I practice my aim. "The more you lose, the closer you get to a win. At least that's what probability and all the quotes on my Pinterest feed tell me."

"What the hell is a Pinterest?"

I release the dart. It lands with a dull, barely audible *thud* just outside the bullseye. Twenty-five points.

I turn to smile at Duke. "It's the place I go to find outfit inspiration and horny book quotes."

"I see what you're doing."

"What's that?"

"Distracting me with your excellent dart-throwing form and use of the word 'horny.' But two can play this game." His bicep bulges as he lifts the hat off his head and flips it to put it on backward. His eyes lock on mine, shimmering like pavement on a scorching summer day. "Now show me what you can do."

Laughter, easy and real, bubbles up in the back of my throat. At the same time, my mouth goes dry.

This man is so fucking hot it almost hurts to look at him. I tell myself that's a good thing, because there's no chance of him ever wanting me as more than a hookup. He's the wild child, remember? Which suits me just fine, because I just want to have fun too.

Is fun all I want, though? Why does my center ping with something like pain when I glance across the bar and see Mollie and Cash dancing cheek to cheek to a Brooks & Dunn song?

I throw my second dart. It lands—*shit*—a centimeter to the left of my intended target. My third ends up dropping pitifully to the floor.

"Now you know how it feels." Duke bends down to pick up the dart.

I shamelessly check out his Wrangler butt yet again because I am indeed quite horny. "How what feels?"

"To be distracted by your gorgeous opponent." He grins. My heart plunges to its death somewhere at the base of my spine when he turns and hits a bullseye on his first throw. "Giddyup, cowgirl."

CHAPTER 2
Hot Damn
Duke

Wheeler's lips twitch. "But I'm not a cowgirl."

"You sure as hell act like one."

"How so?"

"It's the confidence." My eyes flick down her body. "And the strong legs."

"Because you need strong legs for riding?"

Yep, she's picking up what I'm laying down.

Goddamn, I like her. She smells like summer, some kinda perfume that's tropical, juicy even, with hints of coconut and sunscreen. Absolutely delicious.

Yeah, I wanna lay *her* down. That's a given. But I also wanna get to know this girl. People with new ideas, who do something other than work cattle for a living, are few and far between in these parts.

I've dreamed of forging my own path and seeing the world for as long as I can remember. I'm terrified of that world passing me by as I sit in Hartsville and wait for my life to begin. But meeting a person from somewhere else—someone who's experienced things I haven't, who knows things I don't—is a nice reminder that the world *hasn't* passed me by. I still have time to see and do new things.

"For riding, yes." I throw another dart. Not a bullseye repeat, but close.

Really, how could I not like Wheeler Rankin? She's smart as shit. Confident. Well-spoken and witty. She has this way of incorporating interesting thoughts into flirty conversation that makes my dick perk up.

My dick also likes the way she looks in that skirt and those boots. Hard not to imagine what those pretty legs of hers would feel like wrapped around my hips.

Bet I could make you scream, sweetheart.

Didn't know what to expect when Mollie told us she was bringing her business partner to visit the ranch. I think I speak for all of us Riverses when I say Mollie Luck surprised us. We worried she'd be a spoiled brat who'd sell the ranch to the highest bidder. But she turned out to be a deeply kind, incredibly intelligent human who's about to become my sister-in-law.

Wild the way life works.

Also wild that Wheeler—who clearly comes from money and is well educated—is so fucking good at darts, despite this initial hiccup.

Doesn't add up.

She doesn't add up.

Not understanding her feels like an exciting challenge. I like the idea of stretching my wings and being able to explore who she is. What turns her on.

Nice to be on my own for a minute without one of my brothers interrupting me.

I love my family, don't get me wrong. But sometimes I feel trapped in my role as "rancher's son" or "one of the Rivers boys." Being part of our family comes with expectations that I'm not sure really fit. I try to be a good brother. Good cowboy. Upstanding member of the community. But that doesn't leave a lot of time for exploration. For doing something different, something that's better suited to my interests. My personality.

Wheeler's form is flawless. Strategy is solid. Makes me wanna pick her brain, then take her home so I can fuck her senseless.

"Where'd you learn to play?" I pluck the trio of brass-tipped darts off the board.

"I fooled around with darts back in college. I needed some money to get Bellamy Brooks off the ground, and gambling seemed like the most fun way to make it." Wheeler lifts a shoulder, her Shiner in hand. "I only recently started playing on a regular basis again, though. There's this great little bar around the corner from my place in Dallas that I go to a couple times a week. Darts are good stress relief."

"What're you stressed about? Work?" I hand her the darts.

The playfulness in her expression dims. Just for half a heartbeat. Just long enough for me to know I've hit on a sore spot.

I'd know, because I'm plenty sore myself. Losing your parents at fourteen will do that to a body.

"Work. Yeah." Her fingers linger on mine a little longer this time when she grabs the darts. "But now that Mollie's got all the ranch stuff figured out or mostly figured out anyway, I'm hoping we'll be on the upswing."

I sip my beer as I watch Wheeler hit the tiny ring around the bullseye. She lets out a yelp of delight, throwing up her hands.

"See? All cowgirl."

She glances at me over her shoulder. "How so?"

"You got knocked down, but you sure as hell ain't staying down, are you?"

Wheeler narrows her eyes. "You lay it on thick, you know that?"

"Can you blame me?" I sip my beer and glance around the bar. "It's always the same people hanging out in the same places around here. Nice to meet someone new."

I'm happy that Cash found his person. No one deserves happiness more than he does. Not gonna lie, though, I'm jealous he nabbed the only new person to come to Hartsville in what feels like forever.

Really, I'm jealous he has an excuse to get out of town. Mollie and Wheeler's business is still based in Dallas, where the rich ladies who buy their boots live. No one in Hartsville is going to buy a pair of thousand-dollar boots.

I wouldn't say I'm a wannabe city boy. It's just hard not to feel suffocated sometimes by a life as small as mine often feels. I also wouldn't say I'm a playboy like Wyatt, but I do love to get out. Have some fun and work off some of this restless energy I got.

Maybe I can convince Cash we need to get away somewhere for his bachelor party. New Orleans, maybe, or Austin.

Reading my mind, Wheeler replies, "Grass isn't always greener. Especially when the grass is in Dallas."

Easy for you to say.

"Why boots?" I ask.

Her arm hinges at the elbow as she lines up her shot. "Why cowboying?"

"It's what I was born into." I shrug. "I like it just fine."

"But?"

My heart dips. "How'd you know there was a but?"

"I've been staring at it all night." She releases the dart. Twenty points. "You're a Wrangler guy, huh?"

Laughing, I finish my beer. "Just like my dad."

"He was a cowboy too?"

I like how she's the one asking questions now. Is she curious about me like I'm curious about her?

She throws another dart. It lands on the board—another twenty—but I feel it land in my chest too. Aim precise, needle puncturing my breastbone.

"Yep. Just like his daddy and his daddy before that."

Wheeler arches a brow. "That's quite the legacy to uphold."

"Cash is the one who shoulders most of it. The rest of us, we just gotta fall in line. Keep everything running nice and smooth."

"You're smooth." Her eyes narrow. "But you're different too, aren't you?"

"What makes you think that?"

"You're chatting up a stranger in the corner." She glances across the bar. "But your brothers are with people they seem to know. Even your twin."

She's not wrong. Cash and Mollie are canoodling on the dance floor. Wyatt is cozying up to Sally underneath a neon Miller High Life sign, and Ryder is doing tequila shots at the bar with Colt Wallace. I'm close with Colt, but he and Ryder are super tight. Sawyer's the only one missing. Always the responsible parent, he's at home putting his three-year-daughter, Ella, to bed.

I blink, feeling disoriented for a minute. Like I'm standing in the middle of a moving kaleidoscope, the familiar shapes and sounds around me shifting into an unfamiliar landscape.

Wheeler noticing I'm different isn't objectively a big deal. But it's a big deal to me. As a twin especially—Ryder and I were born ten minutes apart, numbers four and five in the birth order—I always felt like I got lost in the shuffle of my brothers.

My parents loved the hell out of us, of course. But Mom and Dad had five kids in six years, and they didn't have much help. Attention, and often patience, were in short supply. Especially when it came to those of us at the bottom. I think by the time my parents had me and Ryder, they were exhausted.

They definitely didn't have the energy to deal with an annoyingly curious son who loved school but was lukewarm on chores around the ranch.

"I'm good at it," I say. "Being a cowboy. When you grow up working cattle, hard not to be. I love a lot about the job. Being outside. Working with my family. There's purpose in it."

Wheeler looks at me from underneath the fringe of bangs that tickles her eyelashes. "It's not your purpose, though. Or not your whole purpose."

Yes. You get it.

You're a fucking smokeshow, and I want to know everything about you.

I never could do anything halfway. Mom used to say I was impulsive. Dad called me wild, and now so does Cash.

They're not wrong. But maybe they were wrong about my curiosity, my restlessness, being a bad thing. A character flaw I needed to work on or change.

Then again, maybe I'm just delusional and a little drunk.

Whatever the case, I ain't about to let this girl slip through my fingers.

"Always thought there'd be more." I tip back my beer, even though there's nothing left. Feels too soon to touch Wheeler, and I need a reason to keep my hands busy. Don't want to scare her off by coming on too strong. "That the world would be bigger somehow. I hate the idea of getting stuck here forever."

She nods, a soft look in her eyes. "I get that. It's one of my favorite parts of my job—all the people I get to meet, the places I get to see. It's the best education there is."

"I loved school."

"Nerd—"

"Hey."

She traps her bottom lip between her teeth. "I was going to say *nerds unite*." She taps her bottle to mine. "I loved school too. It was the one thing I was reliably good at. The one thing I was praised for."

"Seriously?" I grin and tip my chin toward the board. "What about your game? You're a fuckin' rock star at darts."

Her cheeks flush pink. "I'm proud of that, yeah."

"You should be proud you started your own business too. That's awesome."

Wheeler nods, looking down at the mouth of her bottle. "Thanks for saying that."

"Why? Are you not proud?"

"I am."

"But?"

Her eyes flick to meet mine. They glimmer. "How'd you know there was a but?"

"Yours is cute."

"You noticed."

"I have two eyes and a pulse. Your boots are beautiful. Who's not proud of you for taking a risk and doing something different?"

Her eyelashes flutter. "No one's ever put it like that." Turning her head, she glances across the bar and thinks for a minute before turning back to me. "My dad is a lawyer. My grandfather's a lawyer. My older brother went to law school and now works for my dad. My younger brother is the only one who supports what I do, maybe because he's still in college and doesn't want to be a lawyer either. But everyone else…they don't get why I chose this career. *I* know this is what I want to do." She lifts her leg, turning her foot so I can admire her boot. "But as I'm sure Mollie told you, Bellamy Brooks hasn't done as well as we'd hoped it would by this point. If it wasn't for her inheritance, I'm not sure we'd be able to keep going."

"Now you can, though. So keep going."

"You know, I've thought about quitting more times than I can count. But I just…when push comes to shove, I can't do it. I love the job too much. Love our boots. I'm a creative at heart, so I know I'd be miserable if I was chained to a desk all day doing, I don't know, whatever lawyers do."

I offer her a tight smile, moving so that we're standing side by side at the table. "But that's what's expected of you, so it's hard not to feel pressure."

"Yes! Sometimes I think it'd be easier to just fold and do what everyone else is doing. Like, sometimes I think they got it right and I got life all wrong, because look how hard I'm struggling."

Setting my beer down, I wonder if it's too soon to ask this girl on a date. I *like* how honest she is. How fearless. Intelligent. The way she thinks—her doubts—it's like a breath of fresh air.

I understand where Wheeler is coming from. My brothers all seem so certain that the path they're on is the right one. But me? I'm constantly questioning what I'm doing, where I'm going. If I'm asking for too much to want *more* than the admittedly great life that was passed down to me.

Being with someone like Wheeler makes me feel a little less alone. Maybe I'm not asking for too much.

"But really, why boots?" I ask. "How'd you decide on that particular…line of business, I guess?"

Wheeler steps toward me to pick up one of the darts, long forgotten, on the whiskey barrel table between us. She's close enough that her knee brushes my leg. Awareness spreads like wildfire through my thigh and settles low in my middle.

Having chemistry with this woman on all different levels is the best kind of mindfuck there is. I connect plenty with people in a physical sense. But mentally? Emotionally?

Not often enough.

"I was born and raised in Texas. As a baby gift, my

grandparents gave me my first pair of boots. They were powder pink. Soft soled, crib shoes basically, with the cutest white stitching. I always say that's where my obsession started. In preschool, all I would wear was cowboy boots. Pink ones, glittery ones, ones with flowers and butterflies and princesses on them. Drove my mom crazy."

"Cute." I lean forward so that our knees touch against the side of the barrel.

Wheeler meets my eyes. They're alive, liquid with interest. "But as I got older, I could never find just the right pair. I wanted classic shapes—you know, the pointy toes, the ear pulls, all that—but with a fun, fashion-forward twist. So Mollie and I decided to make them."

"Of course you did." I scoff.

She cuts me a look. "What does that mean?"

"Means..." I shake my head. "Most people would just go search online and settle for the least worst-looking cheap pair of boots they could find. But you decided to manufacture your own fucking boots. You know how hot that is?"

Leaning forward, she settles her elbows on the table. "You think I'm hot?"

She's flirting now, the energy between us shifting.

Igniting.

An unexpected shadow of disappointment moves through me. I wanna take this girl home, no two ways about it. But I also wanna keep picking her brain. I see so much of myself in the things she's saying. The struggles she's working through.

For the first time in a long time, I actually wanna... well, take my time.

There's a buzz in the back of my skull. That's the only way I can describe the weird sixth sense I have when it comes to Ryder. Glancing across the bar, I see him watching me. Watching us, more like it.

He cocks a brow. *You like this one, yeah?*

I give him a tiny nod. *I do.*

Grinning, he brings his beer to his mouth. For all his fucking around earlier, I know he'd never step on my toes when it comes to a girl. Not only because he's not a total dick but also because we have completely different tastes in women. He likes country girls who can hold their liquor and who know every word to every Nirvana song. Bonus points if they're brunette.

Me? I like girls who are going places. And yeah, if they have a nice ass, I don't mind that.

Wheeler is definitely going places, and she definitely has the sexiest, cutest ass ever.

I don't wanna fuck this up. If I move too fast, get too deep, I risk scaring her off. My hope is that she and I will be seeing a lot of each other going forward. Gotta keep this chemistry alive without blowing my proverbial load too soon.

Her mouth, though. It's quick and smart and lush. I wanna kiss it almost as much as I wanna listen to the words that come out of it.

Judging by the way Wheeler keeps leaning forward, her leg pressing into mine and her tits on display, I may not have much choice in the matter.

"Surely I ain't the first one who's told you that." I nod at her beer. "Want another?"

Figure that's a good way to slow things down—one more beer, which I'll nurse as long as possible. Gives me an excuse to keep the conversation and the darts going in the world's best, worst game of edging.

"Yeah." Wheeler nods, doing that thing where she digs her teeth into her bottom lip. She's looking at my mouth now. "Sure, I'd love one. Thank you."

"Be right back." I gather our empty bottles between my fingers before gesturing to the board. "No cheating."

"I'd never!" She gives my arm a playful shove. "Well, I would if it meant winning. But I don't need to cheat to win."

"Always so confident."

"Well, yeah." She's grinning as she teases me.

She doing this on purpose? Veering into flirtatiousness so I don't hit on any more sore spots? The shit she said about her parents makes me think that maybe…I don't know, maybe she's going through something. Is she close with her family? Do they talk? Are they fighting? I'm sensing sadness, but she's given me so little to go on that I could be projecting.

I gotta be careful not to overstep. She'll tell me what she wants me to know when she's ready to tell it.

Problem is all of a sudden, I want to know everything.

Ryder picked right up on it: I *like* Wheeler.

She may want me. But that doesn't mean she likes me back. I'm okay with that.

I'm okay with that, I repeat as I order another round and fight the growing crowd to bring the Shiners back to our table.

Only I'm not okay with the idea of hooking up with Wheeler tonight and never getting to talk to her so honestly—so openly—again. What if we sleep together, and then she wants nothing to do with me? What if getting naked makes things awkward?

Still, when Wheeler slides her hand onto the underside of my forearm as she accepts the beer I hold out to her, arousal bolts through me. I try very hard not to let it blot out my desire to get to know her better.

"Thanks, Duke."

"Welcome, Wheeler."

Relax. Shit'll happen the way it's supposed to.

I step into her touch, our legs mingling. I've rolled up my sleeves, so her fingers meet bare skin as she wraps them around my arm. She sips her beer. I sip mine. For the first time all night, I hear the music that's pumping through the speakers overhead.

Garth. An oldie but a goodie.

"Do cowboys dance?" Wheeler starts to rock side to side. Her body, tits to thighs, brushes against mine.

I look down at her, unable to resist putting a hand on her waist to hold her against me. She feels impossibly soft. Impossibly warm. "The good ones do."

"You wanna be good to me?"

Sweetheart, I'd be so good to you.

So fucking good.

My dick throbs. I take a deep breath. Let it out.

"What about our game?" I glance at the darts on the table. "You haven't finished kicking my ass yet."

Her eyes are dark as they rake over my face, catching on my mouth. "We're done with darts, aren't we?"

She's not talking about darts. Well, she is. But she's also talking about…talking. She knows all she needs to about me, and now she's ready to get physical.

I'm not hurt. Just doesn't feel right.

"I like playing darts with you, though." I sip my beer.

Is that a flicker of surprise I see in her eyes? For a split second, I panic. I hope she doesn't think I'm turning her down, does she?

I just don't get why me wanting to get to know her better would come as a surprise to Wheeler. Surely I'm not the first guy to think she's hot *and* interesting. Intelligent. Funny.

"I think I'd like dancing with you better," she replies.

I look her in the eyes. "How 'bout this? You let me pick your brain for the rest of this game, and then we'll dance. That a deal?"

Wheeler blinks, a funny expression on her face. "What do you want to know?"

"Everything."

She goes still.

Very, very still.

So does everything inside me. I swear I can feel my heart trip and fall over the curb of my rib cage.

Shit. I came on way too strong. I've made her uncomfortable, and now she's not gonna talk to me. Definitely not gonna be yelling my name later.

I'm crushed by disappointment.

Crushed by the knowledge that I fucked up my one chance to make this bright, beautiful stranger mine.

CHAPTER 3
Risks Not Worth Taking
Wheeler

That's *not* my cowboy.

It's my one thought as I look up into Duke's blue eyes, alive with all the things: curiosity and lust and hope and disappointment.

The fact that he picks right up on the sudden change in my mood shows how emotionally intelligent this guy is.

Danger.

Run.

Duke is flirting with me, sure. Definitely wants to take me home. The way his fingers knead my side, a steady, warm pressure that makes the ache between my legs throb, tells me that.

He smells so good, woodsy, like juniper and pine.

The kicker: he also quite clearly wants to get to know me. *Know* me. And my knee-jerk reaction is to push him away. I've learned it's better to cut and run than risk letting someone know the real me.

My family and friends have said some...er, not so great things to me in the past. For instance, when I told Dad that I was starting a boot company with my best friend, he said I was crazy. Mom's feedback was slightly kinder, but at the end of the day, she still told me to do something else. Preston, my older brother, called me an idiot and said to call him for a job when Bellamy Brooks inevitably went under. So-called friends made fun of me behind my back.

I've been the butt of jokes, the laughingstock of my graduating class, the shame of my family. *She's really making pink and purple cowboy boots? And she thinks she can make a living doing that?*

Never mind the times I overhead Preston making fun of me with his friends while I was in the throes of my pubescent awkward stage, complete with pimples, braces, and a deluge of emotions I couldn't handle and didn't understand. *Pizza face*, he'd call me. One time, I heard him say to Mom, *What's her deal? Why is she so freaking moody and weird?*

I feel shaky as I disentangle myself from Duke's grasp. I take a step back, putting enough distance between us that his hands fall from my waist. He knits his eyebrows.

"I'm sorry, Wheeler. If you really wanna dance—"

"Don't worry about it." I wave him away and sip my beer, grateful for the excuse to break eye contact.

"Wait. Did I—"

"You're fine." I shake the bangs out of my eyes. Why did I ever think bangs were a good idea? "I'm tired anyway. Lots going on at work right now, and the traffic on the way down here was awful. I'm gonna call it a night."

He tilts his head. "Want a ride back to the house, then? I don't need to stay—"

"Stay. Please don't leave on my account."

Because even if he did want to leave with me, as in take me home and get me naked, that's not something I'm interested in anymore.

Yeah, Duke is asking all the right questions. Saying all the right things. I enjoyed talking to him in a way I haven't enjoyed talking to a guy in forever.

But that's exactly why I need to pump the brakes. I don't want to form any kind of real, serious connection with anyone at the moment. And it's obvious this cowboy is serious.

Most people would bask in his attention. His intelligence. But most people aren't wired to believe the second someone gets close, they'll realize that I'm too sensitive, that I'm just *too much*, period, and run for the hills.

I'm not easy to love. My family has made that abundantly clear.

So I'm the one who runs. I've learned in therapy it's a self-defense mechanism, my way of rejecting people before they inevitably reject me. But *knowing* that about myself isn't the same as *fixing* it.

I'm trying. But turns out rewiring your brain is a really difficult task.

"I'll find a ride." I set down my longneck. "Thanks for the beers."

"We don't have any kind of rideshare stuff here in Hartsville. Just so you know. You sure you don't want me to drive you home?"

I put a hand on his chest. He's solid, hard in a way

that makes my brain short-circuit. I'm flattened by the fact that I don't get to hook up with this fine specimen of a man. I have a feeling he'd be good—excellent—in bed. It's his confidence. The way he's at ease in his big, broad body.

I mean, we've barely touched, and I could wring out my underwear for how turned on I am.

His gaze bores into mine. His face is a mask of concern.

Goddamn it, why does he have to care so much? He's ruining everything.

He's making me feel *everything*, and that scares the shit out of me.

Throat tight, I manage a smile. "Thanks, but I'll be okay. See you around, Duke."

CHAPTER 4
Horse of a Different Color
Duke

Putting my truck in gear, I nearly jump out of my skin when Ryder bangs on the passenger side door and looks at me through the open window.

"You headin' to the Wallaces'?"

"Nah. Just hitched an empty trailer to my truck for shits and giggles."

Grinning, he yanks open the door and hops inside. "Figured you could use an extra pair of hands."

"To pick up one horse?" I eye him. "I know what you're doing."

He yanks on his seat belt. "Oh yeah? What's that?"

"You're not as dumb as you look."

"Dude, stop calling yourself dumb. Sawyer's always telling Ella to be kind to herself, and I think you should too."

Releasing the brake, I let out a sound that's half chuckle, half groan. "I made an identical twin joke without meaning to. Ha."

"Good thing your twin was smart enough to catch it."

"Hey. I thought I was the smart one."

Ryder lifts his Stetson off his head and runs a hand through his hair. "Can't we both be smart?"

"I guess. But I'm smart*er*."

He chuckles. "Still jealous I was the favorite, yeah?"

"You were the favorite only when Wyatt wasn't."

"Salty."

I grin. "Honest."

We bump over the dirt road that leads away from the equipment barn. Digging into his pocket, Ryder pulls out his knife and turns it over in his hands. He doesn't release the blade; instead he admires the wood grain of the handle. "I was bored. Wanted to go for a little drive."

The knife belonged to Dad, his initials stamped on the clip-point metal blade. It was a gift from Mom on their wedding day. Ryder found it in the plastic bag of our parents' belongings that the hospital gave us after they died. He's had the knife on him ever since. I mean that literally—not once in the past twelve-plus years have I seen him without it.

"You're hungover and you want to see Billie, even though I keep telling you that Colt'll rip you a new one if you so much as lay a finger on her."

His grin stays put as he replies, "Only one of those things is true." He glances at me. "How're *you* feeling today?"

I blow out a breath. How do I tell my brother I tossed and turned all night, beating myself up over what I did—and didn't—say to Wheeler at the Rattler?

I also woke up hard. Girl was so fucking sexy. Her sense of humor, her intelligence, those legs—

33

Christ, I'm dying just thinking about it.

I shift my hand on the wheel. The sun glints off the polished handle of Ryder's pocketknife, making me blink. "Been better. Shouldn't have had that last beer."

"What the hell happened? Seemed like you and Wheeler were really hitting it off. Then poof, she just disappeared. Mollie said she slept in her room at the New House, which means she didn't sleep in yours."

Wheeler's car was parked there when I headed that way for breakfast at half past four this morning. She didn't come out to eat with us. But when Wyatt stopped by the New House to chat with Patsy an hour or so ago, he said the car was gone.

My lungs burn. Wheeler and I have chemistry. We were definitely having fun. I'm not making any of that up. Clearly she was looking for a good time. But the second I hinted that I'd be interested in more, she bolted.

Huh.

Makes me think that underneath her flirty exterior lies some kind of wound.

I'd know, because I got one too. Only mine seeks comfort, whereas hers seeks solitude.

"I don't know what happened," I say. "But I'm gonna find out."

"You should. Ain't seen you corner someone that way in an age."

"We don't get much fresh blood in these parts."

He tilts his head. "Don't pretend like it's blood you're after. Seems like she's your equal. Y'all are smart and curious about the world, and you both like to pretend you suck at darts when in reality, y'all are scary good at it."

"Awful observant for a guy who was ripping shots all night."

"Hey. We had a lot to celebrate. And I was just trying to keep up with Billie." He lets out a low whistle as he lifts his hips and tucks the knife back into his pocket. "Girl can drink anyone under the table. Colt says she came out of the womb that way—reins in one hand, bottle of tequila in the other."

Billie is one of the Wallaces' six children. Growing up with five brothers, she learned early to hold her own.

She also learned early that Ryder was the favorite in our family for a reason. He's the baby for starters, a whole ten minutes younger than me. He's got a big heart, although that means he's easily hurt. He's also smarter than he gives himself credit for.

Billie hides it well, but she's been in love with my brother for as long as I can remember. Ryder likes the attention. Who wouldn't? And I think he could fall in love with her too, real easy.

But because he's so smart, he knows that'd just end in disaster. Colt, Billie's brother, hasn't had it easy—like Sawyer, he's a single dad—so we've all made sure not to rock his boat any more than it's already been rocked. Especially since Ryder and I have a bit of a reputation. We're not playboys by any means, but we're also no angels. I'm too restless to sit still and behave, and Ryder's just got too much to offer the world to stay put or stay small.

I clear my throat. "I say this with love—"

"Oh, Jesus, what?"

"You're too smart to torture yourself and Billie, yeah? So don't do it. Not when we just got handed our dreams for the ranch on a silver platter. Combining Rivers Ranch with Lucky Ranch? That's a huge win for us. Let's not fuck it up before it even happens."

Ryder's grin fades. He raises his forearm so that his fingers brush the top of the doorframe and taps it. Once, twice. "Think you can stay away from Wheeler?"

I scoff. "I might not have much choice in the matter."

"You do. And you won't. Stay away from her, I mean. She isn't gonna make it easy for you, but you'll find a way to win her over."

I take the turn onto the long stretch of country road that links our ranch with the Wallaces'. "Since when can you read the future?"

"I can read *you*. And I've been doing that since you and I were womb mates."

"Ha." It's an old joke, one Dad used to make all the time.

A hollow feeling spreads through my center. Same sensation you get after being sucker punched. The grief—it'll hit you out of nowhere like that.

"You think they'd want this for us?" I ask.

"Want what?"

"The life we got. All this." I lift the fingers I have on the wheel and spread them, gesturing toward the pastures we pass.

"Yes and no. They'd be thrilled that we're joining forces with the Lucks. But at the end of the day, I think they'd just want us to be happy. We're all different, so happiness is gonna look different for each of us. For you, this"—he gestures out the window—"it definitely ain't enough."

"Ain't enough for you either."

His grin is back. "Not sure anything'll ever be enough for me."

That's what I'm worried about.

Ryder and I are alike in so many ways. We both liked school. We're both dreamers. In others, we're different. Ryder is obsessed with music. I like it just fine, but I've never played an instrument, whereas Ryder plays several. He's a picky eater, but I love food and will eat anything you put in front of me. I'm able to roll with the punches pretty easily, and I'm good at being spontaneous. Ryder thrives in the structure routine provides.

Problem is everyone sees how alike we look on the outside and thinks we're alike on the inside too. It was always a struggle in school to get people to understand we were two different people with different personalities. I used to get bent out of shape about it.

Hard to feel special when you're always lumped together with your brother. Really, with all four of my brothers. I lived in Cash's and Wyatt's and Sawyer's shadows for most of my life. I think that's part of the reason I want to get out of Hartsville so badly.

If I'm somewhere else, I can *be* somebody else. Someone other than Ryder's twin or Cash's kid brother. Maybe then I'll finally be able to figure out what I want to do with my life.

"Give Wheeler space," Ryder continues. "But not too much space. She likes what she sees in you. Just gotta give her time to learn to trust you and trust herself that she's picking the right twin."

I laugh. "Of course she's picking the right twin. And that sounds an awful lot like threading the needle there."

"I got faith in you."

I turn my head to look at him. "I know. Appreciate that, brother."

Ryder's faith in me is what got me through losing my parents. He always checked in on me. Always made sure I ate, got rest, got home safe. Most of all, he didn't make me feel like a pain in the ass for wanting something different out of life. For being curious about the world and how it worked. When we weren't in the saddle, we were poring over the Rick Steves travel guides I got from the library or asking Garrett Luck how he managed the ranch's finances. Ryder encouraged me to take computer classes in high school, which is how I became a whiz at Excel. I now do the lion's share of the ranch's accounting. He also enthusiastically agreed to spend a weekend with me in Mexico City when we graduated.

Ryder's always been my partner in crime. But while my twin is curious about the world, he doesn't share my burning desire to explore every inch of it. He's content to do his cowboy thing.

No shame in that, considering he's probably the best at it out of all of us. He's just got a special touch with animals. With the land too.

"Now get off my ass about Billie," Ryder says, interrupting my thoughts.

Problem is he's gonna get himself into trouble with that girl. The second we arrive at the fancy new arena old man Wallace built on his property, Ryder's out the door and smiling at Billie like she hung the goddamn moon.

She ushers us inside the arena, where Colt is riding the gorgeous palomino quarter horse we just bought for a newly hired ranch hand.

"Dang, she's pretty," I say.

Billie nudges me with her elbow. "You know I don't date cowboys, Duke."

"You're funny. And I know." I meet Ryder's eyes over her head. "You're too smart for that."

She nods at the horse. "Y'all chose well. Seven panel testing, all negative. Measured her again this morning, and she's fifteen hands high. Gonna throw off big babies."

Ryder chuckles. "We got enough of those in our family." He extends a fist bump in her direction. "Thanks for the guidance. We're gonna need a lot more horses like this beauty in the near future, so let us know if something catches your eye."

"So I heard." She looks at me. "Congrats on Lucky River Ranch. Love the name, by the way."

"Dang." I let out a low whistle. "Word travels fast around here, don't it?"

Billie nods. "One of the perks of living in a small town."

"Or one of the pitfalls," I reply.

"You're lucky sons of bitches!" Colt calls as he trots our way. He dismounts and extends his hand to Ryder. "But really, I'm happy for your family. You deserve the good things that are coming your way."

Ryder pulls him in for a hug. "Thank you kindly. No idea what Mollie sees in Cash, but we're thrilled to welcome her into the family."

I'm glad Ryder has a support system outside our family. Really, I'm glad he has someone else to annoy. The fact that we have our own lives now and hang out with our own friends is a good thing. It's healthy.

Not gonna lie, though, back in the day, I used to get jealous anytime Ryder would hang out with Colt and not invite me. But again, I came to recognize that while

Ryder and I had a lot in common, he had some interests that were different from mine. He and Colt bonded over shit like animal husbandry and land management and football, stuff I could take or leave.

"Trailer's ready." I point my thumb over my shoulder. "Will y'all do us a favor and let us know of any horses you're selling going forward? I know y'all are popular these days, but we really would appreciate you remembering the little people on occasion."

Colt's shoulders shake on a chuckle. The Wallaces are famous for the superb horses they breed and train here in Texas. For years, rumors swirled that they were going to start a barrel racing training program. Those rumors were confirmed when they broke ground on the arena we're currently standing in a year ago.

"You know y'all are always first in line. Well, after Kevin Costner and heads of state."

Billie clucks her tongue. "If Kevin Costner actually bought horses from us, I'd've run away with him a long time ago."

"Wait." Ryder scrunches his brow. "Since when do you like old dudes?"

"Since I began dating young ones," she shoots back.

He adjusts his belt. "We ain't all alike, you know. Us young ones. Except that we got the kinda stamina to ride—"

"Please don't finish that sentence," I say.

His lips twitch. "I was gonna say we got the stamina to ride *horses* all day long."

"Sure you were," Colt says, still laughing.

Does he know my brother isn't joking? Well, Ryder is joking that the sentence included the word *horses*.

He's definitely not joking about offering his stamina-related services to Billie.

Lord above.

"We should get goin'." I grab Ryder's arm. "Cash already paid you, correct?"

Colt nods. "Correct. Thank y'all for your business."

"Business," I hiss to my brother as we head back out into the sunshine. "We're gonna be giving the Wallaces a lot more of that this year, because we'll be hiring a lot more cowboys, which means we'll need a lot more horses. Don't mess that up, ya hear?"

Ryder doesn't answer. He can't, because Billie is hot on our heels, telling us she'll help load up the horse.

"You got an awful lot of energy for someone who drank a fifth of tequila last night," Ryder tosses at her over his shoulder.

I can hear the grin in her voice when she says, "How many times I gotta tell you to stop trying to keep up with me? Admit that you're a lightweight. It's not a crime."

"I'm not a lightweight."

"Aw, but you are. It's kind of adorable, actually."

"Adorable?" He groans. "I don't like that adjective."

"What would you prefer?"

"Oh, you know what I'd prefer."

My turn to roll my eyes. Part of me wants to tell them to just bone already. Another part knows that would lead to a hell of a lot of trouble.

I should be focusing on my own love life instead. Mollie's sticking around the ranch, which means Wheeler is too. I got time. I also got patience.

That woman ain't the only one who can play the long game.

CHAPTER 5
Hard Truths
Wheeler

I try my level best* not *to run into the handsome cowboy I can't stop thinking about in the weeks and months that follow Mollie and Cash's engagement in November.

It's easier than I thought it would be. The cowboys start their day early—like, four a.m. early—and are out with the herd until the sun sets. I stay in a bedroom at the New House, the six-thousand-square-foot main residence Mollie's parents built on the ranch twenty or so years ago.

No one lives at the house now—Mollie and Cash prefer his cabin on the property—but it's become the ranch's unofficial gathering place, and it's where visitors like me typically stay. Mollie and I set up a temporary office for Bellamy Brooks in the house's enormous primary suite, complete with gorgeous views of the ranch. Meanwhile, the cowboys live in houses and cabins across the property.

It takes her and I a bit to figure out our new groove

now that we split our time between Hartsville and Dallas. Before she inherited Lucky River Ranch, she and I used the spare bedroom in her Dallas high-rise condo as our office/Bellamy Brooks's headquarters. We turned it into what we dubbed "the Closet," lining three walls with metal shelves that we used to display our growing collection of boots. On the fourth wall, we hung two huge corkboards above our desks that we crowded with bits of inspiration—fabric swatches, Pantone color palettes, clippings from *Vogue* and *Garden & Gun*.

Up until this point, we've worked pretty much twenty-four seven. There's no such thing as time off when you're an entrepreneur, especially when your company has yet to turn a profit.

But now Mollie has a sprawling ranch to run. She also has acres and acres of vacant land at her disposal, not to mention the money from the trust fund she's finally able to access. She's got a wedding to plan too—she and Cash are eager to tie the knot in a small but exquisite ceremony here on the ranch.

All this is to say she's spending less time working at Bellamy Brooks, and I'm working more.

A lot more.

Not like I mind, because our company has finally turned a corner. We're making real money, our social media is on fire, and it looks like that *Elle* feature might actually happen.

It doesn't take Mollie long to decide to build us a second headquarters and studio in Hartsville. As a surprise, Cash picks a spectacular spot on the ranch for the new studio: a high ridge with the most dramatic views of the Colorado River and the soaring canyons beyond. Construction begins two months after my first visit to Hartsville.

I was born and raised in the suburbs of Dallas, so I'm a little taken aback by how much I enjoy being on the ranch. It's a nice change of pace from the smog-choked traffic of the city.

I also hate working alone, so I try to be with Mollie as much as possible. I end up spending two weeks in Dallas for every one week I spend in Hartsville. It's not perfect, but it works.

Patsy turns out three gorgeous meals a day in the massive kitchen, where everyone sits around the old pine farm table to eat. That's when I see Duke the most. The man never misses a meal.

He also never misses an opportunity to say hi. He always seeks me out, making sure I get enough to eat or that my tea is refilled when my glass is empty. It's sweet, which makes keeping my distance that much harder.

It's also a constant reminder of what I could have but am too scared to allow myself to explore.

When I'm rooting around the pantry after I drive in from Dallas one day, I hear the boys enter the kitchen from the back door.

"Do me a favor, would you?" Cash asks.

My stomach flips when I hear Duke reply, "What's that?"

"For the love of God, can you *please* stop staring at Wheeler like a lovesick creeper? If she wants to be left alone, leave her the fuck alone."

I nearly drop the packet of Goldfish I'm holding. Patsy stocks the crackers for Ella, but like the other adults in the house, I partake in the snack more often than I'd like to admit. They're just so damn good.

I don't dare to so much as breathe. Instead I put a hand on the nearby shelf and listen, heart drumming in my throat.

A pause. Then: "Not to put too fine a point on it. Jesus, Cash. I don't stare at her. I just—"

"Undress her with your eyes?" Wyatt asks.

"Talk about her like that again and see what happens." The threatening rumble of Duke's voice draws my nipples to tight, overly sensitive points. "I'm only making sure our guest is taken care of. Don't want her to go hungry. Or thirsty."

Duke can be so damn sweet.

Something that's not sweet? The memory of Dad looking me in the eye and saying, "You keep being so damn difficult and nasty, no one's ever going to want you. Men don't like nasty women, so I suggest you keep your big mouth shut."

Even now, shame settles like a weight in my gut. I think I'd called him out for being a chauvinist at the dinner table after he demanded "the best slice of meat" because he was "the man of the house." Mom looked miserable as she pushed the food around her plate, but she didn't come to my defense.

No one did. Preston was too much of a jerk, even then. And my younger brother, Haines, was too little to say anything.

Needless to say, it was a relief when Mom finally asked for a divorce last year. Dad moved out of my childhood home a week later, and we've all been navigating their acrimonious split ever since.

I wouldn't say I'm super close to either of my parents, but I'm definitely closer to my mom than I am to my dad. I feel bad for her. But Dad? He's a lost cause in my eyes. He's always been mean and angry, but age has only seemed to amplify his worst qualities. I do my best to keep my distance.

"If you like Wheeler, you should ask her out," Sawyer says, yanking me back into the present. "Mollie says she's single."

My knee feels wobbly. Both my knees, actually. I curl my hand around the lip of the shelf. I should make myself known, but I'm frozen in place. Too scared—too curious—to come out.

"I liked talking to her," Duke replies. "That's it, all right? So y'all can fuck off now."

Ryder chuckles. "Keep talking to her, then."

"Trust me, I've tried. She's busy."

I feel a funny little tug in my center. Regret? I haven't meant to be rude to Duke. I'm just protecting myself from inevitable heartbreak.

Truth is, though, I'd love to hang out with Duke again. Sometimes, after a long, lonely day of work, I want to text him so badly—invite him over for a drink—that I literally ache.

But if my parents' divorce has taught me anything, it's that one, shotgun weddings are never a good idea. And two, my work and my sanity need to be my focus right now. A relationship, marriage, kids—the life I've always dreamed of—will come later, when my business is thriving, I'm one hundred percent financially independent, *and* I've found some semblance of what my therapist calls "self-love" and "inner peace."

"Bellamy Brooks is going places," Cash says.

"Of course it is. Mollie and Wheeler are working their asses off." Duke sighs. "Bet they'll be all over the world in no time."

"You could be goin' with them," Ryder says. "Remember what I told you—bide your time. Good things come to those who wait."

Wyatt scoffs. "Don't you go giving him ideas. We just created one of the biggest ranches in the fuckin' country, remember? I need every pair of hands I can get."

As the ranch's new foreman—he's taking over from Cash—makes sense why Wyatt would say that.

"Seriously, Wy," Duke shoots back with a hard little chuckle. "I ain't your little minion. I got a life of my own, you know. Things I wanna do and see outside Texas."

I bite my lip. I can so relate to Duke's desire to break the mold.

"Aw, c'mon." Wyatt's voice drops, all earnestness now. "You know I love you, right? That's why I wanna keep you around. We're just getting started—as a family, as a business. I'm excited."

"Only because Sally's part of the family now too."

"Well, yeah. Sally makes everything better."

Is there something in the water here that's making everyone and their mother fall in love? These cowboys keep pairing off, and something inside me wishes it were my turn to pair off too.

But it's not in the cards for me right now.

"Sally sure does make everything better." That's Patsy, who must be just getting back. She had to run to her house a little bit ago to grab some fresh mint from her garden, because *of course* Lucky River Ranch's chef grows her own herbs. "Then again, I'm a little biased."

"We're all biased. And real damn lucky that Sally decided to stay in Hartsville," Duke says, and I hear the faucet turn on. "All right, Patsy, what can we help with? I'll chop up those onions."

Ryder laughs. "You always were the crybaby. No, wait, that was me, actually."

"Hey. Cowboys cry too, you know."

I'm laughing, even though I don't wanna be. Duke is cheesy. But his cheesiness is really fucking endearing. So is the way he seems to effortlessly embrace expressing his emotions. He's not afraid to be vulnerable, and I like that.

Too much. Which is why I decide I'll try to sneak out of the pantry and through the kitchen unnoticed. Having lunch with Duke suddenly seems especially dangerous. I figure I'll just grab whatever leftovers there are after the cowboys head back to work.

Yeah, the idea of eating alone is depressing. But I'm used to it by now. I have friends in Dallas, but I'm usually too busy working to meet them for a meal. I make an exception when my little brother visits from college. The best days are when Haines is in town.

I wouldn't say my life in Dallas is depressing in general. But it sure as hell isn't as fun or as full as life on the ranch can be. Living here forces you to work with and see other people. Eat with them too.

I breathe a sigh of relief when I slip into the kitchen unnoticed. Keeping to the far side of the room, I'm about to escape through the little hall that leads to the mudroom when I draw up short at the sound of my name.

"Wheeler! I thought I saw your car earlier today. Welcome back to the ranch." Duke is standing at the counter with a red onion in one hand and an enormous chef's knife in the other. He smiles, his mouth and eyes creasing in the most handsome way imaginable, and I feel weak in the knees again. "I hope you're staying for lunch."

I blush, hard. All the boys plus Patsy are looking at me now. I got dressed in real clothes this morning—jeans, a cute top that's cropped enough to show a sliver of stomach, and my favorite pair of short Bellamy Brooks boots—but I still feel unprepared for the onslaught of attention.

Really, Duke's attention. Damn does he look *good* in his cowboy getup. Dusty jeans that fit just right. A weathered chambray button-up, the sleeves rolled up to reveal deeply tan, slightly sweaty forearms. A bandana and boots and a sun-bleached Stetson that, *wow*, does something to me.

"Um," I manage. "I was—work—I have so much to do. It's month end, so..."

Patsy wrinkles her forehead. "You sure, honey? My pimento cheese and bacon burgers aren't to be missed. They're best fresh out of the frying pan."

"She's right." Duke tilts his head toward the bowl of pimento cheese Patsy's just pulled from the fridge. "Besides, you can't work if you're hungry."

"Please stay, Wheeler." Ryder plucks a bottle of Texas Pete from a cabinet. "If only so I have someone to talk to besides these assholes."

"Hey," Cash barks. "You'd best watch that mouth. Ella's gonna be here any minute—"

"I'm already *here*, Uncle Cashy!"

I glance over my shoulder to see a little girl with big blue eyes and brown hair burst into the kitchen. Mollie is right behind her, smiles on both their faces.

"Shit." Ryder slaps a hand over his mouth. "I mean, shoot. Hope she didn't hear that."

"Oh, I'm sure she did." Sawyer scoops his daughter into his arms and presses a noisy kiss to her cheek.

"Hey, Wheeler!" Mollie pulls me in for a hug. "Drive go okay?"

"It was easy."

"How was school, Elly Belly Boo?" Sawyer asks.

"Ew, Daddy, your scruffies are very scruffy today." Ella runs a hand over his face. "But I still love you."

"Thank goodness. Did you eat your lunch?"

"No. I don't like your sandwiches very much."

Everyone laughs at that. I forgot how cute kids can be. Haines was born when I was five and a half, and I loved having an adorable younger brother to tote around and play with when I was little. My parents joke that he was my first—and favorite—baby doll.

"Well, lucky for you, I made an extra cheeseburger." Patsy says. "And maybe some extra dessert too."

Ella gasps. "Is it cake?"

"Even better. It's chocolate peanut butter pie."

"Oh!" The little girl screams with delight, and I feel that tug in my chest again. "Oh my *goodness*! That's my favorite! Thank you, Miss Patsy!" She leans over, arms outstretched to Patsy.

Patsy lifts Ella out of Sawyer's arms and settles her on her hip, bopping her on the nose. "You're so welcome."

When was the last time I let myself be delighted like

that? The last time I was so happy I couldn't help but holler? I honestly can't remember.

"Lord, and I been tryin' to eat healthy." Ryder pats his stomach. "So much for that."

Patsy *tsks*. "Diets are not allowed in my kitchen. Neither are picky eaters."

"Well, I'm screwed, then," Ryder replies.

"Now y'all go sit while I put these burgers together."

I turn my head, and my stomach takes a tumble when I lock eyes with Duke. He was looking at me.

Is looking at me. He put the knife down, but he's still holding the onion. Am I the one who keeps looking for him? Or is he the one always staring at me?

I look away and head for the island. No one sits down, of course, opting instead to help Patsy finish preparing lunch. Duke chops his onion. Mollie and Cash slather the burgers with healthy spoonfuls of pimento cheese. Sawyer and I arrange a platter of burger toppings: crisp leaves of iceberg lettuce, slices of juicy heirloom tomatoes, pickles, bacon, hot pepper jam.

Turns out food prep is fun when you're doing it with a bunch of cowboys. The camaraderie, the sense of community, of being in this together—it's special, and it makes me long to experience it more often.

Duke sidles up beside me to dump a handful of sliced red onion onto the platter. I smile when I see his watery eyes.

"In our feelings this morning?" I ask.

Patsy serves breakfast at four thirty a.m., which means lunch is on the early side too. We're usually seated at the table by eleven, if not earlier.

"Sorry." He dabs his eye with the back of his wrist. "Food this good just gets me emotional, ya know?"

"No need to apologize. If there's any food that would make me shed a tear, it's Patsy's."

Patsy grins as she sets a sheet pan of burger buns, warmed on the griddle, beside the toppings. "Y'all sure do know how to make a gal feel special. Now eat! Duke, I made enough so that everyone gets two burgers. Don't take a third unless everyone's done, you hear?"

I stare at him. "You can eat three burgers? Just like that?"

"Just like that." Snapping his fingers, he grins. "I meant what I said—you can't work when you're hungry. And cowboying is hungry work. Come to think of it, I'm hungry most of the time."

When I watch him take off his hat before sitting down, his bicep bulging against his shirt as he reaches up to run his fingers through his thick, slightly matted hair, I have a deep, *deep* understanding of that hunger.

Everyone eats. The flow of conversation is steady, sometimes raucous. Ella begs for the biggest slice of pie, but Patsy gives it to me instead.

"For our honored guest," she says with a wink. "It's always nice having you back, Wheeler."

"It's always nice to be back," I say, chest squeezing.

I mean that. It's like they actually enjoy having me around.

Like they enjoy my company.

This is how family is supposed to feel. With my own family—my life—melting down around me, I'd forgotten that fact.

Mollie's phone beeps, making her look up. Immediately, her eyes go wide.

"What is it?" I ask.

She picks up her phone and slides her thumb across the screen. "An email from Bailey."

My stomach drops. Bailey Pappas is our whiz of a publicist. She's helped launch some major brands in the high-end fashion space, and we're hoping she can do the same for Bellamy Brooks. Bailey has been knocking on some pretty amazing doors on our behalf—buyers for department stores, fashion magazines, major influencers, boutiques with huge followings that host trunk shows—and we've slowly but surely gotten traction, especially on social media.

"It's about *Elle*." Mollie scrolls. Then she gasps, her hand going to her mouth. "Oh my God, we're going to be in the feature." Her eyes flick to meet mine as they fill with tears. "Wheeler, our boots are going to be in *Elle!*"

I blink. Blink again. I feel a smile pull at the corners of my lips. My heart pinballs around inside my rib cage.

"Seriously?" I ask.

She throws up her arms. "Seriously. The purple pair of shorties. Apparently violet is the hue of the season."

Holy shit, this is a big deal.

This is happening. Right now.

My dreams are literally coming true right before my eyes. This feature will take us to the next level. Stores and influencers will start knocking on *our* door, which means we'll be selling a lot more Bellamy Brooks boots.

With that kind of money, I can finally pay back my parents. Pay myself a decent salary. Hell, maybe I can even buy out my car lease.

I want to channel Ella's unbridled delight. Jump up and scream and just—yeah, celebrate this huge fucking moment. Mollie and I sure as hell deserve it.

And I do celebrate. Kind of. I reach across the table and grab Mollie's hands, waiting for the tears to come. I manage to smile.

Meanwhile, everyone around us erupts in hoots and hollers. Cash pulls Mollie in for a teary hug. Sawyer stomps his feet, and Ella claps her hands. Wyatt and Sally—when did she arrive?—are jumping up and down. Patsy is crying.

And Duke—

Duke is looking at me, a funny gleam in his eye like he *knows* I'm missing a step here. Like the news isn't hitting as hard as it should.

Really, why can't I be fucking happy for myself for once?

Averting my gaze, I shove that depressing thought aside and let Mollie skip around the table to wrap me in a tight hug.

"We also booked a trunk show at Aspen Leather Company in March," she says in my ear. "I was waiting until you got here to tell you."

My heart does a backflip of genuine delight. Okay, so I'm not *totally* numb. Just mostly. "Oh my God!"

"I know."

"Oh my *God*, Mollie!"

"I *know*!"

Aspen Leather Company is the wildly famous Western wear store that's been a city staple for over fifty years. They sell high-end boots, handmade belts and belt buckles, and an assortment of gorgeous leather jackets, pants, and handbags. Its regulars are well-heeled locals and tourists alike, and over the holidays, it becomes a celebrity mob scene.

They also have two million Instagram followers. There's no doubt in my mind that we'll sell out of whatever stock we bring with us, but the real value of the trunk show will be the exposure we'll get. The hope being, of course, that we make Aspen Leather Company's regulars *our* regulars.

Mollie pulls back, holding my shoulders. "Road trip when I get back from my honeymoon? You and me?"

Seeing her tears up close finally has me tearing up. "Hell—I mean *heck* yes. Wouldn't miss it for the world!"

CHAPTER 6
Road Trips in Rent-a-Trucks
Duke

APRIL

***"No. Fucking. Way."* Hands on my hips, I look at the** U-Haul and shake my head. "You are not driving this thing *by yourself* all the way to Colorado."

"Watch me." Wheeler goes up on her toes to rearrange a box in the back of the truck. "I learned to drive in my mom's Yukon, so..."

"I bet your mom's Yukon had power steering and automatic brakes. This thing"—I nod at the white and orange abomination parked in front of the New House—"I'm not even sure if it has brakes. Or heat."

"You're being ridiculous." Falling back on her heels, she rolls her eyes at me. "Don't you have cowboy things to do?"

I always have cowboy things to do. But whenever Wheeler is around, I have a hard time doing them.

Hard time focusing on anything other than, well, the pretty redhead with a smart mouth and cute ass. Which is how I ended up meandering to the driveway after lunch. Wheeler hadn't shown up to eat, so naturally I wandered around the house, telling myself I was just winding down after a long, boring morning with the herd.

The image of this cute little redhead driving this big ugly truck through the Rockies *in April* gives me heart palpitations. Who thought this was a good idea? I can't believe Mollie is letting her do this.

A lot has changed since the girls booked this trunk show in Aspen. Mollie and Cash got married in a cute little ceremony underneath an arbor of roses in their cabin's backyard. Then Mollie found out on their honeymoon in Australia that she was pregnant.

She's in her second trimester now. She and the baby are healthy. But earlier this week, Mollie's doctor put her on bed rest after she had some spotting, which means she isn't able to travel to Colorado with Wheeler for their trunk show this weekend.

So now Wheeler, being the dedicated entrepreneur she is, is planning to go to the trunk show by herself.

"You know Wheeler," Mollie said last night when I confronted her about the situation. "That girl is gonna do what she wants to do."

"You need to fight her harder on this."

"I've tried."

"Reschedule the pop-up, then."

"I've *tried*, Duke."

It's close to a twenty-hour drive through some pretty treacherous mountains.

I've driven through the Rockies several times with Garrett Luck, Mollie's dad, who passed away last year, usually to purchase quarter horses from a ranch in Wyoming. Those roads ain't for the faint of heart. Especially with the late-season snow they're calling for.

I obviously can't let her drive alone. I don't want her to die for one thing. For another, my heart always skips a beat at the idea of having an excuse to get the hell out of Hartsville. Back in the fall, my brothers and I had a great fucking time in Austin for Cash's bachelor party. Even before we left the Texas state capital, I was itching to plan my next trip.

Really, to get out of Hartsville again.

I get that buzzing sensation at the top of my spine. Ryder. Go figure, he was right. Giving Wheeler space, biding my time, has been the right call. Because all of a sudden, I have an opportunity to finally make this girl mine *and* experience someplace new.

"Y'all got plenty of money now, Wheeler," I hear myself telling her. "Why don't you pay to ship all this shit and fly instead?"

"Because I don't trust anyone but myself to get these boots to Aspen safely. This pop-up is a big deal for us, Duke, and I need everything to be perfect. Plus, this way I don't have to fit all my outfits into one suitcase. Faux fur takes up a *lot* of room." She's reaching inside the truck again, straining to reach the boxes on the tippy top of the stacks of boots piled inside.

Glancing up at the sky—*God give me strength*—I walk over to help. I reach the boxes easily, rearranging them so the stacks fit tightly inside the truck.

I'm hit by the image of her taking a sharp turn and the boxes tumbling down, shaking the truck. She'll jam on the brakes, and they won't work, and she'll be screaming as she tries to pull over, boxes thumping around in the back while she catches the lip of the road and plunges to her death off the side of a mountain.

Wow.

Wow, that was graphic. And specific. And weird.

Mostly, though, it's terrifying.

"How many outfits are you bringing?" I manage.

"Too many. Aspen is fabulous, so I need to be fabulous too."

She's excited. It's cute.

She's really fucking cute. Goddamn, I miss talking to her. Then again, can you miss talking to someone you only really talked to once, in a bar, over the best one and a half beers you've ever had?

"You check the weather?" I ask.

"It'll be fine."

I make a harrumphing sound that makes me think of my dad. "They're calling for snow. Big system moving onshore from the Pacific—"

"You do know Colorado is, like, two thousand miles from any ocean?"

"You indoor people with your indoor jobs. Believe me when I say it's a mistake not to pay attention to the weather."

Wheeler grins, her eyes dancing as she turns to look at me. "I *am* an indoor girl, and I'm proud of it."

Exactly why she shouldn't be driving this truck. Alone. To a destination eight hundred miles from here. A twenty-hour drive ain't for the faint of heart.

"You ever driven in snow before?"

Wheeler reaches for the latch on the truck's sliding back door. "I drove to the gym in a hailstorm once."

I beat her to it, our hands brushing as I yank down the door. "Now you're just trying to get me riled up."

"Why do you let me get you riled up?"

"Because you're an indoor girl visiting a very outdoor place, and I could never forgive myself if you were bit by a rattlesnake and died or, yeah, you drove a U-Haul full of your beautiful boots off the side of a mountain."

"That's dark."

I manage a tight grin. "Just like my mood."

"Lighten up." She pats my chest. "I'll be back in a few days, hopefully with an empty truck. Promise I'll be fine."

But you don't know that. I need to know you're safe.

It's ridiculous how much I care, right? Yeah, I thought Wheeler and I really connected that night at the Rattler. Beyond that, though, we actually haven't interacted all that much outside of group settings. We're friendly, but would I even call us friends?

I don't know.

All I know is there's a good chance this girl ends up hurt—or worse—if she drives to Aspen all by herself this weekend.

There's a good chance I won't get another opportunity to visit a place like that anytime soon.

Wyatt will have a shit fit about me missing work. But Cash and Mollie are in lockdown here in Hartsville now that she's on bed rest, which means he's available to fill in. I can always offer to do admin work remotely—grab one of the ranch's laptops and bring it with me.

But really, I don't care what my brothers say about me going. The idea of staying on the ranch suddenly makes me feel like I'm coming out of my skin.

Figure I'm killing two birds with one stone: by going to Aspen, I keep Wheeler safe, and I get to scratch my travel itch.

Without thinking, I wrap my fingers around Wheeler's wrist. She's delicate here, her bones so slender my fingertips overlap by a good amount. I don't miss the flicker of heat in her eyes that she tries to hide by blinking and looking away.

"I'll go to Aspen with you."

"What?" Her eyes bulge as they lock on mine. She scoffs, dropping her hand. "Stop teasing me."

I release my grip. "I'm not teasing. I'll be your assistant for the weekend. Put me to work, Ms. Rankin."

She scoffs again. "Why the hell would you want to come with me on a really, *really* long road trip?"

"Better question: why wouldn't I come? I've never been to Aspen." I nod at the truck behind her. "Handling heavy machinery is literally my job. Well, a big part of it anyway. And I'm charming as fuck. I'll help you sell out of your boots, no problem."

She's still staring at me. At last, she huffs out a low chuckle, tucking her hair behind her ear. "I appreciate the offer, Duke. But I think it's best if I do this on my own." She offers me a tight smile. "Thanks, though."

"Maybe. Or maybe I don't get out of Texas nearly enough, and I'm dying a slow death doing the same thing with the same people all day, every day. This trip—it could be good for the both of us, yeah?"

Her smile falters. "Since when do cowboys get sick of cowboying?"

"All the fucking time. It's hard work. I've been doing it since I was about yay high." I flex my wrist down by my knee. "You really gonna deprive me of a much-needed break?"

Wheeler rolls her eyes, even as the edges of her mouth twitch. "Way to lay it on real thick."

"Kinda my style."

"I've noticed."

My chest twists. *You paying attention to me, sweetheart? Maybe you really are curious about me, same as I've been curious about you.*

"Say yes, Wheeler. You make me beg, I will. But I promise to be the best damn driver and assistant and model you could ask for."

She's laughing for real now. "You and the modeling. We don't make men's boots, remember?"

"Not yet." I wag my brows. "Maybe I could convince you to give it a shot on the ride up to Aspen. I got some ideas."

"Of course you do." She runs her tongue along the bright pink seam of her bottom lip. "Lemme think about it, okay?"

"Me coming with you? Or Bellamy Brooks's first men's collection, the one that's rugged yet polished and sells out in under a minute?"

She beams. "Both."

I hold up my hands. "I ain't going anywhere. Unless you give me the chance to take a trip that just might change my perspective and my life for the better."

"My *God*, you're shameless!" She gives my shoulder a playful shove.

This electricity between us is back. Suits me just fine. But I know it spooked her the night we met.

I'm determined not to scare her away again. Figure

I'll just be myself, listen to her as best as I can, make her laugh, and hope for the best.

I feel like we're already making progress.

"And I'll work for free," I add. "Just to sweeten the deal. C'mon, Wheeler. You can't say no to that."

She closes her eyes and throws up her hands. "Fine! Fine, you can come. But I really do have to work on this trip. I don't mind you partying—"

"I'm not interested in partying."

"You say that now. You've never been to Aspen."

"And you've never had me as an assistant. Here, how about I get your number?" I dig my phone out of my pocket, giddy that I finally have an excuse to have her contact info in my phone. "I'll start doing some research and send you a route and itinerary. Any snack preferences I should know about? Twizzlers are my favorite road trip food. And are you a podcast kinda girl, or do you prefer to listen to music?"

Her eyes are bright as they bounce between mine. "Since when are you an overachiever?"

"Since forever. Number, please."

We hit the road at four a.m. two days later, on a Thursday.

Patsy, God bless her, pours us each an enormous thermos of coffee and hands us a paper bag on our way out. When I open it, I find that it's filled with foil-wrapped breakfast burritos and homemade crackers with pimento cheese.

"Y'all be safe." Patsy pulls me in for a tight hug before whispering, "And have fun. You deserve it, Duke. I hope you find what you're looking for."

Patsy, as our adopted mother figure, knows as well as anyone in our family that I dream of living life on my own terms.

I think about her words as I drive the rattling U-Haul through the gray light of dawn. The pavement, the flat, sprawling land, the clear sky—it's all different shades of the same color this time of day. Pretty in a weird, moonlike way.

I feel like I should know what I'm looking for, but I don't, other than a change of scenery and maybe a gigantic neon sign pointing me toward the path I'm meant to be on.

I wouldn't say I feel lost. More like stuck. Bored. The restlessness that's plagued me for as long as I can remember is only getting worse.

Is this just what happens when you're twenty-seven? The quarter-life crisis people talk about? No one I know seems discontent with their lot in life. Doesn't help that three of my brothers have paired off in quick succession over the past six months. Not only have they found their purpose, they've also found their people.

I'm happy for them. Truly. But I also wonder why I haven't found my purpose yet or my soulmate. Makes me wonder if I just expect too much. If the freedom I'm seeking just doesn't exist.

All I know is life today sucks a lot less than it did yesterday: I'm heading to Colorado on a Thursday with a pretty girl and a truck full of pretty boots. Not a cow or so much as a whiff of manure for miles.

The highway is empty. The endless space before us opens up a similar space inside my chest, giving me more room to breathe. Feels nice.

Also feels nice to drink coffee in contented silence beside Wheeler. She's bundled up in a pair of sweats and a jacket, her hair in a knot at the top of her head. No makeup, at least not that I can tell.

She sips her coffee and hums. "Patsy makes the best everything I've ever had. I might actually cry over how good this coffee is."

"In your feelings, huh?" I can't help but grin at the inside joke. Really, at the fact that Wheeler and I have an inside joke despite how little we see each other these days.

"Good food makes life worth living."

"Hard agree."

"Y'all seem close." Wheeler eyes me. "Your family and the Powells. Well, your family and really everyone else who works on the ranch."

I nod, sipping my coffee. "Yep. Patsy and John B kind of took us under their wing after our parents died. Garrett Luck too. Not sure what we would've done without all those helping hands."

"That's so nice." Wheeler turns her head to look out the window. "I know you said you couldn't wait to get out of Hartsville, which I understand. But it's not like that in most places."

"What do you mean?"

"That people are willing to help out like that. Also, that you love your family *and* like them too." She lets out a long, low breath. "Mollie adores that about y'all. She feels so lucky to be a part of your family."

"We love her. Dearly. She's been so good for Cash and for the ranch."

"Cash has been so good for her. You all have. I've never seen her so happy."

I glance at Wheeler, who is still turned away from me. There's a wistfulness in her words. She's definitely going through some shit, and that shit's definitely making her unhappy.

Something to do with her family, maybe?

I shift my grip on the wheel, glancing in the side mirror. A thin, pink line has appeared on the horizon. It burns to red just as I look away. *Red sky in the morning, sailors take warning.*

"Hey, Wheeler?" I drop my thermos into a cupholder. "Check the weather for me if you don't mind."

She straightens, grabbing her phone from the purse at her feet. "I did last night before I went to bed."

"I did too."

"Said the worst of the storm is supposed to miss Aspen. The snow won't start until early tomorrow morning, so we'll be fine."

"Check again, please."

Wheeler rolls her eyes, but her thumbs still move over her screen. "Such a Boy Scout."

"You wanna sell these boots? We gotta make sure we can get to the store. Weather up in those mountains is a lot more unpredictable than we're used to."

"Whatever you say." She scrolls for a beat. Then her thumbs go still. "Hm."

"What?"

"It appears the forecast has changed just the tiniest bit."

I groan. "Lemme guess. They're calling for a direct hit?"

"I mean, there's a blizzard warning in effect in Aspen from eight o'clock tonight until—"

"Shit." I hit the gas. The truck shudders, its engine roaring in protest. "I'm glad we got on the road early. I hope you don't need bathroom breaks, because we ain't got time for 'em."

"What? Don't be ridiculous."

"Think you can pee in a soda bottle?"

She reaches across the dash to give me one of her playful shoves. "I can, but you don't want me to because I'd be very, *very* tempted to dump it over your head."

I love getting her riled up. She's cute when she can't help herself.

"Desperate times." I reach for my coffee. "Mind grabbing me one of those burritos?"

Wheeler crosses her arms. "Grab it yourself."

"You really have a lot of faith in me keeping this thing on the road with just one hand."

"Bet you have lots of practice doing things with just that hand. Don't tell me you haven't built up those forearm muscles."

Laughter, real and unexpected, bursts through me. "I have. From playing darts."

"I'm sure that's what you play with." Her lips twitch as she reaches for the bag behind her seat.

Fuck, she's quick. And dirty. I like that.

I haven't stopped thinking about the amazing chemistry Wheeler and I had that night at the Rattler. Which of course has me thinking about whether we'll hook up on this trip. I'm down to have some fun between the sheets, obviously. I haven't had interest in sleeping with anyone else since I met Wheeler, so of course I'd love the chance to get naked.

We're staying at a cabin in Aspen that belongs to a

family friend of hers, which they graciously offered to let her use since they're out of town. She and I will be seeing a lot of each other.

A *lot*.

But the potential for hooking up with Wheeler is not *why* I wanted to come on this trip. Sure, getting her naked would be an excellent bonus. But I'd take just being around her—getting to know more about her and her business.

Let's be real, though. She's made it pretty clear she wants to keep things friendly between us. I still haven't figured out what happened the night we met, but I'm relatively certain she hasn't changed her mind about friend zoning me. Which sucks.

Then again, who knows what will happen on this trip? Maybe a change of scenery will change her mind about me. Maybe it doesn't.

Either way, I got out of Hartsville, and I get to learn new things about a new girl in a new place.

I'll take it.

Just like I take the burrito that Wheeler holds out to me. I smile when I see that she's rolled back the foil and everything. She's even got a paper napkin in her other hand.

"Thank you kindly."

"You're welcome." Sipping her coffee, she glances at me. "Thanks for coming, Duke. I mean that."

"If we don't die driving up Aspen Mountain in this blizzard, I think we'll have ourselves a nice little trip, don't you?"

"Shut up. We'll be fine." She rolls her eyes, but her lips are pulled into a smile as she looks at the hand I have on the wheel. "See? That hand seems to be doing great on its own. You practice that one-handed stuff a lot, huh?"

"Darts? Not as much as I'd like. But I'm a natural talent, so…"

"Don't make me shove that burrito in your face."

"Remember, the whole idea here is staying alive, which means staying on the road. Which means no burritos being shoved in faces."

She glances at the clump of pico de gallo that drops into my lap. "You're a messy eater."

"I prefer 'enthusiastic,'" I reply around a mouthful of burrito.

"Guys usually overestimate themselves in that respect."

I'm laughing again. "You ever know me to go halfway on anything?"

Her eyes glimmer. "We didn't ever find out who was better at darts, did we?"

Fuck me, this girl's got my mind in the gutter. She's not talking about darts, and neither am I when I say, "We're not dead yet. We got time."

She doesn't respond to that. But she's still smiling when she brings her thermos to her lips.

CHAPTER 7
Gas Station Wine and Cozy Cabin Vibes
Duke

We're climbing into the mountains when a gust of wind hits us, shaking the truck.

The steering wheel vibrates beneath my fingers. I tighten my grip, ducking my head to peer out the windshield.

"That doesn't sound good." Wheeler grips the handle on the frame above her door. "Do you think we should pull over, or…"

We've been on the road for over twelve hours now. The afternoon light is fading. Somewhere in the back of my mind, it registers just how bone tired I am. My ass is sore, my back aches, and my eyes are sandpaper, thanks to leaving my damn contacts in for way too long. I'd take them out, but I feel like I look like a dork in my glasses.

I perk right the fuck up, though, when the wind hits us again and I have to yank on the steering wheel to keep us in our lane.

"Duke!" Wheeler's other hand lands on my forearm.

"Jesus, the wind up here. Why didn't they say it would be this bad?"

The highway is mostly deserted, save for the occasional plow and salt trucks. But there's a sheer drop on our left and a wall of rock on our right, so even though we're the only ones on the road, I still need to be careful.

I chuckle, partly as an attempt to keep Wheeler at ease. "They kinda did with that blizzard warning."

"The blizzard's not supposed to start until eight." She glances at the clock that glows on the dash. "It's only five."

I shrug. "Told you the weather up here changes quickly."

"You sure you're okay to drive?"

"Yep. All good."

Truth be told, the weather is deteriorating fast. The snow has started. Just flurries at the moment, but the wind is whipping them around. I know once the snow really starts to come down, we'll be facing whiteout conditions. Especially as it gets dark. The truck's headlights will reflect off the snow, making it virtually impossible to see.

We gotta get to Aspen before that happens. Four more hours. A little less if we get lucky with the weather.

In the meantime, I have to keep Wheeler calm. My cute little city girl clearly ain't used to traveling in adverse conditions.

Luckily for her, I am. Garrett Luck taught me how to drive in rain, shine, and snow while hauling a trailer full of ornery mustangs.

Wouldn't say this is easy in comparison, but I'm only

the normal amount of nervous as we climb our way through the mountains in the deepening darkness. An hour passes. Two. Three.

I keep the conversation flowing in an effort to distract Wheeler, the two of us chatting about a little bit of everything. She asks what my favorite book is—toss up between anything Ernest Hemingway or Anthony Bourdain wrote—and I pick her brain about the World War II fiction she devours in marathon audiobook sessions while driving between Dallas and Hartsville.

We share a love of Excel, Julia Louis-Dreyfus, and colored lights at Christmas. It's my favorite holiday, but hers is Halloween because she loves to dress up and buy Reese's pumpkins in bulk.

The truck doesn't have Bluetooth—hell, it doesn't have so much as a CD player or tape deck—so we find a country station on the radio, and together we sing along to Dolly Parton and Garth Brooks.

"So this trunk show." I bite into a Twizzler. "What are your goals, other than selling all those boots we got in the back?"

Wheeler looks vacantly at the Twizzler she has in her hand. "Network. Meet their buyers, their customers. Get feedback on what people are looking for. Then again, who knows if this trunk show is even gonna happen?" She glances out the window at the swirling snow. "I mean, I know Dallas is totally ridiculous when the weather gets bad. Half an inch of snow, and the whole city shuts down. I imagine Aspen is much better prepared to handle it. Still, if this storm dumps a couple feet of snow on us…"

"They'll clear it, no problem. And if we gotta stay an

extra day or two to make up for lost time, then we stay an extra day or two."

I feel her looking at me. "You'd be okay with that?"

"Wheeler, I am so damn happy to be somewhere other than Hartsville I can't even tell you. Of course I'm okay with that. Ask me to stay a week. Two weeks. I'd love the excuse to be away."

She lets out a soft chuckle. "You really don't get out enough, do you?"

"Out of Hartsville? No, I don't."

The phone in her lap lights up, the ringtone chiming. I glance at it and see *Dad—Work* on the top of the screen.

I lean away, silently giving her space to take the call. Instead, she hits the button on the side of her phone and sends the call to voicemail.

I wait for her to say something. Explain why she didn't pick up her dad's call. Maybe she's too nervous about the weather to chat right now.

Or maybe there's another reason why she doesn't want to talk to her dad. She keeps dropping these hints that her family life isn't the happiest.

Whatever the case, Wheeler pretends like the call never happened. Instead, she drops the phone into her cupholder and puts the Twizzler in her mouth. She bites down, hard, giving the red candy rope a vicious tug.

"Guess we'll cross the bridge when we get there," she says. "If Aspen Leather Company is closed tomorrow or Saturday, then we figure out plan B. Thanks for being flexible."

"Told you I'm gonna be the best damn assistant you ever had."

"The mouthiest for sure."

"But you like it."

The green and red lights of the dashboard catch on her eyes when she looks at me. "Keeps things interesting, I'll say that much."

Conditions steadily worsen. The radio station we're listening to slowly fades out, so Wheeler has to search for something else. She finds a pop station, and we listen to Lady Gaga and the Jonas Brothers—I think—in tense silence.

Wheeler doesn't even to pretend to be relaxed, while I try my damnedest to keep the mood light by cracking jokes and bopping my head to the beat of each song.

The relief I feel when we finally cruise into Aspen city limits hits me like, well, a U-Haul truck.

"We should grab some supplies for the house real quick." I drive slowly, looking out the windows. "If you see a grocery store, let me know."

The only thing we find open is a gas station. Not ideal, but if we don't get our asses up to this house, pronto, we're either gonna get stuck on the side of the road or fall clear off a cliff.

Stepping out of the truck, the cold slaps me across the face. The wind is bitter, biting at any sliver of exposed skin.

Wheeler joins me outside and moans, flipping up the fur-lined hood on her jacket. "Ohmygod I *hate* this."

"My tender little Texas flower." Chuckling, I reach over and tug up her zipper so that her mouth and nose are covered. "We'll make it quick. Booze, snacks, coffee. The rest we'll figure out later."

"I like this plan."

We scurry inside, both of us exhaling audibly as we

stand underneath a blast of heat. I do a quick scan of the aisles. We're not working with much, but it's enough to get us through the next twenty-four to forty-eight hours. Maybe this house we're staying at will have some better food in the freezer?

"Talk to me. I know you drink coffee." I grab a pound of Dunkin' off the shelf and drop it in the basket I picked up by the cash register. "Do you always eat breakfast? That burrito seemed to hit the spot."

Wheeler may or may not have made some porn-adjacent sounds as she polished off her breakfast this morning. I may or may not have had to crack the window to let in some cold air. Told Wheeler I needed a pick-me-up because I was tired. But really, I'd started to sweat. My dick liked those sounds just a little too much.

"I mean." She reaches up for a box of Cinnamon Toast Crunch. "We should probably have something on hand just in case."

I grin. "You just want an excuse to eat that garbage, don't you?"

"Well, yeah." She's grinning too, looking so adorable in her furry hood with her bright pink cheeks that my heart skips a beat. "My parents would buy fun cereal like this when we'd go on vacation. Did you not eat it growing up?"

I grab the box and drop it in the basket. "Lived on the stuff. Cinnamon Toast Crunch just so happens to be among my favorites. Drinking the milk at the end?"

"Best part!"

"Let's not forget to grab milk, then."

"I'm on it."

"See?" I hold out my fist. "Teamwork makes the dream work."

Scoffing, she rolls her eyes and gives me a reluctant fist bump. "Not sure this counts, but okay."

We grab a couple cans of Pringles, some bread, butter, eggs, OJ, and cheese. The solo jar of salsa looks lonely on the shelf, so I grab that too, along with sugar and milk.

We hit the beer and wine aisle last. Wheeler holds up a bottle of wine with a fish on the label. "Feels like a cab kinda night, no?"

"Is that going to be enough?"

"How much are you planning on drinking?"

"No telling how long we'll be snowed in. And far as I can tell, you haven't properly celebrated all those wins that keep adding up for you and Mollie." I pick up a box of cabernet sauvignon. "This is more our speed."

Wheeler stands beside me. "Are you suggesting we play slap the bag?"

Slap the bag is an exceptionally stupid drinking game we'd play back in the day. First, you remove the bag of wine from inside the box. Then one person holds up the bag while the other gets on his or her knees and drinks from the bag for as long as possible. Once they're done, they simply slap the bag and pass it on to the next person.

Mindless? Yes. Does it get you buzzed in a hurry? Also yes.

Not like I want to get Wheeler drunk. I just want her to be able to relax after a long, stressful day.

"I'm absolutely suggesting we play slap the bag." I put the box in my basket, careful not to crush the loaf of

Wonder Bread. "The fancy version, though, since we're in a fancy place, and I'm springing for the fancy boxed wine."

Wheeler ducks her lips and nods. "I could get on board with that. Although you're not springing for anything. Since this is a business trip, our food goes on my business card."

I head for the register. "So you're buying this round, huh?"

"I most certainly am." She's already digging inside her purse. "Just gimme a minute to find that damn card..."

But when it's time to pay, I beat Wheeler to it, sticking my card into the reader just as she finds her Amex.

"Duke!"

I gently elbow her outstretched arm, card in hand, away. "Your money's no good here."

"Seriously, you have to let me pay. You drove, and you brought all that candy..." She looks up at the cashier. "Ma'am, is there a way to void this transaction?"

The reader beeps. Giving Wheeler a bored look, the cashier asks if I want a receipt.

"We're good, thanks."

"We'll take a receipt if you don't mind." Wheeler glares at me. "That way, I know how much I owe you."

"Would you quit? We'll settle up later." I nod at the doors. "Now get in the truck. We ain't got much time, Bluebonnet."

She gives me a look as she adjusts her hood. "Bluebonnet?"

I give her a look right back. "Surely you know what—"

"Of course I know what a bluebonnet is. I just don't get why I have a nickname all of a sudden."

"Because you're my Texas flower, remember?"
"Ew."
"Would you prefer Blue?"
"I would prefer Wheeler, thanks."
"Got it." I step forward, activating the automatic sliding door. "All right, Blue. Gird your loins. It's as cold as a witch's tit in a steel bra out there."

Four miles and two near-death experiences later, we pull into a driveway that must be heated because it's not the least bit icy. My chest feels tight as I put the truck in park. Not sure *I* breathed all that much during the last mile. Those hairpin turns were not fun in whiteout conditions, especially when you're driving a dinosaur of a truck whose tires have a questionable amount of tread.

I look through the windshield at the house. Even in the dark, I can see how enormous it is. How beautiful too. It's exactly what I would picture a mansion in Aspen looking like: stone siding, big steel windows, a soaring, timber-framed roofline. Tucked into the side of Aspen Mountain, the house must have incredible views of the Rockies. It's surrounded by the area's famous aspen trees, some of them soaring twenty, thirty, fifty feet high.

The property must be worth tens of millions of dollars. Exactly what kind of "family friends" does Miss Wheeler Rankin here have?

"Holy shit." I swivel my head to look at her. "You said we were staying at a cabin."

She unbuckles her seat belt and reaches for her bag. "Yup."

"This is not a cabin."

"It's a cabin. It's just a really big cabin." She straightens.

"I mean, it's still made out of wood and stuff. Lots of beams and antlers inside. Lots of fireplaces."

"And you know these people how?"

She lifts a shoulder, then reaches for her door handle. "My parents have very rich, very generous friends. One of the few perks of—God, how am I already freezing? Let's get the hell inside."

We enter through a side door with a keypad. I frown when I hear Wheeler's teeth chattering as we step inside.

"Hang tight, Blue. I'll get a fire going."

"That sounds so nice."

She doesn't call me out on the nickname. Makes me smile.

"Teamwork." I flick on a light switch.

I'm struck dumb by what I see. We're in a mudroom that's about as big as the New House's kitchen. It's neat as a pin, not so much as a speck of dust or pair of shoes out of place.

I follow Wheeler into a kitchen with double-height ceilings and a pair of huge, marble-topped islands. She turns on the lights, and the living room comes into view. A stone fireplace dominates the space, along with a wall of those steel windows that go all the way up to the roofline.

There are two big, cushy sofas in front of the fireplace, complete with plenty of pillows and fur throw blankets.

Not gonna lie, first thing I think of is laying those blankets down on the floor by the fire. Getting Wheeler naked and curling her into the heat of my body. She'd warm up in no time.

"There's plenty of bedrooms," Wheeler is saying, "so take your pick."

My cock twitches. Just hearing her say the *word* bedroom has me feeling some kind of way. As sick as this place is, I almost wish we were staying in a legit cabin with only one bedroom. One bed.

Wonder how that would shake out?

In the still silence of the house, the howling wind sounds enormous. I look up at a loud groan. Apparently the roof likes that wind about as much as I do.

"You think we're okay?" Wheeler asks.

"Gonna take more than a little wind to knock down this house. Here, let me put the groceries away, and then I'll put your suitcase in your room."

"I can do that."

But again, I beat her to it, grabbing her luggage and bringing it to her bedroom. She picked a gorgeous spot that's just off the living area. It's got a big-ass bathroom and a great little nook tucked inside the windows that would be perfect for working or reading.

Can I join you in here? I wanna ask.

"What the fuck do you have in here?" I ask instead, lifting her suitcase onto a luggage rack with an exaggerated grunt.

"The dismembered bodies of my enemies. Why?"

Goddamn, I like how this girl makes me laugh. "If you're sayin' this is my last night on earth…"

"Nah." She throws me a hot look over her shoulder as she unzips her jacket. "I need you to drive me back down the mountain for my trunk show. After that, though, all bets are off."

"I best get to drinking, then. Might as well enjoy my last twenty-four hours on earth." I saunter across the room to help her out of her jacket. "How 'bout we get comfortable? I'll get that bag of wine ready for slapping, and I can make us some grilled cheese if you're hungry."

I don't miss the way she shivers as my thumbs graze the nape of her neck. When she turns around, I see her nipples poking through the fine knit of her sweater.

Her eyes catch on mine. My body pulses. Those eyes move to my mouth, and for a wild heartbeat, I think—

Hell, is this girl gonna kiss me?

"No," she blurts, looking away. "I mean yes. Yes, I'm hungry. Let me get out of these clothes—"

Dear God.

"—and I'll join you."

I bite down on the inside of my cheek. "Great."

"Great."

I don't feel great as I head out of the room with a half-hard dick. Which is why I choose a bedroom in the basement, as far away from Wheeler's as possible. No risk of any nighttime run-ins this way.

If I see Wheeler in any kind of cute pajama situation—I'm imagining one of those nightie things with teeny-tiny straps and lace, nothing underneath it—I just might fling myself off the side of this mountain. End it all, because I can't stand not taking the woman to bed.

I throw on a pair of sweats and a hoodie. My eyes burn inside my head like two balls of hellfire, so I take a deep breath, take out my contacts, and put on my glasses, praying like hell Wheeler thinks they look less dorky than I do. Then I head back upstairs.

Getting snowed in with a smart, funny, ambitious, beautiful woman was not part of the plan. But here we are.

CHAPTER 8
She'll Be Coming 'Round the Mountain
Wheeler

I head into the living room and promptly draw up short.

Duke is facing away from me, crouched in front of the fireplace. His hoodie draws taut over his shoulder blades and back as he makes quick work of building a fire in the massive fireplace.

I watch, transfixed by the bunch and release of his shoulder muscles. Exactly *how* does he fill out that sweatshirt so damn well? This cowboy is thick, solid, in a way few men are.

The logs crackle and pop as the fire grows.

I feel the throb between my thighs grow too. Allowing myself to be honest for a second, I have to admit that there's nowhere else I'd rather be. The ride today was nerve-racking, sure, but it was also a lot of freaking fun. Duke is excellent company. He's also a gentleman. I kept offering to drive, but he waved me off, even though I knew he had to be tired. Even though he joked about not having time for stops, he made sure

I was comfortable, asking several times if I needed a bathroom or stretch break.

I'll only drink a little bit. One glass of wine. Two tops. Surely we'll be ready to go to bed by then, right?

Go to our *separate* beds.

"Hey," Duke says.

I cross my arms over my chest, trying very hard to ignore the way my nipples tingle at the sound of his voice.

"Hey. Hi. Since you're, um, busy with that, why don't I make the grilled cheese?"

He's still crouching, elbows on his knees as he glances at me over his shoulder. "I got it."

Oh, dear sweet Jesus. The man is wearing glasses.

Duke is, I mean. Not Jesus, at least not as far as I know. They're simple, with round lenses and a black plastic frame that fades to brown at the bottom of the lenses.

Damn does he look *good* in them.

Really, really good, like some kind of Robert Redford–coded rugged professor of postmodern literature.

Since when am I tempted to make passes at a guy who wears glasses?

"Teamwork, remember?" Looking away, I head for the kitchen, grateful for the excuse to put some distance between us. "I like the glasses, by the way."

"Really?" He sounds genuinely surprised. "My eyes were killing me, so I had to take out my contacts."

"Really. Why? Do *you* not like them?"

"Hell no. That's why I never wear 'em. I think they make me look like a dork."

"Dorks are cool now."

He grins. "If you say so."

The windows are blank, reflecting the lights inside the house. The wind howls. I nearly jump when the house is hit by a gust, a crackling sound reverberating through the windows.

I freeze. "What's that?"

"Sleet." Duke's knees crack as he rises. "No biggie. Trust me when I say this house has seen much worse."

The ceiling creaks. I look up. "You sure about that?"

"Aspen's snowstorms ain't got nothin' on Hartsville's tornadoes." He casually pads over to the kitchen like we're not facing the real possibility of a snow-induced apocalypse. "I'm sure. Wine?"

"*Yes*."

He smirks as he starts opening cabinets. "You gettin' the shakes?"

"Yeah, I'm getting the shakes." I glance at the windows. "Maybe this really is our last night on earth."

"God's got an awful sense of humor if that's the case, making us drink this shit on our way out." Duke reaches for the boxed wine. "Hopefully it's not too bad."

It's actually decent. I down my first glass while I make the grilled cheese. Duke once again proves himself to be a marvelous assistant. He softens the butter in the microwave. He digs a spatula out of a nearby drawer. He finds plates, napkins, and a serrated knife, which he uses to cut the sandwiches into neat diagonals.

He also looks really cute with wine-stained lips. And the glasses—

It's almost too much.

He picks my brain about the finances of a trunk

show as we eat at the counter. I've never met someone as interested in accounting as Duke is except, well, my actual accountant. It's weirdly sexy.

So is the way he inhales my grilled cheese. I'm glad I made extra. Only when I assure him I'm full does he grab seconds.

"You good?" He wipes his mouth on a napkin.

I nod. "I'm great." I'm just tipsy enough to add, "Should we slap the bag now that we have a solid carb base?"

I mean, why not, right? I've been texting with the owners of Aspen Leather Company, and they said chances are our trunk show is going to have to be pushed back. Last I checked, snow totals for downtown Aspen went from twelve inches to eighteen, with locally heavier snow amounts possible.

Duke grins, and then he takes our plates before standing up. "I thought you'd never ask. Go sit. I'll clean up."

"I'll help—"

"Whoever cooks doesn't clean. Sit."

Heaven help me.

I jump at the thud that sounds overhead. Duke goes still, looking up.

"A tree?" I ask.

Duke waits a beat before responding. "Probably just a branch. I'll check it out."

Dropping the plates in the sink, he heads for the front door. I follow him and turn on the porch lights. He ducks outside, and I find myself praying for the first time in years that he makes it back okay. I stand on the porch while Duke disappears down the front steps, and I marvel at the sound of the wind. It's an eerie wail that's low-pitched but also very, *very* loud.

The snow is coming down with such ferocity that it blurs the world around us. Even here, tucked safely beneath the eaves of the roof, the wind whips my hair into my face.

"You okay?" I shout. "Duke?"

A beat later, I breathe a sigh of relief when he jogs up the steps, his hood up and his cheeks pink. His glasses are fogged over.

"Just a branch," he says, pulling back his hood. "Rolled right off the roof, no problem."

I let him hustle me inside. He locks the door behind us and wipes his boots on the mat before taking them off.

"Yeah, but what if the whole tree comes down?"

"It won't."

"But what if it does?"

He gives me a look before pointing to the sofas by the fire. "Would you go sit? I promise we'll be fine."

"Famous last words."

"Sit."

"Make me."

I'm a little drunk and a lot nervous, and I guess the combination turns me into a brat.

"Oh, Lordy." He puts his hands on his hips and shakes his head. "You've done it now."

"Done what?"

He bends down. "Pushed me too far."

"What? Du—*oh!*" I yelp when he wraps his arms around my legs and abruptly hoists me over his shoulder, Viking raider style.

A literal *hoist*. What a funny little word for the way

he takes command of my body, his arm a steel band around the backs of my thighs. Blood rushes to my head.

His ass—that perfect, delicious, muscular ass—is quite literally in my face. I arch my back in an attempt to create some space between us and, I don't know, keep me from biting one of his butt cheeks.

I am *tempted*.

"Duke!" I don't recognize my voice. It's squeaky. Desperate sounding. "Duke, Jesus, put me down! What the hell? You'll hurt yourself."

"Aw, Blue, you ain't got nearly enough faith in my deadlifting skills." He strides into the living room, my body undulating in time to his steps. "You pick something for us to watch while I finish cleaning the kitchen. Got it?"

"You can't tell me what to do."

He chuckles. "You say that now."

I don't know what to do with my hands. I decide to plant them in the middle of his back so I can half sit up. It seemed like a safe idea, but now I can feel the way his muscles tense as he moves. They're rock-hard. Just like the rest of this man.

The longing in my center coils tighter.

Despite his obvious strength—or maybe because of it—he deposits me gently on one of the massive sofas in front of the fireplace. The heat of the fire feels nice after being outside.

Duke quickly locates the remotes on the mantel above the fireplace and tosses them onto the sofa beside me. "What're you into these days?"

I'm into lusting after cowboys who morph into hot professors.

Licking my lips, I force myself to look away from said cowboy-slash-professor.

"Something funny, maybe?"

"Sounds great."

I pick up the remotes and start to fiddle with them.

"Wheeler?"

I glance at Duke. "Yeah?"

"We really are going to be okay. I need you to know that."

My heart squeezes. I don't know what to say. "Thanks."

I want to believe him. And part of me does. He's confident. As a cowboy, he knows about nature and weather and…stuff. Clearly he's seen worse conditions than the ones currently hammering Aspen Mountain.

But another part is scared to trust a man. Any man. Dad had such a temper growing up that I still, to this day, jump when I hear a loud noise. My anxiety is sky-high during stressful situations because that's when Dad would typically lash out.

Instead of making me anxious, though, Duke's presence today has actually been a comfort. He got us up here no problem, didn't he? He didn't lose his mind or spit obscenities or pout about having to drive. He just got it done, and he made me laugh along the way, clearly hoping to ease my fears.

He kept me safe then. I can probably trust him to keep me safe now.

He's cool as a cucumber as he pads into the kitchen and turns on the faucet. The clank and clatter of dishes is weirdly comforting as I turn on the TV and hunt for something good to watch.

"How about *Veep*?" I ask after several minutes of searching. "Or *The Righteous Gemstones*? To be honest, I haven't been watching a ton of TV lately, so I have no clue what's new or good."

"Why no TV?" Duke turns off the faucet. "You just been building a cowboy boot empire or somethin'?"

"Hardly an empire." But I still smile.

"It's not an empire *yet*." I hear him pad across the hardwood. "All right, Blue. Get over here and get on your knees."

I bite back a laugh. "Excuse me?"

"Ladies slap first." He holds up the silver bag of wine. "Unless you want me to start?"

"You're rude." I unfold my legs from underneath me and stand up.

He smirks. "You can stand if you want. But I always find it more pleasurable if you do it on your knees. Grab that blanket, would you?"

Rolling my eyes, I reach for the fur blanket on the sofa beside me.

Duke catches me fighting a smile, though, because he says, "Aw, yeah, Blue. You agree, don't you?"

"Only in the context of this game."

"Put the blanket on the floor. Then do as I told you."

I drop the blanket, then I fall to my knees one leg at a time. "Try not to spill, yeah?"

He looms over me, looking taller and broader than ever. Immediately my mind goes somewhere it shouldn't. "Aw, Blue, but you just get me so excited—"

"Quit lyin'. I saw firsthand how good your aim is."

His eyes twinkle as he looks down at me. "It's not that often people call my bluff."

"I'm not about to let you outsmart me. Pour." I open my mouth.

"You got it."

Duke's face is a mask of concentration as he opens the little plastic valve on the bag, releasing a thin stream of dark pink wine. I have to duck to catch it with my mouth. The wine hits my chin before I capture it with my tongue.

He starts to count off. "One Mississippi. Two Mississippi. Three—dang, girl, you ain't wasting a drop, are you—"

I slap his leg before he can finish that thought. He laughs and so do I, nearly choking on the wine. Duke shuts off the valve and grabs my hand, helping me to my feet. Awareness zips up my arm from the place where our palms meet.

He doesn't let go. Neither do I as I slap the bag with my other hand, the wine in my stomach sloshing pleasantly alongside the wine in the bag.

"This is such a dumb game." I meet his eyes.

"It's fuckin' stupid." Adjusting his glasses, he holds out the bag to me. "But we keep playing, yeah?"

"Yeah." I'm smiling hard enough for my face to hurt.

Even on his knees, Duke is still a massive presence. I have to hold up the bag pretty dang high to pour it into his mouth. I'm transfixed by the way his prominent Adam's apple bobs when he swallows. At one point, he teeters forward. I catch him at the same time as he catches himself, my hand on his shoulder, his planted on my hips.

His touch sends a charge through me, heat flooding my cunt. A beat of heavy silence swells between us as

I absently turn off the spigot. He's *close*. Mouth mere inches from mine. I'd just have to hinge at the waist, lean in, and then kiss—

Nope. No way. Not happening.

Even though every fiber of my being tells me Duke would be an excellent kisser. When was the last time I made out with someone who knew how to kiss?

Stay strong, sister, I mentally whisper to myself as I help Duke to his feet. He stays close—too close, not close enough—to slap the bag.

We go for another round. Another.

God, I'm buzzed. And horny.

So freaking horny. A little nervous too, because the roof keeps groaning. The windows literally rattle as a particularly vicious gust hits the house.

"Your turn."

I blink at the husky sound of Duke's voice. He takes the bag from my hand, our fingers brushing.

We go through a couple more rounds of the game. My phone buzzes; the manager of Aspen Leather Company texts that the block downtown where the store is located just lost power. It's not looking good for the trunk show tomorrow.

I glance at Duke. "Do you think we'll lose power?"

"Even if we do, I bet this place has a generator."

"Always so confident things will work out." I head to the kitchen to drop the bag of wine back into its box.

"Well, yeah." He follows me, grabbing a pair of tumblers from a cabinet and filling them with water at the sink. "Like I said, you gotta have faith. Looking at the glass as half-empty is no way to go through life." He holds up the tumblers before handing one to me. "See? Mostly full."

"Since when are we drinking water?"

"Since I said so."

I bring my glass to my lips. "You're no fun."

"We're at fourteen thousand feet, Blue. Rules are different up here. You don't stay hydrated, you're gonna wake up with one hell of a hangover tomorrow."

My heart twists. Why does he care so much about, well, everything?

Why does he care about *me*?

Turning away from him, I head back into the living room. "Let's watch *The Righteous Gemstones*."

"Love that show. How good is Walton Goggins?"

"Uncle Baby Billy *makes* the show, right?"

"No question."

I stand in front of the TV, remote in hand, and scroll through shows until I hit the one I'm looking for. Out of the corner of my eye, I catch Duke flopping onto the sofa opposite the one I've been hanging out on, settling onto his back.

I'm gripped by the very pressing desire to join him over there. We could cuddle. Duke's totally a cuddler, right? I imagine his kind of cuddling would be so arousing that it'd quickly lead to more.

Much, much more.

God, I want that.

But I can't. We can't. I did not come to Aspen to cuddle with Duke.

It takes every ounce of my self-control to move away from Duke instead of toward him, but I do it. I curl up in the safety of my own sofa and try to focus on the show, not on the handsome cowboy stretched out across from me. He's got one arm bent behind his head, his straight legs crossed at the ankles. Totally at ease. Is he not about to combust?

I jump at the sudden, howling scream that fills the house. The wind is absolutely ripping outside, the windows rattling again.

Worst of all, the lights flicker.

"Ohmy*god*." I put a hand on my chest, heart pounding. "Ohmygod, Duke, this is bad. My nerves are shot. The drive and the trunk show getting pushed back and all these fucking sounds and..." *Your glasses.*

Duke frowns. He opens his mouth. Closes it, like he thought better of what he was about to say.

Instead, he gets up and walks around the massive coffee table to pick up the remotes off my sofa. "Mind if I put something on?"

"Is it the weather? I feel like we should probably get an update—"

"Pretty sure Mother Nature's giving us all the updates we need." He glances over his shoulder at the windows. "I wanna put something on for you. Trust me?"

I scoff. "Like I have a choice."

"You don't." He grins. "Time to ease your mind, Blue, with a little throwback to the nineties."

CHAPTER 9
Push It
Wheeler

Despite the very real terror that has taken root in my center, I still let out a bark of laughter when a familiar beat plays over the TV speaker.

"Is this—"

"Milli Vanilli?" Duke turns his head to meet my eyes. "Yep. I dare you *not* to dance to 'Girl You Know It's True.'"

I look at him. He looks back, singing along to the song and bopping his head. The music video plays on the TV. It's so bad it's almost good—the kind of entertainment that's compellingly cringe-worthy.

"What in the world made you think of this?" I ask, touched by his very obvious attempt to distract me.

Honestly, what is *wrong* with me that I can't give this cowboy a chance? He is *excellent* in every sense of the word.

And then I remember Preston saying my high school boyfriend broke up with me because I was ugly and stupid and "kind of a bitch." I cried for days after that. Mom made him say he was sorry, but his apology was halfhearted at best.

"When we were kids, we'd get freaked out when the weather was bad," he explains. "Remember how the TV would beep really loud during tornado warnings?"

"That was terrifying."

"My mom would take my brothers and me to the basement, where she'd turn on music and have dance parties with us."

My chest hurts. "She wanted to distract y'all."

"It worked. Just like it's gonna work now." He flexes his fingers. "Up. C'mon."

I really, really should just call it a night and go to bed. My buzz is wearing off, and I'm exhausted.

This flirtation is going nowhere. I won't let it.

But I'm just tipsy enough—just terrified enough—to shove all that aside.

"Great." I take his hands and let him pull me to my feet. "So I just need to dance, and I'll stop thinking about the wind blowing down all those trees and them crashing through the house and us getting pinned underneath them and dying a slow horrible death from internal bleeding and/or asphyxiation before the rescue teams are able to make it up here?"

His lips twitch. "Yup. That's all you need to do."

I don't know how it happens. One minute, the wind howls, the windows to our left literally rattling in their casings. The next, my arms are wrapped around his neck, and he's got his hands on my hips, which are melted into his.

I'm terrified.

I'm turned on.

Duke starts to dance. It's the kind of dancing I'd hoped to do that night we met at the Rattler: flirty, easy, fun.

He's a good dancer, confident as he moves to the beat. His grip on my hips is firm, and he urges me to follow his lead by guiding my body one way, then the other.

The need between my legs flares hotter. Blares louder.

I glance up and see him looking down at me intently. The lenses of his glasses make his eyes look especially large.

Especially blue.

Our lips are inches apart. How does that keep happening?

My own lips throb with the desire to be kissed. He tilts his head—or maybe I'm imagining he does—giving him the perfect angle to go in for the kill.

How good would it feel to let him sink me into the sofa, the weight of his body making me deliciously short of breath as he kissed the shit out of me?

I look away. Look down at my feet, heart pumping.

"We're gonna be just fine," Duke murmurs, his breath warm on my cheek.

I nod. "You know, I'm still not over the fact that these guys were fakes. Milli Vanilli." I glance at the screen.

"The nineties were apparently a wild time."

I move and he moves, and I start to feel slightly better.

Better and so turned on it literally hurts. The more we move, the more adventurous his dancing becomes. I know he's just trying to make me laugh with his exaggerated hip gyrations, and I do. I laugh so hard it leaves me breathless.

I throw up my arms and close my eyes and lose myself to the music, because why the hell not? It really does make me forget everything except the beat and the feel of Duke's body pressed against mine.

It grounds me in the present, time moving heartbeat by wild heartbeat.

Duke must've used YouTube to put on this music video, because another one comes on right after.

I toss back my head and laugh, hard, when I recognize the opening notes of Salt-N-Pepa's "Push It." "I love this song."

Duke bites his bottom lip and knits his brows, really going for a hip thrust. "It's a classic for a reason."

I hip thrust right back, and he bursts out laughing. I do that thing where I put my fists in the center of my chest and pump my arms. I'm sure I look like a lopsided butterfly, but I don't care. What do I have to lose? It's not like anything's going to happen between Duke and me. Since I don't need to play it cool, I can do whatever the hell I want without worrying what he thinks.

Duke turns around and sticks out his butt, shaking it. I pretend to give it several solid whacks, and he pretends to be into it, covering his mouth with his hand.

I do the Bugs Bunny. Or I try to anyway and end up backing into the sofa and falling over.

I don't know who's laughing harder, me or Duke, who once again is pulling me to my feet. Pulling me into his arms.

My sides ache, and so does my face from smiling. I put my hands on his chest.

"You win the dancing competition," I manage.

He grips the backs of my upper arms. "You're terrible at this."

"I know."

"It's cute."

"No, it's not."

His eyes bore into mine. "Yes, Wheeler, it is. You gotta know how cute you are." He licks his bottom lip. "How pretty."

My stomach takes a violent nosedive.

"Thanks?" I manage. The look in his eyes—it's hot and hungry and so very *tender*.

Blinking, I look away and drop my hands from his chest. I step back, everything inside me rioting.

My blood riots at the loss of his touch.

My gut riots at the very real warning coming from my head: *danger*.

"I should probably hit the hay." I bend down to swipe my phone off the sofa. "Just in case the trunk show happens at any point tomorrow."

"Aw, really?" His voice is deep with disappointment. "But you're such a terrible dancer!"

I don't want to laugh, but I do. "Show's over, cowboy. Sorry."

"You're really bumming me out here, Blue." His eyes are earnest now.

He really does want me to stay.

He really is enjoying my company.

A whisper of something new moves through my head. *Maybe I'm not as awful or nasty as I thought.*

Maybe I'm still a bitch, but that doesn't preclude me from also being warm and carefree and a damn good time too. Don't we all contain multitudes?

Don't be stupid. That's another voice, one I recognize. My therapist told me it's my miswired brain being mean—that it's an echo of my dad's voice and my brother's.

"I'll see you in the morning." I grab my water and start heading for my room. "If, of course, we don't get crushed by falling trees tonight."

But truth be told, I'd rather the trees fell than I do.

A loud crash tears me from sleep.

I bolt upright, stomach seizing. My heart hammers as I blink back the darkness. *What the fuck was that? Where am I? What time is it?*

A persistent, roaring howl fills the silence. Glancing at the windows beside the bed, I see nothing but blackness. Occasionally there's a crackle, like sand being thrown against the glass.

It's sleet. And a lot of wind.

I shiver. My nose is numb.

Everything inside me goes still. What happened to the heat? Did the electricity go out?

The ceiling groans. My stomach bottoms out. I reach for my phone on the bedside table, which apparently hasn't been charging. It's two o'clock in the morning.

Dropping my phone and flinging back the covers, I suck in a breath at the shock of cold air that greets me. I'm shivering, shaking, and I—

"You okay?"

Startling, my blood turns to ice at the sound of the voice by the door. Instinctively, I hit the flashlight button on my screen and hold it up.

"You're naked!" I don't know why I'm whispering.

I do know why I'm staring.

Duke stands just inside the doorway.

He is totally, completely, gloriously naked. He also makes absolutely no attempt to cover himself up.

For some reason, that doesn't surprise me. Makes sense that someone who works with animals all day would be totally at home in the animal that is his own body.

Makes sense he'd be totally unashamed.

I wish I could say my gaze lingered on the whorls of dark blond hair that cover his broad chest. Or the deliciously satisfying way his waist tapers into chiseled hips.

But no.

No, my gaze catches on the beautiful cock that hangs between his massive thighs. He's thick, long, a vein running down the side of his velvety-looking shaft. His head is wide and pink. His pubic hair matches the hair on his chest: wiry, dark, lush without being overwhelming.

A rush of saliva fills my mouth. Despite the fact that the room is freezing, a hot bloom of renewed awareness unfurls between my legs. I thought about taking care of that when I climbed into bed earlier, but masturbating to images of Duke in his glasses sliding his hands up my shirt seemed like a dangerous activity, so I did my best to fall asleep despite the acute need that thrummed through my body.

"Heard the crash and came running," he explains impatiently, flattening his palm on his heaving chest.

"No time for clothes." Or glasses apparently, because he's not wearing those either.

He came running.

He heard a crash, and his first thought was to come find me.

My cunt throbs. Heart gallops.

"You sleep naked?"

His hand moves to cover his dick. "Sorry. I just had to make sure you were—"

"No"—I clear my throat—"apology necessary. I appreciate you checking in on me. What the hell was that sound?"

"Has to be a branch. Bigger than before, I think. I was gonna check it out after I made sure you were okay." His pectoral muscle pops. That's when I realize he's shivering too.

"You're freezing."

"You're scared. C'mon, let's go make sure everything's okay. Then you're coming to bed with me."

My heart leaps into my throat. Leaps again into my mouth. "I—"

"I'll sleep on the floor if you want. But my room is in the basement, which seems like the safest place with all these trees around us."

"So you're saying I was right about the trees."

He tilts his head, squinting. "I'm saying we need to be careful."

I laugh. How could I not? Sleeping in a bed with Duke—a very, very naked Duke—seems like the opposite of *being careful*.

But then the wind roars and everything inside me heaves, and I know I should go with him.

I'm shaking so hard my teeth chatter.

"Aw, Wheeler—"

"I'm okay." *I'm not okay.* "Let's go."

We head out into the living room, where I try not to watch Duke peering through every window. He's still holding his hand over his dick, but the rest of him is still very much naked. His ass cheeks hollow out on the sides when he strains to see through the dark windows.

It's freezing.

It's pitch-black. Glancing at the kitchen, I see the clock on the stove isn't working.

"Aha." He jabs a finger at the pane beside the kitchen table. "Big old branch is lying right there. That had to be it. Far as I can tell, the tree is still standing."

"Think it took out the power or something?"

Duke heads for the staircase that leads to the basement. "Maybe. Whatever the case, I was wrong about the generator."

"You were wrong about"—my teeth chatter—"a lot of things."

"At least I can admit it. C'mon, let's get you warm."

"How are you not an icicle?" I follow him down the stairs, holding up the flashlight on my phone so we can see.

Really so I can see the freckles that dot Duke's shoulders and neck. He's got the cutest little farmer's tan. Or would it be cowboy tan?

Either way, I dig it.

"I am." He chuckles. "You had to have seen—well…"

No *way* that was his shrunk-in-the-cold dick.

No fucking *way*. If he's that big when he's cold—

My God, how big is he when he's warm?

A bolt of lust hits me squarely in the clit. I squirm, grateful for the cover of darkness. I bet I'm bright red right now.

It's colder in the basement, the chill slicing through my pajamas. My shivers become violent.

I follow Duke through a door to the right of the stairs. It opens up into a large room with—*oh God*—one bed.

Granted, it looks like it's a king. But it's still the only sleeping surface in the room. Not so much as a bench or sofa in sight.

I'm too cold to care, though. I moan a little, and Duke grabs my elbow and guides me underneath the mountain of covers on the bed.

"You'll warm up in no time." He tucks the duvet around my shoulders and arms, tugging it up so that it covers my nose. *The man is literally tucking me in.* "I'm gonna go grab some clothes and see if I can find extra blankets. I'll be right there on the floor—"

"No." My heart pounds as I bite out the word between chatters. "Sleep here. In bed. Right now. Must…stay warm. Body heat. Jacob the werewolf. He kept Bella warm because…hotter than Edward. Vampire."

Duke chuckles. "I got no idea what you're talking about—"

He's cut off by a shiver that racks his entire body.

"Get the fuck in bed, Duke!"

"All right!" He's still chuckling as he jogs around the mattress and dives underneath the covers. "I'll use a pillow as underwear, I guess."

"Ew, please don't."

"How can you sleep with clothes on?"

"How can you sleep without them?"

I realize the bed is warm.

Well, *this* side of the bed is warm. Did Duke tuck me into his side of the bed knowing the other side would be cold?

I shiver but for a different reason this time. Then a loud screech rends the air, like the wind is dragging metal furniture across the concrete patio outside.

I whimper. Then I'm immediately embarrassed by said whimper, because I'm better than that. Braver.

Except I can't seem to find that bravery now, because I'm shaking like a leaf.

"Wheeler."

"I'm okay."

"You're shaking so hard that the bed is shaking too. Can I—do you need—"

"Yeah."

Danger danger danger.

My heart keeps pounding as I hear him shuffle closer. I know he's naked. I also know he's hot. Literally. And even though he's hot in the proverbial sense too, that's a risk I'm willing to take if it means calming my nervous system, which is currently on the fritz.

If he's offering comfort, I'm gonna take him up on it. We all deserve comfort, right?

I wonder if Duke is going to play it safe. Maybe half-heartedly snuggle with me while keeping his pelvis a respectable distance from my backside.

Ha.

Ha ha *ha.*

I should've known he would definitely *not* do that. Instead, he hooks an arm around my middle with the clear intention of pulling me closer.

"Roll onto your side, Blue."

The endearment. The feel of his hands on me.

I roll right the fuck over, and he immediately pulls me into the cradle of his very warm, very large, very hard body, my back to his front.

"The nickname is growing on me." I don't recognize my voice.

"Good." He bends his legs, and I bend mine so we're in an *S* shape, my ass settling into his lap like his dick isn't right there.

I can feel him. He's not hard or anything, but he is large, and my body lights up like a firecracker.

I nearly moan again when he flattens his palm over my stomach. His hand is huge, his hold on me shamelessly solid and confident. I feel his chest barreling out on an inhale against my back, his breath hot on my nape.

"This okay?" His voice is husky.

I feel myself melting into his heat. His touch. I feel safe here and yet somehow keyed up, wild.

I'm not my normal, often numb self, and I like that. A lot.

The wind gusts, throwing sleet against the windows. The howl it makes is loud enough to have me actually moaning.

"What's goin' on, Blue?" he asks softly. "This kinda shakin'—you're not just cold, are you?"

My brain is short-circuiting. That has to be why I blurt, "My dad. He is—was—a screamer. He's always had a bad temper. You'd never know when he was going to erupt, and when he did, the neighbors could hear it. Loud noises still freak me out."

"Aw, Wheeler. No wonder you're shaking. I wish you'd told me."

"I don't like talking about him. Or my parents in general. They're going through this really nasty divorce that's been—yeah, pretty awful."

His arms tighten around me, cradling me against the warmth of his body. Doesn't say anything. He doesn't need to.

Being here—keeping me safe—is enough.

It's more than enough, judging by the way my weight melts into his. He feels so big, so solid in his mellow silence.

My heart rate slows. At the same time, the hot liquid need between my thighs flares to renewed life. I squeeze my eyes shut.

What if I gave in? Just for tonight? What if I let myself have what I want for once and left nothing on the table? Maybe then I'd stop feeling so damn horny all the time.

Maybe then I'd finally be able to declutter my head, my emotions, and focus on my work. I feel like I've been distracted ever since Mom sat me down and told me she was leaving Dad.

His chest rises against my back again on a deep, unhurried inhale. Jesus Christ, is he not being burned alive by lust right now? How is he so…unbothered?

I hear him move his head on the pillow, and I nearly sigh when something smooth, then prickly, brushes over the nape of my neck.

His mouth. His stubble.

Both.

A lightning bold of need cracks down my middle.

"Sorry," we both say at once.

His chuckle is deep, dark with sleep. "What the hell are you sorry for? I didn't mean to get that close. Sorry."

"Nothing. This. The fact that we're stuck on the top of a mountain during the blizzard of the century."

"Shit happens."

I sigh. "Ain't that the truth."

My pillow smells like Duke, the juniper-scented aftershave or cologne he must wear.

The wind roars, making the house groan in protest. Everything inside me seizes. I'm shaking and I'm scared and I'm so turned on I might actually die if I don't do something about it.

We might die anyway, judging by that wind and snow.

"This is ridiculous," I bite out, stomach heaving as I turn around in Duke's arms. I put a hand on his naked stomach. "We've been dancing around this from day one. Can we just—I don't know, finally fool arou—"

But Duke is giving me what I ask for before I even finish the question, slanting his mouth over mine.

CHAPTER 10
The Good Kind of Second Guesses
Wheeler

His lips are achingly soft and warm, a contrast to the masculine roughness of his beard. My blood ignites as those lips begin to move, a slow, careful caress that has me curling my toes.

How'd he know? My thoughts pound in time to my heartbeat. *Was I that obvious?*

How.

The fuck.

Did he know?

"Thank God," he murmurs into my mouth, tongue toying with my bottom lip. "I been dyin', sweetheart. Dyin' to do this for way too long."

Oh, wow, this guy is good.

So, *so* good at kissing me. My cunt pulses when he opens my mouth with his tongue, and I plaster my body against his, gliding my hand up his chest before tucking my fingers into the hollow underneath his ear.

He groans, the sound drawing my nipples to tight,

almost painful points. I lick into his mouth and taste him. He's hot and clean, like he just downed a bunch of water.

He slips a hand inside my shirt. "Tell me."

"Tell you what?" I pant, arcing my thumb over the sharp line of his jaw.

"To stop." His hand moves ever so slightly north.

"Abso-fucking-lutely *not*." I reach for the hem of my shirt and tug it over my head. Then I reach for his hand and put it on my breast. "Don't you dare stop."

"Fuck." It's more a rumble than a word. His thumb moves over my nipple. At the same time, he massages my breast, another slow caress that has the ache between my legs soaring to new heights. I press against him, eager for the contact, his warmth.

Eager to finally have him.

I'm hit by the acute need to be totally, completely naked with this man. All this skin on skin feels so, *so* good, probably because it creates so much heat. My nipples brush his chest as I roll my hips, and that's when I feel it.

Feel *him*.

His dick has gone full salute. He's hard, and his leaking tip urgently presses into my leg.

He. Is. *Huge*.

"You got me"—he gently tugs my bottom lip between his teeth before ducking his head to kiss my neck—"wild, Blue. You're so pretty and soft and fuckin'—you're wet, aren't you? That's what does it for me. Knowin' I turn you on."

In reply, I make quick work of taking off my pants and underwear, kicking them to the bottom of the bed. "Why don't you find out?"

"Aw, Blue." His hand skates down my side. It curls around my hip before it wraps around my thigh. He lifts my leg and props my knee on *his* hip, spreading me wide.

He reaches between my legs. I sputter when his first two fingertips find my clit. The wind must have died down, because I can literally hear how wet I am.

"God*damn* it," he whispers into my mouth.

I arch my back, pressing myself into his touch. "It's been a long day."

"No shit. You wanna come now?" His fingers work a lazy circle over the place I want him most. "Or you wanna come on my dick?"

The lewdness of his question has my blood rioting.

"That's bold of you."

He bites down on my neck, vampire style, and I literally shudder with pleasure. "Answer the question. Or, if you want, I'll answer it for you."

"Awful cocky, thinking you know what I want."

"Oh yeah?" Those fingers glide through my slit and notch at my entrance. "Give me permission."

"To do what?"

"Touch you how I wanna. If it's too much, you tell me. Otherwise..." He presses his fingers the tiniest bit inside me. "Otherwise, you trust me to give you what you need."

I reach between us to wrap my hand around his dick. His velvety warmth fills my palm, and I can feel just how firm he is. How big.

"What do *you* need?" I give him a slow, easy tug.

He sucks in a breath. "You. I need you, Wheeler."

My stomach contracts. How is he able to be so vulnerable without wanting to shrivel up and die? The man is not afraid to put himself out there. Kinda makes me want to do the same. Just for tonight.

"I'm right here." I kiss his mouth. "Okay."

"Okay, as in—"

I glide my thumb up the furrow on the sensitive underside of his head. "I trust you."

"You'll tell me if anything hurts?" He starts sinking his fingers inside me.

"Maybe I like it when it hurts."

He groans. "Fuck me."

"Gladly," I say with a laugh. The sound dies in my throat as his fingers sink deeper, and a burning stretch comes alive between my legs. My breath catches, my hand fisting his cock.

He audibly swallows. "Sweetheart, you're soaked. And tight. Can you relax for me a little? I know you're wound up right now, but try to breathe, okay? I'm not gonna be able to fit if you don't relax."

I almost come from just the *image* of Duke putting himself inside me. Because we don't even need to play that game, the *will we or won't we actually fuck*.

He's made it clear we're fucking, and I couldn't be more thrilled about it. Which kind of shocks me, considering I was so hesitant to give in at all earlier tonight.

I breathe. At the same time, I smear his precum over his head. Apparently we're going to need all the lube we can get.

"That's it." Duke keeps his voice low and even as he draws his fingers back out of me, then glides them back in. Over and over. "Jesus *Christ*, sweetheart. I'm fuckin' dying here. You're gonna feel—God—so good when I'm inside you. I might come just thinking about it. I love how soft you are. That's my girl. Keep relaxing."

I nod, my eyes fluttering shut when the heel of his hand presses against my clit. "Can you—can we—"

"Lemme grab a condom. I think I got some in my Dopp kit—"

"Do we need one?" My stomach swoops at my boldness.

I'm being silly, I know I am. But I'm scared that if Duke gets out of this bed, I won't let him back in. All it takes is a split second for my self-doubt to return with a vengeance. I'm really enjoying losing myself in the moment. In *him*.

I also don't want him to get cold. He was definitely shivering earlier, and it kills me to think of him being in any kind of pain. Also kills me to think about more of that frigid air invading our warm cocoon.

"I'm on the pill," I continue to blurt, "and I can show you my latest results. I'm negative across the board, and I haven't been with anyone—"

He lets out a pained chuckle.

"What?" I ask.

"The universe is fucking with us. Or it wants us to fuck, I guess, because I just got my results from my annual physical last week."

"We're good?"

Curling his fingers inside me, he presses into the front wall of my pussy. "We're real good, Blue."

Then he's pulling out his fingers and rolling me onto my back. Rolling on top of me as he tosses the blankets over our heads. We're enveloped in complete and utter darkness, and I'm suddenly all sensation.

I feel the give of the mattress and the heat that moves through my skin.

I taste Duke on my lips.

I hear the sigh of the sheets and the throb of my pulse, an insistent beat that sounds between my legs too.

Duke kisses me everywhere: my neck, my mouth, my breasts. He takes his time, holding himself up on his arms as he ducks his head to suck on my nipples. He presses the flat of his tongue against the tight buds, gently lapping me up.

Meanwhile, I'm writhing beneath him. My fingers are curled into his chest, my nails biting into his skin. I bend my knees, spreading my legs so he can settle his body between them.

My hips roll, seeking. His dick catches on the crease between my hip and groin.

"Please." I'm apparently not above begging. "I need—"

"I know what you need, sweetheart." He gives my nipple one last hard, quick suck before reaching for my knee and pressing it into my chest. "Let's get you spread open for me, yeah? Keep breathing."

I realize I'm a little nervous, which just turns me on more.

"Hands on my shoulders. That's right. Good girl." I feel him shift, his hand brushing my stomach. "You can scratch me, bite me, whatever. Do what you need to do. But I'm not stoppin' unless you use your words."

I give his shoulders a squeeze. "I told you I'm good—"

"I know what you told me." He touches the head of his dick to my clit and circles it, making me yelp. Then he notches himself at my entrance. "Now I'm telling you that you're gonna take every inch of me. Every fuckin' inch, you hear?"

I am so frustrated—*so* hungry for him—that for a second, I almost start to cry.

"Give me everything," I pant. "If you skimp out on me—"

My breath catches when he pushes inside me. Just the literal and proverbial tip. But the pressure is already enormous. "I ain't skimpin', sweetheart."

He pushes a little farther. At the same time, he lowers his body onto mine, pinning me to the mattress.

It's hard to breathe.

I *love* it.

He touches his forehead to mine and kisses me, his tongue finding mine. He pushes another inch inside me. Another.

All the while, he kisses me and kisses me and *kisses* me.

The feeling of fullness between my legs makes my eyes prick. It's not comfortable, but it's certainly not painful. Not in the physical sense anyway. Being filled by him, covered by him, feels weirdly…emotional, and I'm not sure why.

"Relax," he murmurs, and next thing I know, he's rolling his thumb over my clit. Over and over. Again and again.

I whimper when my pussy contracts around his girth. It hurts.

It's wonderful.

"Your words. Use 'em if you need to."

"I don't need to."

"Fuck. You feel"—inching deeper, he groans—"like fucking heaven. But I gotta find more space, so you need to breathe for me. In and out. Let me hear it."

I try. I close my eyes and hold on to his enormous shoulders for dear life as my approaching orgasm flickers around the edges of my consciousness.

I feel like I'm being split in two as he pushes and pushes. My hips scream in protest when he settles more of his weight on me, splaying me even wider.

"Last bit." He sounds like he's gritting his teeth. His forehead is damp with sweat. "Yell if you need to."

"I'm not that much of a flowe—*oh!*"

Yup, I yell. Loudly. The burning stretch I feel when he buries himself to the hilt *hurts*. I wonder how sore I'm going to be tomorrow.

I wonder if I've ever felt more aroused in my life.

"Words," he bites out.

I shake my head, even as I sink my teeth into his neck.

He growls. "That hurts. Keep doing it."

His thumb works my clit. When he pulls out a little, then thrusts back in, I feel myself fluttering around him. My back arches, the muscles in my legs drawing taut.

I *come*. Light explodes inside my skull and bones, a release I can only describe as cataclysmic. I'm clawing at Duke, yelling his name as I'm hit with a searing sensation, each throb a heightened echo of the one that came before it.

He softly presses the pad of his thumb to my clit as if to soothe the shock of it. He also begins to move inside me, small thrusts that get deeper and harder as he gains momentum.

"Unreal." His voice is thin. "You. Bare. Coming. Keep coming, sweetheart."

Like I have a choice. The orgasm seems to go on forever, stoked to renewed life with every thrust of his hips. He feathers his lips over mine, the caress heart-stoppingly gentle.

Really, how *does* he know what I need? Want?

How is the sex this good on our first go-around? I usually have to try really hard to come with a guy, especially if he wants to be the one who makes me do it. I can get myself off just fine, especially if toys are involved.

But this? Someone taking total control over my body and making me come harder than I ever have before?

Wild.

It makes me feel like Duke is really, *really* into me.

It makes me feel like I'm desirable and generous and fun.

What if my family's not right about what I am?
What if I'm right?

But really, who do I think I am to trust myself over, well, everyone else? I'm not especially smart. I'm not special. I don't deserve any better than what other people get.

Duke is just lost in the throes of lust right now. Once the attraction wears off a little, he'll see me for who I really am.

The girl who's not pretty or clever or normal enough to want.

The girl who's easy to forget.

CHAPTER 11
Middle-of-the-Night Marathon
Duke

Fucking perfect.

This girl feels so fucking *perfect* I have to bite down on the inside of my cheek to keep myself from coming.

She's hot and swollen and soft, and the feel of her coming on my dick sends my pulse, my thoughts, my will to live into a death spiral.

"Duke." She's whimpering, her hands moving to my face. "Wow. I'm…not okay."

I kiss her neck, trailing my nose up the column of her throat before capturing her mouth with my own. "What can I do to fix that?"

"Nothing," she breathes. "There's nothing that needs fixing. That was…just. *Wow.*"

I let myself chuckle, even as my balls scream in agony. I'm prouder than I probably should be that I finally made this girl let loose. Let go.

She's surrendering to me and to the moment for once. How can I convince her to keep doing that?

"Good," I manage, rocking into her tight heat. *Maybe now you'll give me a shot.* "You feel so good, sweetheart. We fit so good."

I wonder if being under the covers, lost in complete darkness, is why I'm so attuned to her every breath, every noise, every movement. I'm aware of her, of *us*, in a way that's an enormous turn-on.

She runs her thumb over my lips. "Don't stop."

"Couldn't." I kiss the pad of her thumb. "Couldn't ever stop. But I'm close."

Her hands move to my sides, that thumb catching on my nipple. I curse.

She does it again before moving to the other nipple. "What else can I do to make you feel as good as I do right now?"

My chest squeezes. I like how she gives as good as she gets in every sense of the expression. She's generous, invested in this being good for both of us, and I…Christ, I'm flying so fucking high right now.

"I wanna come inside you so bad." I impale her on a hard thrust, our bodies smacking when they meet. "But I also don't wanna get us into trouble."

"I told you, I'm on the pill." She lifts her head to kiss my shoulder before moving to my neck. "We're good."

"Sweetheart, this is so much better than good."

"Yeah?"

I manage to scoff. "Yeah."

"*Please.*" Her voice takes on a desperate edge. And the way she clings to me, fingers curling into my sides—it's like she's worried I won't stay.

Not a chance.

The heaviness in my core becomes unbearable. My

hips jerk, and for several strokes, I rut like a goddamn animal, mindless with lust. Best sex I've had, no question.

It's Wheeler.

How smart she is.

How creative and curious and open-minded.

It's also being in a bed that's not mine in a town I don't know. I love the idea of tomorrow being wide open. No literal or proverbial shit to shovel. No busted tires on trailers or four a.m. wakeup calls.

Nice little break from a routine that's really been wearing on me.

Wheeler moans, pressing her tits against my chest. She runs her fingernails up and down my sides, the pressure she applies *just* right. Goose bumps break out on my arms and legs.

I shove inside her one last time.

The pressure.

The heat.

I can't believe I'm inside Wheeler Rankin right now.

I can't believe she finally let me in.

White light explodes from my center outward. I come with a guttural moan, her name on my lips as the orgasm slams into me.

It knocks the wind out of my lungs. I can't breathe. Can't move. I just *feel*, my entire being a live wire of sensation.

"Duke." Wheeler's voice is a whisper, her lips catching on the underside of my chin. "Take your time. No rush. No rush. I love the feel of you like this."

Raw. Bare. Exposed.

I should have some sense of self-preservation. Yeah, Wheeler is letting me have her tonight. But there's something keeping her from jumping in with both feet. Who knows how she'll feel in the morning?

But I know I'm already in too deep to fight. I don't want any drama. Definitely don't want to play games. Wheeler is one of a kind, and I've been around long enough to know she's something special.

A small eternity later, the shock waves finally subside. My body feels hollowed out.

And Wheeler—she still feels warm and inviting. I kiss her, a slow, deep, lingering pull and press of tongue, lips, breath.

She's breathing hard. I get it. I can't catch my breath either. Our skin is sticky with sweat.

Can't help it. I smile.

"What?" she whispers.

"Mission accomplished."

Wheeler scoffs. "You got in my pants?"

"I got you warm."

She goes still at that. Then, after a beat: "You did. Thank you."

"You okay if I pull out? Might hurt a little, but I wanna get you cleaned up. This is gonna be messy."

"That a problem?" Her finger trails down my chest.

"Jesus *fuck*."

"What?"

"Just—" I straighten my elbows, using my core to lift myself off her. "You wouldn't mind the mess, would you?"

"The mess I'm makin' with you?" Her accent drips with honey. "No, Duke. I don't mind that."

I hang my head. *Stay calm. Stay cool. You like her, but that don't mean you do something stupid and fall too fast and too hard.*

"Deep breath," I manage. "Hold on to me if you need to."

I hear her hair catch on the sheets when she nods, her breasts rising to meet my chest. Her hands are on my shoulders again. "I'm definitely going to be sore."

"You gonna be walkin' bowlegged like me tomorrow?"

She laughs. "Yeah. Maybe."

"Another deep breath."

She does as I tell her. I slowly—*slowly*—rock my hips backward, pulling out of her inch by inch.

Her breath catches. I lean down to kiss her mouth. Moving my lips to her cheek, I taste salt.

My turn to go still.

She's crying.

The calculation happens within the space of half a heartbeat. She's not crying because she's sad or lonely or in too much pain.

She's crying because she's overwhelmed. I know this because *I'm* overwhelmed. In a really fucking awesome way.

My pulse goes apeshit. Does this mean—

I don't know, could it mean this ain't casual for her?

The fantasy unwinds in my mind. Us staying in this bed all weekend. Us driving home and me asking her on a date. Her saying yes. Me going on another trip with her. Another and another and another. Us dancing at the Rattler every Friday night. Us sleeping in at my place every Saturday morning.

Rein it in, asshole.

I'm getting way, way ahead of myself here. But the fantasy is warm and real, same as Wheeler is warm and real underneath me right now.

I want you, sweetheart. So fucking bad.

Kissing away her tears, I pull all the way out of her. I feel a rush of cum follow. Sheets are gonna be wet. Wonder where the linen closet is?

Wheeler whimpers, her grip on me tight. My heart turns over.

"You hurtin'?"

"Yeah. A little."

I brush my nose against hers. "A little? Or a lot?"

"Just a little."

"I'm gonna get you dressed in some of my clothes, okay? That way, you're not freezing when you go to the bathroom."

"You really don't need to—"

"Yes, Blue, I really do need to."

I can't see a damn thing, but I picture Wheeler biting her bottom lip, a smile working its way across her face.

"Okay."

"Stay here. I'll be right back."

———

My dick wakes me up.

Correction: My dick pressing into something soft and warm wakes me up.

I'm warm. So is the woman I'm currently spooning.

Holy fucking shit, it's Wheeler.

Wheeler is in my bed. We fucked. It was awesome.

She's still here.

I am rock-hard. Hungry in every sense of the word.

That's when I realize she's pressing her ass into my pelvis. Opening my eyes, I see that it's still pitch-black. Late, then. Or early.

The world outside the windows is quiet. The blizzard is dying down.

"You okay?" My voice is hoarse with sleep, gravelly with need.

Her hand lands on my side. "I'm sorry to wake you up, but I—I'm sorry, Duke, but I need…well…you."

She gropes for my hand, which she takes and guides over the swell of her hips.

I hiss when she presses our fingertips into her sweet little cunt.

She's slippery with arousal.

"You need me to take care of you?" I circle my fingers over her clit, making her moan.

"Yes, please."

"So polite. How do you want me?"

"I like it best when you—you know, take charge."

Chuckling, I scrape my stubble over her nape as I lift her leg and pull it back and up so that it rests on my top leg. I find her center again and run my fingers up and down the delicious softness of her slit.

I'm gentle when I press my first finger to her entrance. "This hurt?"

"No."

"Good." I use that finger and my thumb to hold her open. It's a little awkward, but I manage to roll over ever so slightly to free my other hand. Then I grab my dick and guide it to her pussy. "Don't forget—"

"I'll use my words. I know."

"Nice and easy." I push my crown inside her, my eyes rolling to the back of my head at the sweetness of her viselike grip on me. "Fuck naw. This ain't nice. This is fuckin' heaven. You—this greedy little cunt of yours—I can't stand how fuckin' good you feel."

"Duke," she warbles, her hand on my hip again as I push in farther. "I'm—it's a lot—but—so good."

I move my fingers to her clit, gathering moisture on my fingertips. "I'm gonna go a little faster this time. You can take it. You trust me, don't you? You know I'll fuck this cunt hard and good. I'll make it so good for you."

"Yeah." She's crying again. I can tell by the thickness of her voice.

"You all right, Blue? This good crying or bad crying?"

"Good. Always. Go. Please."

Inhaling, I firm my abdominals, breathe out, and push all the way inside her. It takes real effort because she's so tiny.

But then I'm there, balls-deep in heaven.

Wheeler makes a choking sound, my name on her lips. But she doesn't tell me to stop.

"I know this is a lot for you." I reach up to paint her nipples with her slickness. They're hard, her breasts firm, filling my hand. "But you're really doing so well. Give it a minute. I feel you stretching for me, yeah? You feel it too?"

"I do. Oh, Duke." She arches her back and reaches behind her, digging her fingers into the hair at the nape of my neck. "This feels amazing. More. Please. Anything you do, I want more of it."

I'm smiling like an idiot in the darkness as I begin to fuck her in earnest. I play with her nipples, her pussy fluttering around me.

"Touch yourself." I take her hand and guide it to her center. "Make yourself come on my dick. You know how much I like that."

"Okay." Her fingers move over her clit.

"Good girl."

She comes a few heartbeats later, her body seizing. I soothe her as best as I can, murmuring her name in her ear while I steadily rock in and out of her.

So much skin. So much closeness, her body wrapped up in mine. We're a cozy, warm mess underneath the covers, and I wonder vaguely if I've ever been happier.

I come inside her with a curse. She laughs. My heart has wings.

I want this to last forever. But I know all good things must come to an end.

CHAPTER 12
One Last Hurrah in the U-Haul
Duke

The weekend does end. But not before Wheeler and I spend the entire time naked in bed, because Aspen Leather Company's trunk show was canceled. They're working to reschedule it for sometime later this summer.

We're officially stranded underneath a blanket of snow that reaches *four feet* in some places. It's bitterly cold outside, but luckily the power comes back on early Friday morning.

When Wheeler and I are not fucking, we're sleeping.

When we're not sleeping, we're fucking.

In between, we manage to shower, eat, and polish off the box of wine. We found a treasure trove of frozen pizzas and burritos in the freezer. Thank God for that, because I need to carb load for the kind of athletic sex Wheeler and I have more times than I can count.

Nevertheless, according to the scale in the primary bathroom, I'm down five pounds by the time Monday morning rolls around. I'm sore in places I didn't know existed.

"I think you mighta given me the best workout of my life this weekend," I say to Wheeler as I load our suitcases into the tiny space behind the seats in the U-Haul's cab. "Gonna need to stop for some Advil on the way to the interstate."

Luckily the roads have been cleared, and temps are steadily climbing into positive Fahrenheit territory. All weekend, we've seen wind chills of up to minus twenty degrees.

Wheeler smiles. "We can do that, sure."

Our breath fogs around us in the air.

All weekend long, Wheeler was open and vulnerable and real. She didn't hold back. She laughed loudly, came hard, and fucked me like the rock star she is. She was down to try all the positions. Have sex in all the rooms at all hours of the day.

There were a few times, like that first night when she begged me with her words and her body to stay close, that I sensed she felt insecure. Why she'd feel that way, I have no idea. Clearly I'm obsessed with her.

Clearly I wanna keep doing this.

I've thought all morning about telling her how I feel. When we're back in Hartsville, I don't want to drop her off at the New House. I wanna take her to my place, the old foreman's cottage on my family's ranch that we recently renovated.

I wanna take her on a date. Many dates.

But it's one thing to hook up when you're snowed in and there's literally nothing else to do.

It's quite another to start a relationship.

I'm down, but I still don't know if Wheeler feels the same.

She frowns when her phone rings. "We should hit the road."

She pulls the phone out of her pocket, her frown deepening when she sees the screen. She sends the call to voicemail.

She keeps doing that. I've been dying to ask what's going on, but it ain't my place. Figure she'll tell me about that divorce she mentioned if—when—she's ready.

"I don't wanna leave." I hold the door open for her.

Slipping the phone back into her pocket, she meets my eyes. "I don't either. I'm bummed the trunk show didn't happen, but..." Her expression softens. "I've had a really great time with you, Duke."

Curling my hand around the top of the doorframe, I cross my left ankle over my right and lean in. "Don't gotta end, you know."

My voice is husky. I'm nervous, no denying that.

Wheeler flattens her palm on my stomach. For a split second, I think she's going to kiss me. Her eyes toggle between mine, and I see the heat in them. The longing.

Same longing that I feel, even though we already fucked twice this morning. Once in bed. Once in the shower.

Not sure I ever wanna shower alone again.

Are we gonna be able to make it down the mountain without me begging her for some road head? I'll happily return the favor. She knows that, surely?

But then she turns away and climbs into the truck. "Mollie wants me to give her a call. I'll drive the second half if that's okay. Just so I can get some work done."

I feel the cold suddenly press in on me, the skin on my face and hands stinging. "I'll drive, no problem."

The winding road that leads us down the mountain is icy in spots. I go extra slow, silently praying the U-Haul's brakes don't give out.

Luckily, I have Wheeler doing boss babe shit to distract me. I legit get hard listening to her talk business strategy and branding management as we hit the highway.

"I think we reframe the conversation as us being more a fashion enterprise than anything else." She's got her computer on her lap now and is busily typing away with her phone tucked between her ear and her shoulder. "That way, we remain open to all kinds of collabs. We could do handbags, jewelry, jackets... Why limit ourselves to just boots, you know?" She pauses, listening. "Yep. That's exactly right. We can do fun branded Western wear. Have a booth at, say, Round Top... Yes! Exactly."

I'd go to Round Top with you.

Really, why stop there? We could do trunk shows all over the world. Maybe open up some stores in places like Aspen and, hell, New York City while we're at it.

By the time she hangs up, the sun is shining, and I'm so turned on I have a difficult time focusing on the road.

"Where are we going?" Wheeler asks when I take an exit that looks like it leads pretty much nowhere.

My hands shake as I turn the wheel. "Quick detour."

"If you need to use the restroom, this doesn't look like the place to—"

"That's not what I need." Reaching across the console, I grab her hand and put it on my crotch. "You.

Being smart and bossy and…confident. It's so fucking hot, Blue. I'm tired, but I ain't too tired for another round. You?"

Turning my head, I see her expression flicker. It's a look I know well now: the blaze in her eyes, the way her nostrils flare just the tiniest bit. The edges of her mouth curl ever so slightly upward. Her cheeks go pink.

Yeah, she's game.

Thank God she's still game.

"You want me to boss you around?" she asks, her hand moving to cup my erection through my jeans. "Oh yeah, you like being bossed around."

The road is empty. I pull onto the shoulder and shove the gearshift into park. Then I hold up my hands. "All right, boss lady. Do what you will."

Her eyes flash with hunger as she pulls down my zipper and reaches for my cock through the slit in my briefs. She wraps her fingers around me, gives me a firm tug, running her thumb up my head, and my other head falls back on the headrest with an audible *thump*.

The engine rumbles as she works my shaft. I love how she flicks her wrist so that her palm moves over my tip. She must've watched me do that this morning when we showered together.

Girl notices everything. Even the tiniest, most insignificant shit.

Maybe she will come home with me tonight.

Nice to feel noticed for once. Growing up, I had a bit of a rebellious streak. An attempt, I think, to get attention.

An attempt to not be forgotten.

Now here's Wheeler, remembering everything.

"Sweetheart." I can barely breathe. "Why don't you come over here? Sit on it for a minute or five."

She smirks, leaning over the console. "I thought I was the boss."

"Not when I want you this bad, you're not. I can't—*fuuuuck*."

Wheeler's head is in my lap now. Holding my dick in her hand, she licks my tip, swirling her tongue over the most sensitive part of my head.

"See?" She sucks my head into her mouth. Bobs down. Bobs up. Licks me again, slowly, savoring me like she can't get enough of my taste. "I'm in charge. I do what I want, Duke, so you best mind your business and let me work."

And does. She. *Work*.

I gather her hair in my hand so I can watch her suck my dick like the motherfucking champion she is. Her cheeks hollow out when she gives me a quick, hard suck. My hips jerk, my balls contracting. How I have any stamina left, I don't know, but I manage to keep my orgasm at bay.

"You're killing me." I don't recognize my voice. "You're so fucking good at this, sweetheart."

My stomach caves when she takes me deep.

"Just so you know," I breathe, "if you wanna fuck me, you'd better do it now, because I'm four seconds from coming in your mouth."

She gently—carefully—lifts her head so that my cock falls out of her mouth. I'm slick with her saliva, my head shining in the light of the sun.

Next thing I know, she's climbing onto my lap, her knees straddling my hips. I grab her, curling my hands around her waist, and I press a hard, hot kiss to her mouth. She laughs.

We're a frenzy of hands and tongues as we try to kiss while yanking down her leggings and underwear.

Then I slide a hand between her legs. Suck in a breath when I part her and feel how wet she is.

I close my eyes and savor her softness.

"Aw, Blue." I circle my fingertips over her clit, just how she likes. Because I know her now. She knows me. "Sucking my dick turns you on, yeah?"

"Everything." Her hands are on my neck as she husks out the words, her forehead resting on mine. "Everything about you turns me on, Duke."

I slide my other hand inside her sweatshirt. Pressing my thumb against her nipple through the lacy fabric of her bra, I draw a happy gasp from the back of her throat.

Her tongue is in my mouth. My mouth is on her chin, her neck. I bite her. She cries out. I kiss her mouth again.

"Get on my dick," I growl, reaching around to squeeze her bare ass. "Sweetheart, I'm dyin' here. Put me inside you. C'mon, now."

I feel her smile against my kiss. "I told you, I do what I want."

"Don't pretend like you don't want me."

She thumbs my cheek. A quick graze that's tender and new, making my chest twist.

"I do. I really do want you, Duke."

I sputter when she grabs my dick and lines me up at her center. Her breath catches.

"Sore?" I ask, opening my eyes.

Hers are open too and wet with pain. "Yes."

"If it's too much—"

"Hush." Putting a hand over my mouth, she begins to sink onto my swollen length.

I almost come from the sheer pleasure of being even just an inch inside her. Her pussy grips me as she sinks lower, her brow furrowed with concentration.

She holds my eyes the whole time, her hand sliding to my throat.

Watching the look in those eyes change—first pain, then curiosity, then satiation—as she gives my throat a squeeze has my heart palpitating. Strands of her hair hang in her face, catching the light so they turn to copper. They move as she breathes, as she sinks lower, lower.

Lower.

"*Blue.*" It's the only word I can choke out when she's all the way down, and I'm so deep inside her I can't breathe.

She's shaking. She removes her hand from my throat and puts it on the window. The other is on my shoulder, her nails biting my skin through my shirt.

"It's too much." I gently kiss her lips. "You're too sore, sweetheart."

"Shh."

"I don't wanna hurt you—"

"But you're not." Her eyes search mine. "You're not the one who's hurting me."

My blood goes still inside my skin. *Who is the one, then? Where can I find him? What did he do to you?*

Before I can so much as utter a syllable, though, Wheeler is rocking her hips. Little circles that become gradually bigger and bigger until she's enthusiastically riding my dick. Her tits bounce. Her hair is everywhere.

She's shouting my name, throwing back her head like we're not in a U-Haul on the side of the road in the middle of nowhere, Colorado. Even the truck rocks in time to her movements.

I just hold on for dear life and roll my thumb over her clit. Her pussy clamps down on me, and a full-body shiver moves through Wheeler as she collapses against me with a sob.

"Oh, Duke. Oh my God. Oh my God. Duke. Duke. Duke."

She chants my name like she's trying not to forget it while she comes.

You ain't forgetting me anytime soon, sweetheart.

I take over. I hug her to me as I piston my hips upward. It doesn't take long for my own orgasm to crash through me. I spill inside her, trying not to shout. I know she doesn't like loud noises. I'll be damned if I scare her the way her dad did.

I hold her for a long time after that. Long enough that my heart rate has evened out somewhat.

Now would be a good time to ask her if she'd like to sleep at my place tonight. Or do I lead with a date? I don't want her to think I'm just using her for sex.

I kiss the top of her head. "Blue?"

"Yeah?"

"You all right?"

She lifts her head, turns it, then scoffs when she sees how we've literally fogged up the windows.

"Ha." She smiles. "We pulled a Jack and Rose."

"A what?"

"You know." She turns back to look at me. In the sun, the brown in her eyes turns translucent, warm like whiskey. "That scene in *Titanic*, when Leonardo DiCaprio and Kate Winslet steam up the windows in that car?"

I laugh. "I'm ashamed to admit I've never seen that movie."

She stares at me. "You're kidding."

"I'm not." My heart pounds. *Do it. Just ask her.* "Would you be interested in coming over to my place tonight to, well, come, and then we could watch it?"

She blinks. My pulse stumbles.

"I totally get it if that's not your, uh, vibe," I continue. "I just really—what I'm trying to—it's not just sex I want. I need you to know that. I'd like to—yeah, maybe date you or…take you out on a date. Many dates. And have sex too, of course. But only if you want to! No pressure. I just…" Spearing a hand through my hair, I let out a pained chuckle. "I like you, Wheeler, and I'd like it if the thing we had happening this weekend kept…well, happening."

Wheeler blinks again. She as shocked as I am by my babbling? I'd like to think I'm a relatively confident guy, but all of a sudden, I'm flustered as fuck.

I'm *nervous*.

Doesn't help matters when the expression in her eyes morphs into something like pain.

Like disappointment.

She looks away, and my heart falls.

Everything in me falls, gathering together in a terrible, weighted certainty in my gut.

She's not coming home with me tonight. Or any night.

My disappointment must show on my face, because when Wheeler turns back to look at me, her expression contracts.

"Look, Duke. This weekend has been a ton of fun. I mean that. And I like you. I really, really do—"

"But you can't date me." I search her eyes. "Or you won't. Why? This is good, Wheeler. I think we could be good together."

Her brows curve upward, her eyes filling. "I admire your optimism. But this weekend…it can't happen again. I'm so busy with work—"

"I love your work. I support it, wholeheartedly." I rock my hips, a reminder that I'm still inside her. "It quite literally turns me on."

"Jesus, Duke, you're not making this easy." She puts a hand on my chest.

I brush the hair out of her face. "Just give me a chance. That's all I ask."

She looks away again. Looks down. I see her eyelashes flutter in an attempt to blink back tears.

Really, why is she doing this? Why make things difficult when they could be easy? I know she's feeling me, same as I'm feeling her.

"I have some napkins in my bag." Her voice is thin as she pushes onto her knees, pulling up her pants before falling into the passenger seat. "Here, I'll clean us up."

My cum is everywhere. It smells like sex in the cab. I feel sticky and cold despite the heat pumping through the vents.

"Did I do something to turn you off or…"

Wheeler shakes her head. "You did everything right."

Then why are you turning me down, sweetheart?

I get my answer when we're back on the highway. We're in east Colorado now, the soaring majesty of the mountains giving way to an endless stretch of high plains.

"Like I told you, my parents are splitting up," Wheeler says. She's holding a can of sparkling water in her hand that we picked up at a gas station after we hooked up. The can's gotta be mostly empty by now.

I adjust my hand on the wheel. "That really sucks."

"I mean, my mom divorcing my dad has been a long time coming." She stares out the windshield. "Part of me is relieved they're finally going through with it. When I was little, I remember them being happy enough. But as I got older, they started to fight more. A lot more. By the time I was in high school, it was obvious they were miserable together, and their relationship has only deteriorated since then. So I'm happy they're, you know, trying to find happiness again."

A beat of silence. I don't know what to say. She doesn't seem to want comfort, at least not that I can tell. Maybe she just needs a sympathetic ear.

"Seems like a step in the right direction," I say carefully. "Can I ask what happened?"

Wheeler nods, dropping the empty can into her cupholder. "I think they ultimately didn't work because they got married for the wrong reasons. They had a shotgun wedding situation, although everyone pretended like it wasn't because my dad comes from money, and they were able to throw this big, ridiculous wedding to cover it up. Long story short, Mom got pregnant with my older brother, so my dad married her. I think they both wanted kids, so it made sense at the time."

"Right. Guess there are worse reasons to get married."

"But there are definitely better ones. They weren't always miserable together, but I'm not sure they were ever super happy either."

I nod. "I absolutely agree. I don't think the point of marriage—or life, really—is to have kids."

"Yeah?" She finally looks at me. "What do you think the point is, then? I'm genuinely curious, because I'm trying to find that out myself."

Lifting a shoulder, I put on my blinker. "Experiencing the world. Traveling. Figuring out who you are. Lending a helping hand when you can."

"I like those ideas. A lot." She looks down at her lap. "Anyway, the divorce was a bomb I was expecting—"

"But it's still a bomb."

"Exactly. I can function okay. Like, work is the thing that's keeping me sane right now. But I'm, like, actually not okay?" Her voice gets high, and I know she's about to cry. "It's hard watching the life you've known explode around you."

How do I know you so well after a single weekend?

How'd we go from fucking in the front seat to talking about serious shit?

There's a vulnerability to Wheeler, a willingness to be real, that has me spinning out. It's so rare to be able to talk about real shit with someone this way. Makes me feel alive.

It's devastating to think this might be the last real conversation I have with this girl.

"I think it'd be weird if you *were* okay." I change lanes, then turn my head to look at Wheeler. "Wish you'd said something, Blue. We can't be there for you if you're not telling us what's going on."

"We?"

"Me. My brothers. Everyone you live and work with on the ranch."

Her face crumples, and so does my heart.

"You're sweet." She wipes away her tears with the flat of her hand. "But we're not that close—"

"Blue, I just spent the weekend inside you. We're close, whether you like it or not."

That makes her laugh. "People aren't like that where I'm from. Don't get me wrong, I have friends back home, but they…yeah, don't care the way y'all do."

"So let us take care of you. Let me take care of you."

She shakes her head, holding her hand to her face. "I need to focus on…other things right now. I'm a mess, Duke. You don't want to deal with this bullshit."

"But I do." I swallow, hard, my chest tight. "You gotta let me decide what I'm up for, yeah?"

But she's still shaking her head. "I can't. I'm sorry."

"I don't accept that."

"You have to, Duke." Her eyes are on me again. "Trust me when I say you want no part of this mess."

My heart screams with the desire to keep pushing her. There's plenty of holes in her argument. I see what she's doing—the way she's pushing me away before I can push *her* away.

Wonder why she automatically assumes that's what will happen?

But it's obvious Wheeler is in a bad place. I have to respect what she wants, even though I think it's a fucking tragedy to give up on the chemistry we share.

Who knows? Maybe she just needs some time to heal. Maybe she'll eventually come around to the idea of being with me. I'll just keep in touch with her in the meantime—a text here or there, a call just to catch up.

Or maybe I'm being a huge fucking idiot, and I need

to take her refusal seriously. I believe her when she says she's beat up over her parents' divorce. Could be that she's not telling me something else, though. She could have her sights set on another guy.

Christ, do I hate the idea of her holding a torch for some finance bro dickhead in Dallas.

I don't realize I'm holding the wheel in a death grip until my fingers start to throb.

"Got it." I try to keep my voice even. Calm. "I'm sorry you're going through all that, and I'm sorry you don't feel the way I do. But I understand."

She sniffles. "Thank you. I'm sorry too, Duke."

CHAPTER 13
Nicknames with New Meanings
Wheeler

"Well, isn't that exciting."

Judging by Mom's tone, the fact that we just sold out of the first drop of our summer collection in *seven minutes* isn't very exciting at all.

A rush of saliva fills my mouth. I put a hand on my middle, wondering why the hell I feel like I'm going to vomit all of a sudden.

Ah yes, it's because talking to either of my parents right now literally makes me sick to my stomach. How could I forget?

"Thanks. Mollie and I are really proud."

"Y'all should be. I know you've worked hard." A pause. "Maybe a little too hard. I still think you going to an office every day would provide more structure. Give you some boundaries, you know? Because it sounds like you're working morning, noon, and night."

Rolling my eyes, I cross my arms over my chest, but I immediately wince. *Wow*, my boobs are sore. I wish my period would come already so I could stop PMS-ing. I've felt pretty awful the past couple days.

"Mom, I tried to do the law thing, and I hated it."

"You should've given it another chance. It's not too late, you know. Barb's daughter just finished law school at the ripe old age of thirty, and she got a signing bonus *and* matching 401(k) contributions at her new firm."

"Well, I'm not Barb's daughter."

I swallow the lump that's appeared in my throat. I know it's just the PMS fucking with me—this time of the month, I always get super emotional. But Mom's old implication that I'm doing the wrong thing—I'm on the wrong path—hits harder than usual.

"I know, honey." Mom sighs. "I'm sorry. I just worry about you is all. I don't want you to get stuck down the road if things don't work out with Bellamy Brooks."

What she doesn't say: *I don't want you to get stuck like me.*

Mom quit her job at a marketing company after she had my older brother, and she never went back to work. To be honest, I don't think she ever had big ambitions for her career. Probably part of the reason why I do. But I know she regrets not having more agency in her life. More financial freedom. Maybe then, she wouldn't have had to tolerate my dad's awfulness for so long. I'm really proud of her for finally having the courage to get a divorce, but I wish she'd done it a lot sooner.

Why do you think I work so hard, Mom? I wish you'd trust me to make the right choices.

No one wishes more than I do that I *wanted* the kind of stable, respectable job my parents pictured for me. I even went so far as to take the LSAT my senior year of college in the hopes I could make that path fit.

I bombed the test. I took it as a sign from the universe that I was meant to do other things, but clearly Mom still disagrees how many years later.

My boobs throb. I put my hand on one, then the other. "I'm doing my best to make sure that never happens. Money's rolling in. If we're smart and we play our cards right, I think we have a real shot at being the next big thing. I really love what we're doing, Mom."

"I'll cross my fingers and toes for you. I'm actually wearing a pair of my Bellamy Brooks right now!"

I smile, even as an arrow of something unpleasant arcs through my middle at the thought of Mom sitting by herself in her boots in the house I grew up in. I really do feel for her—getting a divorce so late in the game has to be an incredibly lonely experience.

"Lemme guess. A pair of the pink shorties?"

"You're good, Wheeler Marie."

"Yup." I smile. "I'm glad you're enjoying the boots, Mom."

"I get so many compliments on them."

Of course you do. I made sure they're fabulous, just like every other pair we design and manufacture.

Another pause. My stomach rumbles. I'm nauseous, but I'm also kind of hungry. Which makes no sense, as it's only three o'clock in the afternoon, and supper isn't until five at Lucky River Ranch. I've been here for a few days now so Mollie and I could be together for our summer launch. She's still not feeling well enough to travel.

Wonder what Patsy is making for supper? I hope

it's meat loaf. Weird craving, but hers is so delicious, especially when she makes it with this sweet pea risotto that's buttery and creamy and just, yeah, out-of-this-world delicious.

"So how's the ranch? You line dance with any cowboys recently?"

My heart somersaults. It's been a little over three weeks since Duke and I parted ways after that incredible weekend in Aspen. I wish I could say I've been so busy with work that I haven't thought about him or his laugh or the way his hands felt on my body.

That I haven't been plagued by a sense of never-ending regret for not taking him up on the invitation to watch *Titanic* at his place.

But that would be a lie. I think about him constantly, which is why I try my best to avoid him. I just don't see a path to happily ever after for us. My sense of self-worth is…wobbly at best. And my career is finally taking off. I have to honor all the blood, sweat, and tears I've poured into Bellamy Brooks over the years by making hay while the sun is shining. That means working more than I have. Ever.

I've made it a point to not sit down for meals in Patsy's kitchen, opting instead for the doggie bags she'll make for me. I'll usually eat in here in the primary bedroom, camped out at the desk in front of the big window that overlooks the front yard.

Duke has texted me a few times. He even called the day after we got back and the day after that. I wanted to pick up the phone so, *so* badly. But that seemed unfair of me, so I sent his calls to voicemail.

He hasn't reached out since.

Part of me appreciates the fact that he's respected my request for space. He's always polite when we do interact. Always friendly but never *too* friendly.

And then part of me wants to grab him by the shirt collar and yank him in for a hard, hot kiss.

What the fuck is wrong with you? I'd breathe into his mouth. *Why won't you chase me any harder?*

Because that's not messed up at all, me wanting him to pursue me despite my very clear instructions to leave me alone.

"Ha. No cowboys, Mom." I'm hit by a vicious swirl of nausea. I put my hand over my mouth. Really, what's going on? Did I catch a stomach bug or something?

"You know, it's important that you take the time to stop and smell the Stetsons. I mean roses."

"You're funny," I manage.

"I'm okay, Wheeler." Another pause. "Really. I want you to keep living your life. I know it's not easy to forget about what's going on with me and Dad, but…" She sighs. "It'll all work out, so you shouldn't put your life on pause. Your love life, I mean."

I wish I could believe that things will work out. Just like I wish I could stop feeling like I'm going to throw up.

"Hey, Mom? I have to run. But let me know how your meeting with the mediator goes tomorrow, okay? I'll be thinking about you."

"Okay. Congrats again on your collection."

You didn't congratulate me the first time, but whatever. I wish our relationship weren't so…complicated.

"Thanks. Love you."

I hang up and sit on the edge of the bed. The mattress

dips, making my stomach slosh. A fist of sudden, violent pressure darts up my throat.

Holy shit, I really am going to puke.

Lurching off the bed, I dash for the bathroom. I make it to the toilet just in time to lose the contents of my stomach with a pair of awful, heaving retches.

Tears prick my eyes. The acidic taste of bile fills my mouth. I retch again and again, my arms shaking as I prop them on the toilet seat.

What the actual fuck?

"Wheeler?" Mollie's voice sounds from the bedroom.

I retch again.

She must hear me, because the next thing I know, she's flying into the bathroom, her brown eyes going wide when she sees me hovering over the toilet.

"Wheeler, oh my God! Are you okay?"

"I have no idea what's going on with me." I fall to my knees in front of the toilet, one leg at a time. "I think I might've eaten something bad. Does anyone have the stomach bug? Maybe Ella brought it home from preschool."

Mollie shakes her head. "No one is sick. Not that I know of anyway. And we've all been eating the same stuff…"

I notice the pair of deep furrows on her forehead.

Falling back onto my butt, I'm overwhelmed by just how miserable I feel. "This is so weird. And awful."

Despite her growing bump, Mollie leans down to run a hand over my back. "Do you want some water? Maybe some crackers? I'm kind of an expert on what to eat when you feel like ass."

Mollie's in her second trimester now. But she was

pretty sick during the first part of her pregnancy, the "morning" sickness they warned her about lasting all day and sometimes into the night too.

"I'm not sure I'll be able to keep anything down." I wince when I'm hit by another wave of what I can only describe as sea sickness.

The furrows in Mollie's brow deepen. Her hand goes still. "Okay, I don't mean to freak you out—"

"Oh God, what?"

"But your little weekend getaway with Duke was, what, three weeks ago?"

Mollie knows all about what went down in Aspen. She may be married to Duke's brother, but she's also my best friend. I don't think it's a stretch to say she knows everything about me.

Really, she's comprised almost the entirety of the support system I've needed after losing the one I had in my family.

Pulse going haywire, I swallow a rush of bile that floods my mouth. "A little more than that, yeah."

"Have you gotten your period?"

"I'm supposed to get it any minute."

"Y'all were careful, right?"

"Of course we were careful. I'm on the—"

The words die in my throat. *Wait a second.*

Wait.

Did I accidentally miss taking a pill?

My brain scrambles to comb through the details of the sex-soaked forty-eight hours I spent in Aspen. I have an alarm set on my phone that goes off at the same time every morning as a reminder to take my birth control pill. I definitely took my pill the day we drove to

Colorado; I remember popping it into my mouth during a restroom stop. But the next day...

My stomach takes a swan dive. I obviously stayed in Duke's room that night. When I went to retrieve my phone up in my room the morning after we first hooked up, it was dead. The power had gone out, so my phone hadn't charged.

Which means my alarm never went off.

I never took that pill, did I?

Leaning forward, I retch. Mollie lunges forward to hold back my hair.

"Oh, honey," she says. "What can I do for you?"

Could I actually be pregnant? Duke and I had so much sex.

So much really great, really athletic, really raw sex. And if I did indeed miss a pill...

Oh my God oh my God oh my fucking God.

My boobs *hurt* as I press them against the toilet seat to throw up again. And again. Mollie runs a hand over my back. I'm dizzy. I have nothing left to throw up.

I don't remember feeling like this the handful of times I got the stomach bug. I'm nauseous, but I'm also sore and so tired and just...

I feel *off* in a way I never have before.

I'm crying when I straighten, wiping my mouth with the back of my hand. "Do you think you could come to the drugstore with me?"

"If you're looking for pregnancy tests, I have some."

I'm gripped by a fierce, full-body sob. "Mollie, what if—"

"We'll cross that bridge when we get there." She pulls me to my feet and puts her hands on my shoulders, looking me in the eye. "Chances are you just have a bug. Let's get the tests out of the way, though, so you can rest easy."

We hop in an ATV, which Mollie drives the half mile or so to the adorable little cabin where she and Cash live. She holds my hand the whole way. It's the comfort I need to keep from getting sucked into an all-out shame spiral.

But really, why didn't Duke and I use condoms? They're easy. Everyone says you should use a backup method.

And why didn't I take my pill first thing when I woke up, same as I always do? It would've taken all of three minutes to dart upstairs and grab the blister packet from my bathroom.

The cabin is tucked into a stand of old oaks that block the ardent spring sunlight, dappling the ground with their new leaves. I feel like a zombie as I follow Mollie up the front porch steps and inside the house.

"Cash isn't here, is he?" I glance left and right. As far as I can tell, the place is empty.

Mollie's boots hit the floor with a comforting *thump* as she heads to the back of the house. "Nope. C'mon, you can take the tests in my bathroom."

I'm shaking so badly that I end up peeing all over the sticks *and* my hand. Mollie is by my side the whole time, a hand on my shoulder. She sets out a towel on the vanity, and I place both tests—she insisted I take two—on the towel, a single blue line already appearing in the window.

"One line means not pregnant. Two lines—a cross—that means it's positive." She taps the start button on the timer on her phone. "We're going to laugh very hard about this in exactly two minutes."

Dropping the lid onto the toilet, I sit down heavily. I rest my elbows on my knees and press my fingertips into my eye sockets.

"I forgot to take a single pill." I suck in a breath. "I can't be pregnant, right?"

"The chances are very, very slim."

I shake my head. "I should've never…"

"What? Succumbed to the charms of a sexy-ass cowboy who's obsessed with you?"

Letting out a mirthless laugh, I straighten and blink the blurriness from my eyes. "Did you know Duke wears glasses?"

"I did. But he doesn't wear them often. I think he's a little embarrassed."

"Why? Glasses look so good on him."

Mollie smiles. "They do."

"These Rivers guys—they're far more charming than they have any right to be."

"Don't I know it." Mollie rubs her belly. "Obviously I'm biased, but I still think you should give Duke another shot. Maybe he's the distraction you need right now with his glasses and his flirting. Or maybe he ends up being more than that, and he shows you the healing powers of—"

"Jesus, Moll, don't make me puke again." I cover my mouth with my hand.

"Just sayin'." She smiles. "I didn't come here looking for love either. But I'm glad I gave Cash a chance."

But you're different, I want to say. She's not a bruised-up mess with a traumatized brain and some serious daddy issues.

Well, that's not entirely true. Mollie actually has some pretty epic daddy issues of her own. She didn't let them stop her from living her damn life, though, did she?

Why am I letting my fucked-up family's fucked-up opinion of me still mess with me all these years later?

I feel like I should've moved on by now. I want to move on. I just—

The timer beeps. My stomach bottoms out. Mollie hits the off button on her screen, and together we peer at the tests on the vanity.

Two blue crosses, clear as day.

My brain scrambles to make sense of what I'm seeing. At the same time, my eyes flood with tears, and my heart pounds. It's my body processing the news before my mind can catch up.

I'm pregnant.

Lord above, I'm pregnant with Duke's baby.

That nickname he gave me now seems horrifically prophetic.

CHAPTER 14
Low Places
Wheeler

Mollie grabs my elbows and lifts me off the toilet. Then she pulls me in for a tight hug.

"It'll be all right." She's running her hand over my back again. "We'll get through this, Wheeler, I promise."

I let out one of those sobs that racks my whole body. It's an animal noise, loud and awful and embarrassing.

Then again, I'm with my best friend. No need to be embarrassed.

"How could I be so stupid?"

"You weren't stupid. You're on birth control, remember? It just didn't work the way it was supposed—"

"Hellooooo! Anybody home? Saw the four-wheeler out front, and I thought I'd sneak in for a little afternoon dee-light."

Except I now have *every* reason to be embarrassed, because Cash just walked into the cabin.

My heart thuds in time to his heavy footsteps.

"Oh God," I whisper.

Mollie slams the door shut. "Cash, I need a minute!" Then she whispers back to me, "He's not supposed to be home for another hour. I'm so sorry."

"You okay?"

I hear him draw to a stop outside the door.

"A minute, please," Mollie calls.

I don't want to sob again, but I can't control it. I'm scared and I'm sad and...yeah, just *so fucking scared*.

Duke's going to be so angry.

Wait, why is that my first thought?

Ah yes. Because the only emotion my father ever expressed was anger. If we were lucky, he'd only bark at us when we were kids. If we were unlucky, he'd bark *and* bite.

I grew up terrified of him. I know rationally that Duke's given me absolutely no reason to be scared of him too. He's not an angry person, and he's not mean. But try telling that to my nervous system, which is currently completely shot.

Mollie holds me tighter. "Oh, sweetie."

"Wheeler? Is that you?" Cash's voice is urgent. "Are you hurt? What's going on?"

"I'm...fine?" I say thickly.

"We're fine, Cash," Mollie adds. "Just—a moment, please?"

"Y'all take all the time you need. But you got me worried."

My heart clenches. I pull back, meeting Mollie's eyes. "If you want me to go—"

"What?" She frowns. "Of course I don't want you to go. You shouldn't be alone right now, Wheeler. Here." She uses her thumbs to wipe away my tears. "Give me a sec to kick my dear husband's ass to the curb." Turning, she reaches for the door and opens it just enough to stick her head through the crack. "We need some privacy, Cash."

"Okay," he replies slowly. "Is there anything I can do, or—"

"You can go back to doing your cowboy things, please and thank you."

Cash is a smart guy. He knows better than to ask what we're doing or why we need said privacy. But he's more than a little overprotective of his wife, especially now that she's pregnant—*holy shit, I'm pregnant too*—so I get why he hesitates.

"Check in with me in a bit, then?" he asks. "Just so I know y'all are still okay?"

"Of course." Mollie opens the door a little wider so she can lean out to give her husband a peck on the lips. "Thank you for understanding."

But when she falls back, she stumbles into me and immediately turns around to apologize. The door stays open for a split second. Just long enough for me to lock eyes with Cash. They're the same shade of cobalt as Duke's.

These cowboys all look so much alike.

I see the flare of panic in Cash's eyes as they rake over my face. No doubt I'm puffy and pink from all the crying I've been doing.

Then his gaze moves to the vanity.

The tests are *right there*, the blue crosses definitely visible from where he stands.

His eyes go wide as they move back to me. A beat of silent, searing understanding moves between us. I have no idea what Duke told his brothers about our weekend in Aspen. Did he say anything at all? Mollie swore up and down that she didn't say a word to Cash, and I trust her with my life.

Judging by the gleam of understanding in Cash's eyes, he knows Duke and I hooked up. My pulse skips several beats. What does it mean that Duke told his brothers about us? What did he say? Does he miss me?

Why does any of that matter? Your relationship with Duke is purely platonic now.

Only these tests might throw a wrench in my carefully laid plans to *be just friends* with Duke. We'll have to talk. A lot. Somehow I know he'd rather die than leave me to deal with this alone.

I have to tell him. Especially now that Cash knows, because judging by the grave concern in this man's expression, he definitely knows I'm pregnant with his brother's baby.

"Please don't say anything," I blurt. "We—I literally just found out, and I don't know—I'm going to tell Duke, but I need a minute to get my thoughts together. More than a minute."

Cash frowns, lines appearing in his deeply tanned face. "I won't say a thing. But I'm here for y'all, Wheeler. If there's anything you need—if you do want me to help you tell him or you need some of those ginger candies that Mollie likes—"

"Those are good." Mollie nods. "They help some with the nausea."

My eyes flood with heat all over again. I close them. "That's very kind of you, Cash. Thank you. I'm okay for now. Just—yeah, I definitely wasn't expecting this to happen. It's a bit of a shock."

"No shit," Cash replies with a scoff. "But these things happen more than you think, so…"

He's talking about the pregnancy scare he and Mollie had when they first started dating. She didn't end up being pregnant, but the experience did bring them closer together.

I doubt that will be the case with me and Duke. It took a minute for Cash and Mollie to open up to each other, but once they did, it was over for both of them. They were saying "I love you" to each other *weeks* into their relationship.

A few weeks after that, they were engaged.

So yeah, a bit of a different story than the one I have with Duke.

Mollie starts closing the door. "We'll be out soon, Cash. I'll holler if we need you."

"All right." He nods, running a hand through his hair. It's matted from the Stetson he undoubtedly just took off and hung on the rack by the front door. "Just—I'm thinking of you, Wheeler."

"Thanks." Goddamn these cowboys and their manners and the way they care and just—

Ugh, I'm crying all over again.

"But you're really going to tell Duke, right?" Mollie asks, closing the door with a gentle *thump*.

"He deserves to know, so yes." I wring my hands. "Mollie, what are we gonna do?"

She wraps me in a hug. "First, we're gonna dry these tears. Then, we're gonna get you some snacks, because eating helps. It will at least make you feel a little less like dying. *Then,* we talk about next steps, okay?"

"Okay." I blow out a breath and shake out my hands,

looking up at the ceiling. "Thank God I have you, Mollie."

"Thank God we have each other." She gently nudges me with her hand. "You know, Duke may not be your guy, but he is a *good* guy."

"He is a good guy. A really good guy who's about to get some really bad news."

Mollie frowns, running her hands up and down my arms. "Y'all will figure this out. One thing at a time, okay? Let's go get you some crackers. Some cheese too if you think you can keep it down. And Patsy keeps a supply of Gatorade on hand. Does that sound good?"

"Sounds great." I manage a tight smile before pulling her in for another hug. "I love you."

"I love you too, friend."

I can barely breathe around the tightness in my throat.

Today started out so well. Sales at Bellamy Brooks are booming. Payroll ran overnight, depositing hefty sums into our checking accounts. It feels so great to have money after many, many, *many* years of barely scraping by. My parents lent us money, but they started turning off the spigot when it became clear that I definitely wasn't going to law school. Today, though, I had a decent conversation with Mom, who seems to be doing better.

Then *this* happens, and suddenly my world is turned upside down. A flare of anger ignites inside my breastbone. *Thanks, universe, for knocking me back down after I'd just dusted myself off and gotten on my feet.*

But really, I have no one to blame but myself.

Myself and Duke's delicious Wrangler butt. And his wit. His filthy mouth too, and his kindness, and his interest in me and my business and my life...

There was no resisting any of that, was there? Not when I was snowed in with him and scared out of my mind that I was experiencing my last hours on earth.

"I think I need to go back to Dallas," I blurt as Mollie and I climb into the ATV. "Just for a little while. Just to get my head on straight. I'm worried…"

Mollie looks at me. "You're worried about what, Wheeler?"

That I'll run into Duke, and he'll see that I'm upset. I'm worried I'll drop this bomb on him but he'll still be wonderful, and I'll say things—do things—I shouldn't.

I need to come up with a plan of action before I talk to Duke. That way, I'll be able to focus on what's best for me and my future first. I definitely didn't plan on having a baby anytime soon. Sure, I think about having kids in a maybe-someday kind of way. I do want them.

But I also don't want to end up like my parents. Settling down with someone just because I got pregnant—having a baby that wasn't planned, that isn't necessarily wanted—that's *not* how my story is going to go.

I know what I don't want. I just need to figure out what I *do* want.

"I'm worried I won't be able to think clearly if I'm here," I say carefully. "These cowboys…they have a way of distracting you, you know?"

Mollie chuckles. "You sure? My doctor cleared me to travel again if you want me to come with you."

I shake my head. "I'll be okay. Haines is in town because his semester just ended, so I'll have him."

"Oh good. You sure?"

"Yeah. I just think I need a few days to figure all this out."

Mollie ponders my words for a second, her hands on the wheel. "You know I'll support you in whatever choice you make, right?"

"Right."

"But I'm telling you, don't keep this from Duke for too long. He's gonna want to be there for you."

More tears, because I know she's right. "I won't. I promise."

"I'm really sorry you're so upset, Wheeler." Now Mollie looks like *she's* going to cry. "I hate seeing you like this. Promise to stay in touch?"

Reaching across the front seat, I loop my pinkie through hers. "I promise. And you promise me you won't say a word. Cash too."

She zips up her mouth with her free hand. "Our lips are sealed."

"Okay," I say, even though I don't feel okay at all.

CHAPTER 15
First Calls and Fuckups
Duke

"Dude, watch out," Sawyer snaps.

Blinking, I glance over my shoulder to see my brother and his horse glowering at me. Did we just cut them off?

Yeah, we definitely cut them off. Giving my reins a tug, I fall in line beside him. "Shit, I'm sorry."

"You okay? You seem a little—"

"Brain-dead." Ryder trots up on my other side. Despite the abundant afternoon sunshine, he's not wearing sunglasses, so I can see the concern in his eyes clear as day. It makes my stomach hurt. "Seriously, now I'm worried. Something happen?"

Pretty sure I fell a little in love with a woman who doesn't want me, and now I can't stop thinking about her.

Will I ever connect with someone like that again?

I can't stop thinking about all the cool shit Wheeler and I could do together. The cool places we could visit. Keeps me up at night, wondering what we're missing out on. Maybe that's why I've felt so wired since we got back from Aspen. I have to drink gallons of coffee to remain upright during the day.

"No." I do my damnedest to keep my expression neutral. "Yes. I don't know."

Of course my brothers asked me a million questions about what went down in Colorado when I got back. Felt wrong to kiss and tell, though, so I just said that Wheeler and I enjoyed our time and let that be that.

My brothers aren't stupid. Especially Ryder. He's read between the lines. But really, what else is there to say? Wheeler and I did enjoy our time. She's not interested in anything beyond a weekend fling, though, so now we're back to being just friends.

Less than that. Acquaintances, because I see her less than I ever did. I know she's visited the ranch often, because I'll see her car parked outside the New House. But I never actually *see* her, which is strange. I can't shake this…unsettled feeling I have.

It sucks, but there's nothing I can do to change that. I tried. I've texted her a bunch since we've been back, and I've even called her a few times. Just making sure she's okay. I know there's a lot going on with her family and her job.

I also can't wrap my head around the fact that she doesn't want to explore the amazing chemistry we have. Doesn't she know how special—how rare—it is?

She hasn't responded to any of my attempts to get in touch. I should let it go.

I can't.

Maybe that's why I blurt, "I think…it's Wheeler. We had a great time together in Colorado—"

"You were a good man to drive all that way with her," Sawyer says.

I give my right rein a tug as we head for the southwest pasture. "Are you kidding? It was an absolute pleasure to travel with Wheeler. Most fun I've had in fuckin' forever. But since we got back to Texas, we haven't hung out much. I…" Sighing, I look down at my gloved hands. "I guess I just miss her."

Cash clears his throat. "You try talkin' to her?"

"Of course I've tried. She won't return my calls or my texts. Haven't seen her at any meals. I get the feeling she's avoiding me. And you know, I accept the fact that she doesn't want to see me again. I just can't shake the feeling that something is wrong."

My oldest brother clears his throat again. A pink flush is working its way up his neck.

I furrow my brow. "You chokin'?"

"Duke, you gotta talk to her," he says, shaking his head.

My heart skips a beat. "What? Do you know something I don't?"

Cash looks away. There's something…off about him. He rides stiffly, and his eyes are narrowed.

My heart skips another beat. *What is going on?* I hate this feeling, like the world is pressing in on me from all sides as I wait for the proverbial axe to fall.

"Talk to her," he repeats.

An icy wash of panic moves through me. "How can I do that if she won't pick up my calls? If you know something, Cash, I need you to tell me."

"Not my place to say. I'll tell Mollie to tell Wheeler to call you."

I reach out and grab his arm. Our horses immediately slow to a walk. My pulse throbs, my thoughts whirring. Is Wheeler hurt? Did something happen with her family? Her dad? I'll murder that man with my bare hands if he did something to make her cry.

"Tell me. I'm begging you. She okay?"

He has a pained look on his face now. "She's fine. Well, she's not fine, but—"

"Jesus Christ." Sawyer stares wide-eyed at me. "She's pregnant, isn't she?"

An explosion detonates inside my rib cage, the blast roaring in my ears and rattling my spine.

We didn't use condoms.

We had so much sex.

So.

Much.

We fucked a hundred times. And every time, I came inside her. Yes, she's on the pill, but there's no fail-safe method.

We should've used backup.

Jesus Christ, why didn't we use backup?

I look for confirmation in Cash's expression. His eyes are full.

Sympathy. Regret. Some embarrassment too from revealing a secret he wasn't supposed to. Wonder how he found out.

Oh shit, Wheeler is definitely pregnant.

Why wasn't I her first call? The idea that she's handled this alone—without me—knocks the wind out of me. I can just imagine the poor thing shaking like a leaf again.

"Fuck." Cash closes his eyes and lets his head fall back. "I didn't say that."

A hand grips my windpipe and squeezes. "Is it true? Is Wheeler pregnant?"

My brother opens his eyes. They're glassy. "Yes, Duke. Wheeler is pregnant."

Somehow, we've all slowed to a stop. So has my heartbeat.

My brothers look at me, their faces blank with naked shock. I may be one of the "wild cards" of the family, but I'm not careless.

Maybe this is the universe's way of keeping me humble.

If so, the universe is one sick son of a bitch.

I am frozen in place. I don't know what to do. What to say.

All I know is Wheeler's handled this on her own, and that's not fucking fair.

Squeezing my legs, I urge my horse into a sprint as I pull hard on my left rein. The pounding of his hooves on the soft ground echoes inside my breastbone as we head back home.

I ride like a bat out of hell. By the time we arrive at the barn, he's foaming at the mouth and I'm soaked head to toe in sweat.

Wheeler is pregnant.

I don't understand why she hasn't told me.

I'm truly and deeply crushed I wasn't her first call. Then again, why would I be? She told me why she wants to keep her distance. Her family—

Shit. This is how her parents' story started, isn't it? Her mom getting pregnant unexpectedly. Her dad doing what he thought was right and marrying her.

My stomach lurches. *Parenthood.* I'm not ready for that. I want to travel. Try new things. Figure out what the hell I wanna do with the rest of my life.

Settling down and having a kid is *not* part of the plan.

My hands shake as I dig my phone out of my back

pocket. I'm a wreck. But as scared as I am, I bet Wheeler's feeling ten times worse, and that's what I need to focus on right now—making sure she's okay.

I only have one bar of service in the barn, but that'll have to do. I shoot off a text to Wheeler. *Call me please.* I know she won't pick up if I actually call.

Then I call Mollie.

"Hey!" she says after she picks up on the second ring, clearly surprised to hear from me. "What's up? Everything okay?"

I don't call Mollie all that much at the moment. She's busy with Bellamy Brooks, my brother, and the baby, and I'm busy…well, pining after her best friend like a lovesick dickhead.

"Where is she?" The words come out as a growl, but I'm too anxious to apologize at the moment. I haven't seen Wheeler's car around the ranch today, so I don't know if she went back to Dallas or what.

"Who? Duke, what's going—"

"Wheeler. Cash just let slip that she's pregnant, which I assume he heard from you?"

Dead silence.

Then: "Oh, Jesus." She lets out a breath. "Okay, Cash wasn't supposed to find out. Wheeler was at our place taking the tests, and he just happened to walk in on us."

I picture the scene: Wheeler crying with her face in her hands. Mollie patting her back. Cash wanting to help but not knowing what the hell to do.

I feel like I just got sucker punched in the throat.

At the same time, my stomach roils, and I feel like I'm gonna lose my lunch. "How long ago was this?"

"Um."

"Mollie."

"Not long. Like...two days ago."

"Two days!" I close my eyes. Bite the inside of my cheek to keep from saying something I'll regret. "You—she—Cash—y'all kept this from me for *two days*? Why didn't she tell me?"

"You'll have to ask her that. This is her news to share. I'm sorry you found out this way—"

"How is she?"

Mollie pauses.

"Please, Mollie." I put a hand on my hip. "I'm literally worried sick here. Is she at the New House? I haven't seen—"

"She went back home to Dallas."

I don't know why that information stings. Or maybe I do. She's running, clearly afraid.

She afraid of me? I've never given her any reason to be on alert, have I?

Granted, this pregnancy was definitely not planned. It's more than a surprise—it's a fucking *shock*. I gotta give Wheeler more credit for not telling me right away. Maybe she needed some time to process the news herself.

Guess I just wanna play a role in her life more like Mollie's. I want Wheeler to trust me. I want to be the person she goes to when shit hits the fan.

But I'm not. And even though Wheeler has told me more than once that she's not interested in any kind of deep relationship, I still want one to happen.

"Can I ask you for her address?"

"Duke...I don't know."

I swallow the tightness in my throat. "I gotta see her,

Mollie. It's killing me not knowing...I need to know she's okay. Or do what I can to make this suck less for her. I imagine she's not doing great if you won't say a word about her."

Another pause.

"You think Cash would sit on this news?" I press. "I know y'all had a scare too. I imagine you told him right away so he didn't have to worry, right?"

Mollie clears her throat. "That was different."

"I'll owe you big time. Please, Mollie. Wheeler won't answer my calls or texts. I don't know when she'll be back. I don't know what's going on inside her head. I care about her." *Too much, but whatever.*

Mollie pauses for what feels like the hundredth time. Sweat pours down my skull and runs into my eyes.

She sighs. "Fine. But you promise you're just going there to check on her?"

"Cross my heart and hope to die."

"I will stick a needle in your eye if you upset her."

There's a pinch in my center. "Why would you think I'd ever intentionally upset Wheeler?"

"Just...she hasn't had great luck with men in general. And I know y'all weren't planning on, well, *this*. How are you doing?"

I squeeze my eyes shut. "I'll be better once I know she's all right."

"You're sweet. But really, Duke—I know you're not okay."

"Of course I'm not okay."

More silence. I appreciate that she doesn't rush to fill it and instead thoughtfully considers what she'll say next.

"We're here for y'all," she says. "I'm here for you. Which is why I'm going to give you this address. But you let her know you're coming, yeah?"

"Of course. Like I said, she doesn't answer me when I reach out, but I'll definitely still reach out."

"I'm rooting for you. Just so you know."

My eyes burn. "Thank you, Mollie." My voice is down to a whisper now. Can't go any louder than that, or my strained vocal cords will collapse. "I really appreciate the help."

"I know you do. Y'all will be okay. Maybe not right away." She takes another breath. "But it'll work out how it's supposed to."

I don't know how that's possible. But I thank her again anyway.

She texts me Wheeler's address after we hang up. Plugging it into my GPS app, I see that I have a two-hundred-mile drive ahead of me.

Best hit the road. I need to know Wheeler is okay. And then I need to fix this, because…

Too many reasons.

I grab a quick shower and throw some shit in a bag. I look up my hotel options in Wheeler's neighborhood. By the time I get to Dallas, it will be nightfall, and I'll be too tired to drive back to the ranch. I know better than to assume Wheeler will let me stay at her place, although I'm more than a little curious about what it's like. Girly? Fancy? Does she have roommates?

How do I not know this about her?

Because she doesn't want me to. Right.

Speeding out of Hartsville, I wonder if anyone in Wheeler's family is with her. She didn't seem particularly close with them. But that's what family is for, isn't it, to be there for you in times of crisis?

Family. I love mine. I always thought I'd have my own in a vague, way-far-into-the-distant-future type of way. Ella is cute as a fucking button, and I loved growing up in a big family. Watching my older brothers pair off has made me realize just how much I want to find my person. Get married one day. Have kids.

I just don't want to do that at twenty-seven. I have too many other things I want to accomplish first. The idea that I'll have to give all that up—

My eyes burn. I blink and roll down my window. The roar of the cool air fills the truck. The sudden drop in temperature is bracing, but it does nothing to slow my wild heartbeat.

I decide to let myself feel all these awful feelings on the drive up to Dallas.

Panic.

Embarrassment.

Shame.

Sadness.

I learned when my parents died that bottling that shit up is not the answer. Cash made sure we were all in counseling for years after the accident, and my takeaway was just how important it is to sit with your emotions. Whether they're good, bad, or ugly, you gotta honor them.

I don't let the panic or the sadness win. But I do allow myself to mourn what might've been. I have no idea what Wheeler wants to do about the baby. Will she want to keep it? If she does, would we co-parent, or…

Hell, I don't know what *I* want to do about the baby. But assuming she does want to keep it, my plans for the future just took a hard left turn. No way I'll be able to travel, at least not for a while. I did get a huge pay bump when Mollie and Cash made my brothers and me equal partners in Lucky River Ranch. But Sawyer's said over and over again that raising a baby in this day and age ain't cheap. Especially if you plan to save for college. I didn't get a degree, but I want to make damn sure my kids have the opportunity to get one if they want. Then there's the diapers, the car seats—*shit, I should probably get a new truck, one that's more reliable*—the cribs, the insurance, the child support…

Not to mention the fact that my world would get a lot smaller. More constrained. If I'm gonna be a daddy, I'm gonna do it right. That's just how my parents raised me. Mom would roll over in her grave if I was a deadbeat who was only kinda sorta involved in his kid's life. I wanna be present for everything: the first smile, first steps, first day of school. My mom and dad were my people, and I wanna be my kid's person too.

That kinda commitment means showing up. All the damn time. And that means no longer owning *my* time.

My life.

The idea sends my pulse into a tailspin.

I know I'm getting close to Wheeler's place when I hit traffic. It's rush hour, and I-35 is a parking lot. Gives me some time to get myself together. I dry my eyes and slow my breathing, which in turn slows my heart rate.

I have to be strong for Wheeler if—when—she falls apart. The important thing is that she knows I'm there for her.

GPS leads me to a busy area near the center of the city. I pass lots of restaurants and shopping along with midrise apartment buildings that look brand new. People my age—younger even—crowd the sidewalks.

I like it here.

I'm also not surprised this is where Wheeler lives. I've gathered that Wheeler's parents have some money, and this part of town can't be cheap to live in. They pay her rent for her? Buy her a place even?

I slow at the end of a quieter street when my GPS tells me I've arrived at my destination. Glancing out my passenger side window, I see a row of cute townhomes made of painted brick with black shutters.

A beat later, I spot Wheeler's white Mini Cooper parked on the opposite side of the street.

My stomach dips. She's home.

I parallel park in a spot nearby and check my phone. Surprise surprise, she hasn't responded to my texts or called me back.

Running a hand over my face, I realize I forgot to shave. Fuck.

Am I making the right call by showing up like this?

I think on that for a minute before the answer comes to me on a hard, certain heartbeat. I am making the right call.

At least I think I am.

Whatever the case, I'm here.

Taking a deep breath, I open my door and walk across the street in the deepening twilight to 209 Meadowood Lane. When I see the words on the doormat, I immediately know it's Wheeler's place.

Everyone Welcome Except Jolene.

I smile. Then I screw my courage to the sticking place and raise my arm to knock on the door.

CHAPTER 16
Comfort Food
Wheeler

"Sit up and finish your water." My younger brother, Haines, holds out my enormous pink water bottle. "I was just reading about how important it is in your condition to stay hydrated."

Shutting my eyes, I burrow farther into the small mountain of pillows on my couch. "I can't move."

"Yes, you can. Up." He grabs my hand, and I let him pull me upright. "You're pregnant, not dying of consumption."

"How much *Bridgerton* have you been watching?" Just looking at the water bottle makes my stomach curdle, but I dutifully remove it from my brother's hand and take two tiny sips.

"You know how I feel about Jonathan Bailey, Wheeler."

"We all feel that way about Jonathan Bailey."

"Those thighs." Haines sighs.

"The way that man looks in breeches." I crack a smile.

"Yes." Haines gets a faraway look in his eyes. "But I like the way he looks when he takes them off better."

I roll my eyes, even as I chuckle. Feels good to laugh. "*Some*body needs to get laid."

"Somebody got laid a bit too well. Or would it be a bit too much?"

"Shut up."

He's teasing, a grin on his handsome face. "Wheeler, surely you know I believe that there's no such thing as getting laid too much or too well."

"Yes, there is. It's called getting knocked up."

Haines's grin fades a little. "Fair. That's not a problem I've run into."

My little brother came out at sixteen and has dated men exclusively since then. I'm thrilled he's happy.

My parents, however? They say they support him, but I know to this day they still wish their son was straight. Preston, my older brother, is embarrassed by the whole thing and pretends it never happened.

"I'm sorry you're feeling so rotten," Haines continues. "I know you're freaked out. But let's not forget you did hook up with a hot cowboy who won't stop calling or texting you."

"I thought city boys were more your type." I try another sip of water. It tastes…ugh, I don't know what it tastes like, but all of a sudden, it doesn't taste like it should.

Nothing does. The food I used to love—smoothies, hummus, chicken—is a total no-go. I literally vomited in my mouth when I tried to eat some rotisserie chicken for lunch earlier today.

And the fatigue, my God! It's never-ending. No

matter how much I sleep, I wake up tired. My boobs hurt, and my nipples are so sensitive to changes in temperature that I howled this morning like a wounded animal when I stepped into the shower.

I've been pregnant for practically ten minutes, and I already hate everything about it.

"I do like city boys." Haines lifts the water bottle from my hands and sets it on the coffee table. "But I think I speak for everyone everywhere who ever existed when I say that I'd sure as hell try out a cowboy too."

"Ha." I fall back onto the pillows. "Duke was just a fling."

"I didn't know people wove their flings so casually into everyday conversation." Haines gives me a pointed look. "For a hookup, you talk about him an awful lot."

My chest twists, my face getting hot. "Well, yeah. He did get me pregnant."

My brother's expression softens. He props my feet in his lap and rests his hands over the blanket on my shins. "I know part of you feels like Duke could never fall for someone as 'difficult' or 'messy' as you—"

"Wow," I say, scoffing. "That's...actually kind of insightful."

"I pay closer attention than you think."

My heart swells. Haines does a good job looking out for me, and I'll always love him for it.

"You also went from hookup to falling pretty damn fast there."

Haines shrugs. "Isn't that how it usually happens?"

"You're twenty-two. Of course that's how it happens at your age."

"Look, all I'm saying is you should give yourself

a chance. Maybe then you'll give this cute cowboy a chance too. Preston is a piece of shit. So is Dad. And Mom..." Sighing, he looks down at his hands. "They're all ignorant in their own ways. Don't let their stupidity keep you from living your best damn life."

My throat swells. "I'm hardly living my best life right now. And seriously, Haines, I'm the big sister. I feel like I should be giving *you* life advice."

"Wheeler, you kept me alive during the darkest time in my life," he says, referring to the years before he came out. "You've done right by me. My turn to do right—"

We both jump at the knock on my door. At the same moment, my Ring camera app announces a visitor. Who the hell is here at this hour? Probably a solicitor. Or the UPS guy.

"Don't answer it," I say, but I sit up so I can see my phone screen a little better. I tap on the app and wait for the camera to pop up. "I must've gotten a package or something."

"And that package *delivered*."

"Ew." I laugh, the constriction in my chest easing ever so slightly. "Too soon, H."

Another knock. My neighbor's dog, an adorably naughty pug mix, starts barking. I can hear him scratching on their storm door.

"You sure you don't want me to get that?" Haines asks.

The camera pops up on my phone, and I freeze when I see the broad-shouldered figure in a backward baseball hat standing on my doormat. My stomach lurches.

What—*how*—my address in Dallas, he's never— fucking Mollie, I bet she—

"It's Duke Rivers." He knocks again. "I promise you, Wheeler, I'm not upset. I just wanna talk."

I start to shake.

Haines meets my eyes. His look like they're liable to pop right out of his head. "Did you—"

"Invite him?" I half whisper, half hiss. "No, Haines, I did not invite Duke to Dallas."

Duke found out about the pregnancy. Why else would he drive two hundred miles to show up unannounced like this? Then again, he did try texting me earlier today. I ignored it, just like I always do, telling myself it's better we keep our distance. No use postponing the inevitable, right?

Who told him about the pregnancy? Did Mollie let it slip? More likely it was Cash. He'd never spill my secrets on purpose, but maybe—I mean, what if he thought Duke deserved to know? Cash isn't wrong. Duke does deserve to know about this, but I just wanted to be the one to tell him.

Shit shit shit.

I put a hand on my forehead. Is Duke angry? I'm not. I'm just overwhelmed. What the hell am I going to say to him? I still don't know how *I* feel about the whole thing, much less how I'm going to handle *his* feelings.

"Please, Wheeler," Duke calls. "Just gimme five minutes. I need to make sure you're okay."

Haines pushes out his bottom lip. *Awwww.*

My mind races. I don't want to see Duke. Really, I don't want to do *anything* except rot on my couch like the waste of life I am.

But he came.

He drove all the way from Hartsville to see me.

Pretty sure he didn't come to yell. Or to fight.

But he did come. And at the very least, I owe him an explanation. An apology too.

Throwing off the blanket, I pivot on the sofa and put my feet on the ground. Haines follows me as I head for the front door, stopping briefly to examine my reflection in the hall mirror.

"Shit," I repeat, this time out loud. I look like hell. Greasy hair. Greasy skin. A smattering of pimples dots my chin, another lovely side effect of this pregnancy.

Haines quickly smooths my hair, tucking it behind my ears.

"Any better?" I ask.

"Meh. Better than nothing."

"Ugh!" Throwing up my hands, I turn back toward the door.

He gives me a soft tap on the hip. "Go get 'em, cowgirl."

"Stop it!"

"I'm just kidding." Haines shakes out his T-shirt. "Although I'd be lying if I said I wasn't excited to finally meet this guy."

I grab the doorknob. Closing my eyes, I take a deep, fortifying breath. I haven't been this nervous since… God, I don't think I was this nervous taking the SAT or meeting my parents' divorce attorneys for the first time.

Go figure. Telling your *very* cute hookup that you're pregnant is a bit of a mindfuck.

You're an adult capable of having adult conversations. You did not do this on purpose. It was an accident, and you can handle it.

The timing, though, couldn't be worse.

I roll back my aching shoulders. Then I open the door.

Duke is *enormous*. The bulk of his body blocks almost the entire opening. He's resting one forearm against the side of the doorframe so that he leans forward a little, the scent of him—clean laundry, piney juniper—filling my head.

He looks up, his blue, bloodshot eyes locking on mine, and everything inside me heaves.

He's so handsome, and he looks so distraught that my vision blurs. Tears.

Lots of them.

"Aw, Wheeler." He steps forward, uninvited, and takes my face in his hands. He thumbs away my tears, his callouses moving smoothly over my skin. "Sweetheart."

My heart swells at the endearment. My pulse slows a little at the gentle tone of his voice, his gentle touch. For the first time all day, I feel…like not dying.

At the same time, electricity darts through me at the feel of his hands on my skin. I could fall into his touch if I let myself.

"You found out." I close my eyes.

"Cash." I hear him swallow. "He didn't mean to tell me—"

"I should've known it would slip. The five of y'all are so close." Rolling my lips between my teeth, I open my eyes and meet his. "I hope you believe me when I say I was going to tell you. I just needed to come home first. Get my head screwed on straight."

"She had to come see me is what she means." Haines steps up beside me and holds out his hand. "I'm the good brother, Haines."

"The good brother?" Duke cocks a brow, but he takes Haines's hand. "Glad I met you first, then."

My chest feels funny seeing my brother and my... whatever Duke is shake hands. Two worlds I've kept totally separate are suddenly colliding, and I'm not sure how I feel about that.

"My older brother is a lot," I explain.

Haines smiles. "Preston is a dick. Pleasure to meet you, Duke. You came all the way from the ranch, huh? Three-hour drive from what Wheeler tells me?"

"Three and a half with traffic." But that doesn't keep Duke from chuckling. "Y'all been talkin' shit about me?"

"Yes." Haines is loving this.

Really, he's loving being in the presence of a startlingly handsome cowboy. I notice Duke's face is scruffier than usual. The heavy five-o'clock shadow looks good on him.

Really fucking good.

I can't believe he's here.

"Well, I think I speak for us all when I say I wish we were meeting in better circumstances." Duke has the grace to look embarrassed as he runs a hand up the back of his neck, his bicep bulging against the sleeve of his worn denim jacket. He picks up a plastic grocery bag I hadn't noticed on the ground. "I, uh, come bearing gifts if that helps."

Haines takes the bag from him. "Listen, Duke, that backward hat is all the gift we need—"

"Haines was actually about to take off." I cut my brother a look.

He looks back. "I was?"

"Yes."

"But the gifts—"

"I'll take those." I grab the bag, surprised by how heavy it is, and open the door a little wider. "Duke, why don't you come in?"

Haines puts his hands on hips. "I really feel like I should stay—"

"I'll call you later, okay?" I blink twice in his direction. *Scram.*

His shoulders fall. "Fine." He looks at Duke. "You be nice to my sister, you hear?"

"Always." Duke's eyes lock on mine. The sincerity in them makes me short of breath.

"And y'all best invite me to brunch tomorrow," my brother continues as he grabs his keys from the tray on the nearby hall table. "If I have to be Mom's entertainment committee for another day, I'm gonna lose my damn mind."

Heat floods my face. "We're not getting brunch. Duke is here to talk."

"Right." Duke's eyes are still on me, I feel it. "We have a lot of that to do."

Haines grins. "Y'all got a lot of somethin' to do, that's for sure. Good luck." He pecks my cheek and walks out the door, twirling his key ring as he disappears into the growing darkness. "Love you, sis."

Then it's just me and Duke and the elephant in the room.

CHAPTER 17
The Good Kind of Blizzard
Duke

"I hope Haines didn't offend you," Wheeler says after closing the door behind him. "He's got a good heart but absolutely no filter."

Putting my hands on my hips, I chuckle. "Wheeler, I have four brothers. I work on a ranch. I think I'm beyond offending at this point."

Her lips twitch. For a second, the haunted look in her brown eyes disappears, replaced by a mischievous gleam I remember well from our weekend in Aspen.

My center aches all of a sudden.

"Just give him time. He'll get you. Here, come on in."

I follow her down a short hallway. There's a set of carpeted stairs to my left, a mirror on the wall to my right. It smells like a new house: fresh paint, new lumber.

It also smells like her. The juicy, summery scent of her perfume. I like how bold it is. How unique. I've never smelled anything like it.

I also like the way she looks in the little getup she's wearing. It's just a pair of baggy sweats, but she's paired them with a crop top that shows enough skin to make my own skin feel two sizes too tight.

My hands itch to reach out. Touch her again. She let me touch her face, didn't she?

I'm leery to go any further, though. I don't want to make her uncomfortable. Yeah, we made a baby together, but that doesn't mean she feels any differently about me. Us.

The hall opens onto one big, open living and kitchen area. The space is tidy, save for the pile of pillows and blankets on the couch and the open box of saltines on the coffee table.

Wheeler sets the grocery bag on the white kitchen countertop and peers inside it.

"Mollie gave me a little list of things you might find useful." I shove my hands into the front pockets of my jeans. "Epsom salts for a bath—"

"Those two and their fucking Epsom salt baths." Wheeler shakes her head. "Mollie and Cash are obsessed."

"Mollie recommended you try it. Supposed to calm your nervous system or something. And then I grabbed Gatorade and some sparkling water. Reese's eggs too. They didn't have the pumpkins, obviously."

She looks at me, eyes bright. "How'd you find the eggs after Easter?"

"Discount pile at the drugstore."

"Ah." She pauses. "You remembered."

"Of course I did." My chest swells. I did *one* thing right at least. "And then Mollie recommended these lozenges that are supposed to help with the nausea. Cherry flavor, because you liked those Twizzlers so much."

Wheeler blinks. For a horrible second, I think she's going to cry again.

Wait, she is crying.

Fuck.

What the hell do I do? Did I get the wrong things? Does she need a hug? Maybe she wanted real food. I should've asked Patsy to pack up some leftovers.

"Hey." I keep my hands in my pockets, but I move closer. Close enough that our arms brush. "If there's anything else I can get you, just say the word—"

"That's not it." She puts one hand on her nose and waves me away with the other. "You're just…so fucking sweet to bring me all this. You came all this way—"

"You really thought I wouldn't come after, well…" I swallow the moon that's suddenly risen in my throat. "Surely you have a higher opinion of me than that?"

Squeezing her eyes shut, she shakes her head. "No. I mean yes, Duke. I think the world of you. I just wasn't prepared."

She wasn't prepared for those positive pregnancy tests.

She wasn't prepared for me to show up like this.

It dawns on me that she wasn't prepared for me, period.

It's killing me not to reach for her. "I tried calling."

"I know. I'm really sorry I didn't pick up. I've been trying to keep boundaries clear, you know? I don't want to lead you on or give you mixed signals—"

"But you're pregnant, Wheeler, and you're scared out of your fuckin' mind." I take my hands out of my pockets. It's the only way I can seem to get air in my lungs. "You can't deal with this on your own. No one can. So let me be there for you." She opens her eyes, and I search them. "Tell me what you need from me, because it really bothers me to see you so upset."

A pair of indents appears between her eyes. "So you're not mad?"

"Am I mad you're pregnant?" I shake my head. "No, sweetheart. But I am bummed I wasn't your first call when you found out."

The indents deepen. "Really?"

"Well, yeah. Takes two to tango, but I'm one of the two. This is scary, Wheeler. I'm scared too. When you run like that...doesn't make me feel any better, I'll say that much."

Her throat works on a swallow. "I get how me running left you alone too. I'm"—she lets out a breath—"really sorry. Guess part of me thought you might not want to deal with any of this."

I flatten my palm over my chest. "Ouch."

"I'm an idiot." She shakes her head for the millionth time.

"You're not an idiot. You're not yourself, and it's hard to make good decisions when that happens. What do you need?" I repeat.

"Honestly?" She takes a deep inhale. "I don't know. I feel so miserable. I'm hungry, but when I eat, nothing tastes good. I'm exhausted, but when I try to sleep, I can't. I'm bored, but I'm also totally overwhelmed."

"Sounds awful."

"It is." Her eyes glimmer, reflecting the overhead lights in pinpricks of white.

"How about we start with a hug and go from there?"

I don't know why I said that. It's the wrong call, isn't it? She *just* said she wanted to keep boundaries clear, and here I am, offering her a fucking hug in the most awkward way possible.

But then she's turning toward me and pressing her body against mine, going up on her tiptoes to wrap her arms around my neck.

"I'd love a hug." Her voice is thick with emotion as she rests her cheek on my chest. "Thank you."

I take my first deep inhale since I got the news and pull Wheeler close, putting my hand on the back of her head. Her hips melt into mine, her fingers in the hair at my nape.

The embrace feels…easy. Comfortable. Broken-in, like my favorite pair of Wranglers.

With Wheeler in my arms, it's the first time I've felt like shit might just be okay. We needed this.

We need each other.

I could get addicted to this.

"Here's what we're gonna do," I murmur into her hair. "I'm gonna order in some dinner. You're gonna sit on the couch or take a bath or do whatever you need to do to relax. Then I'll feed you, and we can talk or not talk. Either way, I just want to be with you. That sound good?"

She nods, sniffling. "Sounds wonderful. Thank you."

We agree on Thai food—we both get vegetarian pad Thai because chicken is grossing out Wheeler—and we eat on the couch while watching the new season of *The Righteous Gemstones*.

"Since we never got to finish it," Wheeler says,

explaining her choice. She's been able to keep her dinner down so far and has even gone for seconds of the spring rolls I ordered.

I eye her. "You didn't watch the rest of the show?" Because I didn't. Didn't feel right to watch it without Wheeler there.

"Didn't get a chance to, no."

Can't help but wonder if she felt the same.

She keeps to her side of the couch, and I keep to mine. But she seems to appreciate me being here to take care of her. When she moves to get up to toss our to-go boxes, I jump to my feet and grab hers. I notice her eyes well up.

"Thank you," she says.

"Anytime. I saw you looking at those Blizzards." I drop the containers in the trash. "Which one do you want? Reese's peanut butter cup or New York cheesecake?"

I may or may not have added a stop at Dairy Queen to our Door Dasher's itinerary. Added fifty bucks to the order thanks to the delivery fee and tip, but it just felt right.

"Reese's, please."

Opening the freezer, I smile. "How'd I know you were gonna pick that one?"

"Because it's the best."

"It is. Did I overdo it with the Reese's?"

"No such thing. But seriously, are you sure you don't want it?"

I pop off the top and tuck one of DQ's long, red plastic spoons into the thick ice cream. "All yours, Blue."

She has this funny look on her face when I hand it to

her, along with some napkins. "For a single dude, you're really thoughtful."

"One, please don't call me dude."

"Why not?"

"Because I'd like to think I'm more than just some 'dude' to you. Second, when you grow up on a ranch, you're taught to always lend a hand. Just the way our world works."

Wheeler blinks, using the spoon to stir the ice cream. "Your parents did a good job raising y'all."

I chuckle. "Well. Wyatt's kind of a degenerate. He used to be anyway, before he and Sally finally got together. And Cash can be a grump." I plop onto the couch next to her. "But I'd like to think the rest of us turned out all right."

"They'd be so proud. Your parents."

I feel the compliment like a bullet to the chest. "Thanks for saying that. How's the Reese's?"

"Excellent." Smiling, she puts the spoon in her mouth and makes an alarmingly porny sound of pleasure. "Jesus, I didn't know this is exactly what I needed."

I tuck into my cheesecake Blizzard. "Gotta give credit where credit is due. Mollie was super helpful."

"Love her."

"Sure do."

We watch another episode of *The Righteous Gemstones*. Another. I put what's left of our Blizzards back in the freezer.

I keep waiting for Wheeler to ask me to go, but she doesn't.

Instead, she dozes off, curled up on her side with her hair splayed over the pillow.

Right now—with a full belly and a happy woman at my side—I feel a flicker of something I never have before. Possibility maybe? It's the opposite of FOMO, or fear of missing out.

Joy of missing out? Like, how there's joy in staying in, eating good food with a good friend while hanging out in our stretchy pants. Is that even a thing?

I'm exactly where I want to be, with exactly the person I want to be with.

I'm still in Texas. I still have some scary shit to deal with. But I feel weirdly calm. Content even.

I don't wanna leave. But I also ain't about to overstay my welcome.

So I turn off the TV and clean up the kitchen, careful not to make too much noise.

Then I carefully lift Wheeler off the couch, cradling her in my arms. She burrows into my chest, her eyelashes dark against her cheeks. She's warm and soft, and I'm gripped by a feeling I can't quite figure out. The shit inside my torso feels tender and achy. But it's not necessarily a bad sensation.

It's just new. And intense.

I head upstairs, careful to keep my footfalls quiet. At the top of the landing, a door to my left opens into a good-size bedroom with a tray ceiling.

Turning my shoulders so Wheeler and I can fit through the doorway, I smile when I see the entire room is done in shades of pink. Pink wallpaper. Pink bedding. Even the bed itself is pink, as are the lamps on either side of it.

Lots of personality, just like Wheeler.

The covers on one side of the bed are already pulled

back, the blankets rumpled. I gently set her down on the mattress. I tidy up the blankets and lift them so that she's fully covered.

My stomach drops when she stirs, her eyes fluttering open.

"Hey." Her voice is thick with sleep. "Did I pass out?"

I reach inside the nearby lampshade to turn off the light. "You did. Get some rest, Blue. Also, I clearly got your color wrong." I glance up at the room as I round the bed to turn off the other lamp.

Chuckling, she yawns. "As long as it's not beige, I like any color."

"The bolder, the better, huh?"

"I like to keep things interesting."

"I've noticed."

I'm reaching up to turn off the second lamp on the other side of the bed when Wheeler says, "Stay."

I go still. "Wheeler—"

"Will you just…lie with me?" She rolls over so that she's on her side facing me. Her eyes are wide open now and clear. "Weird request, I get it. If I'm making you uncomfortable, just tell me to fuck off. But I don't want to be alone right now."

Aw, sweetheart, like I could ever tell you no.

"Sure," I say huskily.

I don't wanna be alone either. Maybe that's part of the reason I wanna stay so bad. We got a lot to talk about. A lot to figure out.

I'm scared she'll want to keep the baby.

I'm scared she won't.

I need comfort as much as she does.

So I toe off my boots and take off my hat, running a hand through my hair as I put the hat on the bedside table. Then I climb on top of the covers and lie on my back. I cross my ankles and put my hands on my stomach.

"Comfy bed."

"I love my bed."

I turn my head a little on the pillow. "You feelin' any better?"

"Much. That ice cream was life-giving." She tucks a hand underneath her cheek. "What are you thinking?"

My heart gallops. "About the baby?"

"Yeah." Her voice is soft.

I lift my fingers. "I…don't know how to answer that."

"Be honest. Please. Because I've had some time to think about it, and I still have no idea what to, er, think about it."

For a split second, my mind races. Then it goes blank, save for a single thought. Well, two thoughts.

What advice would Mom and Dad give me?

Wheeler said they'd be proud of us. Of me.

What choice would make them proud?

"I don't know," I repeat. "This is complicated, Blue. I can't quite wrap my head around it yet."

I can't quite figure out how to tell her how much I like her—how often I think about her—and that if we were five years older, with five years of travel and fun and freedom under our belts, I'd probably be asking her to marry me right now.

Wow.

Just…wow. No idea where that thought came from. But in my gut, I know it's true. I'd take this pregnancy, unexpected as it is, as a sign from the universe that Wheeler and I were meant to be together.

I'd make having this baby and being together the right choice. I think it *would* be the right choice. If, that is, Wheeler was willing to give me a chance. Which I don't think she'd do.

I think she'd want love and friendship first. *Then* marriage, *then* baby.

Never mind the fact that we're not five years older, and I haven't seen or done nearly as much as I'd hoped to by this point.

See? Complicated.

"That's how I feel too." Her eyes squeeze shut. "I really wish this wasn't happening. I'm so mad at myself."

"Hey." I reach over to tuck her hair behind her ear. "This was an accident. No one to blame, all right? And your doc said we got time to make a decision."

She nods, eyes still shut. "I just hate being in limbo. I can't focus on anything else right now, which is a big problem because work is so busy."

"Are you…" I clear my throat. "Open to all options?"

She opens her eyes. "I am. Are you?"

"Yes."

"Good."

I let out a silent sigh of relief. We're on the same page in that at the very least.

"Do you want kids?" I ask.

"Like in the bigger picture sense?" She sniffles. "Yeah, I think I do. Be nice to have my own little family. One that's hopefully happier than the one I grew up in."

"My family was happy. Is happy. Not to brag—"

"Ha."

"But it is awesome. That sense of belonging."

She opens her eyes. They look different. Thoughtful. "Sounds so nice."

"It is. Most of the time anyway."

Taking a deep inhale, she lets it out. "I have a doctor's appointment tomorrow at ten. Guess they want to confirm the tests, and I want to figure out what my options are." Her eyes toggle between mine. "I know you probably have to get back to the ranch for work, but—"

"Absolutely." My heart drums inside my chest. "I will absolutely go with you. Ryder's got my shit covered back home. I'm here for as long as you need me, yeah?"

Her lips pull into a soft smile. "Yeah. Okay."

I have no idea how to make this okay.

I got no clue if things are going to *be* okay.

But right now, Wheeler is okay, which means I'm okay.

I'll take it.

CHAPTER 18
Hot Cowboy in the City
Wheeler

I've known Dr. Martinez for over a decade. She's seen me through my first Pap smear, my first birth control prescription, and my first slightly panicked STI screening.

I have never, not once, seen her blush. Or giggle.

But she does both during my appointment the next day, her eyes wandering to Duke over and over again as she bangs on the keyboard at the computer in our exam room.

"So you're a real life cowboy, huh?" Her fingers pause over the keys.

Duke crosses his arms, his chambray button-up stretching across his wide shoulders. "Yes, ma'am, born and raised."

She bites her lip. "I didn't know y'all actually existed."

"I assure you, we do. Someone's gotta do the dirty work."

Our nurse, Laura, stares. "I bet you do it *right*."

"And you wear the jeans and the boots and…

everything." Dr. Martinez's gaze flicks over his long legs, moving up to his glasses and the backward hat he's wearing again today. "God bless America."

"Amen," Laura whispers.

To be fair, Duke does look especially delicious today. Being the thoughtful kinda-sorta gentleman he is, he packed an overnight bag for himself "in the off chance" I needed him to stay. And in that overnight bag was a pair of slim-fitting jeans and that fucking button-up, which he wears over a worn white T-shirt. It all looks so good on him I kind of want to scream.

Don't get me started on the glasses.

He's wearing a pair of square-toed, perfectly broken-in Ariat cowboy boots and a five-o'clock shadow that's really growing on me—he said he forgot his razor. The man looks like an absolute *snack*.

I don't know if it's the low ceilings in the office or what, but he also looks enormous. Bigger than usual. They just don't make them like this in Dallas: six two and handsome in a rugged, broad, deeply tanned way. He just looks so…capable, his big, strong body able to handle anything the day throws at him.

Hell, *I'm* having trouble not staring, and I've been with Duke all night and all morning. Literally. He fell asleep next to me in my bed, and when I woke up, he was smiling at me, his hair sticking up every which way.

"What?" I asked, nausea already rising through my center.

"You were snoring."

I felt my face flush. "Shut up."

"It was cute."

"No, it wasn't. Why are your eyes red?"

He squeezed them shut. "I forgot to take out my contacts. I didn't mean to fall asleep—"

"It's fine. Please tell me that means you'll be wearing your glasses all day."

He opened his eyes and his smile grew, showing me a flash of even, white teeth. "You really like the glasses, huh, Blue?"

I love them.

I might've orgasmed just *watching* him make me coffee in my kitchen while wearing the glasses (I messaged Dr. Martinez earlier this week about caffeine, and she assured me one cup of coffee per day is fine). He remembered how I took my coffee and then asked me not once, not twice, but three times if I was sure I didn't want anything to eat. I swear the man was ready to run out for whatever I asked for.

A gal could get used to that kind of treatment.

Just like I could get used to having someone with me for what turns out to be an intense conversation. To her credit, Dr. Martinez is kind as she patiently walks us through our options.

In Texas, there aren't many.

"Unfortunately, the laws in our state are such that you'd have to seek abortion care elsewhere." I can tell she's trying very hard not to roll her eyes. "New Mexico is going to be your closest option if you decide to go that route, which—let's be honest—isn't that close at all."

I've followed the depressing developments in women's health care over the years in the news, and I anticipated Dr. Martinez saying something along these lines. Still, I want to vomit. I ask for a barf bag, which Laura silently places in my hand.

But Duke doesn't flinch at the word *abortion*. Instead, he takes my other hand and holds it while he listens as Dr. Martinez continues to fill us in.

At one point, he looks at me and says, "As luck would have it, Wheeler and I are excellent road trip buddies. I'd be up for another twenty-hour drive if that's what she wants. My only request is that we don't take a U-Haul this time."

I crack a smile, even as my throat closes in. I'm about to cry, not because I'm upset this is happening, although I'm still pissed at myself. My boobs hurt so, so bad, which doesn't help.

I'm about to cry because it's really nice not to feel alone in any of it after days of trying to figure it out on my own. Duke is a steady, comforting presence, keeping my hand warm in the mitt of his. Leave it to him to make me smile during what might be the most difficult conversation I've ever had.

It's all right. This sucks, but we'll figure it out.

He doesn't say the words. He doesn't need to.

"I think we need some more time." I glance at Duke. "Right?"

He nods. "More time sounds good."

"Of course," Dr. Martinez replies. "I'll put the information we talked about in your MyHealth portal so you'll have that to reference as y'all make your decision. I know it's a lot, so please don't hesitate to reach out with questions." She stands and looks me in the eye. "Whatever you decide, I fully support you. Trust yourself to make the right call, okay?"

I nod. "I really appreciate that. We'll be in touch."

"And you keep doing that dirty work." She taps Duke on the arm with the manila folder she's holding.

He smiles. "Yes, ma'am."

"*And* he's polite. Good Lord." Laura uses her hand to fan herself. "I need to take five, Christina."

"I think we all do," Dr. Martinez says as she ducks out of the room. "Karl! Where's my fan?"

Duke keeps a hand on the small of my back as we leave the office. I don't miss the way the women in the waiting room check him out.

I feel myself biting back a smile. Having arm candy is kinda fun.

Duke's vintage Chevy stands out in a parking deck packed with shiny Range Rovers and souped-up BMWs. It's old but immaculately restored and maintained. There's not a speck of dirt or dust on the white and cocoa-brown colored paint. My chest does that squeezing thing when I wonder if he ran the truck through the car wash on his way to Dallas.

Did he get her all dolled up for me?

I climb onto the vinyl-covered bench that runs the length of the cab. It smells like Duke inside, and I have to close my eyes and remind myself to keep breathing as a wave of longing rips through me.

Nausea too.

What a mess.

We're quiet on the ride back to my house. I have no idea what Duke is thinking. I have no idea what *I'm* thinking.

All I know is that he looks so damn sexy when he's driving. One hand on the wheel, the other draped casually over the gearshift because *of course* he drives stick.

I swear, the man is out to give me a legit heart attack.

"I'm not tryin' to be weird or quiet or whatever," he says at last over the faint strains of Lainey Wilson playing on the radio. "I just don't wanna say the wrong thing. Put my damn boot in my mouth. Because I'll support you in whatever you decide too, Wheeler. I meant what I said about another road trip." He turns his head. His eyes look so, *so* blue in the sunlight that slants through the windshield. "I also don't want to put the burden of making that choice solely on you, because that sure as hell ain't fair."

Truth is I don't know how I feel. Maybe because I'm still in shock? Am I in some kind of state of denial, even though a medical professional just confirmed that I am one hundred percent pregnant?

I think part of it is Duke's hotness scrambling my brain. I can't think when he's around.

At the same time, I don't want him to leave.

"Duke, I have no idea what I'm thinking." I press my fingers to my forehead. "First off, these laws are fucking stupid."

"No shit."

"And the timing couldn't be worse, right? You have all that exciting stuff happening at the ranch, and Bellamy Brooks is finally doing well. You and I aren't dating or anything. Having a baby right now…" I shake my head. "It's a terrible idea."

Adjusting his hand on the wheel, Duke is quiet for a beat. He shifts gears. The engine roars.

"Timing's not great," he says. "We obviously weren't planning for this to happen. And I know with everything going on with your parents…"

I scoff. "Right. That shit. Another reason why having this baby wouldn't be the smartest move."

Why then does my chest hurt when I think about not having this baby?

I move my hand to my breastbone, pressing my fingers into the phantom soreness there. What the fuck is that about?

Now is not the time to be dumb. Or sentimental. Or *soft*. Not when my dreams for my career and my life are finally coming true.

"But you know I'll be there for y'all, right? You and the baby? If you wanna have it?" Duke looks at me again, all earnestness. "Smart move or not, I'll be the best damn daddy I can be. You sure as hell won't be raising this kid on your own, Blue. I couldn't live with myself knowing I have a kid in this world who didn't feel loved the way I felt loved by my parents."

My heart spasms. Probably why I feel short of breath. Just—

This *man*. He's a good one.

A really, really good one. And I keep running into this feeling that I'm doing something stupid by keeping him at arm's length.

But that's just the thing, isn't it? He's smart and he's kind and he's handsome as all get out, and because of that, *he makes me stupid*. That's how I got myself into this mess in the first place. In the heat of the moment, I suggested we have unprotected sex, which I never do, and then this happened.

What other stupid shit will I do because those fucking blue eyes of his make me weak in the knees?

I never knew Duke's mom and dad. He's talked

about them in a peripheral sort of way. But like I said last night, I can tell they were good parents. Happy parents.

Would Duke be the same kind of parent?

Could he teach me how to be too?

What if, deep down, that's a piece of the puzzle of what I've been looking for? To be the kind of supportive parent I always wanted—needed—but haven't really had?

I shove the thought aside. I'm too young to be thinking about that kind of thing. Of course I want to be a good mother. A happy mother.

But that comes later, *after* I build my empire and I'm able to stand on my own two feet the way my own mother was never able to. I can only imagine what she and my dad would say if I decided to have a baby with a guy I barely know—someone they've never heard about, much less met.

"You're going to be a great dad," I reply carefully. "I think we all know that. But I also know you want to travel. Take more time to figure yourself out. You're not ready to settle down yet."

His Adam's apple bobs. "Ideally not, no. No, I'm not."

"Neither am I. I don't see how I'd be able to work the way I do and raise a kid. Especially with Mollie having *her* baby."

"Right. Yeah, that'd be tough."

Silence.

Terrible, awful silence fills the truck. We didn't make a decision, but...

Did we just make a decision?

I'm filled with a sense of forlornness. It's the only word I can think of that describes the sinking feeling in my stomach.

Which makes no sense. I don't want a baby right now. I definitely don't want Duke to have to be tied to me for the rest of his life. I know how important his freedom is to him. That's why he volunteered to come to Aspen in the first place, isn't it? Because he wants to experience the world. Do what he wants, when he wants.

He's a good guy, though.

Thoughtful.

I tell him to take the next right. He puts his blinker on.

"So." He slowly makes the turn.

I shift on the bench, tucking my hair behind my ears. "So."

"What are you up to the rest of the day?"

"Ugh. Work. I got a flood of invoices this morning I need to pay."

"First of the month. Fun, ain't it?"

Chuckling, I shake my head. "I forget the ranch is a small business too. Not so small anymore actually."

"Blue, is there anything about me that strikes you as 'small'?" The tendons and thick sinews of his neck pop against his skin as he turns his head to flash a flirty smile at me.

Without thinking, I reach across the cab and give him a shove. "Why you gotta be so gross?"

"'Cause it makes you smile."

Shit, it does. "I want you to know it's not a voluntary smile."

"But it's there." He splays the fingers on the hand he's got on the gearshift. "Sorry for the bad joke."

"No, you're not."

"I do dirty work for a living. Of course I'm not sorry." He shifts gears. "How 'bout you and I take our laptops to a coffee shop or somethin'? Get out for a while, get some work done. If you start feeling bad, I'll take you home. If you want, I'll help you pay your invoices too."

My heart leaps. I don't feel great, but I don't feel *terrible*. I also like the idea of having some company right now. I thought I'd feel more settled after seeing Dr. Martinez. Don't get me wrong, she was great. But I'm still sick, and I still feel so mixed up inside.

I didn't realize how much I wanted Duke to stay until right now.

Oh, girl, you're in trouble.

I'm able to ignore the small voice inside me that warns I'm getting in over my head. This is Duke's issue to deal with too. Maybe if we spend a little more time together, we'll be able to parse out our feelings on the issue a bit more. Can't hurt to keep talking about it, right?

"I can pay my invoices. But coffee sounds great. Actually, it sounds kind of awful, but I could totally go for a croissant the size of my head."

Duke grins. "You got it. Point me in the direction of the nearest laptop-friendly bakery."

My heart's doing a goddamn pirouette now. "Next light, we'll take a left."

CHAPTER 19
Coworking Space
Duke

"Oh, God, yes."

Wheeler's eyes practically roll to the back of her head as she bites into the biggest croissant I think I've ever seen. The thing is the size of a football.

I pop open my laptop, try not to pop a woody. "You and the enthusiastic sounds while you're eating."

"That was you." She nods, chowing down on the croissant. "Although yeah. I kinda do everything with enthusiasm."

Ain't that the truth. The way this girl sucked my dick that morning in the U-Haul—

Yeah, can't go there right now. Not while we're in public, even if we are at a coffee shop named the Drip Drop.

It's actually a cool little spot. Tucked into a corner in a hipster neighborhood that bustles with pedestrians and traffic, it's a got a vibe that I'd say is part kooky French bistro, part cozy southern porch hangout. There's an actual porch with rocking chairs and a couple big porch swings, each one occupied by tattooed twentysomethings typing furiously on their phones. Inside, groupings of cushy upholstered wingback chairs and a row of high-top tables occupy a space with beamed ceilings.

It smells like coffee and chocolate. It's filled with the low hum of conversation, and as I sip my ridiculously priced latte, I decide I love it.

Almost as much as Wheeler loves her croissant.

"Some things have tasted *really* bad lately." She takes another bite. "But I'm just discovering that other things taste *really* good. Like, I can't remember the last time I had a plain croissant like this. But the butter? And the flakiness? That little hit of salt too?" She touches her fingertips to her lips. "Chef's kiss."

I discreetly adjust my jeans underneath the table. Seeing this girl smile—enjoy herself after last night's tears—is definitely gonna get me hard.

What can I say? I like it when she's happy.

"Guess pregnancy takes you back to basics." I pull up my email in an effort to distract myself.

"In this moment, I don't hate it." She nods at my coffee. "How's the lavender haze latte?"

"Amazing. I love me some good old drip coffee—"

"But you can be a fancy bitch on occasion." Wheeler smiles at me over her laptop, and something catches in my chest. "Welcome to Dallas. I think you'll fit in just fine here."

Don't tempt me, sweetheart.

I have mixed feelings about the conversation we had in my truck on the drive here. On the one hand, we got the facts laid out, which needed to happen so we have a clear picture of the reality of our situation. She's building her business. I'm figuring out how to handle this sense of wanderlust, of boredom, I can't seem to kick.

A baby does not fit into any of that.

Wheeler and I are also not together. We didn't even need to mention marriage, because it's so laughably far off the table. Wheeler's working through some tough stuff with her parents and their marriage, and I know she has no interest in following in their footsteps by having a shotgun wedding situation.

Gonna be honest, though—the thought of us pairing off in any way makes my heart skip a beat. Marriage makes my heart skip another beat, and not in an entirely bad way. Seeing Cash marry his best friend has shown me that a wife doesn't tie you down. She becomes your partner in crime. The person who's by your side as you make your dreams come true together, whether those dreams mean traveling or making babies.

Why not both?

But that's a road that leads nowhere with Wheeler. Girl won't date me, much less let me put a ring on her finger.

Wheeler taps on her keyboard, then lets out a little yelp of delight.

"Good news?" I ask.

She nods, her fingers flying. "Because we still haven't been able to reschedule our Aspen trunk show, the store there put our boots up on their website for preorder yesterday." Her eyes flick to meet mine. "They sold out within minutes. Two hundred pairs!"

I hold up my hand for a high five. "Fuck yeah they did. Congrats."

"Thank you. And you'll appreciate this." She slaps my hand. "Apparently the store got a zillion questions about our men's boot collection. Which obviously doesn't exist—"

"But it could. Clearly there's interest. And imagine if you had a hot cowboy starring in your first marketing campaign? Y'all would sell out in *seconds*." I hold out my arms. "I'm still available. I'll take my shirt off and everything."

Wheeler arches a brow, her gaze flicking down my body. "Pants too?"

"For you? Honey, I'd drop trou in a heartbeat."

"How hilarious would it be if the whole ad was just you, naked, in a pair of Bellamy Brooks boots with you holding a cowboy hat over your—"

"Longhorn?"

She bursts out laughing. "See! Gross."

"You're still smiling."

She purses her lips, clearly trying to fight the big old grin she's wearing. "I like the idea of men's boots. Mollie and I just need to clone ourselves to get it done."

I shrug, grabbing my phone to open my banking app. "Or you could hire that hot cowboy as a consultant. I got ideas."

"Well, by all means, share them." She sets her elbows on the table, her hair falling over her shoulders. "To be fair, you are kind of an expert in this area, so I'm all ears."

My chest lifts at her openness. Her confidence in me.

I like that she's as jazzed by new ideas as I am.

I lift my leg and give my Wranglers a tug, revealing the pair of Ariats I'm wearing. "Y'all would make what we call 'indoor boots'—the ones you wear when you're feelin' a little fancy. Seems to be your wheelhouse."

"As opposed to work boots?"

"Barn boots, yes. I think making everyday boots would bore y'all, and plenty of other companies make excellent boots for cowboying. But Bellamy Brooks—you make boots for special occasions."

Wheeler nods, her brown eyes lighting up. "First date boots."

"Boots you wear to prom."

"Right! Boots you wear when you wanna get laid. Also, boots you wear on your wedding day. Sexy *and* sweet." She glances down at her laptop and runs her fingers over the mouse pad. "I like this, Duke. I'm gonna take some notes."

"My hourly rate is one viewing of *Titanic*, front to back."

Wheeler looks up and grins. "You're not gonna let that go, are you?"

"You got plans tonight?"

"Guess I do now."

My pulse leaps. For a day that began with a trip to an ob-gyn's office to confirm an unexpected pregnancy, today is actually turning out to be…not all that sucky.

I don't know what that means. Am I being reckless—or just plain stupid—to allow myself to have some fun right now, to allow myself to enjoy Wheeler's company? Shouldn't we be discussing what the next few weeks will look like? Should we feel, I don't know, some kinda shame for the pickle we got ourselves into?

But here we are, talking business ideas over some really fucking delicious treats in a really pretty spot.

"Deal." I tilt my foot one way, then the other. "I like the idea of doing two versions. One square-toed for the honky-tonk. The other a little more timeless for the altar."

Wheeler holds up a finger. "Classic round toe. Yes. Maybe in a goatskin leather, with a riff on classic stitching—tone on tone, so it's subtle but still very Texas."

"Could be cool to stitch the state flag on the heel, since that's where y'all make the boots?"

Wheeler claps. "Sexy! Yes. You think we do a tall shaft? Midcalf? Or shorties?"

I hold my hands about a foot apart. "Seems about right, yeah?"

"Not *that* big." Her lips twitch.

"Everything's bigger in Texas, Blue." I snap my fingers. "There's your tagline for the marketing campaign."

She cuts me a glance. "It's so bad it's almost good."

"You're welcome," I reply, chest swelling. "I say you do both—midcalf and short. Winter and summer."

"And then we keep the designs simple. Offer two shaft heights—"

"Okay, you gotta stop saying 'shaft.'"

"What's wrong with the word 'shaft,' Duke?"

"You know what's wrong with the word 'shaft,' Wheeler."

She's smirking. "Am I making you uncomfortable with my talk of shafts in all different shapes and sizes?"

"Don't make me answer that." I drop my leg, my half-hard dick catching on the fly of my jeans. I bite back a wince. "One design's gotta be ridiculous. Ostrich or alligator or some shit. The other is the goatskin. Hardworking but nice. Your ideal customer is a guy's guy who appreciates craftsmanship but isn't flashy. He's got money, but he ain't gonna shove that fact in your face. I wonder if it wouldn't be a smart idea to host some trunk shows at country clubs. Hunt clubs too."

"I didn't know such a thing existed."

"They do, and y'all definitely wanna hit those up." I rub my hands together. "You pitch your boots as heirlooms—the kind you pass from one generation to the next. Maybe you offer free refurbishment services every, I don't know, five years or whatever. Resole the boots, give the leather a polish. I know that's how Garrett kept his boots in such great shape."

Wheeler's fingers slow to a stop as she looks up at me thoughtfully. "Cash wears those boots nonstop."

"Well, yeah. They're boots with meaning. There's a story there. And I think it's a sign of respect to wear the boots of a man you admired."

"Were y'all close? You and Garrett?"

I tip back what's left of my latte. Even lukewarm, it's delicious. "We were. He came into our lives when we really needed a father figure. If it wasn't for him…" I shake my head. "Well, you'd like me, but you wouldn't *like* me."

"I like you?"

"Oh, Blue, you *like* me." I drop my empty cup on the table. "But yeah, Garrett was awesome. Was he perfect? No. But he wasn't like anyone else I had ever met up to that point. He was a rancher, obviously, like pretty much everyone else in Hartsville. But he was also interested in other shit. He was curious about the world. He loved ideas. I distinctly remember him telling me the story of how he struck oil on his land after years of research and prospecting. After that, he got really into bringing back biodiversity to the ranch, and we undertook this huge project he designed to make the property green again. He loved music. Loved to fish." I shrug. "Guess he was a little restless too."

"Just like you."

I scoff. "You give me too much credit. Garrett was one of a kind. He'd definitely wear Bellamy Brooks boots, though."

"Mollie would love to hear that," Wheeler replies with a smile.

"He'd be proud of y'all."

"He'd be proud of you too, Duke. All of y'all." It's her turn to scoff. "I've truly never met men like the five of you."

"Men with large shafts?" I hold my hands apart again.

She laughs, and a burst of warmth moves through me. "Kind men. Thoughtful men. Men who give a shit about the right things."

Christ, are my eyes getting a little misty?

"Y'all should make it happen." I nod at her laptop. "The men's collection."

She leans back in her chair. "You did get me awfully excited."

"I know your buttons."

"Your innuendos are shockingly vulgar."

"And a goddamned delight." I smile.

She smiles back. We sit like that for a beat too long, the space between us alive.

I feel alive. Didn't sleep all that great, but you wouldn't know it from the energy that thrums through my veins.

Are we stupid to not have this baby? What if he or she is not the end of our story but the start of it?

My rational mind knows our situation is much more nuanced than that. But I keep getting these thoughts about, well, giving the decision more thought. More time.

If I'm being honest with myself, I'm *not* sure I want to end the pregnancy. Is that just because I have a crush on Wheeler, though, and I'd do anything to keep her around? Because that's just plain fucked up.

I clear my throat and look down at my computer screen. "I, uh, should get to these invoices."

"Right." Wheeler sits back up. "Me too. I probably need an hour. Then you wanna head home? I'm already tired, even though I've done, like, practically nothing today."

If only home was the same place for both of us.

"You mean you only planned out the future of your company *and* went to an all-important appointment?" I tilt my head. "Totally nothing."

"I haven't been productive is what I'm saying."

"There's gotta be more to the day than that, yeah? You're doing better than you think."

Her expression softens. "Thanks."

"And sounds like a plan about going back to your place."

Only when Wheeler closes her laptop and stands up an hour later, putting her hands on her lower back to stretch, I'm hit by the image of her with a pregnant belly.

A very pregnant belly, our baby tucked snugly inside.

We made a baby. Still can't get over that fact.

What would our daughter look like? Because in this

fantasy, I guess we're having a girl. *Who* would she look like? Hopefully more like her mama than me.

I'm suddenly gripped by a fierce urge. One that feels an awful lot like protectiveness. I'd take damn good care of Wheeler and the baby. If, of course, Wheeler would let me.

"You okay?"

I blink, Wheeler's voice yanking me back into the present.

"Yeah. Sorry. Spaced for a minute there." I fold my laptop and tuck it into my backpack. "How are you feeling?"

She makes a face and puts a hand on her stomach.

Her *flat* stomach.

"I'm starting to feel nauseous again. Just my luck, I'm part of the minority of women who get morning sickness this early."

I grin. "That's why you have me. You like peppermint?"

"I do." She furrows her brow. "Why?"

"Was just reading about how it might help with nausea. I'll stop and grab some on our way back to your place."

She blinks. "Okay. Great. Thank you."

"I wish you'd stop doing that," I say with a chuckle, putting my hand on the small of her back as we head for the door.

"Doing what?"

"Acting all surprised and shit when someone does something nice for you." I follow her outside.

She chuckles too, although the sound has an edge. "It's cute how you assume being shown respect is a given in everyday life."

"Shouldn't it be?" Despite the ardent afternoon sun that shines directly into our faces, I meet her eyes. "Who in the world ever made you feel unworthy of something as basic as respect?"

She waves away my question. "Still up for *Titanic*?"

I debate whether to press her for an answer. Her brother seemed nice enough—I could tell they're close. But what about everyone else in her family? Now I'm thinking about those times on the drive to Aspen that she sent her dad's calls to voicemail. And the fact that Haines said their older brother was a dick.

My hand tightens into a fist around the strap of my backpack. He a dick to Wheeler? Was her dad also an asshole?

I don't like that idea.

But then Wheeler is reaching out to open the passenger side door of my truck. I beat her to it just in time. She calls me a pain in the ass, but she's smiling as she says it. I take her bag and put it behind the bench, then help her climb inside.

Jogging around the hood, I send up a silent prayer that she lets me spend the night again.

Maybe this time she'll let me sleep under the covers.

CHAPTER 20
Desperate Times Call for Shirtless Measures
Wheeler

Jack is heading up to first class for dinner with Rose and her terrible fiancé when I'm hit by an especially violent bout of nausea.

Bile surges up my throat in a bitter-tasting gush of heat. I launch myself off the couch and make it to the powder room just in time to throw up the peppermint tea I've been sipping all afternoon.

"Oh, Jesus, sweetheart." Duke's somehow right behind me already. "You all right?"

Wiping my mouth with the back of my hand, I nod. "I'll be okay. This shit comes out of nowh—"

I retch. More puke.

I'm shaking, and *oh Lord*, Duke is pulling my hair out of my face and holding it in his hand as I continue to lose the contents of my stomach in the toilet bowl.

The force of my sickness pushes tears from my eyes. I'm shaking.

I'm also so, *so* embarrassed that I'm vomiting in front

of Duke. The smell, the noises I'm making, the way my body convulses—it is literally the unsexiest thing on planet Earth.

Why, God, why?

But Duke, being the stellar human he is, just takes it in stride.

"I imagine this really, really sucks for you," he practically coos while gently placing his free hand on the small of my back. "I'm so sorry. Let me know if you wanna rinse your mouth out with water. Sometimes that helps."

I nod, too embarrassed—too tired—to do anything else.

Next thing I know, he's turning on the sink. Keeping my hair in his hand in a kind of ponytail, he gently guides me to the water. He even goes so far as to cup his hand underneath the faucet, allowing me to drink from his palm like some wounded baby animal.

"I hate you seeing me like this." I sound as miserable as I feel.

Duke chuckles softly. "Blue, this is nothing. Ever witnessed a five-hundred-pound bull having explosive diarrhea?"

"That happens?"

"I've seen it firsthand. You're fine." He shuts off the water and grabs the nearby towel to wipe my mouth. "Well, you're not fine, clearly. But this don't bother me one bit."

Suddenly we're face-to-face. His brows are pinched together, eyes full of concern.

"Promise?" I ask.

Those eyes stray to my forehead, my nose, my

chin. Like he's checking to make sure I'm not dying or something.

"I promise."

I start to cry. The physical misery of this, the emotional turmoil, but also how *good* it feels to be looked at this way, cared for—it slams into me with the force of a freight train, and I can't hold it in anymore.

I have never been more overwhelmed in my life. This is so bad but also so wonderful, and I just—none of it computes.

"Aw, Wheeler." Duke does that thing where he pulls me into his chest, practically smothering me with his warmth and solidness and *goodness*.

The T-shirt he changed into after we got home smells like Tide detergent. Same kind Mom used when we were growing up.

It's a small comfort but a comfort nonetheless.

I breathe in the scent and feel my heart rate slow as he cups the back of my head in his enormous hand.

He holds me. I let him.

"Tell me something," he says after a beat.

"Yeah?"

"Is Haines going back to SMU?"

I nod, smearing snot all over Duke's T-shirt. For a split second, I'm mortified, but then I remember that this is a cowboy, and he's used to being dirty. He just said he's not bothered by a mess.

He *would* care if I said something or pulled away. So I don't.

I melt into him and say, "Yeah. He's taking some classes there over the summer."

"And Mollie's sticking around the ranch for now."

"As far as I know, yes." *Where is he going with this?*

"Are your parents around to help you at all?"

"My parents." I scoff. "I'm not going to say anything to them unless we decide to keep the baby."

I feel him stiffen. "You're not gonna tell your parents—"

"Well, maybe I'll tell my mom. But I definitely won't tell my dad. It's easier this way, trust me."

My head tilts back as Duke's chest barrels out on an enormous inhale. "So you're gonna be on your own here."

"I have friends," I say defensively, lifting my head to look at him.

He's looking down at me, deep grooves in his forehead. "Don't shoot me down right away, all right?"

"Duke—"

"I want you to come back to the ranch with me. Just…only until we figure out what to do. You're sick, Blue. You gotta let someone take care of you, and that someone should be me and my family."

Aaaannd now I'm literally weak in the knees. Great. Just freaking great.

This guy is so freaking great.

"But work—"

"You do it at the ranch. You haven't mentioned any trunk shows or meetings you have in the next couple weeks."

My breath catches. "You really pay attention, don't you?"

"Yes, ma'am, I do."

"I don't know if I like it when you call me ma'am."

"Yes, *Blue*, I do pay attention to you." He lets go of

my hair and slips that hand around my nape. "I'm not leaving you here alone. So either you invite me to stay in Dallas until we make a decision—"

"But *your* work—you can't just—"

"Leave the ranch to take care of something important? Yes, I can. And I will."

I flatten my hand on his chest. I feel his heart beating thickly, strongly, against the wall of muscle there. "Maybe we should just make the call then? Get this over with."

"Are you ready?"

No.

I shake my head.

"Me neither," he says softly. "Come home with me, Blue."

My instinct is to say no to that too.

I can handle this on my own. I don't need help. Chances are I'll be heading to New Mexico sooner rather than later, and Duke doesn't need to be with me for that. Then this whole thing will be over, and we can all move on with our lives.

But I just—God, he makes me feel so *safe* and seen and cared for. I don't want to be alone right now.

I'm so sick of pushing people away. So sick of my bullshit. I learned early to be hyper-independent—to take care of my own needs so I didn't inconvenience anyone or cause them to blow up—but now, that identity chafes.

It feels too tight. Too…stupid. Why am I wasting my time punishing myself this way?

"You should've been a lawyer." I trail my fingertip over the nubby fabric of his T-shirt. "You're really good at convincing me to do things."

"That a yes?"

"That's a yes."

He falls asleep in my bed again. This time, I make sure to tuck him in.

Parking my Mini Cooper beside Duke's truck, the breath leaves my lungs.

In front of us is the cutest fucking house I think I've ever seen. Or would it be a cabin? It's small, but it's got a front porch that's dominated by a massive limestone fireplace, rocking chairs drawn up to the hearth. Shingled wooden siding and a tin roof give it a rustic edge. A pair of farmhouse windows look out on a yard studded with soaring oaks.

My heart soars too when I see a field of bluebonnets off to our right.

Is this real? Or am I on a movie set?

I pop my trunk and open my door. Stepping out into the afternoon sunshine, I'm immediately hit by the smell of freshly cut grass. The air is warm, soft without a touch of humidity.

I feel the knot of tension in my gut loosen ever so slightly.

"Repairs just wrapped up. It's the old foreman's cottage," Duke explains as he lifts my bags out of my trunk. "Been a dream of ours to restore it, but we never had the cash to do it until recently. Now—"

"It's a dream that came true," I breathe, clinging for dear life to the top of my car's doorframe. "Duke, this is magical. Holy shit."

Chuckling, he tucks the strap of my pink Vera Bradley bag over his shoulder. "It sure as hell ain't Aspen—"

"It's better." I turn my head to look at him. "It's *you*."

He's wearing a pair of gold-rimmed aviators. When he smiles, the world tilts beneath my feet. "It's still a work in progress. Inside's pretty spare. But yeah, I really like living here. Big improvement over the bunkhouse, that's for damn sure."

I hold the doorframe in a death grip. Is it possible to stay here and not fall head over heels in love with this man?

Is it possible to leave after, well, everything he's done for me?

He pushes the front door open—no one locks up around here—and I follow him inside the house. It smells like new paint and Duke.

The furnishings are sparse but cozy looking. There's a smaller version of the New House's table in the kitchen, and a leather couch is paired with some upholstered chairs in the living room.

My eyes catch on the stacks and stacks and *stacks* of books lined up neatly on a far wall. Paperbacks. Textbooks. Recent bestsellers I recognize, all in hardback. Even some cookbooks are in there.

"You cook?" I ask.

"Those are my mom's. After she died, Wyatt took all her books except the cookbooks. No one really wanted those, so I took them. Can't say I've referenced them a ton over the years, but I like collecting books, so." He shrugs. "Seemed a shame to toss 'em. I like having a piece of her around, ya know?"

My heart twists. "I've always wanted to learn how to cook."

"I'd say we could learn together, but I feel like that'd

probably be a bad idea right now—making food that could potentially make you barf. How are you feeling, by the way?"

I turn away from the books. "I'm fine. Same as I was twenty minutes ago when you checked in."

Duke's powers of persuasion only went so far. He wanted me to drive with him in his truck back to Hartsville, telling me I had "pregnant passenger princess" privileges and that I should take advantage of them. *Rest while you can*, he'd said.

I wanted to have my own car, however—he offered me the use of his truck, but I can't drive stick—so we ended up driving together but in separate cars from Dallas. He called me every twenty minutes on the dot to check in on me. And this was *after* he loaded me up with enough snacks and drinks to literally fill my passenger seat and all the cupholders in my car.

He'd be a good dad.

So different from my own. I grew up thinking all dads were mean because, well, mine was as mean as a snake.

Duke is the opposite of mean. He's patient. He has appropriate reactions to things. He's able to talk about his feelings, and he seems to genuinely care when I talk about *my* feelings.

"Here, I'll show you the guest room." He nods toward the back of the house. "That way, you can get settled."

He leads me down a short hallway that dead-ends in a trio of doors. Straight ahead is a bathroom, covered in gleaming white subway tile. To the left and right are bedrooms.

I nearly jump out of my skin when I catch a glimpse of Ryder tucking a sheet underneath a mattress in the room to my right.

He looks up and smiles. "Well, hey, y'all!"

He looks and sounds so much like Duke that for a second, I have a total brain fart. *Where am I? What's happening?*

"He—hi, Ryder." I give him a little wave, heat flooding my face. Does he know I'm pregnant?

He has to know. Duke has a great relationship with all his brothers, but it's obvious he and Ryder are especially close.

Besides, me staying here is a dead giveaway that something's up. Like all guests who visit Lucky River Ranch, I always stay at the New House.

"How was your drive?" Ryder straightens.

"Easy." I step into the room and look inside. "Are you—"

"Oh, I'm just the caboose, Wheeler. There wasn't a stick of furniture in here when Duke called us yesterday, so Wyatt and Sally went to Austin for the bed frame and mattress, Mollie lent us some of her fancy-ass sheets, and Patsy gave us the pillow inserts and the comforter from Sally's room in their house. Now that she's living with Wyatt, Patsy and John B don't have a need for 'em. She assured me they were clean. Ava and the girls came over to hang those curtains Mrs. Wallace was able to whip up. I'm just bringing it all together."

"Ryder." A moon lodges itself in my throat. "Y'all didn't have to do that. I could've just stayed at the New House—"

"All by your lonesome? Naw, that ain't right. You're

better off here." His eyes slide to Duke, who's setting my bags on a pair of luggage racks by the door. "Patsy wanted to know if we could expect y'all for dinner? Think she's making vegetarian pasta. Something simple."

Duke looks at me. "Sound good?"

"Wait a second. *Wait*. Did you—"

"Ella loves Patsy's pasta," Duke replies. "Since you're grossed out by chicken and stuff right now, I asked Patsy to make it tonight. I think it's basically just butter, cheese, peas, and, yeah, more butter."

"She was probably gonna make it anyway," Ryder adds. "You know, meatless Monday."

I stare at them. "It's not Monday."

They shrug, mirror images of each other. Ryder is slightly shaggier, with longer hair and a legit beard.

Dear God, what if I'm pregnant with twins?

How cool would that be?

Or would it be a nightmare? I imagine caring for two newborns at the same time isn't for the faint of heart.

None of this experience is.

"I don't know what to say." My voice is thick. "Y'all—your family—really, this is all too much—"

"Wheeler, this is just what we do." Ryder walks over and wraps me in a hug. "Welcome. We hope you'll stay a while." Then he glances over his shoulder at his brother and walks out of the room, calling, "See y'all at dinner!"

"Sorry about him," I hear Duke say. "I think he misunderstands—well, he wants...he thinks I'm lonely or maybe just lost, and..."

My lips twitch. "I like how we both apologize for our big-mouthed brothers."

"I swear, I'm not trying to push you one way or the

other. To keep the baby, to not." His eyes bore into mine. "Ryder laid it on thick, but I won't. I respect your, um, autonomy. That's not quite the right word, but…"

"Are you?"

"Am I what?"

"Lonely." I have a sudden, urgent need to know.

Duke tucks his hands into the front pockets of his jeans. "I don't know. Maybe."

I think maybe I've been lonely too.

"I'm glad I had an excuse to get the guest room together," he continues. "Kinda depressing having empty rooms in your house."

I swallow, taking in the room with its mismatched furniture and cute little curtains. "It's perfect." I swallow again. And again. "Sometimes I wonder—I know we're doing the right thing, chasing our dreams. I'm just not sure that it's enough. Like, maybe the dream is incomplete, you know? Because my career is taking off, and that feels really, really great, don't get me wrong. But there's a loneliness that comes with being so focused on one thing." My eyes burn. I blink and look at the floor. "I keep coming back to your idea that there's gotta be more to the day than just being productive. Like, what are we waiting for, an invitation from God or whoever to finally *enjoy* life? To enjoy each other's company rather than sit in front of our laptops all damn day?"

Duke's voice is different when he replies, "I feel that. Just swap out the laptop part for a horse."

I laugh, meeting his eyes. "Sorry. Getting way off topic here—"

"I love it when you get off topic. Picking your brain

is fun. And enlightening."

I have to look away again. "I'd say I like picking yours too, but it's always in the gutter, so..."

"So?" His voice is teasing now.

A familiar lick of heat moves through my skin. I don't know how I can be horribly sick one minute and turned on the next, but that's pregnancy for you.

"So we're on for dinner, I guess."

One side of his mouth kicks up. "Sounds good."

"Thank you. For asking Patsy to make pasta. And for this." I motion to the room. "I'm feeling the love."

Duke taps the doorframe on his way out. "That's the point, Blue. Take your time unpacking. I'll be in the kitchen."

God, he's good.

So good that I wanna be good to him too. Yes, life is an absolute disaster right now. Yes, we have a monumental decision to make after a series of horrible mistakes. But somehow, throughout it all, Duke has made me feel so much less lost and lonely than I did before that fateful trip to Aspen.

I feel like I'm starting to get a sense of clarity about life because of him. Or maybe it's the pregnancy, I don't know. Either way, I wanna show him the love.

I also wanna run. But I'm trying my damnedest to ignore that feeling—that sense of fear—and lean into being good to Duke the way he's been good to me.

Closing the door, I grab my phone and shoot Mollie a text.

WHEELER: We should seriously think about doing a men's collection now that we have momentum.

Came up with some cool ideas I'll share.

MOLLIE: *Interesting you send me this text after you and Duke spent some time together [side eye emoji]*

WHEELER: *No comment.*

WHEELER: *But he has been wonderful*

WHEELER: *Haines says he'll take Duke if I don't want him*

MOLLIE: *My sweet angel baby, you want him. You just have to let yourself have him.*

WHEELER: *Easier said than done.*

MOLLIE: *That's why I'm here [purple devil emoji]*

CHAPTER 21
Patterns
Duke

"You're awful chipper this morning." Ryder unhooks his horse from the crossties. "Any reason in particular you're Mr. Fucking Rogers today?"

I hadn't realized I was whistling until…well, right now.

The tune dies on my lips. That's when I realize the base of my skull is buzzing. Jesus, even my Ryder radar can't break through my good mood today.

My brother screws up his face. "Is that—Lord, it's the Jonas Brothers, isn't it?"

"I don't know who that is."

"Yes, you do. Mr. Rogers would be appalled." Ryder grins. "Boy, you got it bad."

"Shut up." I climb into the saddle and take the reins. Much as I loved being away for a bit, it's nice to be back. "I told you, Wheeler and I aren't together. She's just staying with me so I can keep an eye on her. Make sure she's okay. Morning sickness has hit her pretty hard."

"So she stayed in her bed, and you—"

"Stayed in mine, yes." Although it near about killed me. Knowing Wheeler was right there on the other side of the hall had me seriously considering all kinds of stupid shit.

Sucks to be a gentleman sometimes.

"And y'all didn't have, like, any kind of shared shower situation or—"

"Remember that time in sixth grade when I punched you in the mouth?"

Ryder grins, and we head outside into the gray dawn. "How could I forget?"

"Let's not have a repeat today, all right?"

"All right, all right."

We're quiet as we head for the southwest pasture, where we're going to meet John B to check on some calves. Mollie has an early doctor's appointment this morning, so Cash is sleeping in and going with her. He'll be at the ranch office a little before lunch. Wyatt and Sawyer drove over to the Rivers side of the ranch, where they're overseeing the installation of some new irrigation.

So it's just me and Ryder and the quiet clap of our horses' hooves. It's barely past five a.m., but the horizon is already starting to turn to gray. Spring is in full bloom. The branches of the old oaks we pass are covered in new leaves. The ground is soft, fragrant from recent rain. The air is cool. A breeze will keep the day from getting too hot.

It's my favorite time of year on the ranch. Fall is branding season, so we're always crazy busy. Winter is boring and cold, and summer is an absolute nightmare thanks to the heat.

But spring? Spring is just right. Glancing across the acres and acres of land that stretch out before us, I'm struck by just how beautiful this place is. Dallas was pretty in its own way, with its hipster hangouts and buzzing energy. But I love this too—the wide-open spaces, the canyons, the brush, the quiet.

I've always been a country boy who dreamed of the big city. I thought I'd like the city better. And I do like it.

But I like this too. No wonder I've had such a hard time pinning down what I want exactly. I like... everything.

Correction: maybe I like to *experience* everything. New shit and familiar shit too. A combination of the two. Is that my definition of freedom? The ability to see and feel and do it all? Well, maybe not the ability to do it all, but the ability to live fully in the moment wherever I am. The ability to put myself in the way of feeling *this* alive.

"So how're you feeling?" Ryder asks, voice low. "You were pretty upset when you left the other day."

I lift a shoulder. "I'm scared. Really scared. Ain't like me to be reckless, and I hate—" My voice catches. "I've been worried that I made a mistake that could derail my life, as terrible as that sounds."

"Not terrible. It's totally understandable why you'd feel that way."

He pauses. I realize he's waiting for me to say something.

"But I like her, Ryder." I pull my horse to the left to avoid what appears to be a small sinkhole. We'll have to fill that in later. "The more time I spend with her, the more I like her. Weird thing is I can see us together. Like, *together* together."

Ryder's eyebrows pop up. "Like, get married and have a family together type shit?"

"Yeah. She's smart and she's cute and she's just so interested in the world. Life with her would never be boring." I shake my head. "But life with a baby? That might be."

Ryder tilts his head to one side, then the other. "Yes and no. I'm no expert, but seeing what Sawyer went through—yeah, there's gonna be a period where you're homebound and you're not sleeping and it's just a ton of work. But now he's kind of living his best life, and that wouldn't be the case if Ella hadn't come along. Life doesn't end when you have a kid."

Sawyer and Ava kept running into each other because their kids go to the same preschool. One thing led to another, and now they're living together, happy as clams.

I cut him a look. "Do you want a kid?"

"One day, I do, yeah. I just haven't found my person. Sounds like you have."

My pulse skips several beats as his words sink in. "Wheeler's not interested in anything serious."

"Not even now?"

"Especially not now. Her parents got married because her mom got pregnant. Now they're going through this really shitty divorce. Sounds like they were never really happy together. And I know Wheeler is connecting the dots."

"Right. She thinks if y'all go down the same path, you'll end up unhappy too."

"Yup."

Ryder shakes his head. "That's tough. But she does know y'all are different people, right? Obviously, I've never met her parents, but somehow I doubt they had the connection you and Wheeler do."

"You've seen Wheeler and me together all of, what, a handful of times?"

"Dude." He cuts me a look.

"What?"

"It's obvious to everyone that you and Wheeler got somethin' special. Hell, y'all eye fuck nonstop when you're in the same room."

My stomach dips. "No, we don't."

"Then how'd she end up pregnant?"

Laughter bursts through my middle. "You do know a different kind of fucking needs to happen for that to, er, happen."

"I know. And that kind of fucking starts with the eyes." He uses his first two fingers to point to his. "You also ain't ever talked about a girl this much. Ever. You get bored so easily…"

I chafe at that. "So do you."

"It's not a dig. Just a fact. But being with Wheeler seems to do the opposite. She energizes you. Like, she gets you excited about things."

Bull's-eye.

That's exactly why I enjoy her company so much.

Exactly why I like her and could see myself falling for her.

Back in high school, I thought I was in love with a cute girl in chorus named McKenzie Stanhope. But now I'm starting to think that wasn't love at all. With McKenzie, I felt like I had to follow a script—like we had to hit specific milestones at specific times. First date, first dance, first kiss. When I suggested we veer from that script a time or two, she wasn't interested. Everything had to be by the book, which I found suffocating.

Lonely too.

With Wheeler, though? I don't feel lonely. There is no script. We're just figuring it out as we go, deciding what feels right as we experience it. No pretense. No pressure to be anyone other than ourselves. I always thought relationships tied you down, but the relationship I have with Wheeler is actually…liberating. I feel safe to be myself with her.

Is this another part of freedom? Not travel necessarily or the ability to do what I want, when I want. Maybe freedom is more about self-expression. The ability to be who I am with people who love me for it. Who *see* me.

In other words, is freedom simply the opposite of loneliness? Is it being seen and known and understood?

Also, how the hell did I make it to twenty-seven without ever being in love?

Does that mean it's finally my time?

Glancing up at the sky, I can't help but wonder what Mom would say. She'd love Wheeler, no question. Wheeler is open-minded like Mom. Curious about the world. Confident and kind and loving.

What about the baby, though? What would Mom have to say about that? I know she wouldn't want me to sacrifice my dreams out of some misguided notion of "doing the right thing."

What is the right thing, though? I don't want to be lonely again.

I don't want to come home to an empty house ever again. I *love* having Wheeler there. I'm already itching for four o'clock, when the day is done and I get to go home to her. I don't know what we'll do. I do know that whatever activity we decide on—TV, a porch hangout session, whatever—it'll make me think. It'll make me smile.

It'll make me happy. The idea of *that* being my life going forward—

Yeah, doesn't suck. And somehow, I could see a baby fitting in just fine.

"I want Wheeler," I say quietly. "I don't know if I want this baby. What would you do?"

Ryder is quiet for a minute. "I can't answer that. I know you wanna do something different with your life. But have you thought about what you really want out of all that? What are you really lookin' to get out of your time on earth? I don't think it's money or partying or anything like that."

I reach up to push my hat a little farther onto my head. "It's not."

"I think we're here to find our people. Look at Sawyer and Ella—our babies become our people. What if…how cool would it be if you got to travel *with* your babies? Maybe not when they're, well, babies. But as they grow up, that kid could very well become your best travel buddy."

And that's something I'd miss out on if Wheeler and I decided not to have said kid.

The thought lands heavily on my chest in a way I'm not expecting.

"Hadn't pictured it that way," I manage.

"Even better if you got to travel with your babies *and* your girl."

Yep, my heart leaps at the thought of Wheeler riding

shotgun on every road trip I take going forward. Of her sitting beside me on a plane, the two of us pouring our beers into those stupid plastic cups they give you while we plot how we're gonna spend our first day in New York, Charleston, Paris, Grand Teton National Park.

Because Wheeler, as much a city girl as she is, would be just as excited to explore a European city as she would a national park. Granted, I don't think I could convince her to spend the night in a tent or anything, but I'm good with staying at a swanky hotel by night while hiking or fishing by day.

I'd love to teach Wheeler how to fish.

I'd love to teach my kids too.

Huh.

A slow, rolling rumble fills my ears. A beat later, I'm hit by a familiar smell I can only describe as manure mixed with dust and sweat and that distinct, tangy animal scent I know so well.

The herd is close.

"You're getting my hopes up," I say.

Ryder looks at me. "Isn't that my job as your brother and best friend? Pump you the fuck up so you make good decisions?"

"Whoever said you're my best friend?"

"Hey." He points at me. "I know you got the hots for Wheeler, but I'll always know you best. Don't you dare disappear on me, ya hear?"

I laugh. "I'm going places. But I'm not *going*."

"What the hell does that mean?"

"I'm not, like, leaving for good."

Ryder arches a brow. "You sure about that? Feels like leaving is all you've talked about."

And now I'm starting to think that maybe I can leave and *I can stay. What if they're not mutually exclusive concepts?*

Just like having a kid and having freedom aren't mutually exclusive concepts either. Sure, having a baby takes some forms of freedom away.

But I hadn't considered that it might give you other forms of freedom in exchange. Like the freedom to be myself with my people. The freedom to explore the world with them.

The freedom to start my damn life, whatever that looks like. Because I'm not really sure I've been living up to this point. Sure, I go through the motions just fine. I'm good to my family. Good at my job.

But I've had all the "freedom" in the world when you think about it. And what the hell have I done with it? I'm alone.

That's something Mom and Dad wouldn't want for me.

"By the way, I'm not saying that if you decide not to have this kid, you're making the wrong choice," Ryder continues. "Maybe that is the right choice at this point in your life. I just want to make sure you're considering all angles. We're not getting any younger, and people like Wheeler—they don't come around all that often."

I scoff. "No shit. I want to make the right call, and I want to keep Wheeler around. But I don't want to have a kid just to make her stay, ya know?"

"I get it. You gotta get her to fall in love with you, so you gotta do what you do best." He gives me a shit-eating grin. "Eye fuck the shit out of her."

"Not funny."

"Why're you laughing, then?"

"Last time I come to you for advice." I roll my eyes.

He trots over to give me a hard slap on the shoulder. "You know I'm just messin'. I think you just keep showing up for her, yeah? She says her family sucks, so show her how great family can be. Shouldn't be hard, considering how fucking awesome we are—"

"There's as good of a chance of y'all convincing Wheeler to stay as there is of y'all chasing her off."

But Ryder just keeps grinning. "You're lucky to have us, and you know it. I'll turn on the charm for Wheeler no problem. Could be fun to have a two-for-one situation happen—Wyatt and Sally's wedding is coming up, and I bet they'd let you and Wheeler join 'em up at the altar."

My pulse spasms. Not because the idea of meeting Wheeler at the altar makes me panic.

It's because it gets me *excited*.

Shit.

Just…shit.

Now I'm smiling too as we join the herd, John B waving us over to a calf and its mama.

I still haven't figured things out, but it all seems a lot less heavy all of a sudden.

CHAPTER 22
God and Grilled Cheese
Wheeler

I don't see the little parcel on top of my laptop until I sit down at my desk beside Mollie at the New House.

"What's this?" I ask. It's about the size of my hand and is carefully wrapped in the wax paper I recognize from the kitchen. Patsy will use it to wrap up leftovers for us after meals.

The parcel is warm.

Mollie shrugs, pops another Ritz cracker into her mouth, and makes a muffled sound that I interpret as *I don't know*. We just got back from taking a quick ATV ride to check on the progress of the new Bellamy Brooks studio we're building here on the ranch. It's coming along swimmingly, and the views from its perch above the Colorado River are especially stunning this time of year.

"Something tells me you *do* know." I carefully unwrap it, my face splitting into a smile when I see the grilled cheese sandwich inside. It's cut on a diagonal, and when

I split the two sides, the cheese oozes out in a yummy golden avalanche.

A rush of heat hits the backs of my eyes. This morning, I woke up craving grilled cheese. No clue why. Maybe because I dreamed about Aspen? My dreams have been vivid—and vividly horny—lately.

Whatever the case, I shared that info with Duke while we had coffee earlier this morning. Well, he had coffee, and I had peppermint tea, because sadly coffee has become one of the many things that doesn't agree with me at the moment.

I fully expected him to be gone when I woke up at seven. The cowboys start their day early so I thought I'd make myself breakfast, then head up to the New House to work with Mollie.

And Duke *was* gone. But when I responded to the "good morning, how are you feeling?" text he sent me at four forty-eight a.m., he showed up ten minutes later at the door in his full cowboy getup and demanded I sit while he made me tea and buttered toast.

That's when I told him about the grilled cheese craving.

Now, several hours on, I'm wondering where the hell he found the time to make it for me.

I pay attention to everything, sweetheart.

"Aw." Mollie runs a hand over my back. "Are you gonna cry?"

I shake my head, even as tears leak out of my eyes. "I'm not gonna cry. This is just a sandwich. I don't cry over sandwiches."

"I've been instructed to tell you that while Duke didn't make the grilled cheese himself because there's a lot of fences to mend before the summer grazing season begins, he enlisted Patsy's help."

"And Patsy would like you to know that she'll happily make you anything you want, whenever you want it."

I jump at the sound of Patsy's voice. Glancing over my shoulder, I see her poking her head in the door, a wide smile on her face.

Does she know I'm pregnant too?

Does everyone on this goddamn ranch know?

My stomach clenches. It doesn't bother me that everyone around here is knit so closely into such an, ahem, communicative community. It's actually pretty sweet. But now everyone is going to know whether Duke and I keep the baby, and the last thing I want or need is people's judgment.

Guess we'll cross that bridge when we get there. In the meantime, I'm going to enjoy the hell out of their excellent hospitality.

"You're too freaking kind." I quickly wipe my eyes and stand, crossing the room to wrap her in a hug. "Thank you so much. How have you been?"

"Busy but good." She gives me a squeeze. "With the wedding coming up, we've got a lot on our plates. We hope you're planning to come."

My stomach clenches again, for a different reason this time. "That's right! How exciting. I'll do my best to make it. I appreciate y'all thinking of me, truly. Sally and Wyatt are so cute together. I'm happy for them."

"Of course we thought of you." Patsy pulls back and puts her hands on my upper arms. "You're family, Wheeler."

But I'm not.

Really, though, I feel more at home among the Lucky River Ranch crew—more comfortable, more seen, more taken care of—than I have in years at my actual home with my actual family.

Hi, God, it's me, Wheeler. Question for you—can one ditch their biological family, perhaps with the exception of a younger brother, and adopt the Rivers-Powell-Luck people as their new family? Asking for a friend.

"How are you?" Patsy asks.

Do I beat around the bush? Or do I let her know that I know that *she* knows that I'm pregnant?

"I'm...okay."

She nods, her eyes kind. "It's literally my job description to feed you all, so really, if anything sounds good—or bad, for that matter—just say so." She reaches up to thumb away a tear. "I'm also here if you ever want to talk."

I'm gripped by the urge to do exactly that. At the same time, I feel a pang of sadness. I want my mom. She's the one who should be here right now wiping away my tears. She's the one I should be able to confide in, to look to for guidance.

I also don't want to overwhelm her any further or upset her. She's been through so, so much. Why add to the pile if in all likelihood I'm going to end up not keeping this baby?

And in all honesty, I'm not sure I want her advice. I love my mom dearly, and she was a good parent to us. But I definitely don't want her life, which is why I'm so invested in making different decisions than she did.

I also don't want my dad to find out. Even though he and Mom aren't getting along at all right now, I know she'd tell him. And I know he'd flip his shit. I don't need him to scare me; I'm already terrified.

"I appreciate that, Patsy. Thank you. And thanks for the sandwich."

"Anytime. I gotta get lunch going. Holler if you need anything, all right?"

I smile. "All right. Tell Sally I said hey."

"Tell her I'm brainstorming her wedding day boots!" Mollie calls after Patsy's retreating back.

I land heavily in my chair and take a bite of the grilled cheese. It's all I can do not to moan. Patsy knows what's up. The sandwich is buttery, rich, just the right ratio of bread to cheese.

"That looks really good," Mollie says. "Can I have the other half?"

I nudge the wax paper toward her. "All yours. I get hungry, and then I eat because if I don't, that's when I start to feel nauseous. But then I get full really quickly so I can't finish the meal I started. I'm finding it's best if I kind of graze throughout the day."

"Exactly how I felt my first trimester. Keep snacks handy. Or, really, keep a thoughtful cowboy around who feeds you just when you need it."

I close my eyes, tears spilling over again. "Fucking Duke."

"Fuck that guy. How *dare* he think of you?"

"Rude."

She scoffs. "Dump his ass."

"Good thing we're not dating."

Mollie pauses as she takes a bite of grilled cheese. "Damn, that's good. You know what's not good?"

"What?"

"You sabotaging yourself like this. I know you like him. I know you're wildly, indecently attracted to him. He's good to you. You're good to him. Why *not* date the guy? I mean, even your biology is begging you to make him your boyfriend." She nods at my stomach.

I roll my eyes while I polish off another bite of my sandwich. "You know why."

"You and Duke aren't gonna end up like your parents, Wheeler."

"But that's just it, Mol. This is exactly how my parents got together. Their marriage—they did it for all the wrong reasons."

"But think about it. You've been trying to sabotage your nonrelationship with Duke since before you were pregnant. You were clearly into him before this all happened, so it's not like y'all hit it off just because a baby is in the picture." She drops what's left of her grilled cheese onto the wax paper and grabs a tissue from a nearby box, which she uses to wipe her hands. "Look, I know your parents well, but obviously I wasn't around when they met and got together. From my understanding, they thought they were doing the right thing. It was a different time, and it happened under different circumstances."

"True."

"But I think the biggest difference is that your parents weren't friends. Obviously they were lovers—"

"Jesus Christ, can you *please* not use that word in reference to my parents?"

Mollie grins. "You get what I'm saying, right? Maybe Tim and Frannie had chemistry, but they weren't *friends*. They didn't talk to each other the way you and Duke talk. They didn't have shared interests. I think they did love each other at one point, but did they ever *like* each other?" She shrugs. "I'm not sure."

My heart hammers. I've never thought about my parents' relationship that way. I always knew they weren't well suited for each other. Dad is obsessed with work and golf, while Mom loves music and her sisters and books. My parents would occasionally go out to a concert, and every so often, they'd get us a sitter so they could attend parties in our neighborhood when we were little.

Beyond that, though, I don't ever recall them doing something fun together. I really don't remember them talking to each other about anything other than work, my brothers and me, or the house.

They had a shared life, but shared interests? Not really.

"Now you and Duke, on the other hand—wouldn't you say y'all are friends?" Mollie asks.

I can barely hear her above the thump of my pulse in my ears. "I mean…I don't know. I think he's a hookup more than anything else, right?"

Mollie shoots me a look. "Do hookups take note of your cravings and then call in a favor to have that craving fulfilled?" She nods at my half-eaten grilled cheese. "Do they drive twenty hours across the country during a snowstorm so you can make it to a trunk show for your business? Do they move you into their adorable cottage—"

"The cottage is really freaking cute."

"And make sure you have a bed and clean sheets and curtains and peppermint tea?"

I furrow my brow. "How do you know about the tea?"

"Where do you think he got it from? I had a stash at my cabin."

My stomach is doing somersault after somersault. Oddly enough, I don't feel nauseous, however. I feel...

Like smiling. And crying.

I want to give Duke a hug. Then I wanna strip him down and take him to bed.

"Y'all both have big dreams," Mollie continues. "You both want to see the world. Do something different with your careers and your lives. You're both scary good at darts."

"I'm better, actually," I say with a grin.

"You make him laugh, Wheeler." Mollie reaches over to tuck my hair behind my ear. "He loves being around you. Cash and the guys were always rolling their eyes over how much Duke talked about you. He's obsessed with you, friend, and I think that's because y'all have managed to create this beautiful friendship. Yeah, y'all slept together. But you were friends first. Still are. And *that* is why you guys won't end up like your parents."

A feeling, warm and light and real, rises through my center.

Mollie is right.

Deep down, I know she's *right*. Maybe I got pregnant just like Mom did, but that's where the similarities between our circumstances end. Duke *is* a good friend. I'm a good friend to him.

Which means I have to keep putting myself out there. Keep being vulnerable and keep opening myself to his wonderfulness. And damn is he wonderful. I could easily fall in love with this man.

What if that's what's meant to happen?

And if I'm meant to fall in love with Duke, does that mean we're meant to have this baby? Raise him or her together in his cute little cottage, surrounded by the family and friends we know and love?

"It's a beautiful idea." I have to look away from Mollie's kind eyes, or I'll burst into tears all over again. "But what about—he's not ready to settle down, and I'm not sure I am either."

Mollie nods. "The baby would kind of blow up those plans to be free."

"Yes."

"I mean..." Mollie tilts her head. "I can't help but think about my mom. Not that she's someone we necessarily want to look up to, but she had me in her twenties, and then she got a whole bunch of freedom later on, which she used to build her business. Ask her if she'd do it any differently, and I don't think she would."

I nod. "I like that idea—that having a baby doesn't mean you're stuck in the house forever."

"Something else to consider—I'm splitting my time between the ranch and Dallas, so y'all could too if you wanted. There's lots of helping hands around here, Wheeler. Lots of people who'd adore that sweet child and babysit anytime if you asked them. Trust me—everyone's already offered to babysit this little one." She rubs the swell of her belly. "Even Ella and Junie."

My chest squeezes when I imagine those two loving up on a newborn. The ranch would be a pretty damn great place to raise kids. The isolation would be hard in the beginning, but I imagine a childhood spent running wild, riding on horseback, and learning a trade that goes back generations would be nothing short of magical.

It'd be so different from the way I was raised.

"But you and Cash knew you wanted babies right away." I pick up my grilled cheese. "Why? How?"

Mollie grabs her sandwich too and takes a thoughtful bite. "As cliché as it sounds, it just felt right. I never imagined falling in love with someone and marrying them and then getting pregnant would happen so quickly. But before coming to Hartsville..." She takes a breath, lets it out. "I was really unhappy. Well, unhappy in some areas of my life."

"I remember."

"When I got here, got to know Cash—it was like the world cracked open. I understood myself and my dreams in a way I never had before."

"Yes." *Yes.*

"And I realized that some of the dreams I'd always had weren't actually making me very happy. It was the worst, best surprise ever. So I ditched those dreams, kept some others, and got a few new ones."

"Your story is beautiful. Just like you." I toss the last bit of crust into my mouth. I hadn't realized how bad I felt until just now, physically and emotionally. Because all of a sudden, I feel *so* much better.

The powers of grilled cheese. And a guy's thoughtfulness. And a friend's wisdom.

I'm not glad I got pregnant, but I am glad to be here right now. In a room with my best friend on a beautiful ranch that's run by indecently good-looking, deeply kind cowboys.

"You can make your story beautiful too, Wheeler."

The light in my center dims. I'm coming around to

the idea that it's possible—probable, even—that I won't repeat my parents' patterns, whether I have this baby or not. But me deserving happiness?

Deserving a guy like Duke?

Something inside me still balks at that.

"Remember when you first pulled into town?" I say with a laugh. "We were on the phone, and you told me you swore you saw Buffalo Bill or whoever getting off his horse. You thought you'd gone back in time."

It's an obvious change of subject, but Mollie doesn't call me out on it.

Instead, she laughs too. "That was Wyatt. He was collecting his poker money at the Rattler."

"Little did you know he'd end up being the best man at your wedding."

"Small world."

"Small town."

Mollie's smile touches her eyes. "Since when are you a cheeseball?"

"The baby," I say, patting my own stomach. "It's making me stupid."

"Hm." Mollie taps a finger against her chin. "Better answer: it's the guy who put that baby in your belly who's making you so adorably mushy."

I grab a tissue to wipe my hands. "I don't do mushy."

"But you are doing mushy. Right now, I see it. And it looks good on you."

I don't want to smile, but I do.

That keeps happening. Why is my first impulse to fight good feelings? Maybe I don't trust them. Or, more likely, I don't believe I deserve good things, period.

That's ignorance talking.

"I heard back from Rory," I say. He's our master boot maker out in San Antonio. He's the guy who turns our designs into reality: he'll handcraft several samples of each of our boots until we're all obsessed with the result.

"Really?" Mollie gasps. "And?"

"And he's going to fast-track those prototypes for the men's collection. He had a cancellation, so we should have them by the end of the week."

Mollie smiles, biting her lip. "Bet Duke's gonna be happy."

I'm smiling just thinking about how thrilled he'll be. And isn't that the definition of friendship? Going out of your way to thrill someone? *Knowing* how to thrill them because you've learned who they are and what turns them on?

I wonder if Duke would be open to some kind of official collaboration. Maybe...hell, maybe he'd like the idea of joining us full-time. I could draft a proposal, then run it by Mollie. I think she'd be open to expanding our company, right?

My gut seizes. *Fear.*

My heart flutters. *Hope.*

Just for today, I try on something new.

I let hope win.

CHAPTER 23
Caught in the Act
Wheeler

The next evening, however, it's my, ahem, **need** *that* wins out.

I blame Duke for showing up to lunch with a Stetson on his head and a three-year-old on each hip.

Ava had the day off from her job as a barrel racing trainer over at the Wallace Ranch, a nearby property where the Wallace family has bred horses for generations. So she brought the girls with her to the New House to eat.

I was walking into the kitchen after a call with Rory when I stopped dead in my tracks. My mouth legitimately went dry as I took in the tall cowboy holding two giggling toddlers.

"Tickle monster!" he said over and over as he somehow managed to tickle them with his one or two free fingers.

June and Ella were in stitches. When it was time to sit at the table, neither of them let him put them down. Instead, they both squeezed onto his lap, and Ella put her head on his shoulder. Duke, being the fucking magical human being he is, leaned his cheek on her head. He let both girls continue to sit on his lap throughout the meal, and it was all I could do not to burst into a fiery ball of want as I watched him coax them into eating their "pea peas."

Somehow, I managed to work for a few hours at the New House afterward. I blame the nice chunk of change that hit our business checking account earlier today for the burst of motivation. Because the presale for the Aspen trunk show did so well, we decided to try it again for another pop-up we're doing in Nashville.

It sold it out in *three* minutes. The best part? We just got a five-figure payout.

A growing sense of certainty—of peace—settles in my center. Maybe I was crazy to start a boot company with my best friend, but it's working. More than that— Mollie and I and our business are *thriving*.

For so long, I wasn't nearly as successful, financially speaking, as my peers who became lawyers or bankers. But I'm getting there.

"I'm so damn proud of y'all," Haines says.

I decided to give him a call on my short drive from the New House to Duke's cottage. I want to check in on him—how his last couple days with Mom were—and I also want to share my good news with someone.

"I'm proud of us too." I hit the brakes when I see a snake slithering across the dirt road. Despite how warm it is, I shiver. Not sure I'll ever get used to *that*.

"Not that I'm surprised. Between Mollie's creative talent and your brain power, I always knew y'all would knock it out of the park."

My center—hell, my entire being—glows. "I'm learning, slowly but surely, to have that kind of faith in myself."

"I hope you know how much I admire you for chasing your dreams. You think you took the easy way out by not going to law school, but I beg to differ. Think y'all will be hiring this time next year?"

I grin. Haines is taking an extra year at college to graduate with dual degrees in business and history next May. Like me, he doesn't want to follow in Dad and Preston's footsteps and pursue a career in corporate law. Problem is my younger brother isn't sure what else he'd want to do.

"I love the idea of you coming to work for us." I mean that. Haines is smart, well-spoken, and hardworking. He also loves fashion as much as I do. "If business keeps going in the right direction, we can definitely talk about it."

"I'd offer to intern as a model, but you already have a hot cowboy in your stable. I mean, on your roster."

"Ha."

"How is Hottie in the Backward Hat?"

So. Fucking. Hot.

"He's good."

"Have y'all…"

"Made a decision yet? No. But."

I turn into a grove that's bursting with green, and I feel a familiar flutter when the cottage comes into view. Will I ever get over how *beautiful* this little slice of heaven is? I half expect Snow White to walk out the front door, birds landing on her shoulders as she steps into the afternoon sun.

Haines scoffs. "Hello? You can't leave me hanging like that!"

I put my car in park and kill the engine, keeping the windows rolled down. Snow White's birds chirp and sing as I let my head fall back on the seat.

"When this first happened, I thought there was no way we'd keep the baby."

My brother gasps. "But now you're thinking about keeping it? Him? Her? Sorry, it feels wrong to refer to a baby as 'it.'"

I laugh. "Agreed. I still can't wrap my head around the whole thing. But I talked to Mollie, and...I mean, is it crazy to think having a baby with a guy I'm not even dating might end with us making the happy family I've always wanted?"

"Aw, Wheeler. You're getting me choked up. What a beautiful idea. Not crazy. It would be crazy if you wanted to have a baby with a deadbeat. But Duke is..." Haines scoffs again. "Not that."

I close my eyes, heart thumping. "I haven't told him what I'm thinking."

"Somehow I don't think he'll react poorly to this development."

"Seriously? If I say I want to keep the baby, I'll be upending his life. He's already said he wants to be involved, which means—"

Another gasp. "He said that?"

"He did."

"Be still my beating heart. My God, Wheeler. Maybe he wants to keep the baby too."

My stomach flips at the idea. "Would you...be there? If I had this baby and we, like, needed you?"

"Of course." No hesitation. No qualifications.

In many ways, Haines bore the brunt of my parents' divorce. My parents' relationship got worse and worse—borderline abusive—as the years went on. Preston and I were able to escape the worst of it since we were in college. But Haines was stuck at home, witnessing the awfulness firsthand on his own.

It's kind of a miracle he didn't turn out to be a douche like Preston. Instead, he's an awesome human being brimming with empathy.

Reminds me a lot of Duke, come to think of it.

"Thank you." My voice trembles. "I'm scared, Haines."

"I know you are."

"Can you imagine what Dad's gonna say?"

"Fuck him. If he wants to react like a lunatic, let him. It's his loss."

I nod. "You're right."

"I think Mom would be happy. Mostly because you found such a great guy. You know she's gonna go bananas over Duke, right?"

Laughing, I slide a hand over my mouth. "You're jumping twenty steps ahead here."

"Because it's gonna happen—Mom is gonna meet Duke, and she's gonna love him. She's also gonna be thrilled about the baby."

"You think so?"

"I know so. Mom might be a little leery that y'all's relationship is so new, but she'll see right away that Duke is special. And she loves kids, Wheeler. Why do you think she had three of them with a guy as awful as Dad? That's how bad she wanted to be a mom. She's going to love the excuse to be busy too. You need help, Mom's gonna be there."

I blink, the realization hitting me. Haines is kind of right. I assumed she wouldn't want to be embroiled in more messiness. I assumed she'd want to enjoy her newfound freedom, not spend her time babysitting my kid.

Why can't she do both, though? Could I afford the childcare we need? Duke would pitch in, I'm sure, which means we wouldn't have to rely on Mom to watch the baby full-time. She could enjoy being a grandma.

My chest twists. All things considered, Duke and I are lucky we're in a decent enough position to consider these things. The childcare piece is huge now that I'm thinking about it. Mollie and Cash are going to hire a nanny. Could we nanny share, I wonder? Or are there options for day care in Hartsville? I know Ella and Junie go to preschool in the mornings.

Duke might know more. If he doesn't, I'm relatively certain he'd be more than happy to find out.

"We could make some pretty delicious lemonade out of these lemons if we wanted to, huh?" I ask.

"Duke will bring the sugar."

I burst out laughing. "You're gross."

"You want him. Go get your cowboy. Maybe have his baby while you're at it."

That's the thing, though. Just because I may want to have Duke's baby doesn't mean we're going to end up together. But I am warming up to the idea.

I go inside, munch on some crackers, and then grab a shower. Duke didn't show up until after four yesterday, so I have some time to myself.

The crackers keep my nausea at bay, and I actually

feel pretty damn good as I tilt back my head and let the hot water rinse off the day.

Rinse off the dread and guilt that's plagued me for what feels like weeks now.

In their place rises a sense of effervescent possibility.

Yes, this all could blow up in my face. That's the most likely scenario.

What if it works out, though?

What if I take a chance on me and on Duke and on our ability to say fuck what everyone else thinks so we can live life on our terms?

Live a life different from everything we've known. Everything we've seen.

Soaping up a washcloth, I run it over my chest. A bolt of heat moves from my nipple to my clit. I think of Duke. How perfectly his ass filled out his Wranglers. The way his shirt drew taut over his shoulder blades and back as he grabbed his hat from the rack by the kitchen door and dropped it on his head before going back to work after lunch.

I run the washcloth over my nipples again, the nubby fabric catching on their overly sensitive peaks. My boobs are sore, but it feels kinda good to touch them this way.

That heat spreads between my legs, making my clit throb. Closing my eyes, I revel in the fact that I feel like myself again and not some perpetually sick, chronically confused mess.

I feel sexy. At home in my body, even though it feels different.

I miss the feel of Duke's hands on me. My God, can that man fuck. Best sex of my life, no question. And that big, beautiful dick of his—

Next thing I know, I'm tossing the washcloth aside and grabbing the showerhead off its holder. When was the last time I had an orgasm? I don't remember. Before I found out I was pregnant, I was trying not to masturbate, because every time I did, I ended up thinking about Duke. That was a problem then.

Is it still a problem now?

I tuck the showerhead between my legs. The multiple streams of water hit my center all at once, sending a shock wave through me that has me gasping for air. My cunt spasms, once, and I bite my lip.

How I'm this turned on this quickly, I don't know.

That's a lie. I totally know why I'm about to come in two seconds. It's that fucking cowboy I'm living with. Him and his smiles and his shoulders and those *lips*.

I thumb my nipple, imagining him taking it in his mouth. The water hits my clit, my heart rate spiking. I roll my hips, seeking more, the intensity of how hot the water is and how badly I want to come almost overwhelming.

This feels *so* damn good.

Spreading my legs a little wider, I notice they start to shake. Pressure grows in my center. I can't breathe. Can't think.

I want him.

I want you, Duke, so bad it's killing me.

I adjust the showerhead so that it's aimed directly at my clit now. My hips buck. I roll my thumb over one nipple, then the other, and imagine the pressure between my legs is Duke pushing inside me.

I'll make room, sweetheart. Let me in.

"God, Duke, I want to let you in," I breathe. "I want that more than anything, but I—"

Pleasure—pain—it rips through me in a way it never, ever has before. This orgasm has teeth, and it takes over the entirety of my body. My toes curl. My calves flex. My thighs shake and my hips roll, and my tits feel hard and overly large in my hands.

I *scream*. "Oh my *God*!"

What—

How—I read about this, I think, orgasms being better when you're pregnant—

A loud *bang* has me opening my eyes, my heart leaping to my throat as I let out another scream.

Duke is standing in the doorway. He's still wearing his cowboy hat, and even through the slightly fogged-up glass, I can see the sweat that stains his shirt, causing it to cling to his chest and stomach.

That chest is heaving, like he just dominated the hundred-meter dash. Eyes wide. Mouth open.

I stand there and shake, facing him, the showerhead poised between my legs as my cunt's spasms slowly begin to die down. I have the other hand on my breast.

Duke can see everything.

Oh my God, he can see everything.

And still I don't move as his eyes rake down my body, stopping to linger on my tits. I blush violently, my cheeks and neck and chest prickling.

I should have some shame here. I do, clearly. But I also…don't?

I *like* his eyes on me.

He puts a hand on his chest. "What the hell was that? You okay?" His voice echoes in the room.

"I—" *Have no words, because you just walked in on me coming harder than I ever have in my life while thinking about you.* "I'm fine."

His eyes dip to the showerhead. I lift it, settling it back in its cradle. The gentle patter and slap of the water on the tiled floor fills the silence.

"Why'd you scream, then?"

I put my face in my hands. "Um."

"Almost sounded like you were in pain."

"I wasn't. I just—I felt good. Well, not sick, so I—I decided to—stress relief, and I think because I'm pregnant—"

"Your orgasm hit you like a ton of bricks?"

I blink. "Yeah."

"I read about it. How they can be more intense because of the increased blood flow to"—he clears his throat, a pink flush working its way up the thick column of his throat—"that area."

I surprise us both by laughing.

"What?" he asks.

"Of course you read about it."

I want you more than words can say, but I'm still scared.

He runs a hand over his face, his expression pained. "I just wanna know what's goin' on with you is all. So I can, you know, be there for you."

My heart dips. "You've been wonderful, Duke. Thank you. Sincerely."

"Thanks for saying that." His Adam's apple bobs. "I'm trying my best."

I know you are, cowboy.

"And don't worry. I asked Dr. Martinez if it was okay—"

"I'm not worried." He runs his hand over his face again before dropping it to his hip. "Or I should say, that's not what I'm worried about."

I finally have the peace of mind to attempt to cover myself, crossing my arms over my chest. "What are you worried about?"

God, I wanna ask you to come in.

"How fucking gorgeous you look," he replies hoarsely.

Now it's my stomach dipping, a sudden drop that gives me a wobbly feeling in my knees. Heat flares to renewed life between my legs.

"That's something to be worried about?" I manage.

"Yeah, sweetheart. Me walking in on you making yourself come in my shower and looking fucking beautiful while doing it is definitely something to be worried about."

I don't know what to say, so I drop my arms and blurt, "My boobs are bigger."

Do I just freaking ask him to take off his clothes already and get in here? I shouldn't.

I really, really shouldn't.

He runs his tongue over his bottom lip, his nostrils flaring as his eyes lock on my breasts. "I can tell."

"And sensitive. Really sensitive. Everywhere."

He makes a strangled sound and drops his head.

"Are you okay?" I breathe.

"Naw, Blue." He shakes his head. "I ain't okay." And then he looks up, the naked hunger in his blue eyes sending my pulse into a tailspin. "You gonna ask me to join you? Or am I gonna have to beg?"

Oh God. Oh my fucking God.

I don't know what any of this means or where this is going. All I know is I want this man more than I want my next breath.

He's already making this fun.

Already being playful and intense and all the things that I apparently find irresistible in the opposite sex.

Maybe because I like being playful too.

"You as desperate as you look, cowboy?"

He reaches for his belt. The muscles in his forearms bunch and release as he unbuckles it, yanking it through his belt loops with a single, vicious tug. He drops it on the floor, the buckle hitting the tile with a metallic *thud*. "Been desperate for you all damn day. Every day. All the days, ever since Aspen."

"Would you get on your knees for me?"

His jaw twitches, one side of his mouth curling upward. Without a word, he drops down one leg at a time. "What else you want, sweetheart?"

"Your hat. Your shirt. Take it all off."

Reaching up, he takes off his hat and sets it on its crown on the vanity. Then he bends his elbow and gathers the back collar of his shirt in his fist, tugging it over his head in one smooth, wildly sexy motion.

My eyes catch on the wiry, dark blond hair that covers his chest. He's thick everywhere, shoulders and arms and abs, and my entire being pulses with the knowledge that I get to have all that.

I get to have *him*. I feel downright giddy. And relieved.

He runs a hand through his thick hair, which is matted thanks to the hat and likely some sweat too.

"Now your jeans. Take all that off, and then"—I lick

my lips—"I want you to take yourself in your hand. Get yourself ready for me."

He chuckles, a dark, low sound I feel in my nipples, and unzips his jeans. "Blue, you best believe I'm ready. Hard as shit already. See?" He reaches inside his briefs and pulls out his dick.

He is hard.

He's also huge and already leaking.

He pumps his hand slowly, his stomach caving as he sucks in a breath. "You know how many times I've done this thinking of you?"

I put a hand on the glass. "I was thinking about you too."

"You were?" His expression softens for a beat, even as the tendons in his neck pop while he strokes himself a little faster. "What was I doing?"

Loving me.

"You were just…you." I swallow thickly. "You said you were willing to beg. So beg."

He smirks, his chest heaving. "Please. Please, sweetheart, let me make you feel good. I can't—" He makes a choking sound as he thumbs his tip, the playfulness in his expression morphing into hard, almost pained need. "I can't take it anymore. Bein' apart from you. I dream all the time about touching you again. Hearing you say my name while I make you come. The look on your face when I come inside you—I miss it. I miss you. So fucking much. So please, Blue, put me out of my goddamn misery already and ask me to touch you."

Well, damn. That's some A-plus begging right there.

I struggle for air. "Will you come in now? Please?"

"So polite after being so fuckin' bossy."

"I'm done waiting." Turning, I open the shower door. "Aren't you?"

CHAPTER 24
Shared Shower Situation
Duke

This is happening.

I blink. And blink again, giving my dick a hard squeeze just to make sure this is real. My balls contract, the ache there making me groan.

Wheeler is naked in my shower.

She's asking me to join her after getting off with the showerhead while thinking about me.

I get up, ignoring the way my knees burn from being on the floor as I shuck off my jeans and briefs and socks with hands that shake.

We lock eyes. Hers are wide and full of white-hot feeling.

An ache with sharp edges hollows out my torso as I devour her glistening body with my eyes. Her shoulders are proud, pushed back, which puts her tits on prominent display. They're fuller now, the nipples slightly darker.

Her body's already changing.

My dick screams. I make a sound I don't recognize.

The urge to protect her, fill her, care for her, is so fierce it nearly knocks me over.

"You look so fuckin' pretty with my baby inside you."

Her eyes go even wider, her breath catching in her throat.

It's a totally inappropriate thing to say. Last we spoke on the subject, it was pretty clear that we're most likely not going to go through with the pregnancy. I don't wanna push her one way or the other. Push her into doing something she's not ready for.

But fuck, maybe I'm ready.

"Duke—"

"I'm sorry, that was—"

"You make me feel pretty." Her chest falls on an exhale. "I love the way you make me feel. So put your hands on me already."

My pulse thunders. She's not turned off by what I just said.

In fact, she's quite clearly turned on by it.

What does that mean?

"Fuck, Blue. Just…fuck." Taking the door in my hand, I close it behind me as I step in the shower. The water is hot enough to sting. I love it. "You know that's my job, right? To make you feel pretty and make you feel safe?"

Wheeler moves back, her eyelashes fluttering as her gaze rakes down my chest and stomach, landing on my dick. When she looks back up, I realize how much taller I am than she is. I tower over her, the two of us barely fitting inside the shower, even though it doubled in size during our recent renovations.

"Such an overachiever, crushing both those things," she whispers.

I notch my finger underneath her chin. Use my thumb to pull her bottom lip open, cursing at her softness. "Nerds unite."

She smiles.

That's it.

That's fucking *it*.

I move my hand to the back of her head and bend my neck and slant my mouth over hers, the water coursing down the sides of our bodies. Her familiar taste and feel flood my senses, drawing a groan from the back of my throat.

Her hands find my neck, her thumbs caressing my jaw, and my arms break out in goose bumps as she licks inside my mouth.

"Oh, baby," she breathes. "Thank God. I missed you. I missed you so much."

Baby.

Wheeler just called me baby.

Also, she missed me.

My heart—I'm not sure it's working anymore.

My dick, however, most certainly is. I step into her, pressing myself against her belly, and she bites the corner of my mouth before kissing the shit out of me. Our kiss is hot and deep, the two of us drinking each other in like we've been in the desert for forty days and forty nights and we've just stumbled on an oasis of abundance.

I run a hand down her back, my fingertips trailing along the knobs of her spine. "I've missed you too."

She's got her hands on my chest, my shoulders, my stomach. Exploring. Memorizing.

Loving.

My balls are in agony.

I gently cup her breasts. "You still hurting here?"

"Uh-huh." She kisses my neck. "But it also feels good when you touch them. Just be careful."

I break the kiss to look down. I tenderly feather the pad of my thumb over one nipple, cupping the weight of her breast in my palm.

"*Oh.*" Wheeler's hand lands heavily on my shoulder.

I go still. "Too much?"

She shakes her head, looking at me through heavy-lidded eyes. "Good. Great. See? You're so—*yes*, baby."

I start thumbing the other nipple. "Say that again."

"You're so good at—"

"No. The other part." I hold her eyes.

She bites her lip. "You like it when I call you baby."

"Uh-huh." I love when she smiles, recognizing that I'm repeating her breathless words. "I like it a lot."

Keeping her eyes on mine, she reaches between us. Wraps her hand around my dick, thumbing my head just the way I like. Desire, urgent, cracks down my middle.

"I see that."

"I'm not coming in your hand." I reach for the showerhead. "I'm taking over, yeah? Lemme just give myself a quick scrub—"

"I'll do it." She grins. "You need it."

The spiraling need between my legs becomes acute. "You sure?"

"Of course I'm sure."

"All right, then. Soap. Hands. Now."

Laughing softly, she does as I tell her, lathering up her hands with a good amount of soap. I watch as she washes me. She starts with my chest and shoulders. My eyes nearly roll to the back of my head when she washes my hair, applying just the right pressure to my scalp to make my cock feel like it's going to fall off.

She's taking care of me. Same as I've cared for her.

I jump when her hands move to my armpits and jump again when she fists my dick and gives it a hard, slippery tug.

"Anything changed?" I grunt.

"What do you mean?"

"I got condoms under the sink—"

"Nothing's changed." She gives me another tug and another. "What about you?"

Wrong that I'm fucking thrilled she hasn't been with anyone since me? Granted, she's pregnant, but we only just found out. Aspen was, what, four weeks ago? She could've easily gone out and hooked up with someone new.

She didn't, though. I'd like to think I know what that means.

I drop my hands to her ass, giving her a gentle squeeze there. "Blue, you think I been able to so much as think about anyone else since I was with you?"

She's biting her bottom lip again.

Shit, she's biting back a smile, isn't she? She *likes* that I haven't stopped thinking about her.

I know—fuck *yes*, I know—she hasn't stopped thinking about me either.

How do I convince you to let that feeling win, sweetheart?

Wheeler is turned on, but she's also sore. Tender might be a better word. Much as I wanna fuck her senseless against the shower wall, I think that might be too much for her right now.

I put the showerhead back in its cradle. Giving my hair and body one last rinse, I sit on the little tiled bench Cash insisted we install in the shower.

"Mollie says it helps her shave her legs," he'd explained at the time. "Might be good to have in case, you know, a woman lives here someday."

I thought it was a waste of money, but now I'm mentally thanking my older brother up and down for insisting we put the bench in the shower. I wave Wheeler over with one hand and take my cock in the other.

"How do we do this?" she asks.

"I want to make this as easy as possible for you. I also wanna make you come again, and I think I'll be able to do that pretty quick if you sit on my lap. Face the other way so that your back is to my front."

"Oh, I see."

"Yep. You're gonna sit on my dick, and I'm gonna play with that pretty little cunt while you ride me."

"So rude."

"Mind in the gutter. Turn around, Blue."

Giving me one last, hot look, she does as I tell her. I lean forward to loop an arm around her waist.

"I'll hold you up so you can take as much of me as you want. Don't try to be a hero, okay?"

The unspoken words hang between us: *Let's not hurt you or the baby.*

Wheeler nods. I dip my fingers between her legs. Her back arches when I glide them over her clit. She's soft and swollen and slick.

Ready for me.

I use my knee to nudge her legs a little wider. Use

my hand to angle my dick just right. Then I readjust my arm so that it's looped tightly around her waist and start to guide her down.

"Sit, sweetheart. You're gonna feel some pressure. Use your words if it's too much."

She nods, looking down. My tip meets with her entrance, and we moan together at that first bit of contact. She sinks a little deeper, then starts to shake.

I tighten my grip on her waist. "Too much."

"You gotta trust me, baby." She shakes her head and sinks lower. "I can take it."

Fuck.

Fuck fuck fuck.

"Then take it," I grit out.

I can tell she's in pain, her back and shoulders tensing. But she doesn't stop. Her thighs flex as her cunt swallows me bit by bit.

Heaven.

Soft, excruciatingly tight heaven.

Her hands are on the arm I have around her waist. She digs her nails into my skin, but she doesn't fucking stop.

Curling her pelvis outward so that her ass sticks out, she sits all the way down.

"*Duke*," she whimpers, a strangled sound.

I love the feel of her. Even her back is soft, and I pull her against me, skin to skin.

I kiss the spot where her neck slopes into her shoulder and move up my hand a little to caress her breast.

"So brave," I whisper against her neck. "Take all the time you need. Then I want you to fuck me."

She lets out a breathless laugh. "I am fucking you."

"Naw, sweetheart." I thumb her nipple. "I want you to fuck me like you mean it. Lemme feel how hard you come."

Her head falls back on my shoulder, her weight settling against my chest. Now that I have a free hand, I snake it over her hip and belly.

When I feel her pussy splayed around me, I just about lose my shit. She's split wide open, totally at my mercy. It takes every ounce of strength not to impale her on a handful of hard, merciless thrusts in a bid to chase down the orgasm that presses in on me from all sides.

"We fit," I choke out, rolling my index finger over her clit. "Perfect. Perfectly. You feel perfect, sweetheart."

Reaching back, she digs her fingers into the hair at the nape of my neck. "I love how you feel. Full. Not an inch to spare."

She rolls her hips. It's a tiny movement, and she hisses at what I imagine is the fullness she's talking about. But I keep playing with her clit and her tits, a different fullness filling me as her hips move a little faster. Her thrusts become a little deeper.

Then all of a sudden, she's riding me. Her hands find my knees, which give her some leverage as she lifts her hips, brings them back down, over and over again, her cunt's firm grip on me almost unbearable. Her tits bounce in my hands.

"Baby." Her hands are on my hands now, both of us massaging her breasts. "You're the best. Best I've ever had. I'm so close already. I never come twice in a row, but I—*oh*, baby, you're just—you're different in all the best ways."

I knocked you up, and now you're coming more. You're coming harder.

You're only gonna come with me, sweetheart.

I watch in awe as her body rises on a wave of ecstasy. Her ass moves in these delicious little circles, and I can't help it. I grab her hips and guide her in a few especially deep rounds, thrusting my hips to meet her at the apex of her own thrusts.

She reaches down to touch her clit. Playing with herself just like I told her to. Then—

Bam. Her cunt spasms, clamping down on me.

Blinding white light obscures my vision. She cries out my name and then whimpers *baby, baby, baby* over and over again as her body shakes and her cunt's contractions milk me to the edge of my own orgasm.

She's a shaking, shuddering mess when she comes down.

We both are.

But I gotta be the one to keep it together. I meant what I said about keeping her safe. I wanna be her rock. Prove that I have no intention of hurting or abandoning her the way others clearly have in the past.

Curling my hands around her ribs, I run my thumbs up the sweet little furrow of her spine.

What's it gonna take to convince you I'm for real?

Wheeler collapses against my chest, boneless, breathing hard. Her hand finds my thigh. She gives me a hard, almost painful squeeze.

"You okay?" I pant.

She shakes her head. "Yes. No. I don't know, Duke."

Her voice is thick. My heart trips to a stop.

She's crying.

Steam billows around us. I should probably get her out of here sooner rather than later—the heat can't be good for her or the baby.

Look at that. I'm already thinking of both of them. Not just Wheeler. Does that mean I'm in this for them both now? That I'd have this baby not just to keep Wheeler around but because I really wanna be a daddy too?

This about-face I'm doing gives me whiplash. Twenty-four hours ago, I was sure I wasn't ready to be a dad. At the very least, I was sure it was the right call to prioritize other things—work, travel, friendships.

Now?

Now I'm thinking I want everything, all at once. This girl and our baby and my evolving notion of freedom.

Am I nuts to think that could happen? Or is that just how life works—you make choices, and you work your ass off to build a dream life out of them, however messy or chaotic or exhausting it might be?

Because I ain't afraid of hard work.

I am afraid of fucking this up and losing my chance with Wheeler.

"Aw, sweetheart." I nudge her head to the side with my nose and kiss her neck. "Imma make it okay. Give me a minute, yeah? Then I'll dry you off and take you to bed."

She nods. "Sounds nice."

She starts to rock her hips again, but I use my hands to still the motion.

"Let me take over. You relax. Unless you wanna come again?"

Wheeler scoffs. "I think I might literally die if that happens."

"We'll wait a bit, then," I say into her neck. "I need you to stick around."

Then I start to fuck her in earnest. Holding on to her hips, I lift her a little so I can rock into her cunt. The friction is delicious and deliciously maddening. She moans, her head falling back even farther.

"You feel so good, baby," she whispers.

Sensation, searing and hot, rips through my center. The white light returns. I squeeze my eyes shut and surrender, the pressure in my balls releasing in a series of agonizing pulses. It feels like falling off a bike or a skateboard, the pavement rising up to meet me before I slam into it in a burning collision of skin and blood and bone.

I black out. For a second, an hour, a year, I have no fucking clue. All I know is when I come to, Wheeler's got my hands in hers, our fingers twined over her belly.

My heart thunders. *The baby.*

Our baby.

I'm gripped by that fierceness again.

I think I wanna have this kid. And if we have it, there's no way I'm letting another man raise her.

No way I'm letting another man touch Wheeler the way I'm touching her right now.

These girls—I'm still assuming we'll have a daughter—are *mine*. Maybe staking my claim makes me a caveman, but I don't give a fuck. I couldn't live with myself knowing I wasn't there for them. Knowing I didn't work my fingers to the bone to make them happy.

Take care of them the way they deserve to be cared for.

So I care for Wheeler the only way I know how—with everything I've got. I turn off the water. I help her gently to her feet. She wobbles, still orgasm-drunk, and her arms fly out in a desperate bid for balance.

"I got you." I keep my hands placed firmly on her waist. Pressing my front to her back, I use the bulk of my body to nudge her out of the shower. I grab a clean towel off a nearby shelf and wrap her in it. She shivers when I press a kiss to her nape.

"Cold?" I ask.

She glances at me over her shoulder. "Overwhelmed."

My chest cramps. Grabbing another towel, I make quick work of drying myself off, then wrap it around my waist.

Wheeler looks at me in the mirror above the vanity, its corners fogged over from the heat of the shower.

Her lips are swollen, eyes hazy as they rake over my bare shoulders and chest. "You're the pretty one."

"Glad you think so. You can admire me all you want when we're in bed." Bending down, I scoop her up into my arms. "Preferably with your hands."

Her lips curl into a small smile. She reaches up to play with a tendril of my hair as I walk the three steps to my bedroom. "What about dinner?"

"What about it? Thought I'd have you."

"Ha."

"Ain't gonna be funny when you're begging me to let you come again."

I set her on her feet, and before I know what's happening, she's letting the towel fall to the floor and she's stepping into me, pressing her tits against my chest at the same time as she wraps her arms around my neck.

Looking down at her, it strikes me how *happy* she

looks. Tired, sure. But her brown eyes are bright, the tears gone, and her skin is flush with color.

"I don't need your permission." Her eyes glide to my mouth.

I smirk. "But you do want my help."

She bites her lip. "I kinda do. I haven't been feeling my best lately, but you…" Her eyes flick to meet mine. "You really do make me feel beautiful and sexy, even though I'm bloated and sick and my body is—"

"Sensitive." I reach up to cup her breast, and her breath catches. "I know that's not always a good thing, but it is right now. So lemme make you feel good, Wheeler. I'll feed you. Then I'll fuck you. Rinse and repeat as many times as you want. 'Cause you're outta your mind if you think I'm letting you out of my sight tonight. Or my bed."

She blinks, expression softening. "I can't make any promises, Duke."

"I'm not asking you to. Tonight, all I want is your company. We'll talk about the rest tomorrow."

"Sounds too easy."

"Surely you know that *I'm* too easy when it comes to you."

She laughs, scrunching her brow. "I'm not sure that makes much sense—"

"Does it have to make sense if it feels this good?" I swallow. "Because you gotta admit, this feels really fucking good right now, sweetheart."

She cups my face in her hand. The tenderness of the gesture makes my stomach flip. "It does. I don't want it to end."

"Doesn't have to."

She searches my eyes. "I love what an optimist you are."

"Try it on. Optimism. Bet it'll fit you just fine."

She grins. "It doesn't come naturally to me. But I'll try."

"Good." I shape her waist with my hands, and she lets out a happy little yell when I toss her onto the bed. "You sleep here on one condition."

"Name it."

Aw, yeah, she wants to sleep beside me as much as I wanna sleep beside her.

"Keep calling me baby."

Her eyes ignite. "Consider it done. I know how much you like that."

"I do."

But that's a lie. I don't like it.

I fucking love it.

CHAPTER 25
Found Family
Wheeler

"Ho-ly shit." I force air into my lungs, feeling flattened in the best, most thorough way by the orgasm that just rocketed through my entire being. "Baby, that was—how—did I—I think I came for an hour? Is that why it's light out now?" I glance at the windows across from the bed, where thin gray light slants through the gap in the curtains.

Duke, who's currently moving over and inside me with my legs hiked over his shoulders, just grins. "Wish it was an hour. You feel"—he grunts, grin fading as he pins me to the mattress with an especially hard thrust—"so fucking good."

"Don't stop."

"Can't." He wraps a hand around my throat. He doesn't squeeze, just holds me there, eyes locked on mine in the semidarkness. "Won't."

I snake my hands to his waist and marvel at the play of muscles there. He's rock-hard, thick, and warm, his belly covered with a smattering of that dark blond hair.

His strength—his size—they're sexy. And kinda scary.

This is the fourth—or fifth or sixth, I've lost count—time we've had sex since we fell into bed yesterday afternoon. I'm sore, my pleasure tinged with a little more pain each time, and I never, ever want it to end.

We've only stopped screwing to eat, sleep, or snuggle. We made a quick supper of scrambled eggs and hash browns, and then we were back at it. You'd think we hadn't fucked for years for how insatiable we are. Duke's alarm just went off at four, but I was already awake and ready for him.

The bed sighs, a quiet, somehow happy sound, as Duke moves between my legs. I love—*love*—his bed. It's comfortable and warm, and it's not so big that we end up sleeping several feet apart. Instead, Duke insists we spoon, using an arm around my waist to curl my body into the bulk of his own.

He hasn't stopped touching me since the shower. He's always got a hand on my hip, a hand on my breast, a hand between my legs.

It wasn't lost on me that he fell asleep with his palm pressed to my belly. My throat closed in at the perfect tenderness of the moment. How safe I felt, surrounded not only by the heat of Duke's body but also by the growing sense that he might be changing his mind too.

He could easily avoid the subject of my pregnancy. Instead, he says shit like *you're so pretty with my baby inside you* and then keeps his hand on my stomach all night long. It makes me think he might *want* to be a dad.

He might want to be with me.

No question, Duke is going to be an awesome father. He's also going to be awesome to the mother of his children. How could he not be? He's been awesome to me, and I've been pregnant for all of a few weeks.

He's awesome in a way my dad never was to my mom. Which makes me think…

Duke and I might actually have a shot at a happy ending.

"These"—he leans down to take my nipple into his mouth—"still feel okay?"

Panting, I nod. "They feel fine."

"Good. That's where I'm gonna come."

Then he's pulling out of me, my legs dropping from his shoulders. My body cries out at the loss of him, but then he's taking himself in his hand, giving himself a few quick pumps while his eyes tear over my body.

"Fuck. So fucking pretty. Love your tits bigger like this. Love how sensitive the baby makes—*fuck*."

He shudders, and the next thing I know, ropes of his cum cover my breasts. It's warm, a little sticky. He looks down at me, and his nostrils flare.

What were you saying about our baby?

I'm dying to know.

I'm dying for him to ask me if I want to keep it. Because I think I do.

I really think I do.

Looking down, my insides clench. I'm covered in him. The sight of my nipples glistening with his release is obscene. Why do I get the feeling that he's marking me? Claiming me even?

I'm *hurting* between my legs, but I feel a renewed bloom of heat there anyway.

Meeting his eyes, I move my hand up. I use my first two fingers to gather up some of his cum off my nipple, my breath catching at the need that bolts through me when I touch myself there. Then I put those fingers in my mouth. He tastes salty. Hot.

He watches me, eyes going dark.

I like this. I want this. I want you.

Gently, he pulls my fingers out of my mouth. Leaning in, he kisses me, his tongue slipping between my lips. The kiss is tender, sweet, a startling counterpoint to the lewdness of a moment ago.

Oh, cowboy, this is exactly how I want to start my day every morning.

The thought turns me on. It also terrifies me.

He breaks the kiss and rests his forehead on mine, our noses touching. "Lemme take you to dinner."

My heart twists. "Are you asking me out on a date?"

Am I actually going to say yes this time?

"I am." He presses his lips to mine. "You gonna run again?"

My first instinct is to fight the smile that pulls at the edges of my lips.

Today, I let the smile win. "I'm not going anywhere, am I?"

"'Persistence pays off' is our new motto, huh?"

"I am all about the long game."

"501." I feel his mouth move into a smile against mine. "I remember. So is that a yes?"

My pulse thumps. My every instinct screams at me to turn him down. Dates are dangerous. If he gets too close, he's going to see my ugly parts. It's safer to keep him at arm's distance. We can still sleep together. We can even have a baby together. But we don't have to date.

I call bullshit.

I'm so sick of my bullshit. I don't know how to let

go of my fear of letting people in. But I think a date—an honest-to-goodness date—is a good place to start.

"Yes."

"Aw, yeah." He ducks his head to kiss my neck. "There's a fundraiser at Ella and June's school on Saturday at five thirty. What if, after that, I come grab you—"

"Wait. What's this fundraiser about?"

"You bid on the kids' art, they sing some songs for you, and everyone feels good about it. It's an hour, tops. I can be at your front door by seven at the latest."

I swallow. I don't know why—*oh, girl, you totally know why*—but the thought of going to the girls' fundraiser gives me butterflies. "Could I possibly come with you? To the fundraiser, I mean."

Dinner sounds really nice—that's a given. But I'm surprised that the butterflies flap their wings a little faster when I think about going to the fundraiser too.

I imagine the entire Rivers family will be there, along with a good chunk of the community here in Hartsville. Duke and I showing up together as a couple—that is a *hard* launch.

But if we decide to have this baby, people are going to know we are—were—together anyway. Who am I kidding? They probably already do.

I just get this absurd and absurdly warm and fuzzy feeling when I think about attending the fundraiser as *part* of the Rivers family. Ella is a doll and so is Junie, and they'll be thrilled by a big turnout. I imagine very few kids in their class will have ten people show up for them at this thing.

How cool would it be if the Riverses showed up for our baby too?

If they showed up for us?

Duke straightens and looks me in the eye, brow scrunched. "You really wanna come to that?"

"I do, yeah."

"It is really cute. I think you'd like it."

"I'm in. If you'll have me, of course."

He chuckles. "Oh, sweetheart, I always wanna have you. This time, though, I'd love to take you to dinner before we get naked." He pushes up on his arms so he can meet my eyes. "So it's a date? A real one?"

I wrap my arms around Duke's neck and pull him down for a kiss, too scared to look him in the eye as I say, "It's a date. A real one."

I have limited experience with first dates.

With dating in general, really.

But the few first dates I've been on have been awkward as hell. Do you hug when you meet? Or is a kiss on the cheek better? And the chemistry—if it's not there at first, do you cut your losses and run? Or do you give the connection a chance to grow?

Duke puts all those concerns to bed before our first date even begins.

I emerge from the guest room—all my stuff is still in there—dressed and ready to go. I catch a glimpse of Duke standing in the hall by the front door, which is open to the delicious spring breeze. His back is to me, and he's looking down at his phone, so he doesn't notice me yet.

My stomach nosedives when I take in his handsomeness. He's wearing a clean pair of jeans and the "going out" boots he had on back in Dallas. A crisp white button-up shirt, freshly ironed, is tucked into a thick leather belt, the sleeves of the shirt rolled up to reveal enormous forearms that are crisscrossed with large veins and dotted with freckles.

And then—*fuck me*—there's the cowboy hat.

It's one I haven't seen on him before. Dressier than the one he usually wears to work, this hat is dark brown, felt, and in pristine condition, not a smudge or speck of dirt in sight. Duke looks *good* in it.

The kind of good that has me putting a hand on the wall to steady myself. I can't get over the way his biceps fill out those sleeves. Or how his tapered waist slopes into the firmest, cutest ass in existence, the pockets of his jeans just the tiniest bit faded.

I'm going on a date with a cowboy. A real one.

He looks up and sees me. His lips part as his eyes move over my floral-print skirt and matching top. I'm wearing a short pair of blue Bellamy Brooks boots to complete the look, along with big earrings and a straw bag.

Looking at myself in the full-length mirror attached to the back of the guest room door, I felt pretty. But when Duke looks at me like this, his throat working, eyes sharp—

I feel *beautiful*.

"Blue." It's the only word he says.

I lift my leg to show off my appropriately colored boots. "Thought you'd appreciate that."

"*Blue.*"

Walking toward him, I open my bag and drop my phone inside. "So clever, I know. Mollie and I are debating whether to include this pair of boots in our first winter drop, but I…"

The words die in my throat when I see Duke stalking toward me. His jaw twitches. His boots mark a hard, quick beat on the wood floor.

He's huge.

He smells fucking *delicious*, like freshly showered man.

He tucks his thumb and first finger underneath my chin and tips my head back. Then he leans in, neck bending in the most mind-bogglingly sexy way imaginable, and kisses my mouth.

"Blue *balls*," he murmurs against my lips. "I'm gonna have 'em all night with you lookin' so fuckin' gorgeous."

I kiss him back, rising up on my tiptoes. "I'm not fucking you before we leave. I don't want to mess up my hair."

"But you will fuck me after." He gives my bottom lip a bite, then pulls back. "And I *will* mess up your hair. Ain't apologizin' for it either."

I smile. "I look forward to it. You look so handsome, Duke. Love the hat."

He looks at me for a beat. I look back. I feel like an emoji, the smiley face with the stupid heart eyes.

What the hell am I doing?

How can I do more of it?

Duke grabs my hand, my chest lurching at how dry and warm and big his feels wrapped around mine.

"Thank you." His voice is quiet. "For agreeing to come to the fundraiser. Ella's gonna get a big kick out of you being there. So are Sawyer and Ava."

"I'm happy to."

He nods at the door. "You ready?"

"I'm ready, cowboy."

CHAPTER 26
Bidding War
Wheeler

My heart twists when Duke pulls into the parking lot beside a cute little building just off Main Street.

There's a playground to our left, and to our right is a series of raised garden beds that burst with greenery and flowers.

The sidewalk is covered in rainbows drawn in chalk. A game of hopscotch is underway nearby, a handful of little boys and girls attempting to skip on one leg, their faces split into smiles.

"Adorable," I breathe.

Duke puts the truck in park and turns off the engine. "Nice little spot. It's Hartsville's only preschool—used to be a church—and with all the newcomers we have, they need to add some more classes. That's what they're raising money for tonight, to fix up the new classrooms."

There'd be room for our baby, then.

The thought takes me off guard.

I can only stare as Duke hops out of the truck and

walks around the hood to open my door for me. He looks *so* good.

So fucking handsome in his hat and his jeans and those gold-rimmed aviators, and so different from everything I thought I wanted. Everything I thought I knew.

When I was younger, I thought I'd end up with someone like Dad or Preston. The type of guy who had a corporate job and went to work in khakis and a polo emblazoned with a prep school logo. That's how all my guy friends from high school and college ended up. I imagined I'd pair off with one of them, date him for a while, get married at thirty, have a baby at thirty-five. That path, that way of life, was all I knew.

All I thought existed.

When I decided not to pursue a law degree and started Bellamy Brooks instead, I knew I was forfeiting the chance to ever be with a guy like that. After all, a successful man who came from a good family would never want a broke creative type for a girlfriend or wife who was, by all accounts, going nowhere fast.

For a long time, that fact stung. I felt embarrassed. Shameful even.

Now, I'm so glad I didn't end up with one of Preston's prep school friends. Maybe I get to end up with a cowboy instead.

Maybe I finally get to embrace who I really am and what I really want, something I'm not sure I could do if I still lived in my parents' world.

Duke opens my door and holds out his hand. Taking it, I am brimming with a profound sense of gratitude. Who knew coming to a small town in the middle of nowhere would broaden my horizons in such an epic way? There's a whole *universe* outside the place I'm from and the people I grew up with.

A whole different way of life that isn't objectively any better or worse than how I grew up. It's just different.

The kind of different I'm really starting to like.

"Thank you." Holding on to Duke's hand, I step onto the cracked pavement. Beside us, Ava and Sawyer are unloading the kids from his black Silverado.

Ella and Junie scream when they see us.

"Uncle D!" Ella makes a beeline for him, wrapping her arms around his legs. "You're here! Daddy said you were coming."

Junie eyes me. "Mommy didn't say Miss Wheeler was coming too."

Sawyer shuts the car door and grins. "We didn't want to jinx it. So happy you made it, Wheeler." He comes over and wraps me in a hug. "Thank you for coming. Means a lot."

I give him a squeeze. "Thank you for having me. I'm so excited to see this art I've been hearing so much about." I let go of Sawyer and hold out my hands to the girls. "Y'all wanna show me what you made?"

Junie and Ella bounce on their toes, all smiles. Junie takes my right hand, and Ella takes my left.

"I love your beautiful shoes," she says.

"And your jewels," Junie says, staring at my earrings. "Can I wear those?"

Ava laughs and starts walking beside us. "Those are for pierced ears, Bug. When you're a little older, we'll get yours pierced, and then you can wear any earrings you want."

I give Junie's hand a squeeze. "How fun is that gonna be? I'll save all my favorite earrings for you."

"I love you, Miss Wheeler." She beams at me.

I burst out laughing. "That's all it takes, huh?"

"She's got a big heart," Ava says.

Sawyer chuckles. "And expensive taste."

"You're in trouble, brother." Duke claps Sawyer on the shoulder. "You lucky bast—bum. You lucky *bum*."

The girls see a friend, so they drop my hands and take off running. The guys hang by the open doors at the front of the school where several teachers are handing out paddles for bidding.

Ava nudges me with her elbow. "I love your outfit."

"Thanks. Duke and I are heading to dinner after this, so figured I'd put some real clothes on."

She grins. "I heard y'all are going on a date. I'm happy for you guys."

For a split second, I think about keeping up the pretense that she doesn't know I'm pregnant. It's easier that way. Less awkward if we stick to polite topics of conversation. I'm still getting used to the fact that all Duke's family will probably know all our business for, well, ever.

But all of a sudden, the idea of pretending makes me feel suffocated. I'm not going to get anywhere in any area of my life if I don't talk about anything real. Look how far Duke and I have come in such a short amount of time, largely because I've tried my best to be open and honest with him.

Something tells me Ava doesn't mind *real*. She was a single mom before she moved in with Sawyer, and I've seen firsthand just how much she appreciates honesty and authenticity. She loves to cut loose at the Rattler every so often. Last time we were there, seemingly ages ago, she and I shut the place down, Tallulah shaking her head at us as we worked the dance floor despite us being the only people left in the bar.

So what if Ava judges me for whatever choice Duke and I end up making? Maybe she'll think less of me if I get an abortion. Or maybe she'll understand and offer some crucial insight into parenthood and kids and pregnancy and relationships and—well—everything.

Because the more I think about it, the more I'm convinced I want this baby.

I keep my voice low. "I'm sure you've heard I'm pregnant?"

"I have." Ava's grin doesn't waver, and a sense of calm comes over me. She's not freaking out, so why should I? "How are you feeling?"

I seesaw my hand. "I feel pretty good right now. But the morning sickness hit me hard pretty early. When it happens, it's awful."

"Truly the worst. I never threw up, but I felt like I had the worst hangover of my life for ten straight weeks."

"Yes! That's exactly how it feels—like a bad hangover. The exhaustion, the headaches, the brain fog."

Ava nods at Duke, who's chatting happily with an older woman wearing a name tag. *Mrs. Hobson.* "How's he doing? Ryder told me he caught him whistling the other day while they tacked up their horses. Mind you, it was five a.m. Ryder couldn't believe how chipper Duke was."

My pulse riots. "Does Duke not usually whistle?"

"Not that I know of. Definitely not at five a.m."

I feel my lips pull into a smile. "He's been…in surprisingly good spirits. We haven't made any decisions. Like, we're obviously not together—"

"Oh, sweetie, y'all are together." She looks at me. "You're sick, but you're still glowing. Tells me all I need to know. He's taking good care of you, isn't he?"

My heart's doing several backflips per minute at this point. "He's been absolutely wonderful, every step of the way."

"Duke's an excellent human being. All the Rivers boys are." She nods at Ryder, who waves to us as he approaches from the parking lot. "My ex—Junie's dad—he was definitely *not* excellent. Makes all the difference when you're with someone who adores you for who you are and who pulls his weight."

I nudge her with my elbow. "You're the one who's glowing."

"I am." She crosses her arms and looks at me. "Ella and Junie are at a great age. It's lots of fun, plus we got to ditch the diapers. I love my man. Love my job. For so long, I felt like life wasn't coming together the way I'd hoped. I wanted my marriage to be something it wasn't, and I couldn't figure out what I wanted to do career-wise. The stuff that was supposed to make me happy didn't. It was only when I veered off the beaten path that I found what I didn't know I was looking for."

I swallow, hard, and watch Duke scoop Junie onto his hip. "What was that?"

She takes a deep breath through her nose, pondering. "Freedom."

"You found freedom in settling down?"

"I wouldn't call what I'm doing with Sawyer 'settling

down.' It's more like…settling *in*. Settling into who I really am, chasing after what I really want, and doing it all with a super handsome cowboy by my side."

Chuckling, I watch said handsome cowboy chase Ella down the sidewalk. "So your career is working out? How are y'all making that happen? Because I feel like I'm just hitting my stride…"

"And you don't want to shoot yourself in the foot by having a baby." Ava nods. "I'm not surprised Bellamy Brooks is heading for the stratosphere. I love my pair." She kicks out her foot, revealing the tan-and-coral midcalf boot Mollie and I gave her to wear on *her* first date with Sawyer. "I won't lie to you. Having a career and a baby at the same time is not easy. But it's definitely doable if you're having that baby with the right guy. He'll make sure you get the help you need. He'll pull his weight. Be a real partner. Because at the end of the day, he doesn't want to hold you back or trap you. He wants to make your dreams come true as much as you do."

A happy, achy feeling takes root in my center. I recognize all that in Duke.

He's doing all that already.

"What if I want to make his dreams come true too?" I manage. "He loves to travel and try new things. See new places. I'd hate to think the baby and I would keep him from doing that."

Ava nods again. "Totally understandable. But here's another way to think about it: yeah, y'all aren't gonna be doing a ton of travel with a two-year-old. But newborns? Psssh, you put them in the carrier and go on your merry way. It's not a walk in the park, but it's totally doable. And then when your kids go through the hairy toddler phase where they don't want to sit or be told what to do—" She shrugs. "You travel a little less. Maybe you ask your family and friends to take the baby overnight so you and Duke can get away. But then all of a sudden, they're out of diapers, and they'll sit with their iPad for a few hours, and you're able to go on a trip that doesn't totally suck."

I laugh again. "Guess you adjust your expectations and set the bar pretty low."

"Yes. But not forever." She smiles. "It gets easier as they get older. Well, in some respects. Travel is one of them. Who's not to say that one day, traveling with your kids will blow your expectations right out of the water? I think all the time about how cool it'll be to experience the world all over again, this time through Junie's eyes."

My turn to nod, my heart lodging in my throat. "I hadn't considered that angle."

"Something to think about."

"I'm thinking."

Her eyes go soft. "Trust yourself to make the right decision. I wish I'd trusted myself earlier. I would've avoided a lot of unnecessary heartache."

A beat of silence moves between us as we look toward Sawyer and Duke. They're the ones playing hopscotch now, Duke showing Ella and Junie how it's done.

I scoff. "I keep waiting for the other shoe to drop. Like, a man that good can't possibly exist, you know?"

"Oh, I know," Ava says with a mirthless laugh. "Why do you think I settled for my ex? It's what I was taught—that men just aren't as kind or thoughtful as women. But they can be." She points to the boys. "Those men are."

I think I knew the night we met that Duke is one in

a million. Every interaction with him just hammers that point home. I want him.

I'm falling for him. *I can't fuck this up.*

I just need to figure out how to like myself a little more, so I can let him in without being terrified that he'll be turned off by what he sees.

Am I kind enough? Smart enough? Do I love hard enough? I think so. But everything I learned growing up told me otherwise. I'm so, so scared Duke won't love me back because of that.

Ryder comes over to give us a hug.

"I'm so glad you came," he murmurs in my ear. "You bein' around is making my brother a very happy man. Kinda grosses us out, actually, how chipper he is."

I lean in to whisper in his ear. "It's the sex."

"Figured as much," Ryder replies with a smirk. "How're you feeling?"

Wrong that I appreciate how everyone's asking me that question tonight? Seems silly, but their genuine concern makes me feel…safe. Taken care of.

Out of the corner of my eye, I see Wyatt approaching.

"I'm feeling all right tonight," I say.

Ryder's smirk stays put on his handsome face. "Duke makes everything better, huh?"

"Are you bein' a perv again?" Cash appears over Ryder's shoulder. He's holding hands with Mollie, who beams at us with a knowing twinkle in her eye.

"Probably shouldn't say the word 'pervert' when you're at a preschool." Wyatt glances around.

Cash rolls his eyes. "You just said it."

"What? Pervert?" Duke strides over wearing a cocky smile. "Yeah, that's definitely inappropriate."

Sawyer groans. "Can y'all be polite just once in your lives?"

"Nope." Ryder holds out his arm. "May I escort you inside, Miss Wheeler? My brothers may be heathens, but I'm a gentleman."

Cash lets out a bark of laughter. "I call BS."

"Case in point," Ryder sniffs. "C'mon, pretty lady."

I meet Duke's eyes, and my heart takes a tumble. They glimmer with happiness, the kind you can't fake. Happiness and…is that pride?

Why wouldn't he be proud of you?

Why am I not more proud of myself? I'm pregnant. Scared. Sick. But I'm showing up anyway.

I'm trying my best anyway.

I smile at him, and he smiles back.

"I'll allow him to take you inside." Duke tips his hat at Ryder. "But then I take over, yeah?"

Ryder chuckles. "We'll see about that."

"Your brother *is* cute." I slip my hand into the crook of Ryder's thick arm.

Duke shrugs. "Well, yeah, because he looks exactly like me."

Ryder and I introduce ourselves to the teachers at the door. One of them, Ms. Blair, looks to be about my age, and she tells us how much she and her teaching partner Ms. Sherman enjoy having Junie and Ella in class.

"I hope my daughter is as kind and happy as those two are."

"Oh?" I ask. "How old is your daughter?"

"She just turned four months old yesterday."

"Aw."

Ms. Blair wiggles her shoulders. "She's chunking up."

"She's absolutely delicious," Mrs. Hobson adds with a smile as she hands us each a paddle. "And sweet as pie."

"Probably why I could eat her with a spoon," Ms. Blair replies. "Welcome, y'all. We're so glad you're here."

I have the strange urge to hug her. Will this be our first and last interaction? Or will she become a new friend? A *mom* friend?

The event is taking place in a large central hall with a stage on one side and more chairs than I can count on the other. It's already loud inside. Kids are running around, and parents chat while holding beers and plastic cups of wine. My smile grows when I see Tallulah tending a makeshift bar in the far corner.

Sally and Patsy are on the stage. Sally plays the violin, while Patsy sings a twangy version of "Somewhere Over the Rainbow" into a microphone.

Large bulletin boards are set out across the space, each one pinned with dozens of pieces of the children's art. There are paintings of strawberries and houses. Centipedes constructed out of egg cartons. Hats that look like bunny ears.

"All right, this is really adorable," Ryder says.

"The most adorable," I agree. "It's perfect."

Never thought I'd want to spend a Saturday night at a preschool function, but this is actually sweet and very well done.

There's nowhere else I'd rather be right now.

I can't stop smiling as we approach a bulletin board that a placard tells us belongs to Ella and Junie's class. "The finger painting." I gesture to the kaleidoscope of colors that make up a finger-painted heart. "I remember loving that as a kid."

"Well, yeah. It was an excuse to make a huge mess with no one gettin' mad at you." Ryder pulls me a little closer. "Can I ask you a favor?"

"Always."

"Be good to my brother, would you? Duke grew up feeling like the odd one out, even though he's probably got the biggest heart out of all of us. He's always been lookin' for something more, you know?" Ryder's eyes bore into mine. "I think he mighta found it in you."

My eyes prick. "Duke is...kind of amazing, isn't he?"

"He's my best friend. Of course I think he's amazing. Although if you ever tell him I said that, I'll deny it up and down." Ryder's smile is kind. "We love havin' you at the ranch, Wheeler. I hope you know that. But I also love how you push Duke out of his comfort zone. Give him an excuse to get out of town. He needs that."

I have to look away. Otherwise, I'm liable to burst into tears. "You're a good friend and brother to go to bat for him like this."

"You're a good friend too, Wheeler." Ryder pats my hand. "Duke doesn't let just anybody in. He's picky. Probably why he's been single all this time. But you stood out to him, for all the right reasons."

"Jesus." I wipe my eyes. "Since when are you the relationship whisperer?"

Ryder shrugs. "Heck if I know. Not like I have any real experience in that area."

But he does. Maybe not romantically speaking, but Ryder has good relationships with all four of his brothers, despite the fact that they work together *and* live within a five-mile radius of each other.

Just like Duke, he loves hard.

I want to be loved that way.

I turn around at the tap on my shoulder.

"Can I borrow you for a sec?" Ava asks. "There's some friends of mine I want you to meet."

Ryder huffs out a sigh. "Fine. But I get her back, ya hear?"

"Wyatt's already claimed her for the auction."

"What?" I laugh. "Since when am I in such high demand?"

Ava furrows her brow. "Since forever." She says it like there should be a *duh* at the end of that sentence.

Next thing I know, she's whisking me toward a circle of women. She introduces me to Sarah, who has four-year-old triplets and a side gig illustrating erotic scenes from romance books. Then there's Paige, who has three kids three and under, and Mona, who is eight months pregnant with her second boy. She works three days a week as a physician's assistant at the family medicine practice down the street.

"We've all heard about your boots," Sarah says.

Mona nods. "I'm asking for a pair for Christmas. The red ones with the hearts."

"Oooh, I love those. Y'all are truly so, so talented," Paige adds. "I wish I was creative like that."

Sarah grins. "If you ever want me to illustrate a scene for you where the people are wearing your boots and your boots only, just say the word."

Laughing—*so much laughing tonight*—I grab my phone and open up a blank notes page. "I think our Instagram followers would definitely get a kick out of that, Sarah. All right, gimme your email. And then I need all y'all's shoe sizes."

I'm buzzing by the time the auction begins, and I haven't had so much as a drop of alcohol. Wyatt elbows Sawyer out of the way to claim the seat beside mine. Duke sits on my other side, draping his arm over the back of my chair.

"You okay?" he asks, voice low. "I know this is a lot."

Bending down to grab my paddle out of my bag, I shake my head. "Are you kidding? This is so much fun. Thank you again for the invite. Everyone is so friendly."

He smiles, a funny look in his eyes. "I saw you working the room, taking names and selling boots."

"The boots will be a gift. I really like those girls."

He swipes his thumb over my bare shoulder. Once, twice. "You fit right in. No surprise there, though."

But Duke is the one who really shines during the auction. He drives the prices up on everything, from a tie-dyed butterfly made from coffee filters to a snowman constructed entirely from buttons. Goody, Tallulah's wife, is running the auction, and she kindly but firmly asks Duke to give other family members a shot at winning the next handful of items.

Mollie buys a cardboard cowboy hat decorated with glitter. I purchase a princess party the threes teachers will host for Junie, Ella, and ten of their very best friends, letting out a squeal of delight when I beat Paige by fifty bucks.

Duke gives my thigh a squeeze, then leans in to brush his lips over my neck before murmuring in my ear, "You wanna be one of the best friends that goes to that party, right?"

I bite my lip. "You know me well."

"I'm learning, Blue." He gives my thigh another squeeze before resting his hand there.

And I'm learning what life could be like if I chose Duke. Chose the baby.

Chose love.

CHAPTER 27
Baby Steps
Duke

Tonight's plan: hang with Ella and Junie for a bit, buy some cute art, and then get the hell out of here so I can take my girl to dinner.

However.

I had not accounted for the approximately seven hundred and eighty-five people I'd run into trying to squeeze out of the preschool. There's Colt, who has a five-year-old little boy in the junior kindergarten class here. I stop to chat with him and introduce him to Wheeler.

"Great to meet you." Colt cuts me a look after shaking her hand. "Y'all just about gave me a heart attack with all your bids."

Wheeler shrugs. "We're overachievers. We can't help ourselves."

"Duke's been making the rest of us look bad for about as long as I can remember." Colt grins. "Hope we'll be seeing more of you around, Wheeler."

It's his way of asking if we're dating. My gut clenches.

But my girl doesn't miss a beat. "Hard not to fall in love with Hartsville. Tonight's been—"

"Total chaos?" He chuckles.

"A lot of fun," she replies with a smile. "The love y'all have for each other is…something I've never witnessed before."

Stay, then.

Wheeler also runs into some new friends she's made. I meet Paige and her husband, Crosby, who are really cool. So are their kids, who wrap Ella in a series of tight hugs that have her giggling.

I don't miss the way Ava and Sawyer greet nearly everyone who attends. They're both super involved in the preschool—Sawyer's on the parent council, and Ava helped organize this event—and they seem to have a genuinely good time visiting with other parents, teachers, and the zillion kids who are here.

They're still in the hall when Wheeler and I manage to slip out the front doors. I feel dizzy as the warm evening air hits me.

Did Wheeler enjoy that as much as me?

Did she start to understand that becoming a parent is an end to some things but the beginning of others, the way I just did?

Mom homeschooled us, bless her. Dad had a ranch to run. We rarely ventured into town.

Really, we didn't leave our property much at all. Mom and Dad didn't seem to mind that. I think they were too exhausted to be social or make plans to get out.

The parents I saw tonight, though? They definitely get out, as evidenced by the way everyone seemed to know everyone. I knew Ava and Sawyer did weekly date nights, but I hadn't realized that they might invite other couples to join them.

What if parenthood doesn't make your world smaller?

What if being a father leads me to meet new people? Experience new things?

Granted, that's not always the case. But it could be for me.

For us.

I only realize my hands are shaking when I let go of Wheeler's to open the passenger side door for her.

Starting the truck, I wonder what the hell to say.

Do I keep it casual? *How great was that? I'm glad we won the papier-mâché heart. Great running into Colt too.*

Or do I tell her the truth? *I think we keep the baby. I think we make that official, and I think we make us official too. The thought of you being with anyone else kills me. I don't want you sleeping in any bed but mine, sweetheart. I want you with me, always.*

She's quiet on the ride to Main Street, rolling down her window and resting her elbow on the ledge of the door. We're going to a restaurant that just opened next to the Rattler. One of Colt's brothers is a big foodie, and he invested a chunk of change in a farm-to-table spot some fancy chef from Austin wanted to open in the country.

I'm not hungry, though.

I'm not sure I can keep all this inside anymore.

I pull into one of the angled parking spots on Main Street. It's Saturday night, and with the new restaurant opening, there's lots of people downtown. Couples stroll along the sidewalk hand in hand. People sit outside the

Caffeinated Cowgirl at its little bistro tables, sipping coffee, enjoying dessert. I can smell something delicious wafting through the restaurant's open windows a few doors up the street.

Turning off the engine, I reach across the bench and put a hand on Wheeler's thigh. Funny how a week ago, touching her like this would be weird.

Now, it feels like the most natural thing in the world.

She turns her head to look at me. For the hundredth time tonight, I'm struck dumb by how beautiful she is. Pouty lips, tan skin. Bare shoulders and lush breasts.

It's her expression, though, that has my pulse tripping to a stop. She looks…serious. Earnest.

She looks like she's bursting with something she wants to say too.

"Duke?"

"Yeah?"

"I…"

Swallowing, I press my thumb into her leg. "Whatever it is you wanna say, I hope you know you can say it. I'm not goin' anywhere."

She nods. Blinks. Her chin wobbles when she says, "I want to keep the baby."

I startle at the warm explosion inside my chest. I put my free hand there, just to make sure this woman didn't just blow a hole through my center with her achingly vulnerable confession.

"Blue," I sputter.

She's crying now. "I'm sorry if that's not what you wanted to hear, but I just—I had to tell you, Duke. I know I said that I wasn't sure. I know this makes things super complicated—"

"I don't care. I'm so glad, sweetheart." I reach up and thumb away her tears. "So glad you want that, because it's what I want too."

Her brows pop up, her wet eyelashes glistening in the thin, late light. "Wait, are you saying—"

"I want to keep the baby. Yes."

She lets out a bark of laughter. "Seriously?"

"Of fucking *course* I wanna have a baby with you, sweetheart."

Without warning, Wheeler launches herself into my arms. Her hands find my neck. Mine find her belly. She pulls me in for a teary, salty kiss—we're both crying now, tears leaking out of my eyes left and right—and we hold each other like that for one heartbeat. Then another and another and another.

We're having a baby.

Holy shit, we're having a fucking baby!

Because she's apparently turned me into a fucking animal, I'm hard by the time she breaks the kiss.

"What helped you make up your mind?" She whisks away the tears on my face with the flat of her hand.

"In a nutshell?" I tuck her hair behind her ear. "You." I tilt my head. "Them. My family. Our friends."

She nods, rolling her lips between her teeth. "Me too. I didn't realize—you and me, we're friends. You're a *good* friend. We're more than that too, but we were friends first, right?"

"I'd like to think we'll always be friends, Blue." I run my hand up her side. "I like you too much not to want you around all the time."

That makes her smile. "I like having you around too."

"Glad to hear it."

"Point is my parents *aren't* friends. They never were. Obviously I don't know everything about their relationship, but I'm pretty sure it wasn't Mom getting pregnant that torpedoed it."

I meet her eyes. "It was the fact that they didn't have a connection as friends that explains why it didn't work out."

"Right."

"I see Mollie's fingerprints all over *that* lightbulb moment."

Wheeler's smile grows. "You know her well too."

"Well, yeah. She is my sister-in-law."

"She wants us to be together." Wheeler's eyes toggle between mine. "Everyone in your family does."

"Can you blame them? You walked into my life, and everything's changed for the better."

She laughs. "You mean I walked out in the middle of our first game of darts, then dragged you on a twenty-hour road trip to Colorado, and *then* got pregnant, all while doing my damnedest to push you away?"

"Can we work on the pushing away thing?"

Wheeler nods. "I want to. I'm trying. This—our friendship, our relationship"—she flattens her palm over my chest—"it means a lot to me. I want it to work. So I'll put in the work I need to do to make that happen."

My heart feels downright drunk, skipping around my torso without a care in the fucking world.

"If that's not the sexiest thing anyone's ever said to me," I growl.

Wheeler laughs. "*So* sexy, me promising to go get therapy and look on the bright side."

I grab her hand and put it on my crotch. "But seriously."

"Wow." Her mouth forms a neat little O. "You... aren't kidding."

"I wanna feed you, Blue. But I also wanna fuck you."

Her eyes go hazy. "Tell me why you wanna be a daddy."

Because I'm falling in love with you, and I want to follow that feeling to the ends of the earth.

"Because a baby is a big responsibility but also a big adventure. Because freedom can be many things, and I've realized that the kind that's important to me is the kind where I have the freedom to be with my people. Because this baby *is* my person. Our person. Because I'm not sure I'll ever have life figured out, but I can try to figure it out *and* be a dad all at once. Because being a dad is a dream I have. Because..." I blow out a breath. "I don't wanna live small anymore. You made me see what's possible. You'll keep chasing your dreams, and I'll keep chasing mine. The baby won't change that."

Her throat works on a swallow. "You promise?"

"You have my word." I press my hand into her belly. "I'll always take care of you and this baby. I wanna be with you every step of the way, sweetheart. I'm in. Both feet."

She's crying again, fisting my shirt in her hand. "Please don't fuck me over. Because this all sounds so, *so* nice, baby. You're right. It is a dream. But if you take that away from me—"

"My brothers'll take me out long before you do if I ever fall down on y'all. That's not part of the game plan, Blue. Trust me."

She looks at me. I look back.

"I'll try. To trust you."

"You need some convincing, that's not gonna be a problem. Surely you know that."

"Oh, I know," she says with a laugh. "You can be relentless."

"We call that grit around here."

"Whatever it is, I like it."

"I'll make sure our baby has plenty of it."

She takes a sharp breath through her nose. "We're doing this. We're going to have a baby."

"Yes, sweetheart." I smooth her dress over her thighs. "We're having a baby. But first, we're having dinner. Then I think I'm gonna have you in the shower again."

Her laughter is a warm gust on my lips as she leans in to kiss me. "This is wild."

"Exactly why it's right." I kiss her back. "Maybe wild is what we're looking for."

She pulls back. "What do we tell your brothers? And my parents…"

"Lemme ask you a question."

"Okay."

"Introduce me to them as your boyfriend."

Wheeler chuckles. "That's not a question."

"Would you? Call me your boyfriend?"

"Only if you call me your girlfriend."

My stomach dips. She's trying, and I appreciate that more than she'll ever know.

"Deal." I hold out my hand. "Might lessen the blow if they think your boyfriend got you pregnant instead of some random-ass hookup in Aspen."

"Gross. Who gets knocked up that way?"

My turn to laugh. "Not you now, seeing as we're dating and shit."

"I think I like this dating and shit thing."

I grin. "I think I do too."

What I don't say? That I wanna be more than the boyfriend.

I wanna be the one.

Her man.

CHAPTER 28
Three's Company
Wheeler

Taking a deep breath, I square my shoulders. "So I have a proposal."

Mollie holds up her left hand, her engagement ring twinkling in the overhead lights. "Sorry, I'm taken." With her right, she pops a potato chip into her mouth.

"Ha. Trust me, I'd never step on Cash's toes." I set my laptop on the kitchen island, then dig into the bag of chips. I've never been particularly turned on by sour cream and onion, but these are delicious. "This is a business proposal. You have a minute?"

Chomping on her chips, Mollie grabs a napkin and uses it to wipe her hands. "For you? Always. Talk to me, partner."

"You and the cowgirl stuff." I smile as I open my laptop. "Suits you."

She wiggles her shoulders. "I know. You've been

looking mighty comfortable around the ranch yourself these days. I'm not the only one who's noticed how at home you are here."

I've been smiling so much lately my face literally hurts. "Y'all take good care of me. Don't get me wrong, I do miss Dallas sometimes—"

"Same. Which is why we go back every so often to scratch our city girl itch."

"Right. But life on the ranch...I don't know what I was expecting, but I really like it."

Mollie digs for more chips. "That have anything to do with why you and Duke decided to keep the baby?"

"It absolutely does, yeah." I scroll through my docs before I find the right one. Clicking on it, I pull up the PowerPoint presentation I've been working on day and night. I think I make a convincing case, but this is a big ask, so who knows. "I feel supported here. Seen. And I imagine that's really important when it comes to where you choose to raise your kids. Imagine how cool it would be to grow up here, riding horses, hanging outside all the time, being surrounded by a zillion aunts and uncles and cousins."

Mollie's eyes are bright when she replies, "Why do you think I got pregnant so fast?"

"Because your husband is super hot and you can't stop riding his mustache?"

"You don't get pregnant from riding their mustaches, Wheeler."

Laughter works its way up my sides. "Really? Never would've guessed."

"It's still a good time, though. The mustache rides. You should ask Duke to grow one. I'm sure he'd be more than happy to oblige. Honestly, what wouldn't that man do to make you happy?"

The knowledge that she's right gives me this weightless feeling in my center. Duke *really* cares about how I'm feeling.

He cares about me, period.

Time to show him that I care just as much about him.

"That's actually a great segue into what I wanted to talk to you about." I angle the laptop so Mollie can get a better look at the screen, my pulse banging inside my ears. "Duke does make me happy, so I want to make him happy too. Which is why I'd like to bring him on board at Bellamy Brooks."

Mollie's hand flies to her chest as her eyes move over the first slide of my presentation. "Oh, Wheeler. *Wheeler.*" Her gaze meets mine. "You're serious?"

"I hope I'm not taking you off guard—"

"Hell no!" Next thing I know, Mollie's sliding off her stool and wrapping her arms around me. "I had an inkling you'd want to do something along these lines after we decided to do a men's collection. I can put two and two together. I know Duke's not satisfied doing just the cowboy thing. Cash told me he's always been on the hunt for something more. Something different."

Tears flood my eyes. I really hit the best friend jackpot. She gets it. Gets *me*. "So you like the idea?"

"Wheeler, I fucking love it."

Relief, enormous and immediate, unfurls inside my rib cage. "I think Duke will be a really great addition," I continue. "He really knows his shit when it comes to authentic cowboy boots. He's clearly a team player. And he'd clearly be a great personality fit."

Mollie releases me, her arm curling around my waist now. "Keep going."

Turning, I glide my fingertips over the mouse pad to pull up the next couple slides. "I ran the numbers, and with all the money we've got coming in, we can definitely afford to hire him. We're also expanding so quickly that I think we can both agree we need all the help we can get."

Mollie leans her head on my shoulder. "Not a bad call to hire that help before these babies come. And you're right, I don't want to miss out on any important opportunities just because we don't have enough hands on deck."

"Doing a men's collection is one of those opportunities, Mollie. I mean, we literally live and work with cowboys all day."

"We love them all night too."

"I don't know if it's the boys rubbing off on you or you rubbing off on them, but everyone here has their mind in the gutter."

"It's me. Which is why you'd better make me your baby's godmother, because I'm the reason you made him or her." She grins. "Yes, my matchmaking skills are the reason people in Hartsville are so horny."

"The hot cowboys who live here are the reason everyone's so horny," I correct. "As I was saying, I think this is the perfect time to bring someone on board, and I think Duke is the perfect someone. He's creative. Driven. Easy to get along with. He knows his shit, and he's good at relationships. He's got great ideas, and yes, he'll look really fucking hot in whatever advertising we decide to do."

"A jack-of-all-trades, if you will." Mollie nudges me with her hip. "You're putting on the hard sell, friend."

"Because I truly believe this is the right move for Bellamy Brooks. If you don't agree, I completely understand, but—"

"Aw, Wheeler." Mollie's eyes glisten with tears. "You really think I'm gonna miss out on hiring that man after all the amazing ideas he came up with for the men's collection? Oh. He is also amazing to you, amazingly hot, and just all around amazing, so those are other reasons why I definitely think we should hire him."

I blink. Blink again. "So you're in? I know Bellamy Brooks has been our baby from day one. I need you to know I don't take changing things up lightly. I've loved our time as a twosome."

Mollie wags her brows. "But I hear threesomes can be fun."

"Okay, you need to get laid ASAP. You're turning into a sixteen-year-old boy."

"How great are the orgasms while you're pregnant?"

It's all I can do not to groan. "The best. I don't know who enjoys them more, me or Duke."

"You gotta enjoy the perks of our condition while they last." She curls a hand over her belly. "So what's your plan for the grand gesture? How're you going to ask your man to be part of our threesome?"

Wiping my eyes, I chuckle. "I haven't come up with something I love yet. Like, do we take him out to dinner and ask him then? Maybe make him a poster board that says 'Will you join my company' and give him a boutonniere?"

It's Mollie's turn to laugh. "While I love the prom

theme, I think we can get a little more creative. What if…" She taps a finger against her chin. "Hm. The samples we ordered—the ones for the men's collection—those are supposed to arrive when?"

"Pretty soon, actually." My heart thumps as I start to pick up what she's laying down. "Do you think—"

"Yes." Her expression lights up. "Here's what we do."

CHAPTER 29
Brand-New Kicks
Duke

"I didn't know I had a sexy mechanic fantasy until... yup, right now."

I smile at the sound of the familiar voice. Glancing up from the trailer tire I just replaced, I see Wheeler standing inside the garage. It's been a few weeks since our first date, but I still can't get over the fact that she finally agreed to be my girlfriend.

I can't get over the fact that it was her idea.

"You're welcome," I reply.

"You can fix tractors and wheels and engines and... shit?" She motions to the heavy equipment parked behind me. A stack of spare tires is tucked into a nearby corner; a toolbox the size of a small house sits beside it.

I wipe my face on my sleeve. "I'll get any engine goin', no problem."

"You're funny."

"You're pretty."

She nods at the flat tire. "What happened?"

"A nail. We bought this dang trailer less than a month ago, and it's already gotten three flats."

Then again, that's the hazard of working and living in a giant construction zone. Stray nails, broken glass, and splintered wood are everywhere these days. Seems like the whole damn ranch is under construction. Between the new studio Mollie and Wheeler are building for Bellamy Brooks, the massive irrigation repair we're doing over on the Rivers' side of the ranch, and the renovations we've started on several outbuildings, our property is a fucking mess.

It'll be worth it. But it's a huge pain in the ass in the meantime.

Speaking of asses, Wheeler is currently devouring mine with her eyes.

"The grease." She blinks. "Your sweat. But the jeans—"

"What about my jeans?" Rising, I grab my gloves off the top of the tractor's wheel basin and tuck them into my back pocket. "You sayin' they're dirty too?"

"Very dirty. And I like them very much."

"Would you say I"—I pick up a tool and toss it in my hand—"threw a wrench into your plans for the afternoon, Miss Rankin?"

"Ha."

"You all right? Feeling any better?"

Wheeler was hit by a vicious bout of nausea after breakfast this morning. Dr. Martinez informed us that the morning sickness can get worse before it gets better, peaking between nine and eleven weeks, and that's definitely been the case over the past few days.

Luckily Mollie was with her at the New House

when it happened, but I still rode like the devil from the north pasture to check on her. She assured me she'd be all right and insisted I get back to work. I stayed with her for some lunch, then headed back to the herd.

Not long after that, the trailer tire blew out. Took me over an hour to drag it back to the garage. Another hour to change out the tire, because someone took it upon themselves to hide the tools I needed underneath the baler nearby.

I really hope it's quitting time soon. If only so I can go home with my girl.

"I'm feeling all right. Just had a snack, which helps."

"Good." I toss up the wrench one last time before catching it. Then I put it back in the toolbox.

She blinks again, straightening. "I will *not* let your hot mechanic look distract me. I have a surprise for you."

I gesture to the front of my Wranglers. "And I have one for *you*."

Her face creases into a smile at that, tongue darting out to move over her bottom lip. "Mine first."

"Aw, Blue, I'm not sure I'm gonna be able to wait that long." I close the distance between us in four long, lazy strides. "I've a mind to dirty you up too."

Those brown eyes dance. "Don't you *dare* get grease on this dress. Shower first. Then we can do all the surprises."

"Deal."

"Meet me at the cottage when you're done."

I have no idea what to expect when I pull up to my house ten minutes later. Giving myself a good scrub in the quickest shower ever, I dry off, then pull on a clean T-shirt and jeans.

When I emerge from the bathroom, I hear Wheeler and Mollie chatting on the porch. The front windows are open, so I'm able to catch what they're saying.

"He's gonna flip his shit when he sees these boots," Mollie squeals, trying—and failing—to keep her voice down. "Wheeler, I am *obsessed*."

"I am too," Wheeler gasps. "I mean, feel this goatskin. It's smooth as a baby's bottom."

My stomach takes a hard tumble, landing somewhere on the ground between my feet.

Boots.

Goatskin.

Baby.

"Have I told you yet how happy I am that we're having our babies together?" Mollie asks.

I hear the smile in Wheeler's voice when she replies, "Just a few hundred times."

"Thank God we have each other."

"And our cowboys. Speaking of, did you ever call Miss Lee back?"

Now I'm smiling. Miss Lee is Sawyer and Ava's nanny. Last night, Wheeler and I chatted about our childcare options on an after-dinner stroll. We both want to continue working full-time, so we agreed we'd ideally hire a nanny. It's a huge privilege to be able to afford that kind of help, but I can swing it.

We can swing it. Still getting used to us being, well, an *us*.

My face hurts. Not sure I've stopped smiling since Wheeler enthusiastically agreed to be exclusive.

Thank fuck.

"I did!" Mollie says. "We spoke for a while last

night. She knows a woman who's looking for a full-time nannying position—"

"Amazing news."

"I'm not sure the timing will work out, but it's a start."

"I'm relieved to hear there are options available at all."

"You know it's not a crime to get what you want, right?" Mollie's voice is soft. "And it doesn't make you stupid to hope for the best."

Wheeler chuckles. "As long as I can still expect the worst too."

"Now, that's something we gotta work on." I step onto the porch. The late afternoon light streams through the new leaves on the trees overhead, dappling the ground with gold. The air is warm but not humid.

Gonna be another gorgeous evening.

Mollie and Wheeler look up. They're bent over the picnic table Ryder and I recently built out of leftover lumber. Wheeler is holding a boot in her hand.

It's square-toed, the shaft—heh—made of smooth brown leather, but the toe box is covered in this cool ostrich-type leather that's the same shade of brown.

A little Texas flag is stitched onto the side of the heel.

Pressure, hot and sudden, appears behind my eyes.

Wheeler smiles. "Hey, baby."

"Oooh, I like the way that sounds," Mollie says. "And she's working on her optimism, Duke. I'm doing my best to convert her."

I'm choking on my heart, but I still manage to gruffly reply, "Thank you kindly. We'll make a believer of her yet."

"So." Wheeler turns the boot in her hands one way, then the other. "What do you think of your creation?"

I try to clear my throat. "*Our* creation."

"Y'all are making beautiful babies *and* beautiful boots together." Mollie beams at us. "It's so perfect I almost hate you for it." Then she goes up on her toes to press a kiss to my cheek. "Thanks for the ideas. You get a ten out of ten from me, no notes. Wheeler did say you were willing to go naked in the advertising campaign. That true?"

"I'm always willing to get naked."

Mollie laughs. "For once in your life, that's a good thing."

"There's been other times that it's a good thing," Wheeler shoots back, giving me a saucy look.

But Mollie just waves us away. "Y'all can go bone in a minute. First, we need to get your approval on these masterpieces. And then we need to ask you something."

Wheeler holds out the boot, and I take it. Thing's got heft. Leather really is soft. Proportions look right. Bet it's comfortable.

She puts her hand on my shoulder. "It's your size. Wanna try it on?"

"My size?" Shit, I'm really gonna cry. "How'd you—"

"I snooped through your closet, of course."

"Did you find the old *Playboys*?"

Wheeler bites her lip and nods. "Hot."

"I think Wyatt stole them from my dad, and I stole them from him."

Mollie makes a face. "That's not weird at all."

"Hey." I shrug. "Our internet was slow. Needs must."

Toeing out of my sneakers, I drop the boot on the

ground. I bend over and carefully tuck my foot inside it, using the ear pulls to finish the job.

I straighten. Put my weight back in both feet.

Perfect fucking fit. There's just enough cushion to make me think I could wear these all damn day but not so much that the sole feels mushy or my foot feels cramped.

When I open my mouth to say as much, I find I can't breathe.

Instead, I meet Wheeler's eyes. They're uncertain but hopeful too.

She's trying.

A tear slips out of my eye. I don't know what else to do, so I take her face in my hands and pull her in for a kiss.

A messy, warm, trembling kiss.

I'm in love with you, I want to say.

"You made the fucking boots," I say instead.

She nods. "You wanna travel—do something different—well, come make these boots with Mollie and me. Come sell them with us. Come do this thing with us, Duke. Not as our employee but as our partner."

"We'd love to have you on board," Mollie says. I can tell by the way her voice shakes that she's crying too. "Sorry to be the third wheel, but I'm too obsessed with these boots not to be involved."

I let out a gruff chuckle. "I'll allow it."

Wheeler pulls back, keeping her eyes closed as she rolls her forehead against mine. "If you can't make it work with your cowboy schedule, I totally understand—"

"Ella's graduating preschool soon. She can fill in for me."

That makes Wheeler laugh. "She'd whoop all y'all's asses."

"God, I love that kid," Mollie adds.

I run my thumbs over Wheeler's cheeks. "I'll figure it out. I wanna do this with you, Blue. I'm—Christ, so honored y'all would go out of your way to…"

I can't finish.

"You're making my dreams come true," she replies steadily. "I want to do the same for you."

"Oh yeah?" I sniffle. "What would those dreams of yours be?"

"For starters, having not one but two amazing best friends. Obviously you and I are more than friends too, but you get my point." She searches my eyes. "I needed a friend like you more than I knew."

"She means a friend with a penis," Mollie explains.

I laugh. "Got it."

"And then there's this." She grabs my hand and puts it on her belly. "We've got our work cut out for us. I'm still figuring my shit out when it comes to my parents and their whole…situation. But I really do feel hopeful for the first time in a long time, and that—it's all you, baby."

The words are on the tip of my tongue.

Just three of them. Simple enough.

I've said them before, but I've never actually meant them.

I open my mouth. *Just say it.*

"Answer's yes." Aw, now I feel like a chickenshit. I just don't wanna ruin this moment. Everyone's in a good place. One major milestone at a time, right?

Wheeler wraps me in a tight hug. I wrap my arms

around her waist and pull her against me, burying my head in her neck so I can inhale the familiar smell of her skin.

Maybe one day, she'll say yes to me too.

For right now, though, this is enough.

I got my girl, and now I got a plan to pivot my life and my career in a way I've always wanted.

I'm bursting.

I'm happy.

CHAPTER 30
What Happens Next
Wheeler

Tha-wunk, tha-wunk, tha-wunk.

The loud, insistent beat of the baby's heart suddenly fills the room, and I'm filled with a sense of overwhelming gratitude. And joy. And disbelief.

I burst into tears.

"Aw, Blue, you're doing great." Duke runs his thumb over the back of my hand and nods at the ultrasound screen. "Look how perfect that little nugget is."

The ultrasound tech nods, smiling. "He's right, Mom. Everything is looking great. Heart rate is 155 beats per minute, and we're measuring a little ahead at nine weeks and six days."

Mom. First time someone's called me that.

I cry some more.

"That's good?" Duke asks, sniffling.

"That's excellent." The tech moves the wand over my belly. "Your doctor will likely keep your current due date, but we could be looking at a big, healthy baby."

"Big, huh?" Duke squeezes my hand. "Runs in the family."

The tech and I both laugh, even as I roll my eyes. "Think it's a boy, then?"

"I think girl, all the way."

"Y'all can find out the sex at your twenty-week anatomy scan," the tech says. "It's a really fun ultrasound. You'll see the brain, the chambers of the heart, the little bones."

"And not so little—"

"Parts." I cut him a look. "If it's a boy."

"I was going to say not so little *heart*. Our daughter's going to be a lover."

"Just like her daddy." I grin at him through a film of tears. "You'd be such a great girl dad."

"Sawyer just learned how to braid Ella's hair. Said he'd be happy to teach me."

My heart twists at the image of Duke brushing a little girl's hair.

I can't believe we're doing this.

I can't believe this man and this baby are mine.

I really, really hope I don't mess this up. Duke and the baby are nice reminders to focus on the positive. They're also the best excuse to think ahead instead of dwelling on the past.

Looking up at the screen, I see a tiny, bean-shaped blur that floats in a transparent sac. The beating heart is barely visible as a pulsing white light.

In thirty-some-odd weeks, I'm going to have my own my little family. Before meeting Duke, I would've felt this overwhelming sense of disbelief. *All this goodness is happening to me? The girl who's been told all her life she's too sensitive, a pain in the ass, a strange, shameful, ultimately forgettable human being? What right does she have to happiness?*

Now, allowing myself to enjoy that goodness just feels like the next right step.

Duke grabs my hand again as we head out of our appointment after meeting with Dr. Martinez in an exam room following the ultrasound.

"Since it appears this nugget is sticking around, I'd like to officially share the news that we're expecting with my family." Duke looks at me. "Maybe host a little get-together at the cottage or something?"

Those butterflies appear again in my center. The doctor informed us that with such a strong heartbeat and good measurements, our baby has a very good chance of making it to the all-important twelve-week mark, when the instance of miscarriage goes way down.

Even if that wasn't the case, I still want to officially tell Duke's family. Yes, they already know, but this way, no one is tiptoeing around the news. We can finally all celebrate together, and they can be there for us if anything ever happened.

I'm learning how valuable support like that is.

I'm learning how much I need it and how good it feels to accept it.

"I love that idea. Maybe we have a fire on the porch? Have s'mores for Ella and Junie. And Mollie. And definitely for me too."

I've never had much of a sweet tooth, but all of a sudden, I've been craving chocolate and ice cream and Patsy's Texas sheet cake.

Duke nods. "Consider it done."

He doesn't broach the subject of my family until we're in his truck and heading back to my townhome.

"I know this is a sore subject." Adjusting his hand on the top of the wheel, he meets my eyes. "But we're gonna have to tell your parents about us and the baby at some point."

I grab his forearm as he shifts gears. "You're not a sore subject."

"I'm gonna be when your daddy finds out we've only been dating for, like, two seconds, and you're already pregnant."

Dad is gonna be *pissed*. Not only because he has a terrible temper and even worse impulse control, but this is also how his sad story began.

Mom's too. Which makes me think she's also going to be less than thrilled. Sure, she loves kids, and I know one day she'd be excited to be a grandmother.

I also know she wants me to learn from her mistakes. How do I make her see that the mistake wasn't having a baby but having a baby with someone who was never going to be a friend to her?

"Haines is happy for us," I say. "And my parents... well. They'll just have to come around, because I'm doing this."

He takes his hand off the gearshift and puts it on my thigh. "*We're* doing this. Together."

"You wanna get laid, don't you?"

He grins. "Well, yeah. But that's not why I'm saying that."

"I know."

"Good."

I put my hand over his and squeeze his fingers. "I

want them to meet you. My parents. I hope you know I'm not ashamed of you or anything. They'll…love you eventually."

"Like, in a month? Or we talking years?"

My stomach flips at the idea of us being together that long. I had a boyfriend in college I dated for a year, which felt monumental at the time. Shocker, I ended up running when things got serious. Am I really capable of *staying* this time?

Really, the question should be am I capable of letting someone in and trusting that they'll stay? Because that's what needs to happen if I want a relationship that lasts a lifetime. Which I do. You wouldn't necessarily know it, but I'm a romantic at heart. I want to believe that happily ever after exists and that my story can have a different ending than my parents'. Just like I want to believe that I'm not as awful or difficult to love as my family made me feel.

I just wish I could trust myself.

"Pretty sure you'll win my parents over quicker than that." I let my head fall back on the seat. I'm tired. And yeah, kinda turned on too.

"I'll start my campaign right now. Invite them to the ranch."

My heart hiccups. "What? I'm not sure—"

"Let them see how well we take care of you there. They can also meet my family. Not to brag, but they're pretty awesome. Well, maybe we let them meet Cash last since he's so grumpy. But Ryder will show them a good time. Wyatt'll take some money off your dad and older brother if they're poker players. Even if they're not. Especially if they're not."

That makes me smile. "I like that idea."

"What about weekend after next? Weather's supposed to be good, and as far as I know, everyone will be at the ranch."

The hope in his voice has my pulse skipping a beat. I feel like most guys wouldn't be champing at the bit to meet their girlfriend's parents. Least of all if that girlfriend got unintentionally pregnant.

But here's Duke, ready to tackle the issue head-on.

This man—the guy with character and intelligence and grit—*really* likes me. His level of devotion is bewildering in the best way.

Doesn't make sense for a person of Duke's caliber to want to be with a bitchy, difficult person, right?

What if I'm not that person?

Or what if I can be bitchy and difficult, but I'm also kind and caring and fun to be around? It seems unfair and unrealistic to expect someone to be on their best behavior all the time.

What if I'm a good person who's just trying her best? Fucking up but learning from it and trying better the next go-around?

I didn't realize I've been holding myself to a ridiculous standard of perfection until now. Like I was supposed to look perfect and act perfectly and do things perfectly right out of the gate. That's a ridiculous goal for anyone.

What if I'm right about who I am, and Preston isn't?

Only one way to find out.

"Let's do it." I reach for my phone. "I'll start with Mom. Do you think I should give them any kind of heads-up? Maybe tell them you and I are dating and I want them to meet you?"

Duke nods, shifting gears. "I think that's a good call. Might make them a little more amenable to that news." He nods at my midsection. "Your daddy doesn't own any guns, does he?"

I laugh, even as an icy spike of fear lodges itself in my chest. "He doesn't."

Duke cuts me a look, his eyes flashing. "Good. Even if he did, I hope you know you're safe with me, Blue."

My heart swells and so does my throat. I look out the window so I don't burst into tears all over again.

Because truth is I do feel safe with Duke. Not just in the physical sense. In the emotional sense too. And that feeling of security is something I've been missing in my life.

I'm grateful I found it with him.

The fire crackles.

A breeze blows through the trees, filling this little slice of heaven with the rustle of leaves.

The sun has begun to set. It's the golden hour, my favorite time of day, when the air is pleasantly cool and the light is ardent, painting everything in shades of yellow and amber.

The sky is clear, its fiery colors vibrant.

And the rocking chair I'm currently sitting in? It's so comfortable I melt into the seat, the ache in my back lessening as I use my big toe to rock myself back and forth. Back and forth.

I'm not feeling great. I've been hit by a bout of insomnia, another lovely symptom of pregnancy. Paired with the nausea I've been experiencing, it makes for a pretty miserable end to my first trimester. But I'll take it if it means having a healthy baby.

My boobs still hurt, and I feel bloated. Even so, it's such a beautiful evening I almost forget about all that.

I'm also really, really excited to welcome our visitors. Everyone on the ranch already knows I'm pregnant, but it's still going to be fun to share the news.

Duke's family is going to be so happy for us. They already are, despite the, ahem, less than perfect circumstances that led to us getting together. It's nice to know we're not going to be judged for what happened.

It's nice to know we're going to be *celebrated* for it instead.

My boyfriend—*I still can't believe this delicious specimen of a man is my* boyfriend—emerges from the cottage. He's carrying a large metal tray that contains all the accoutrements we'll need for our s'mores: a box of graham crackers, stacks of Hershey's chocolate bars, and a big bag of marshmallows. In his other hand, he holds a bottle of Coca-Cola, which he holds out to me.

"Sally and Wyatt swear it tastes better in the glass bottle," he explains. "So I grabbed some at the grocery store. I know the carbonation helps settle your stomach some."

Taking the bottle, I shake my head. "You're lucky your family's about to be here. Otherwise I'd be climbing you like a goddamn tree." I take a sip of the Coke. It's sweet, ice cold, and so delicious I can't help but moan. "Thank you."

He grins. "You say that like it's a bad thing. You're welcome to climb me anytime, sweetheart." Leaning down, he presses a quick, hot kiss to my mouth before setting the tray on the nearby picnic table.

Ryder is the first to arrive. He's wearing a Bellamy Brooks T-shirt and a big smile.

He's also holding a gift that's wrapped in pale yellow paper.

My throat closes in as he mounts the steps. I stand, and he loops an arm around my neck and pulls me in for a hug.

"Hey, mama," he says. "Congratulations."

I can only whisper a reply. "Thank you."

"I'm thrilled for y'all."

I see Duke approach over Ryder's shoulder. "You whisperin' sweet nothings into my girlfriend's ear?"

"Just some words of wisdom for the mother of my niece."

Leaning my head against Ryder's shoulder, I swallow. "So you're convinced it's a girl too?"

"Definitely a girl. We need more of 'em in this family." Ryder pulls back, and my heart twists when I see that his eyes are wet. "Glad you're one of them, mama."

Duke glances at me, brows knit. He's not sure if I like being called that.

I don't like it. I love it.

"We'll see if you and dad are right." I lean over to curl my hand over Duke's shoulder. "I'm still thinking it's a boy."

"It's definitely a boy!"

I glance to my right and see Mollie and Cash approaching. She's got a bouquet of flowers in her hand, and Cash is carrying a huge box.

"What's that?" My heart begins to pound.

Mollie grins. "Just a little something I know you'll like. I'm sorry I didn't have time to wrap it."

"Dang thing is heavy as hell." Cash sets down the box on the porch with a grunt. "Means it's gonna be sturdy."

Ducking to get a better look, my eyes blur over when I see that it's the dream stroller Mollie and I gushed about the other day. We're obsessed. She likes it in heather gray, and I liked it best in bright red.

She and Cash got me the red.

"Y'all." I cover my face with my hands. "You did not need—"

"Yes, we did." Now Cash is pulling me in for a hug. "I love that our babies are gonna be almost the same exact age. It'll be like having twins."

Wyatt's face splits into a grin. Where the hell did he come from? "I think we got enough of those in the family. Hey, Wheeler. Welcome to the family."

"Please don't make this weird," Duke says. "Wheeler and I are dating. Yes, we're also having a baby, but we're not—I'm not—"

"Gonna wife her up?" Ryder rolls his eyes. "We all know it's happening."

Duke does that thing where he looks at me, gauging my reaction.

I'm crying and I'm smiling and, wow, Sawyer and Ava are here, and so are Ella and Junie, who are currently wrapping me in the world's sweetest little group hug.

"Y'all ready to make s'mores?" Duke squats in front of them, a handful of sticks in his hand. "I know I am."

"Yes!" Junie jumps up and down. "But what is a more?"

Duke smiles. It's so handsome and so genuinely happy that I feel short of breath. "It's only the best dessert ever invented. Here, I'll show you how we make 'em. You start with the marshmallow, which we put on the end of this stick…"

Sally insists Mollie and I sit in the pair of rocking chairs in front of the fire. Ryder insists I open his gift. Everyone breaks out in *awwws* when I hold up the little onesie dotted with cowboy hats and horseshoes.

"Dude." Duke sets a plate of s'mores on my lap. "Where the hell'd you find that?"

Ryder shrugs. "Billie helped me pick it out."

"Billie?" Cash raises his eyebrows. "Colt know about y'all hangin' out?"

"There's nothing to know." Ryder's voice has an edge. "I asked her for a favor, and she helped me out."

Wyatt claps his hands. "Oh, Lord, there's more to that story, ain't there?"

"Shut up," Ryder says.

"Tread carefully is all we're sayin'." Wyatt holds up his hands. "You know how the Wallace boys are."

Sally pats his stomach. "Almost as bad as the Rivers boys are."

"True story." Duke sets down his stick and wipes his hands on a towel. "I'd like to think we're more handsome, though, right?"

"Of course you are," I say, picking up my s'more.

Ella and Junie are happily munching on their treats, their little faces already streaked with melted chocolate and marshmallow. I take a bite of mine and nearly moan again.

"You're also really good at making dessert." I lick

some chocolate off my thumb. "This is delicious, Duke. Maybe you're not so far off from cracking open those cookbooks."

He meets my eyes. "Ready when you are."

"I hope that means y'all are ready to officially share your 'surprise' news." Cash swipes a s'more off the tray by the fireplace.

Duke slips his hand through mine. "Ready?" he asks me.

"Not like everybody doesn't already know." I set down my plate and stand up. "You wanna tell them?"

"I mean, I do. But if you have something you'd like to say..."

I squeeze his hand. "You first."

"All right." His broad shoulders rise on an inhale before he glances at his family. "Y'all will be happy to know Wheeler finally agreed to be my girlfriend."

Wyatt throws up his hands. "Hell yeah, she did!"

"What a shocker." Sawyer smiles as he slips his hand into his front pocket. "The two of you have only been making eyes at each other for how many months now?"

Ava gives him a playful shove. "You know better than anyone that timing is everything."

"So do you." He leans in to kiss her.

Duke gives my hand a squeeze. *Your turn.*

I also take a deep breath. "We're also going to have a baby. He or she—"

"She," Ryder says.

Wyatt nods. "Definitely a she."

I'm smiling so hard my face hurts. "She—or he—is due a little after the New Year."

The patio erupts in hoots and hollers. John B and

Patsy have snuck their way in, and they clap, absolutely delighted. I watch, eyes brimming, as Ryder extends a hand to Duke. He takes it, and then Ryder is pulling his twin in for a hug—the kind where guys slap each other on the back because they're so overwhelmed they don't know what else to do with themselves.

Ava and Mollie are crying, and Sally is taking both my hands in hers, eyes gleaming as she tells me how excited she is to see the family grow.

"Gimme a bump." Mollie sticks out her stomach. "C'mon. Don't make me wait, Wheeler. I know you wanna."

It's my turn to roll my eyes, but I give her the belly bump she's looking for. Then she pulls me in for the fiercest, tightest hug she's ever given me.

"Proud of you, friend," she says in my ear. "Keep doing what you're doing."

"Getting knocked up by cowboys?" I say with a laugh.

"Yes. Also, loving yourself as hard as you love him."

My heart lurches. Yes, I'm well aware that I've been *in the process* of falling for Duke.

Falling hard and apparently falling fast, because hearing that word—love—in relation to him feels... right.

It feels true. Which should scare the ever-loving shit out of me. I mean, it wasn't long ago that I was terrified to *date* the guy. Now I'm in love with him, and I'm not panicking or running for the hills?

"Who the hell am I?" I manage.

Mollie gives me one last squeeze. "You're exactly who you've always known yourself to be. I'm legit thrilled you finally have the courage to acknowledge her. Also, congrats on the superhot stud. I mean that literally."

"Ha. Funny cowgirl joke."

"I am a cowgirl now." She pats my back. "Only a matter of time before you become one too."

Cash, who's been shamelessly eavesdropping, gives me a smile. "Howdy, mama."

CHAPTER 31
New Hire
Wheeler

From: nick.kelce@aspenleather.com

To: wheeler@bellamybrooks.com, mollie@bellamybrooks.com, duke@bellamybrooks.com

Subject: Re: Bellamy Brooks Men's Collection

Y'ALL I'M NOT EVEN GONNA SAY HEY I'M JUST GONNA SCREAM IN ALL CAPS ABOUT HOW MUCH WE LOVE YOUR BOOTS! The City Boot is killer in that ostrich. Our fancy customers are gonna LOVE those. And the Country Boot is exactly the classic-with-a-twist silhouette we're always looking for. I know you said the samples were fresh from the boot maker, but if you're game to accept orders we'd like to place one. See attached for the details. Send me an invoice whenever is convenient for you.

Peace, love, and damn fine cowboy boots,

Nick

PS—any chance we could convince you to come to Aspen again for another trunk show? Maybe we try for the summer this time ;)

I yell.

Mollie shouts.

I hear the thump of footsteps, and then Duke, Ryder, Cash, and Patsy appear at the door, eyes wide.

"Y'all okay?" Patsy puts a hand on her chest.

"Is it the baby?" Duke and Cash blurt at the same time.

Mollie laughs, smoothing her dress over her bump. "Babies are just fine."

"Come here!" I wave frantically at Duke. "Big news!"

He hustles across the room in his full cowboy getup, hat and all, and bends at the waist to look at the laptop screen over my shoulder. I can smell the sweat on him. The clean air too. He and his brothers just arrived at the New House for lunch—Patsy's barbecue chicken, which she's serving with cornbread and collard greens.

My stomach grumbles just thinking about it. *Hell yes.* Chicken is no longer the enemy. In fact, it's something I suddenly crave. Now that I'm finally in my second trimester, I'm starting to feel worlds better.

Hungrier too.

Duke points to the screen. "Still makes me smile to see my new email address."

"And Wheeler and I are still your bosses." Mollie elbows him. "No horsing around, you hear?"

I laugh. "Love the cowgirl jokes."

"I got lots of 'em." She nods at the laptop. "Now read the dang email, Duke, so we can freaking celebrate already."

Duke squints, the edges of his eyes crinkling in the most adorable way imaginable as his smile grows and grows and grows.

He looks at me, tapping the bottom of his fist on the desk. "Well, hot damn. How many did he order?"

"Only *two hundred* pairs of each." Running my fingertips over the mouse pad, I click on the order. "Which means—"

"You're well on your way to building a women's *and* men's cowboy boot empire." He laughs. "Congratulations, Blue."

"It's *our* empire, dummy." I wrap my arms around his neck. "You're still good to go shirtless in the ad campaign, right? Because that was part of our pitch to Nick."

Duke laughs, a velvety chuckle that I feel in my nipples. "How many times I gotta say you could pay me a hell of a lot less to show a hell of a lot more?"

"We didn't offer to pay you," Mollie teases.

I kiss his cheek. "We just brought you onto the team and made you partner."

"Oooh." He ducks his lips. "That's one sexy title."

"You're one sexy cowboy."

Patsy laughs. "Y'all need the room? I gotta finish up the cornbread anyway—"

"I mean, if y'all are willing…" Duke's eyes gleam.

I give him a shove. "Success turn you on?"

"Yours does, yeah." He kisses me back. "I can grab a shower—"

"How 'bout we celebrate first?" Cash asks. "Then we 'nap.'"

Mollie bites her lip. "I like naps."

"Who doesn't like naps?" I rise, putting my hands on the small of my back. I'm achy and I'm tired and I'm so freaking happy.

And relieved.

And *happy*.

"You're glowing, Blue," Duke says later when we're at home, naked in bed after the slowest, most delicious sex ever. "I'm proud of you. Proud of us."

I turn onto my side and tuck my hand underneath my cheek on the pillow. "We've had an awesome year so far at Bellamy Brooks. So many wins we've been working toward for such a long, long, *long* time." I shut my eyes. "For a while there, I wasn't sure we'd make it. We were spinning our wheels year after year, trying to catch a break."

He nudges my knee with his underneath the covers. "But you stuck with it. Remember our motto—perseverance is everything."

I nod, opening my eyes. "It really is. And today's win—it hits different for some reason. Like, I suddenly feel like our success isn't a fluke. We're not just going to hit it big once with one collection. People are banging on our door, asking for more. Which is how you build a career out of something like this, right? People wanting more of what you're creating?"

"Absolutely. It's how you create longevity."

"Yes." *Yes.* "And I think I'm seeing for the first time how we're not a one-hit wonder. Our success isn't a fluke. It's happening for a reason, and that reason is—"

"You were right." Duke's blue eyes bore into mine. "You knew you could build a successful business doing something you love."

My heart flutters. "Yes. Even though everyone told me I couldn't."

I was right.

Holy fucking shit, I was *right*.

Everyone told me I would fall on my face trying to make it as an entrepreneur in the fashion world. But here I am, making a damn good living doing exactly that. Have I loved every minute? Hell no. There were entire years I dreaded going to Mollie's condo in uptown Dallas to work. I feel like I spent a good chunk of my twenties feeling ashamed to tell people what I did for work when they asked me.

But I couldn't quit. I knew in my heart of hearts that this is what I wanted to do—be a successful entrepreneur in a creative field. It just took me a lot longer than I thought it would to figure out how to make that happen.

Took me a lot longer than I thought to realize I was doing the right thing.

I want to shout. I want to smile. I want to kiss the shit out of the man beside me.

I do all three, Duke and I giggling like lunatics as we make out.

"I was right," I keep saying into his kiss. "Duke, I was *right*."

"You know what else you were right about?" He takes my hand and guides it to his dick. He's hard again, his velvety warmth filling my hand.

I give him a pump. "What's that?"

"Me." His lips move into a grin against my own. "You knew the night we met you liked me."

I'm laughing as I toss a leg over his hip and guide him to my center. "Just had to get out of my own way to let you in."

"Glad you did, sweethe—*oh*, fuck you feel good." He glides inside me on a smooth stroke. "You meant that literally, yeah? Letting me in?"

"Ha."

He rolls on top of me. "So now the question is, Blue—what else are you right about?"

I'm hit by a flood of thoughts—of certainty—as he fucks me to orgasm.

I was right about my ability to teach myself how to be a designer.

I was right that I could learn to run a business too.

I was right to keep going when everyone else told me to quit.

I am right about being lovable. I'm not the problem. Preston is the problem. Dad is the problem. The world is the problem. Perfectionism is the fucking problem.

I. Am. Loved. Look at this man, loving the shit out of me every day and every night. He never lets up. Never wavers in his worship of me and the little life we're building together.

I am kindhearted. I am messy. I am fun and funny and a joy to be around—most of the time anyway. And when I'm not? That's okay. That's called being human.

A feeling bursts through me. It's light. It's laughter. It's an orgasm I can feel in every corner of my being.

I'm going to let Duke all the way in, because I know he's going to love what he finds.

No more holding back. No more pushing him or anyone else away. I'm moving toward connection now, not running away from it, breaking my own heart before anyone else can.

After we get cleaned up, I head for the kitchen. I play Milli Vanilli on the little speaker by the window above the sink while I make grilled cheese and Duke, who put on his glasses, throws together a salad with the season's first tomatoes, fresh from Patsy's garden.

"Wow, that's good," Duke says after taking his first bite of grilled cheese. "Just as good as the first time you made it, Blue. Thank you."

"I always want to make you grilled cheese." My voice wobbles, but I push forward. "Just like I always want to dance with you to the nineties' best lip-synched hits."

Duke's eyes lock on mine across the table. He smiles. "I love the sound of this."

"I love you." A tear slips out of my eye. "So freaking much, baby. It terrifies me to think I could've missed out on all this if I'd kept being stupid—kept pushing you away. But I didn't and now I'm happier than I thought I ever deserved to be. I feel so lucky, and I am so grateful, and—"

I don't get to finish, though, because Duke is pushing up to his feet and rounding the table and grabbing my face in his hands. He kisses me, hard, and I feel his cheeks go damp as he keeps kissing me, his tongue in my mouth, his hands in my hair.

"Thank fuck," he finally breathes, breaking the kiss. "Because I'm in love with you too, Blue. I always wanna dance with you and make you s'mores and go on treacherous road trips with you."

"Dear Lord, let's hope we don't have any more of those," I say, giggling like an idiot because I *am* an idiot for this man.

I am stupid in love with him, and I don't care who knows it.

"Most of all, though, I always wanna be the one who makes you smile." He runs his thumbs underneath my eyes. "You and this baby—y'all are my world now. Grateful doesn't begin to cover how I feel about that fact."

I kiss his mouth. Softly this time. "Can we dance now?"

"Yes, Blue." He pulls me to my feet. "Answer's always gonna be yes if you're the one asking."

We dance in the kitchen until my feet hurt from busting several terrible moves and my sides hurt from laughing. We dance to Billy Joel and Whitney Houston and old school Tim McGraw. Duke sings totally off-key along to Kenny Loggins, while I know every word to Reba's "Fancy."

The whole thing is silly and stupid and quite possibly the most fun I've ever had stone-cold sober. When we finally collapse into bed, I fall asleep almost immediately, curled up in my usual position as little spoon.

Sometimes, love really does win.

Thank God for that.

CHAPTER 32
Quittin' Time
Duke

The week Wheeler's parents are due to visit, I take Thursday and Friday off to prepare.

Even though they're staying at the New House, I still clean the cottage top to bottom. I pay a small fortune to have three new rocking chairs and a pair of side tables for the family room rush delivered. I mow the grass, stock the fridge, mop the floors, and practice making a few recipes from one of Mom's cookbooks. I refresh the tape we use to hang Ella's and Junie's art on our fridge, including the three pieces we won at the auction. Wheeler and I figured we'd have her family over to the cottage for dinner the night we tell them about the pregnancy, so I planned a simple but hearty meal: skillet pork chops with shallots, cheesy grits, and roasted brussels sprouts.

Wyatt brings over some wine. Ever since Mollie taught him all about Barolo so he'd sound smart on his first date with Sally, he's become obnoxiously helpful on that front.

Ava and the girls bake us chocolate chunk cookies for dessert. Patsy drops off some homemade vanilla bean ice cream, along with a note. *Good luck! Please remember that firearms are to be used for life-and-death situations only. Don't pull a John B! Much love, P.*

John B and Wyatt had a—well, we'll call it a "charged moment" when John found out Sally wasn't going to take some big veterinary job in New York. He mistakenly thought she wanted to stay in Hartsville because Wyatt was holding her back, when in reality, he was planning to leave his whole life behind and move to New York with her.

A shotgun was involved. So were some choice words about Sally's decision to forgo the job offer. Luckily, Sally, Wyatt, and John B were able to quickly work through the misunderstanding, and no one was shot. Still left us all a little shaken. How could I not be, seeing one of my favorite people in the world pull a gun on my brother?

Ryder, being Ryder, doesn't bring anything except advice I don't need.

"They may *say* you and Wheeler are dead to them, but I doubt they'll actually mean it."

I set one of the new rocking chairs in front of the hearth on the porch. I cluck my tongue when I see it's not the exact same shade of black as the other two I already have. "So helpful. Thanks for nothing."

"Hey. I'm just trying to lighten the mood a little. You're clearly nervous."

"What makes you say that?" I pull the rocking chair an inch to the right. Nope, now it's too close to the fireplace. I pull it two inches to the left and curse when I see that it's too far.

Ryder nods in my general direction. "You're obsessing over stupid shit. Her parents don't care if your rocking chairs are in a perfect fucking circle. They just want to know that you love their daughter and that you'll be there for her when this baby comes."

Straightening, I wince at the soreness in my middle. All this prep is doing a number on my back. "What if they're not? Like, if they're not there when the baby comes, I mean. Wheeler's not super close with her parents or her older brother. But I know she'll be crushed if they pretend like none of this is happening and don't participate in our kid's life."

Ryder pulls off his baseball hat, smoothing back his hair before putting the hat on backward. "Fuck them if that's what they do."

"No shit. But that won't bring Wheeler any comfort."

"Us being there will." He hops down the steps to grab another rocking chair. "They ain't the only family she's got now. And you bet your bottom dollar all eighty-seven of us Riverses and Powells and Bartletts and Lucks are gonna be in that hospital waiting room."

I chuckle. "How much you wanna bet Wyatt'll get kicked out for sneaking in a flask?"

"Not if they don't kick me out first for the same offense." He carefully sets down the rocking chair beside the others, stepping back to eyeball it before moving the chair a little ways back.

Ryder may talk a big game about not giving a shit, but deep down, he cares. A lot. That thought makes my heart twist.

"Thank you." My voice is gruff. "For being with me

through all this. Wheeler talks a lot about what a good friend I am, and I think…I know I learned it from you."

"You getting all sappy and shit on me?" Ryder smiles. "Good."

"I hate you."

"That's not very nice. I love you. Very much. And I can't wait to love up on your sweet baby." He claps me on the shoulder. "Why you think you want a girl so bad?"

"I don't know. Maybe because I'm obsessed with Wheeler, and I can imagine just how fun it would be to have a mini version of her running around." I look up at the cottage. Then I glance at my truck. "Think I'm gonna need something newer."

Ryder chuckles softly. "Might be good to have a car with a back seat, for both safety and making out purposes."

"I'll call Rod at the dealership." I pull out my phone to make a note of it. "Sawyer said he gave him a good deal on his Silverado."

My brother squints up at the sky. "You gonna marry her?"

There's a squeezing sensation inside my chest. Have I already asked Mollie what kind of ring Wheeler would like? Maybe. Am I already thinking about dream destinations, places like Paris and Jackson Hole and the British Virgin Islands that would be the perfect place to get down on one knee? Definitely.

But I don't want to overplay my hand. Wheeler and I just said "I love you" to each other. We've been together for practically two minutes. It's not my intention to rush her or rush into something neither of us is ready for.

Thing is I am ready. Would be even if we weren't having a baby. I remember Garrett saying something along the lines of "when you know, you know."

I know I wanna make a life with Wheeler. It's that simple. Being with her is exciting and easy. All my dreams seem within reach when she's around. I'd like to think neither of us is settling or playing small by being in a relationship and becoming parents.

Instead, the world feels so much bigger. That's never happened with anyone else before.

"I ain't lettin' her go," I say.

"That ain't what I'm asking."

I eye him. "Ever consider my love life isn't your business?"

"Everything you do is my business." He holds my gaze. "You're my person. Like, literally. We are literally the same person, genetically speaking at least. And I want you to be happy. Maybe then…" His throat works. "I don't know. Maybe then I got a chance to be happy too."

Aw, shit, now my throat's closing in. I hadn't considered that me pairing off with Wheeler is a big change for Ryder too, especially now that he's the only one of us who is still single. We've done everything together. Been through everything together. I wouldn't say I'm moving on now, but my life is moving forward, and Ryder's is staying in the same place.

"Your time'll come." I put a hand on his shoulder.

He blinks. "I know. Life is fine, don't get me wrong. Just seeing you and Wheeler…nice to know that kinda connection is possible."

"I am gonna marry her."

"I know you are."

Next thing I know, I'm pulling him in for a hug. The kind where we quietly cry into each other's shoulders, holding on so tight I can barely breathe.

It all comes out. The joy and the grief. Last time we hugged it out like this was at Mom and Dad's funeral.

"Hartsville will always be home base for us," I manage thickly. "You know that, right? I wanna travel, but I'm also not goin' anywhere. I've learned freedom ain't necessarily about going places. It's about having the space to be myself. To live a life that feels right."

Ryder nods. "I like that idea. And you'd better be sticking around. Could you imagine if you left me with Cash and Wy and Sawyer? They'd eat me alive."

"Cash would, yeah."

"They'd be so happy for you." Ryder pounds my back. "Mom and Dad. And Garrett. I'd like to think they're rooting for us all from up there in the sky."

I like that idea too.

Who knows what happens to us when we die? I do know, however, there's real power in believing your people—past, present, future—have your back and are making shit happen for you behind the scenes.

I feel Mom's presence as I prepare some chicken salad for lunch before moving to the pork chops we'll be having for dinner. Know Garrett's in the room when I turn on my favorite Brooks & Dunn album, singing along while I chop shallots and try not to cry again. And Dad—

Dad is everywhere too. As I cook, I think about how he handled meeting his in-laws—my grandparents—for the first time. Apparently it took a minute for Mom's family to warm up to him, a hardscrabble rancher who talked a big game about keeping his family's legacy alive on the property they'd owned for generations.

I think about him scooping one of us up and putting us in front of him in his saddle every damn day. Rain or shine, he was gonna teach us everything his daddy taught him about working cattle and raising a family.

Can't wait to teach my baby the same.

I look up from sticking a toothpick in the cornbread and nearly have a heart attack when I see the time on the clock above the stove. *Shit*, Wheeler's parents are due to arrive any minute.

I jam my best hat on my head and hop in my truck. The New House is quiet when I let myself inside and head for Wheeler's makeshift office, where she's pretending to work. I know she's pretending because she keeps typing the same sentence over and over again on her computer, then hitting the delete button every time.

"Think it's quittin' time, Blue."

She whips around in her chair, her expression relaxing when she sees me. "He—*hey*, cowboy." Her eyes rake over my Stetson, white button-up, and Wranglers, stopping when they reach the boots I'm wearing.

Her face lights up with a smile. "Our Country Boots. Nice choice."

"I know. Can't wait to show 'em off to your mama and daddy."

Wheeler's expression falls. "At least one of us is excited to see them."

Frowning, I close the distance between us. Lean down to kiss her mouth. "You not feeling great?"

"You smell good."

"I got important people to meet."

Her lips twitch. "And one important person, I mean thing, to do."

"Don't tempt me, Blue." I tilt my head and feather my lips over her throat. "Last thing we need is your parents walking in on you yellin' my name."

She puts a hand on my chest. "At least then they'd know how much I like you."

"Or they'd think you're using me for my body." Straightening, I adjust my belt.

Closing her laptop, Wheeler stands. She goes up on her toes to tap my hat. "That's the only thing I'd ever use you for. Well, that and your perfect—"

"Company's here!"

We both glance toward the door at the sound of Patsy's voice.

"Look at me, Wheeler." She does as I tell her. I take her face in my hands. "You and me—we're gonna be just fine, regardless of how the next forty-eight hours goes, all right?"

Blinking, she nods, curling her hand around my wrist. "I know. I also know I keep apologizing in advance for whatever comes out of my dad's and brother's mouths—"

"Good thing I'm not easy to offend."

"They'll find a way, trust me."

Wheeler lets go of my wrist. I grab her hand. "C'mon, we got good news to share. Remember that."

She brightens a little at that. "Yeah. Yeah, it is good news. I just hope you don't fall out of love with me after meeting them." She motions to the door.

"Ain't gonna happen, Blue."

She must know I mean that, because she squeezes my hand.

Together we head out to the front hall. My heart pounds, but I keep my footsteps steady in the hopes it keeps Wheeler steady too.

Patsy is at the door. "Y'all excited?"

"Trying to be," Wheeler replies.

"Aw, honey. It's going to be a nice visit." Patsy reaches for Wheeler's arm. "Not to toot our own horn, but Lucky River Ranch's hospitality is second to none."

I nod. "She's right."

"I'm not as much of a city girl as Mollie is," Wheeler replies, "but I wouldn't say I was a fan of the country. Then I came here, and now—"

"You're one of us." I bring her hand to my lips. "We'll win every last one of 'em over, you'll see."

I just wish I felt as confident as I sound.

CHAPTER 33
A Can of Whoop Ass
Duke

Holy shit, Wheeler looks exactly like her mom.

That's my first thought.

My second: *Who the fuck is the asshat in the pink polo and boat shoes?*

"Preston Rankin." He gives me a once-over before shoving his hand in my direction. "Huh. A real cowboy." He glances at Wheeler. "Didn't think you were telling the truth."

I give him a handshake that's firm enough to border on pain. "I'm a real cowboy, yes. Nice to meet you, Preston. I'm Duke Rivers. Welcome to my family's ranch."

"It's so beautiful!" Mrs. Rankin lifts her arms, clearly inviting me in for a hug. "You are too, Duke. Goodness, Wheeler, you should've warned me he was this handsome."

"Fran," the man behind her groans. He's a rotund version of Preston, right down to the polo embroidered with a country club emblem and those dumbass boat shoes.

Who wears those things to a ranch?

"It's all right." Laughing, I give her the hug she's looking for. "I see where Wheeler gets her good looks from. Y'all could be sisters."

"Shameless," Wheeler says, but when I lean back, I see that she's smiling. "Haines! Hi!"

Her younger brother launches himself into her arms. "God, I've missed you."

"I've missed you too." Her voice is a little thin.

Haines gives me a hug next. "You sure you're ready for this?" he whispers.

I laugh. "I'm sure."

He steps aside, but Mr. Rankin stays awkwardly in place.

"Sir." I extend my hand. "It's a pleasure to finally meet you."

Eyeing me, he takes my hand. "Tim Rankin."

"I'm grateful y'all took the time to come all the way out here. How was the drive?"

"Oh, I drove. Please call me Frannie, by the way." Wheeler's mom smiles up at me. "And the ride was fine."

Interesting. This man has the gall to not even split the drive with the woman he's put through hell.

"Glad to hear it. Why don't y'all come inside?" Patsy opens the door a little wider. "We'll get you settled, and then we'll get you fed."

Tim makes a noise, like he's already fed up. "Not sure that we're hungry."

"Dad, if you wanna lie down, go lie down. The rest of us will eat." I can tell Haines is trying very hard not to roll his eyes.

I grab Wheeler's hand again. Preston watches me do it, his expression carefully neutral.

"I need to use the facilities," he says, then brushes past me inside. Tim follows closely behind.

"I'll be there in a minute," Frannie says. "I just need to get our luggage—"

"I'll get your luggage." I glance over my shoulder. Were Tim and Preston going to come out after lunch to get the bags? Or were they really going to let Frannie carry it all in?

"Tim has a bad back," she says, reading my mind. "And Preston will help after he uses the restroom. I don't mind, really—"

"But I do mind you carrying everyone else's bags." I meet eyes with Wheeler. Her jaw twitches. I get why she's pissed. "Y'all head inside. I'll set your luggage in your rooms and meet you in the kitchen."

Wheeler's brows curve upward. "You sure? I can—"

"You won't. And yes, I'm sure."

"I'm sorry they suck," she says.

"Wheeler." Frannie gives her a look.

Wow, lots of family dynamics happening here. No wonder Wheeler's been such a mess.

We have the world's most awkward lunch ever with my brothers and their wives and girlfriends in the kitchen. My family is predictably loud, but they also go out of their way to be friendly. Ava tries to engage Tim on his work, but he responds with one-word answers. He also takes one bite of his chicken salad—I made it with red grapes, walnuts, and celery, and it's out-of-this-world good—then drops his fork and pushes away his plate, clearly pissed.

Sawyer meets my eyes across the table. *What's his deal?*

Wheeler, meanwhile, is literally sweating as she tries to keep the conversation going. Preston quietly sips his water as his gaze wanders around the kitchen. I'm sure he's assessing how much everything costs and in turn how wealthy we are.

A lot richer than you, dickhead.

Haines is the first to jump up and offer to help do dishes. Grateful the meal is finally over, I start to grab plates too. Wheeler tries to help, but I shoo her away.

"Rest." I place her plate in the crook of my elbow. "Go put your feet up if you need to, yeah?"

That's when I catch Tim watching me, his eyes narrowed.

Shit. Did I just give us away? Wheeler told her parents we were dating, but they obviously don't know about the baby yet.

"I know everyone's tired," I add swiftly. "Your rooms are ready, so feel free to lie down for a bit."

Cash stops me on the way to the sink. "You got this?" he murmurs, glancing over his shoulder. "Seems like a tough crowd."

"I'm fine. It's Wheeler I'm worried about." I look at my girlfriend, whose posture tells me everything I need to know: stiff expression, shoulders slumped. Defeat is written all over her.

My chest clenches. If I didn't know why Wheeler loved travel before, I do now: she wanted to get the hell out of the house she was raised in.

"Mollie is on standby," Cash replies. "She's known the Rankins for a long time. Which means she knows Wheeler is gonna need extra TLC this weekend."

I tap his chest with my free elbow. "Appreciate that."

"And you know you just gotta say the word, right? We're all available if you need to, ahem, end the weekend early."

My chest clenches again, for a different reason this time. I've always loved my family, but now, I appreciate having them more than ever. Growing up one of five kids was no picnic, but being part of such a close-knit crew certainly has its perks—my brothers having my back among them, no questions asked.

I want that for Wheeler too.

I want that for our baby too.

———

Thankfully the Rankins retreat to their rooms in the New House for the afternoon. Mollie whisks away Wheeler, the two of them disappearing to Mollie and Cash's cabin.

Meanwhile, Wyatt gets a call from our contractor that there's an issue with the new irrigation we're installing on the Rivers' side of the ranch. He and I hop in his truck and drive that way. We get stuck, literally and figuratively, in a ditch that's ten feet deep and a hundred feet long trying to help the crew fix it.

So much for staying clean.

Back at home, I grab a late afternoon shower, then get dressed in my—our—bedroom. That way, Wheeler has plenty of time in the bathroom to get ready for dinner while I finish prepping the food.

She arrives at the cottage a few minutes later, looking tired but better than she did at lunch.

"You all right?" I pull her in for a hug.

She nods against my chest. "Yeah. I went back to the New House and spent some time with Mom and Haines. They love you."

"Your mom okay? Your dad is…interesting."

"Mom hasn't been okay in thirty years, but she's surviving." Wheeler sighs. "We all are. I'm excited for dinner."

"You're a terrible liar."

She laughs. "Correction: I'm excited to eat the food you're making. Already smells good in here. Thank you."

"For what? Making you food?" I scoff. "Kinda my job, sweetheart."

"And for pretending to enjoy my family's company. I know they're painful."

"More painful for you."

She nods again. "Sometimes I miss them. Other times, I…well, I don't." Looking up, she meets my eyes. "Makes me appreciate having you and your family that much more. What y'all have here is special, Duke."

I brush her hair out of her face. "You're special too. You survived twenty-seven years with your family. You can make it through dinner too."

"Maybe."

"Definitely. Don't forget you also have the best excuse to, ah, excuse yourself from dinner if you need to. Once they know I knocked you up, you can do whatever the hell you want."

She grins. "I know."

"Go get ready." I give her ass a gentle slap. "I got everything handled."

I finish the food, double-check that the table outside is properly set, and light a fire.

It's all ready.

Cracking open a beer, I decide to relax on the couch in the hopes my nerves don't overwhelm me. I'm careful not to wrinkle the button-up I ironed earlier as I sit heavily on the cushions and turn on the TV.

I keep the volume low enough so that I can still hear Wheeler in the bathroom. There's something comforting about the sounds that are slowly but surely becoming familiar: the water slapping on the shower floor, the blow dryer, the music she plays on her phone while she puts on her makeup. Tonight, she's listening to The Lumineers. I don't mind that one bit.

After a while, I hear her emerge from the bathroom. Looking up, my mouth goes dry. Dick perks up.

I can only stare. She looks like a fucking bombshell with her red lips and curly hair. She's wearing a pretty blue dress with tiny straps and a neckline low enough to get me going. Even though the dress is long, hitting her midshin, I can still see how hot those high heels she's wearing make her legs look.

Her toenails—those are red too. I'm hit by the image of Wheeler seated on the bathroom floor, her head bent as she teaches our little girl how to paint *her* toes.

Shit, now I really can't breathe.

Wheeler grins. "Hey, baby."

God, I fucking love it when she calls me that.

"Blue."

Raising her brows, she waits for me to finish the thought. Her grin becomes a smile. "You all right there, cowboy?"

"You're feelin' *much* better."

She nods. "Amazing what a shower and some nail polish can do for your mood."

I set my empty beer bottle on the coffee table and stand.

"You're gorgeous." I head her way.

Grinning, she crooks her finger. "You are too. Promise me you'll kick my dad out if he offends you? Same goes for Preston."

"I'm not kicking anyone out." Curling my arms around her waist, I bury my face in her neck and inhale her scent. "I will gladly kick some ass, though."

She reaches around to squeeze *my* ass. "I like the sound of that."

Wheeler's family arrives a few minutes later. We make more awkward small talk over drinks by the fire on the porch. Wheeler sips a fake tequila and soda I made her that's just soda with lime.

"So Wheeler's staying with you here." Preston lifts a finger in the general direction of the cottage.

"She is."

"And how long have y'all been dating?"

"Long enough." I sip my beer. Watch Wheeler laugh at something Haines says. "The minute I met your sister, I knew I wanted to date her."

Preston chuckles. "Yeah. Right. Sure you did."

"You sayin' something?" I eye him.

"Just saying you didn't know her then. Like, *know* her know her. She's always been so..." Shaking his head, he tips back his tequila soda.

I hold my bottle in a death grip. "So what?"

"How do I say this nicely?" He squints. "She's not an easy person. Like, she's a little off, you know? Just really hardheaded. She wouldn't even hear out my dad about going into law, even though he has really great connections at a bunch of big law firms and could get her a plum job, no problem. She gave up a lucrative career to do what, make stupid cowboy boots for Barbie?"

I see it: me calmly setting my beer down on the table. I'd push up my right sleeve a little bit more. Curl my fingers into a fist. Then I'd turn around and hurl that fist into this smug bastard's face.

He'd cry.

I'd smile, satisfied I let him know *exactly* what I think of him talking about my girl this way.

Talking about *any* girl this way. Who the fuck does this kid think he is? God's gift to the world, just because his parents are rich?

But decking Preston in the mouth would upset Wheeler, so instead I paste on a smile and say, "I know Wheeler pretty well. Just like I know the quality and craftsmanship of her boots is top notch. She's smart, she's capable, and she does amazing work. I'm proud of her."

But Preston just raises his brows and rolls his eyes, letting out an annoyed breath. "Whatever you say. Good luck with that one."

My turn to chuckle. "You know, it's funny."

"What?"

"You went to law school, right?"

"I did, yeah."

"And now you work with your dad?"

Preston nods. "I'm the youngest partner in the firm's history."

I bet you think you earned that too, don't you? When really it was handed to you on a silver platter.

"Congrats. But really, we should be congratulating your sister, because she's going to make more money doing her 'stupid' cowboy boot thing than y'all ever will pushing paper behind a desk for ninety hours a week for the rest of your lives. Because turns out that 'stupid' cowboy boot thing isn't so stupid. It's actually really cool and really lucrative too."

Preston blinks, a pink flush working its way up his neck. "Dude, I'm not, like, attacking you—"

"But you are attacking Wheeler." I put a hand on his chest. "And that's something I'm not gonna tolerate. You understand me, *dude*?"

He blinks again. "Whatever."

I pat his chest. "Good." I turn to face everyone else. "All right, y'all. Time to eat."

I look at Wheeler. *Ready?*

She looks back. *Ready.*

Everyone serves themselves in the kitchen, and then we head outside to sit at the picnic table. I notice Tim is slapping his leg, a scowl on his face.

"You all right there, Mr. Rankin?" I put my napkin on my lap.

"I'm getting eaten alive out here. Christ."

I nod at the bug spray on the ledge of the window behind him. "Mosquitoes are starting to get bad. Help yourself to the spray."

He doesn't thank me, but he does grab the bottle and spray down his legs. I notice his movements are sluggish. Is he already drunk? He's still scowling when he turns back to his plate.

Frannie frowns as she sets her plate beside Wheeler's at the other end of the table. I'm sure she saw Tim's face. We all have. His bad mood is a dark cloud that hangs over the meal.

I do my best to ignore it, making polite conversation with Haines. The light begins to fade. Dinner is delicious if I do say so myself. But dessert is even better.

"God, that's good," Wheeler says, spooning the last of her ice cream into her mouth.

Preston makes a face. "Since when do you have such a sweet tooth?"

She looks at me. My stomach drops.

Time to spill the beans.

Honestly, it's kind of a relief. I've been waiting on tenterhooks for Wheeler to give me the go-ahead.

I clear my throat. "Funny you should mention that."

"Duke and I have some news." Wheeler drops her spoon and grabs my hand. It's the first—only—time her palm's felt clammy.

Frannie claps. "Oh my God! Are y'all engaged?"

"Mom! Jesus fuck, they've known each other for, like, a week." Preston shakes his head. "Now let her finish."

I wait for Tim to chastise his son for talking to his mother like that.

Instead, he looks blandly at me, his nose red from the tequila he's been swigging like it's his job.

"Preston, have a little respect, okay?" Wheeler says. "Mom's just excited."

"For what?" Preston tips back his empty glass, crunching loudly on the ice. "What's this big news?"

If he was sitting next to her, I can tell she'd give him a hard shove. Is he the type of guy who'd shove her back?

"I'm pregnant."

Dead silence. Frannie's eyes look blank in the growing darkness. Preston stares. Haines fights a smile.

Tim blinks. Blinks again. The fire crackles behind us.

Then, suddenly, Tim shatters the silence by banging his fist on the table and shouting, "Fuck! You gotta be fucking kidding me! What the hell are people going to say?"

There's something about the way he spits out the words, his tone suddenly harsh and venomous and loud, that almost makes me jump. I don't, because I'm not afraid.

But Wheeler is. She actually jumps, her shoulders up by her ears, body stiff, like she's bracing herself.

Oh no.

No, no, *no*. She's got nothing to be afraid of. Not when she's with me.

"Tim," Frannie says. "Please calm down. I'm sure that's an explanation—"

"For what? Her having a fucking kid with a fucking stranger?" Tim stands, staring me down. "Where do you get the balls to—"

"Love your daughter the way she deserves to be loved?" I stare right back. "That's how I was raised, Tim. I'd never, *ever* talk to her the way you just did. Same as I'll never talk to our kids that way. No one deserves that kind of disrespect."

"Dad." Even Preston sounds nervous now. "It'll be fine. I'm sure she's not keeping it—"

"I'm keeping it." Wheeler's voice shakes, but she still speaks. "Duke and I made that decision together."

Tim bangs his fist on the table again. "You wanna talk about disrespect? How do you think this is gonna look? You're a stranger—"

"He's no such thing." Wheeler squeezes my hand.

"Duke is my best friend."

Frannie's quietly wiping the tears from her cheeks. "Are y'all going to get married?"

"They'd better be!" Tim roars. "It's the only way our friends won't think our daughter's a total—"

"Do yourself a favor and don't finish that sentence." My voice is deadly calm. I feel all eyes at the table move to me. Glancing at Frannie, I see her eyes glimmer with shock. They're not used to Tim being put in his place.

Wheeler looks up at me. "Thank you."

"Again, I will not tolerate that kind of disrespect in our home," I continue, looking at Tim. His gaze simmers with barely contained rage.

"Dad, we haven't talked about getting married yet," Wheeler says carefully. "But we're in love. Duke loves me like no one ever has. He's a good friend—"

"And a shitty excuse for a man if he doesn't put a ring on your finger."

"That's our decision," Wheeler shoots back. "Baby or no baby, we'd be together. We'd be building a future—a life—together."

"Never wanted something more," I say.

"You." Tim jabs his finger at me, spit flying from his mouth. "You'd best do what's right here. I've got nothing to say to any of you until that happens."

Then he turns, pushing back the picnic bench so that everyone on that side of the table lurches forward.

"Dad, you're going to regret this tomorrow," Haines says.

"Fuck off," Tim replies.

Standing, I keep my voice even but loud when I say, "Sit down, Tim."

He pauses, then looks at me over his shoulder.

"I'm not asking," I continue. "Listen to what your daughter has to say to you. It's important. She loves you, and she wants to include you in this very happy moment in her life."

He looks at me. And looks. Jaw set. Nostrils flaring.

"You walk away now, you'll never be welcome in this house again. Which would be a shame, considering this is where we wanna raise your grandbaby."

Tim has the grace to look ever so slightly sheepish.

"Fine," he says at last and sits back down.

So do I, and I calmly reach down to grab my napkin off the ground. "Another thing. You ever speak to my girlfriend that way again, we're gonna have a problem. A big one."

Tim waves his hand and mutters something.

"Did you hear me?" I ask.

He gives me a nasty look. "Yes."

"Good." I put my hand on Wheeler's leg. "You were saying?"

Her eyes are full. For a second, I panic. But then she's putting her hand on my leg too. She's smiling—it's a small one, but it's still there—and it hits me that the tears in her eyes are happy ones.

Grateful ones.

Relieved ones.

Wheeler doesn't need a protector. She's strong enough to fend for herself.

But I'll always come to her defense anyway. I'm her man now, and it's just what I do.

It's what I'll do for the rest of my life.

"Thank you," she says.

"Don't need to thank me for making sure you get respect when respect is due, Blue."

"Blue?" Haines's lips twitch. "That's cute."

Everyone listens as Wheeler explains our decision to be together and to keep the baby. Frannie continues to cry, but Haines wraps her in a side hug and rubs her back. Preston keeps drinking, but really, who cares? He's a lost cause. We're never going to be close to him. Like father, like son.

To Tim's credit, he sits until Wheeler is done talking.

"Good for you," Haines says quietly. He raises his class. "Congrats, y'all. Duke, I gotta tell you, my sister— she's different since she's been with you. I mean that in a good way. She's truly come into her own. You let her be herself, and she's finally stepping into who she was always meant to be."

"Oh yeah?" Wheeler laughs, even as she dabs at her eyes with her napkin. "Who's that?"

"A badass, bighearted human who works hard and loves harder and isn't afraid to go after what she loves." He tilts his glass toward her. "You inspire me every day, Wheeler."

Frannie nods. "You inspire all of us, honey."

I wonder if she means Wheeler inspired her to leave a miserable man. Whatever the case, I couldn't agree more.

I give Wheeler a nudge. "You inspired me too. And now look. We're living the dream. Multiple dreams, all at once."

"You've made so many of my dreams come true, baby." Her voice is barely above a whisper. "Thank you."

I'm crying.

Wheeler is crying.

Tim appears to be blinking back tears. I'm honestly shocked that I may have finally gotten through to him.

Whatever the case, everyone gives Wheeler a hug as they're leaving a little while later.

Preston and Tim refrain from giving *me* hugs, but Preston does shake my hand.

"She seems happy," he says. Then he trots down the stairs.

Tim keeps his hands in his pockets. "Don't forget us back in Dallas."

"We won't," Wheeler replies.

It's not *congratulations!* or *I'm so happy for you*. But it is better than *fuck off*. And maybe, for now anyway, that's a win.

Wheeler and I watch her family drive away.

"I hope they don't get lost in the dark on their way back to the New House," she murmurs against my shoulder.

"I got Cash lookin' out for them."

"Of course you do." She lets out a breath and burrows farther into my side. "Thank *God* that's over. It went just as badly as I thought it would. But also…better somehow?"

Chuckling, I curl an arm around her shoulders. "The right people are gonna be happy for us. The wrong ones—"

"We ditch the wrong ones. Even if the wrong ones are—were—family."

I look down at her. "You really do know what you want."

"I do now." She hooks a finger into my shirt. "I want you, baby."

I let her have me, all night long.

CHAPTER 34
Pickle Tickle
Wheeler

I glance out the window at the knock on the door. My heart does a backflip when I see that it's Mom.

Peeling myself off the couch is no small feat, especially after the emotional roller coaster of the past twenty-four hours. I woke up feeling sore inside my rib cage, like I'd just run a marathon in cold weather.

But it was a good sore. Like the weight that was bearing down on my heart and lungs is no longer there, and my body's adjusting to the new lightness.

I push myself up to my feet and head for the door.

"Hey, Mom."

She smiles when she sees me. Her eyes are bloodshot, her face pale.

My stomach drops. She didn't sleep.

"Hey, honey. I'm sorry to just show up like this, but I—I had to talk to you in person. Do you have a minute?"

I motion her inside. "Of course I do. You want some coffee? Duke always has a pot going."

"I'd love some, thanks."

I pour her a mug, and we settle on the couch.

"Duke in the bathroom?" she asks.

I nod. "Man takes more showers than anyone I've ever met. Not like I mind."

"I imagine those cowboys get filthy."

"They do. They work hard. He was up cowboying at five."

"His work has paid off. This place is spectacular."

Smiling, I let my head fall back on the cushion. "I love it here."

"Have you thought about what it's going to be like?" I can tell Mom is choosing her words carefully. "Raising a baby on a cattle ranch? Probably gets lonely. There's a lot of distance between you and, well, everyone else."

"Might be, at least at first. But Duke's family is super close, literally and figuratively—"

"I've noticed." Now she's smiling. "I like that. A lot."

"And they all help each other out. It annoys him sometimes how far up his butt they are, but I think it shows they care." I grab her hand. "I've got a solid support system here, Mom."

She nods, then sets her mug on the coffee table. "I'll be honest, Wheeler. I was surprised when you said you were keeping the baby."

"Makes sense. I was surprised too when that slowly but surely became the right decision."

"And you're sure?"

The bathroom door opens, and Duke emerges. He's wearing a towel wrapped around his waist and absolutely nothing else.

God, he's handsome. His wet hair sticks up every

which way. His well-muscled torso still glistens—with water, steam, who cares, honestly?—and my eyes follow the happy trail of dark blond hair that arrows downward toward his groin.

I can't help but smile. "My mom's here."

"I can see that." He gives her a little wave. "Hey, Fran. Gimme a second to get dressed, all right?"

"Sure thing." Mom puts hand on her face.

"Aw." I pat her leg. "You're blushing."

"Duke is…really something else, Wheeler."

"I know. That's why I'm having a baby with him." I lower my voice. "He's thoughtful and emotionally intelligent and—"

"A friend." Mom blinks, her eyes filling. "The way he defended you last night…your father never went to bat for me like that. Ever. He's too self-involved."

Swallowing hard, I look down at my hands. "I'm sorry you're going through what you're going through, Mom. But I need you to know that I'm not following in your footsteps by committing to this man and having a baby."

"I know you're sorry, honey." She reaches over to tuck my hair behind my ear. "And I know you're on a different path than mine. Duke is wonderful, Wheeler. Heck." She scoffs. "I might be in love with him too!"

"I heard that!" Duke shouts. "And I'm very flattered, Fran, but unfortunately I'm taken."

"Lucky woman!" Mom shouts back, all smiles now. She turns to me. "I mean that, Wheeler. You're lucky, but so is he. You're lucky to have such good friends in each other. But I'm your mother, and I'm always going to worry about you. Now I know, though, that I don't need to worry about you being with someone for the wrong reasons. I can't let you make the same mistake I did, and as luck would have it, you're not."

"Aw, Mom. Thank you for saying that."

"I know you love it here, but please don't be a stranger, all right? I didn't sleep much last night because of…well, everything. But my excitement also kept me up." She takes my shoulders in her hands. "I'm going to be a freaking *grandma*, Wheeler!"

"Correction: you're going to be the best grandma *ever*." Duke saunters into the room as he pulls a clean T-shirt over his head. "From what Wheeler tells me, you're going to be a natural."

She's laughing and crying and, shit, so am I.

All this crying. At least it's happy tears now.

"Y'all be good to each other," Mom says hoarsely. "But I don't need to tell you that."

Duke plops onto the couch beside her. "You got it. Now tell me something, Fran."

"You name it."

"Ever seen the Colorado River by ATV before?"

Mom laughs. "I haven't, no."

Duke meets my eyes. "How about we go for a little ride? Give grandma-to-be here a lay of the land. Hopefully she'll be visiting a lot more often."

Mom's smile is bigger than I've seen it in years. "Only if you visit me in Dallas."

"You have my word." Duke holds out his hand.

She takes it. "Congratulations. And thank you for, well, being a cowboy. And for being you. But mostly for being a cowboy. We clearly need more of y'all in this world."

"Luckily for us, a cowgirl is on the way." Duke nods at my stomach.

I shake my head. "Cowboy."

"What do you think, Fran?"

Mom pretends to think for a minute. "It's a boy."

Clapping my hands, I laugh. "Told you, Duke!"

"Do y'all have names picked out?"

Duke looks at me. "Not yet."

"I have some ideas," I say.

He smiles. "I love them already."

Mom and I wait in the rocking chairs on the porch while Duke grabs an ATV from the equipment barn. It's a gorgeous day, warm and sunny, although I can tell it's going to get steamy this afternoon.

Mom puts her hand on mine on the armrest of my chair. We rock like that, both of us quiet, for several minutes. I watch fat, fuzzy-looking bees zoom across the yard, stopping to rest on the wildflowers that continue to bloom as summer rolls on. The trees rock with us in a refreshing breeze, bending lazily this way and that.

Mom closes her eyes. "I get why you love it here."

"I really do. I love Dallas too, though. Mollie and me—we're a little too fancy to stay here all the time."

Her lips curl into a grin. "A little bit country, a little bit city. You in a nutshell. Duke too, from what it sounds like."

"We're good for each other." I put a hand on my stomach. "I'm excited for what's ahead."

Mom opens her eyes and looks at me. "You're going to be a great mom, Wheeler."

"Aw, thank you." I wrap my fingers around hers. "I learned from a really good one."

"I know I wasn't perfect, but I hope you know I love you. More than you'll ever know. When I found out I was having a girl, I was so happy I burst into tears." She gives me a watery smile. "You're a dream come true."

A bubble of joy expands inside my chest, making it difficult to breathe. "I love you, Mom."

"I know." She squeezes my hand before glancing out at the yard. "There's your cowboy. Crazy to think you'll have two of them soon."

"Life is good."

Mom's smile grows, and for the first time, I see a glimmer of something like hope in her brown eyes. "It is. It really is, honey."

TWO MONTHS LATER

I feel a funny little flutter in my center just as Tallulah pronounces Sally and Wyatt husband and wife.

A hundred guests burst into applause. Cash shocks everyone by bursting into tears. He sobs at his place by Wyatt's side, all five Rivers boys lined up underneath the gorgeous arch of white and yellow flowers where the ceremony is taking place.

I watch, pulse pounding, as Duke pulls his brother in for a hug. His eyes are misty too.

These men may be rough-and-tumble cowboys, but they're total softies at heart.

I go still at another flutter, low in my belly.

Mollie, who's seated beside me in the front row, puts a hand on my shoulder. "Are you all right?"

I can barely hear her over the cacophony of joy that surrounds us.

"Mol, I think I just felt the baby move."

Her face splits into a smile. "Did it feel like bubbles? Or someone was using a paintbrush to tickle your stomach from the inside?"

"Yes."

"Friend, that is your sweet baby." Now Mollie's wrapping me in a hug. So many hugs happening. "Isn't it the coolest feeling?"

"It makes me want to laugh." I give her a squeeze before letting her go.

"So laugh. You deserve it after months of nonstop nausea."

I was one of the unlucky moms-to-be whose first-trimester symptoms lasted well into my second trimester. I'm *finally* feeling like myself again at nineteen and a half weeks.

Mollie, meanwhile, has popped in a big way. She's due in the fall, and her dress stretches over her adorable baby bump.

She's also hot all the time, especially now that we're in the thick of summer. Wyatt and Sally originally planned to get married on the ranch in the spring, but thanks to some delays in projects around the property, they had to push it back to August.

Luckily we got a rare, moderately warm evening after a big line of storms moved through earlier this morning. Still, Mollie and I are sweating bullets.

"Thank God they gave these out." Mollie nods at the straw fan she's currently whipping in front of her face. "I'm looking forward to getting in that air-conditioned tent."

The ceremony took place in one of the pastures by the New House. Wyatt and Sally's wedding planner set up a huge Sperry tent behind it for the reception, complete with farm tables for supper—Sally's request—and a spot for the cigar roller Wyatt hired to make cigars for the poker they'll be playing at special tables set up beside the bar.

The bride and groom are all smiles as they process back down the aisle. Sally looks absolutely radiant in a classic A-line gown and the custom Bellamy Brooks boots we designed for her. They're yellow, her favorite color, and stitched with her and Wyatt's initials.

The rest of the Rivers brothers process behind them. Duke stops to hold out his arm to me.

"Beautiful ceremony." I curl my hand into the crook of his elbow.

He tucks his arm against his side, holding me close. "Cash really fell apart there."

We start walking toward the tent. "Hey. He was in his feelings. To be honest, I am too. There's lots of love in the air tonight. Also...I think I felt the baby move."

Duke goes still, eyes flying wide. "You serious?"

"Hell yeah, I'm serious." I take his hand and put it on my stomach. "You're not going to be able to feel it from the outside for a while. But it felt like butterfly wings. Or a tickle."

One side of his mouth quirks up. "Wanna give me a tickle later?"

"Can you not be horny for five seconds?"

We may have had morning sex earlier. Twice. And I would've snuck in a quickie if we'd had time after lunch. But Sally invited me, Mollie, and Ava to get our hair and makeup done with her, so I was too busy drinking nonalcoholic sparkling cider to get, er, busy with my boyfriend.

"Absolutely not. That's a double negative, right?" Duke pretends to think on this for a second. "Whatever the case, I cannot not be horny. Not when you're around."

I give him a nudge, and we start walking again. "Nice boots, by the way."

Duke is wearing a pair of our City Boots. All the Rivers boys are. We had five matching pairs custom made in navy blue leather for today to match their navy blue suits. They topped it all off with brown Stetsons.

It's a good look for them.

Duke nods. "They're comfortable too. Already got asked by Doc Hamilton where he can get a pair."

"Way to mix work and pleasure."

"Aw, Blue. It's all pleasure these days."

The breath leaves my lungs when we step inside the tent. It's a summertime wonderland, the poles that hold up the tent covered in whimsical greenery and yellow flowers. Wooden chandeliers hang from the ceiling, coating everything in low, sexy light. A huge bar is set up on the opposite side of the tent, where a dance floor waits.

I wonder what our reception will look like. Mine and Duke's.

Not long ago, I would've banished that thought to the far corners of my brain. I didn't want to date this man, much less marry him.

Now, though?

Now, I like the idea of Duke making an honest

woman out of me. It doesn't have to happen anytime soon. But I'm pretty sure I've found what I've always been searching for in my life with Duke.

Now, I'm finally able to trust that sense of deep knowledge inside me—that I'm exactly where I should be, doing exactly what I should be doing. Because with that deep knowledge comes a deep sense of joy.

Moving farther into the tent, we're greeted by dozens of familiar faces. Ava and the girls are nibbling on the mini sliders that servers pass around on pretty china plates. Sawyer makes sure everyone's hands and mouths are clean before they go for the sweet little lemonade stand set up in another corner.

John B can't stop laughing, and Patsy is about as happy as I've ever seen her.

We're turning back toward the bar when I see the dartboards. They're hanging on a makeshift wall made of greenery nearby, and they're done in shades of white and yellow to match the rest of the wedding decor. I come to a halt, my heart beginning to pound.

"Duke."

"Yeah?"

"Did you—"

"Give Wyatt and Sally dartboards as a wedding gift?" He chuckles. "No, I got them a toaster. But I may have mentioned that darts would be a fun wedding day activity. You know, keep people busy during cocktail hour. Sally loved the idea, and of course Wyatt agreed because he can win money off people."

A bolt of excitement moves through me. "We haven't played since the night we met, have we?"

"Nope. We never did finish that game."

"Prepare to get your ass kicked."

Duke holds out an arm. "Only if you do the same. After you, Blue."

We grab a quick drink at the bar—club soda with lime for me, tequila on the rocks for him—and then we head for the dartboards.

The weight of the yellow-tipped darts is thrillingly familiar in my hand. I'm tired, and my feet have started to swell, but you wouldn't know it by the way I bounce on my feet and shake out my arms, bending my head side to side in preparation to dominate this game.

"All right, Rocky," Duke says with a laugh. "Time to get down to business. 501?"

I drop a pair of darts but keep one in my hand. "Like you even need to ask. Giddyup, cowboy."

He smiles at the line, clearly remembering when he said it to me that night at the Rattler.

The band starts playing. I hit a bull's-eye. Duke hits two.

"Do I get a pregnancy handicap?" I sip my club soda.

He presses a hard, quick kiss to my mouth, the brim of his cowboy hat tapping my forehead. "You get whatever you want, sweetheart."

My heart pops around in my chest. He tastes like tequila and smells like heaven, and I'm hit with the certainty that I've never been happier in my life.

This is it. This right here is what I've always wanted.

Family. Friends. Good music. Darts. Cowboys.

"How about this, then?" I tilt my chin to peck him on the lips. "I hit a bullseye, and you promise to marry me in a tent just like this."

A glimmer of surprise moves across his eyes. "You

wanna marry me?"

"One day, yeah."

"Just yeah?"

"*Fuck* yeah any better?"

"It is." He nods at our surroundings. "So you want a tent like this, huh?"

"Yup." I reach around to put my hands on his ass.

"Can it have dartboards in it too?"

"Yes."

He puts his hands on *my* ass, pressing me into his body so that our hips melt together. "And our people—can they come?"

"Absolutely."

"Can we serve Twizzlers? And grilled cheese? Not sure I could afford Milli Vanilli, but I could always try."

I laugh, joy pouring through me. "Maybe we could even ride off into the sunset in a U-Haul."

He laughs. "Now that, I'm gonna have to say no to." His smile softens. "You just let me know when, Blue. I been ready to make you mine for good since that first round of darts. Before Aspen. Before the baby. She just sped things up a little bit."

My pulse hiccups. "You still think it's a she."

"She's absolutely a she." His eyes search mine. "She's gonna make a beautiful flower girl, you know."

I blink back a rush of tears. "Of course she will. She's gonna look just as gorgeous in her boots and hat as her daddy does."

"Where we doin' the honeymoon?"

"Anywhere we want."

Duke leans in and kisses me again. This one is soft, ardent, full of feeling. My body lights up, and I'm not surprised when someone nearby—pretty sure it's Ryder—singsongs, "Duke and Wheeler, sitting in a tree, K-I-S-S-I-N-G. First comes boning, then comes baby, then comes making out in public places."

I laugh.

Duke smiles.

"Then comes happily ever after?" I ask him.

He nods. "If this ain't a happy ending, I don't know what is."

I win the game, although I have a sneaking suspicion Duke let me have the W because I'm sober and he also wants to marry me.

We sit with his brothers and their wives and girlfriends at a long farm table and share a delicious meal that's right out of Patsy's kitchen: steak, sweet potatoes, and green beans sautéed in a creamy sauce that's just the right amount of spicy.

When I feel another flutter, I grab Duke's hand and put it over my belly. "Your flower girl likes those green beans."

He blinks, hard, a cute little smile on his face. "Think she'll like to dance too?"

"I think she will, yeah."

He motions to the dance floor. "Let's get to it, then."

The band is excellent, their cheery renditions of wedding classics like "September" and "Shout" making it impossible *not* to dance. Sawyer, Ava, Junie, and Ella join us out there, and my heart twists at how adorable Sawyer looks when he puts Junie on his hip and twirls her around the dance floor.

Duke is all smiles as we move, keeping his eyes on the girls.

"What are you thinking?" I ask.

He turns to look at me. "That you're beautiful. That our daughter will be beautiful." He nods at the happy little family beside us. "One day, I'll get to dance with her like that."

"I can't wait," I say. "Soon."

He pulls me close. "Never soon enough when it comes to you."

We dance and we laugh, and together with the people we love the most, we send off Wyatt and Sally with sparklers and lots of hollering.

When the commotion dies down, Duke grabs my hand. "Off to our next adventure?"

Grinning, I take it. "If by 'adventure,' you mean going home to sleep for twelve hours, I'm in."

"Sounds like a mighty fine adventure to me."

THE END

EPILOGUE
Brand-New
Duke

"Good Lord, can everyone just slow the fuck down?" I motion to the truck that speeds through the intersection. "He's gonna kill somebody."

Wheeler chuckles from the back seat of my new king cab Silverado. It's not a yacht in the Caribbean, but somehow it's a million times better. Maybe because the truck is getting us through the kids' very first ride.

"All right, grandpa. Most people don't drive ten under the speed limit."

"Well, they should. I'm hauling precious cargo today." I glance in the rearview mirror, and my heart just about bursts.

Wheeler sits in the center of the back bench between two car seats. A blue ribbon is tied to the top handle of one car seat, and a pink ribbon is tied to the other.

While identical twins don't run in families, apparently fraternal twins do. Turns out Wheeler's grandmother was a twin, and so was *her* grandmother.

No one was more shocked than me when we discovered a second heartbeat at our twenty-week anatomy scan. It's not common to miss twins at the first ultrasound, but it does happen.

It happened to us. And now here we are, bringing home a girl *and* a boy.

"How does it feel to be right but also wrong? About us having a girl?" Wheeler meets my eyes in the mirror. Hers are tired but happy.

Exactly how I feel after a stay in the hospital that was exciting but not exactly restful.

"Feels pretty dang great." I smile. "How are you feeling, Mama?"

She chuckles quietly. "Still not over the fact that we have not one but *two* babies now. How lucky are we?"

"The luckiest. And also the most tired."

"No kidding. Thank God we've got lots of helping hands."

"Is there such a thing as too many helping hands? Because I think we might have that problem."

"Definitely not a problem when you've got two newborns. Kudos to your mom for doing this with three other kids in the house."

My heart twists. I really wish Mom and Dad were here. Not only would they love up on our babies, but I'm sure they would have some good advice for us. We've got plenty of help lined up, but it'd still be nice to get some wisdom on raising twins from people who've done it.

"She and Dad were rock stars, no question."

Wheeler's voice is soft when she replies, "You're a rock star too, you know. Have been from the moment we met."

My throat swells. I adjust my hand on the steering wheel, resisting the urge to honk at a guy who hits the gas through a yellow light instead of stopping. "I mean, I did impregnate you not once but twice in one night."

This time, she full out laughs. "That's not how it works."

"Still gotta give my sperm some credit."

"It did its job."

On cue, our daughter lets out a wail.

"Aw, honey, we'll be home soon," I say, looking up into the rearview mirror again.

Wheeler has her hands inside the baby's car seat, a sated smile on her face. "You're cute when you coo."

"You talking to me?"

"Pretty sure our babies can't coo yet."

"Isn't 'coo' kind of a weird word?"

"When you say it this much, yes." Wheeler's laughing, and I'm hit by a surge of deep, almost painful gratitude.

This woman brought two babies earthside earlier this week after a difficult pregnancy. We've been through some shit—how unexpected this all was, her family's disapproval—but we've still managed to laugh together through it all.

Wheeler was right. We really are friends. Best friends. And turns out doing life with your best friend by your side provides exactly the kind of freedom I've been looking for. This is life on my terms. *Our* terms. I'm able to be who I am and do what feels right because Wheeler and I value the same things.

Our relationship isn't perfect. We had a messy start. And I imagine life's about to get messy in a whole new way with two babies in the house. We've talked plenty about where we're going to take the kids as they get older—the beach, Aspen, California—but it's going to be a while before we travel again.

It will happen, though. And once we get over the hump of the babies being too tiny or difficult to go places, we're going to have travel buddies for the rest of our lives.

I'm going to have Wheeler as the best travel buddy ever too. The connection we have is real and honest, and that makes me think we can find our way through any mess as long as we have each other.

We decided that we wanted to get settled at the cottage before everyone came over to see the babies, so I'm not surprised to see that the driveway is empty when I pull up a few minutes later.

I am surprised, however, to see a pair of signs shaped like storks in our front yard. One is blue and printed with our son's name. The other is pink and printed with our daughter's. A bunch of balloons in pink and blue are tied to the porch, and there's a big bow taped to our front door.

"Aw," Wheeler says thickly. "How cute is that? Had to be Mollie, right?"

I groan, even as my eyes smart. "And Cash. And Sally and Wyatt, come to think of it. And you gotta know Sawyer and Ava and the girls had a hand in the balloons and bow."

"I love it."

"I love you." I cut the ignition. "Ready to start life as a family of four?"

In the mirror, I see Wheeler nod, a huge smile splitting her face. "I'm ready."

Jumping out of the truck, I'm careful to close the door quietly behind me. I've been practicing taking the car seats in and out of the truck for weeks now, just in case Wheeler went into labor early, so I make quick work of lifting our son's car seat out of the back. I hold out my hand to Wheeler, and she gingerly climbs out of the truck.

"Almost time for another dose of ibuprofen." I give her hand a squeeze.

"You're sexy when you stay on top of my meds."

"But sexier when I'm on top of you, right?"

She shakes her head, but she's still smiling. "I *just* had your babies. Two of them. Can you give me a minute to recover?"

"Take all the time you need, Blue. Just know I think you're beautiful."

Wheeler looks up and holds my gaze. In the thin winter light, her eyes shimmer with something I can only describe as joy. "Even when I look like, well, this?" She motions to her disheveled hair and rumpled pajamas.

Leaning in, I press a tender kiss to her mouth. "Especially when you look like this. You're a miracle worker. Literally. Now let's get you comfortable inside, yeah?"

I carry both car seats into the house. A scent hits me—something pretty, fresh. Wheeler is ahead of me, and she draws up short with a gasp.

My stomach plunges into a bucket of ice. "You okay?"

"Duke." She points to the family room. "Look."

Turning my head, I see several bouquets of flowers are set out on the mantel, the coffee table, and the console behind the sofa. Each bouquet is topped with a card.

I don't need to open those cards to know who sent the flowers. It was everyone in Hartsville.

We get the babies settled in their bassinets in the family room, and then I help Wheeler go to the bathroom. It's currently a two-person job. I've gotten pretty damn good at making the "padsicles" Wheeler uses to help with pain and swelling.

She says she's hungry, so after I get her settled on the couch, I head to the kitchen and open the fridge.

I scoff, my throat closing in.

"What?" Wheeler calls from the family room. "Everything okay in there?"

"Yep. Just—we got a fully stocked fridge." I mean that quite literally. There's not an inch to spare inside the fridge or freezer; they're packed so tightly with all manner of containers and bottles of wine and stacks of yogurt cups that I wonder if I'm going to be able to close the doors.

I grab the Post-it stuck to a foil-covered casserole dish on the refrigerator's top shelf. *Hi Mom & Dad! Feeding two babies is going to make y'all hungry. Here's my riff on the grilled cheese y'all love so much! XO, Patsy.*

A drawing of a unicorn is stuck to a Tupperware dome that appears to contain a cake. I smile, sniffling, when I imagine Ella and Junie helping their parents frost the cake in Sawyer's kitchen.

"Your family moves fast," Wheeler says. "I love them."

Closing the fridge, I rest my forearm on the door and try to gather myself.

Actually, fuck that.

I let myself cry. It feels good.

Being loved this way, cared for this way, feels really fucking good.

Wheeler and I dig into some enchiladas Wyatt made, eating on the couch while staring at our sleeping babies, because—ugh, I truly cannot get enough of them.

"He looks like you," I say.

Wheeler nods. "She looks like you."

"Funny how that works."

We both look up at the knock on the door.

"Don't hate me," I blurt.

Wheeler frowns. "Why would I hate you?"

"I know we said no visitors today, but…"

She sucks in a breath through her nose. "Duke."

"I promise you'll like this one."

Her lips twitch. "Okay."

"That was easy." I rise from the couch with a groan.

She lifts a shoulder. "I trust you."

My chest puffs out a little, the way it always does when Wheeler tells me that. Her trust isn't easy to earn, and I know what a big deal it is that she's given it to me.

I've barely opened the front door when I'm pulled into a hug.

"You look like hell," Haines says in my ear. "I'm so happy for you!"

Laughing, I reply, "Nice to see you too, brother."

"Oh."

"What?" I pull back to look him in the eye. "Do you not like—"

"I love when you call me that. Don't be silly. I guess I'm still mourning the fact that it'll always be 'brother' but never 'boyfriend.'"

"Haines Michael Rankin."

Glancing over my shoulder, I smile when I see Wheeler standing in the hall, arms crossed over her chest.

"Are you trying to steal my children's father away from me?"

"Yes." Haines moves around me to hug his sister. "You're officially a mom! Can you believe it?"

"No." Wheeler's laughing and crying all at once, and suddenly, so are Haines and I.

We bring him into the family room.

"Haines, allow us to introduce Margaret Rose"—Wheeler gestures to our daughter—"and Robert Haines Rivers."

Her brother's eyes go wide, his hand landing on his chest with a thud. "Are you serious?"

"Yes, Haines, we seriously named our baby after one of the best, most stand-up men we know." I clap him on the shoulder. "Thank you for being so good to us. We love you."

Haines wipes his eyes. "Let's hope little Robbie here takes after me in the looks department too."

Wheeler gently elbows him. "He already does."

Ryder is the next to visit. He comes over the next morning, bearing gifts of lattes from the Caffeinated Cowgirl downtown and a pair of kids' cowboy hats.

"For later, obviously," he says, blinking away the moisture in his eyes. "When they get older and follow in our family's footsteps. We're always looking for more cowgirls and cowboys."

Too choked up to reply, I just give my twin a tight hug.

"Can't breathe," he gasps.

"I love you," I grunt.

I startle at the sound of a car door being slammed. Glancing across the room, I see a familiar truck parked in front of the house.

"Colt Wallace?" I look at Ryder. "Did you—"

"Invite him?" A pink flush works its way up Ryder's neck. "I didn't. No clue why he's here."

I follow Ryder out to the front porch, where Colt is waiting. He has one hand on his hip. In the other, he holds up a small, rectangular object.

My stomach plummets. I'd recognize that pocketknife anywhere. The slight arc of the handle, the dark grain of the wood. Why does Colt have Dad's—Ryder's—knife? And why does he look like he wants to kill someone?

I turn to look at Ryder, hoping for answers, but he's staring straight ahead, his face a mask of…

I don't know what. Fear? Defiance? For the first time ever, I can't read my brother's expression.

"What are you doing here?" Ryder asks.

Squinting against the morning sun, Colt spits out, "Care to tell me why I found your pocketknife on my sister's nightstand this mornin'?"

BONUS EPILOGUE
Sun & Sand
Wheeler

FIVE YEARS LATER

"Mommy! Mommy mommy mommy!"

Tucking my feet into my flip-flops, I grin at my daughter's high-pitched call. "Yes, lovie?"

"Come see!" That's Robbie. I can hear the smile in his voice. "We look *cuuuuute*."

"As a button!" Maggie cries.

"Two cute little buttons," Robbie singsongs. "Ready for the beach!"

Maggie giggles. "I love the beach. There's dolphins there."

"And sharks!" Robbie is *obsessed* with great whites thanks to *Finding Nemo*, his current favorite movie.

"Maybe I like the pool better." Maggie sounds slightly less enthused than her twin brother about the prospect of encountering wildlife at the beach. "We can play in the pool too, Robbie, right?"

"Of course we can! We're on vacation!"

I turn my head and meet eyes with Duke, who's

brushing his teeth in the sleek hotel bathroom. He grins, his eyes crinkling at the edges.

"We've created two little monsters," he half-whispers around a mouthful of toothpaste.

My grin broadens into a smile. "That's kind of inevitable when you get a passport at three weeks old."

"Don't regret it for a minute." He turns on the sink and ducks down to cup his hand underneath the faucet. My pulse skips a beat at the way his shirt draws taut against his shoulder blades. The back of his hair sticks up every which way. We may have snuck in a little quickie this morning before the kids were up, and it ended up being a bit more, er, enthusiastic than I think either of us anticipated.

Not to brag, but we've kind of mastered the art of hotel sex. We've had *lots* of practice since the kids were born five years ago. We traveled a ton when the twins were really little—Duke wasn't joking about the kids getting passports as soon as they were earthside—right up until they hit the terrible twos, when we hit pause for a minute. But for the first year or so of their lives, we put them in their carriers and made a point to take them on the road with us as much as possible. We hit up Montreal in the summer, Florida in the winter, with stops in Mexico and Grand Teton National Park in between, where Duke and I got married when the twins were just shy of six months old.

Once they turned three and got a little better about sitting still in a car or on a plane, we really went for it. Over the past two years, we've been across the world: Paris, Prague, Japan.

Has it been easy? Not by a long shot. But it's always

(well, usually!) worth it. The kids know the gig by now, and they love experiencing new places with us.

Gathering my hair in a clip, I reply to my husband, "I have no regrets either."

Then I hustle through the doorway into the adjoining hotel room, gasping in the most exaggerated way possible when I "stumble" upon my children. They're busy admiring themselves in the full-length mirror inside the closet.

"Y'all really are the cutest." I mean that. My heart swells taking in their matching little swimsuits and sun hats. They even went so far as to smear sunscreen on each other's faces, zinc whitening their noses and cheeks.

We've only been in California for two days now, but already freckles are popping out on Robbie's cheeks, and Maggie's strawberry-blond hair looks lighter.

She jumps up and down, making the back of her bathing suit ride up. "Can we go to the pool now, Mom? Please? I pooped and everything."

"She did." Robbie nods solemnly. "Right after I did. That's the rule, right? You have to poop and put on your swimsuit before you go in the pool."

Laughing, I bend down to help Maggie with her wedgie, but she wiggles out of my touch. "Don't fix it, Mommy. I like it like that."

"With your cheekies hanging out?" Duke groans from somewhere behind me, his footfalls quiet on the carpet. "Lord save us."

Maggie shimmies her bottom, making the ruffles there dance. "I like my cheekies."

"They are the most delicious cheekies ever," I reply,

giving her bathing suit a quick tug. "You'd better put them away before I eat them for lunch!"

She lets out a peal of laughter. "Don't eat my cheekies, Mommy, please!"

"I'll do my best to refrain."

Duke puts his hand on the small of my back after I straighten. "Beach bag is packed. Goggles—"

"You packed my *Bluey* ones, right, Dad?" Robbie asks.

Duke's face splits into a smile. "Yes, Robbie, I packed your *Bluey* ones, and the *Paw Patrol* ones, and the ones with the sprinkles on them, and—"

"The Ariel ones?" Maggie pipes up.

"Those, I think I forgot."

"No, Daddy, no!"

Chuckling, he bends down to swoop her up into his arms. "Of course I remembered your Ariel goggles. They were the first thing I packed."

"You're good," I say.

He turns that smile on me. "I know."

The kids lead the way down the hotel's long hallway to the pool deck. We're in San Diego for the first leg of a two-week trip to California that's part business, part pleasure. Bellamy Brooks has grown by leaps and bounds, and we're stopping at stores and suppliers up and down the West Coast for meetings and trunk shows galore. We're also making stops at places we know the kids will love: San Diego for the sun and sand, Santa Barbara for the zoo, Big Sur for the whimsical vibes.

Is it going to be manic? Yes. Will it also be a ton of fun? Absolutely.

Case in point: the kids literally scream with delight

when we head outside to the hotel's enormous pool, which glitters beneath a wide-open sky. The sun is warm on my chest and shoulders, while the breeze is just cool enough to keep the temperature pleasant. There's not a whiff of humidity.

"Can we set up a third Bellamy Brooks headquarters here?" Duke grunts as he sets down the beach bag that weighs about as much as our two children combined. "What was the temperature back in Hartsville yesterday? A hundred and eight, I think Cash said?"

"A hundred and nine, actually. Mollie told me her shoes were literally melting onto the pavement downtown."

Duke turns his head to flash me a wide, white smile. "Not sad we're missing that."

"Not a bit." My heart squeezes at his handsomeness. His *joy*. "I do miss our people, though."

"They'll be there when we get back."

My entire being lights up when Duke straightens and pulls off his shirt. My husband still cowboys part time on the ranch back home, so he's as thick and strong as ever. The server passing by does a double take, both of us devouring Duke's sculpted arms, wide chest, and narrow waist.

"He-hi. Hello." The server's voice cracks. "Would you be interested in any food or beverages?"

"Piña coladas!" Robbie shouts as he helps Maggie press her goggles to her face. "Please, can we have one? Please, Dad?"

Maggie throws up her arms. "With extra cherries?"

Laughing, Duke nods. "Sure. Two virgin piña coladas with extra cherries, and two regular piña coladas with extra rum." He looks at me and shrugs. "It's five o'clock back home."

I give him a playful shrug. "It's actually ten a.m. in Texas."

"Exactly." He grabs my wrist and pulls me in for a peck on the lips. "In ranch time, that's basically five o'clock."

"If you say so."

We head into the pool with the kids. Thankfully, it's heated—we've learned the hard way to always make sure the hotel we're staying at heats their pool. At first, I was a little annoyed that our kids were such water bugs, because it meant I always had to get into the pool too.

Now, I don't mind it one bit. Somewhere along the way—probably in high school—I stopped going in the water, whether it was the ocean, a lake, or a pool. I was just too lazy, or maybe too self-conscious, to jump in, so I'd just sit beside said body of water and scroll on my phone. But having kids forced me to get back in the water, literally and figuratively, and it made me remember just how *fun* it is.

Setting our piña coladas on the lip of the pool, Duke, Robbie, Maggie, and I start with a game of Marco Polo. The kids howl with laughter when Duke runs into the steps with his eyes closed, pretending to stub his toe.

"Can we do a cannonball competition?" Maggie asks.

I smile. "Only if I win."

"Bet you I'll win," she replies, then takes off toward the ladder.

Maggie does her cannonball first, followed by Robbie and Duke. When it's my turn, I take a running leap into the pool—much to the chagrin of the lifeguard—laughter bubbling up my sides as I pull my knees into my chest and land in the water with a satisfying splash.

"Mommy!" Robbie screams when I come up for air. "You win! That splash was *epic*."

I laugh harder. "Since when do you know what *epic* means?"

"Since he realized how epically hot his mom is." Duke loops an arm around my waist.

I lean in to give his neck a quick bite. "That's not weird at all."

"It's just facts, Blue."

My heart flutters. The nickname still hasn't gotten old after all these years.

"You're pretty hot too." This time, I'm the one kissing him.

"Ew, can you guys stop kissing so we can go to the beach now?" Maggie asks.

Robbie has a disgusted look on his sweet little face. "You guys kiss a *lot*."

Duke slips his tongue inside my mouth. "Yup. And that ain't changing, so you'd best get used to it."

We grab some towels and head out to the wide, flat beach, careful to avoid a volleyball game in progress on one of the courts in the sand. I gather seashells with Robbie. Duke and Maggie race to the water. Watching them laugh together has me feeling short of breath.

Could this day be any more perfect?

Could this life be any more perfect for us?

We dip our toes in the ocean—"too cold!" according to Robbie—then take a walk to look for dolphins and/or sharks. We work up an appetite playing volleyball when we're invited onto a court, and then we demolish lunch by the pool.

I don't know if it's because of the sun, the time change, or all the activity happening, but the kids end up conking out in the room later that afternoon. While they nap, Duke and I run through a checklist for an upcoming trunk show, and then we shower—together, because why the hell not?—before waking up the kids and heading into town.

They're eager little explorers, ducking into shops and nibbling on appetizers we order as we progress from one cute restaurant to the next. They get into a spat over a stuffed whale at a store, and we have to separate them, but the whale is quickly forgotten when we encounter a frozen custard shop.

Scooping my peanut-butter-and-chocolate custard into my mouth, I nudge Duke with my shoulder. "Did you ever think you'd be having a blast doing such wholesome things?"

He smirks. "Not everything we've done today has been wholesome."

"So, it's been the perfect day, then."

He takes a big bite of his cheesecake custard. Ever since he had that Blizzard at my place ages ago, it's become his favorite flavor.

"Every day with you is the perfect day." He squints, watching the kids devour their treats on a nearby bench. "But yeah, today's been pretty epic, as Robbie would say."

"He is so dang cute."

"Just like me. You happy, Mama?"

"The happiest. And no, I still refuse to call you Daddy."

He chuckles. "We'll see what you're saying later tonight when I got you—"

"Are you talking about kissing Mommy again?" Robbie pulls a face. "Gross."

I grin at my husband. "Not gross at all."

My body warms when he ducks his head and kisses me for the five thousandth time today.

"We're doing it, Blue. This is a dream, yeah? *The* dream."

I nod. "Dreams do come true."

"Cheeseball."

"Yep. And I'm not sorry about it."

His grin makes my stomach dip. "Good. I'm not either."

READ ON TO GET A SNEAK PEEK AT THE FIRST BOOK IN THE LUCKY RIVER RANCH SERIES, *CASH*

CHAPTER 1
Kiss My Ass, Cowboy
Mollie

SEPTEMBER

I'm deep in cowboy country, but I still jam on the brakes when I see an actual cowboy park his actual horse outside an actual saloon.

Have I gone back in time? Or is the whole scene a mirage? My dashboard does say it's 109 degrees outside.

The cloud of dust that's followed me since Belton billows around my SUV, temporarily obscuring the view of a building marked *The Rattler*.

The Hill Country dust clears. Yep, that's definitely a horse. And that's definitely a guy in slim-cut jeans and a cowboy hat sliding off the saddle with an ease that makes my breath catch.

Mom's words echo inside my head: *Hartsville is a one-horse town.* I didn't know she meant that literally.

I feel a whisper of recognition as I take in the building's facade behind the cowboy and his horse. It's two stories, brick, with windows whose uneven panes glint in the hazy afternoon light. A faded green-and-black-striped awning bears the image of a white rattlesnake, its forked tongue protruding from between its fangs.

I was six years old the last time I was in this tiny town, smack-dab in the middle of nowhere. Why would I remember a bar of all places?

"Mollie? Did I lose you?"

My stomach seizes, the sound of Wheeler's voice on the phone yanking me back inside the Range Rover. Without looking, I immediately hit the gas, then send up a silent prayer of thanks that Main Street is deserted. No one to hit, thank God.

Well, except for the cowboy and his horse, who I glimpse in my rearview mirror. I'm less than two hundred miles southwest of Dallas, but I might as well be on another planet for how different this place feels.

I reach for the vent beside the steering wheel and aim a blast of AC at my face. "Sorry, I'm here. I just got to Hartsville and…I think I may have just had an *Outlander* moment? But a Western-themed one, with a saloon and a cowboy."

My best friend and business partner's raspy laugh pours through the speakers. "Bring cowboy Jamie back to Dallas. Tell him city life is better."

"No shit." I peer out my windshield as my GPS tells me I'm approaching my destination. "Mom wasn't joking when she said there was nothing out here."

"Get your money and get the hell out of Dodge. Call me when you're done, okay? I'm thinking of you."

I smile, even as my stomach seizes again. "Thanks, friend. I can't wait for the pop-up."

"Same. I'm so curious to see how it goes."

One of Dallas's better-known boutiques is hosting a

pop-up shop for our cowboy boot company this week. The boutique's clientele is fashion-forward and well-heeled, so we'll hopefully make a decent number of sales. Lord knows we could use the revenue.

Hanging up, I slow down in front of the last building on the left before Main Street continues down a desolate stretch of nothingness ahead. The chalk-colored dirt, dotted sparsely with trees, cacti, and brush, wavers in the midafternoon heat.

A brass placard beside the building's door reads *Goody Gershwin, Attorney at Law, Est. 1993*.

"You have arrived at your destination," my GPS informs me.

I pull into an angled parking spot beside an enormous candy-apple-red pickup truck. It also appears to be from 1993, its windows rolled down to reveal a front bench seat upholstered in faded gray fabric. A box set of Brooks & Dunn's greatest hits sits on the passenger side of the bench.

It's a box set of *cassette tapes.*

Maybe I really have gone back in time.

The heat hits me like a slap to the face the second I hop out of my car. It radiates off the blacktop and singes my bare legs.

At the same time, the sun bears down on my head and shoulders from above. It's like being pressed inside a griddle.

Looping my bag over my shoulder, I wonder why the hell anyone would live out here. What did Dad see in this place?

I can't believe I'm actually here. I can't believe he's actually gone.

Most of all, I can't believe I lost the chance to ever make things right between us.

Grief, mixed with a hefty dose of anger, sits on my chest like an elephant.

A literal bell jangles above the door as I enter the building. It's blessedly cool inside the office. The familiar scent of brewing coffee makes me feel slightly less discombobulated.

A young man with round glasses smiles up at me from a nearby desk. "You must be Mollie Luck. Welcome! I'm Zach, Goody's paralegal." He rounds the desk and holds out his hand. "Can I get you anything? Water? Coffee? I hope the drive wasn't too bad."

I take his hand. "Three hours. Not terrible. Nice to meet you, Zach. And I'm fine, thanks."

He eyes my metallic-pink boots. "Those are *spectacular*."

"Aw, thank you. They're part of my boot company's most recent collection."

"You own a boot company?" A woman with short, dark hair in a light-colored linen suit emerges from a door to my left. She appears to be wearing a bolo—black, silver buckle—without a trace of irony. "How amazing!"

"They're manufactured right here in Texas."

The woman's eyes crinkle as she smiles at me. "Even better. I'm Goody Gershwin. Nice to finally meet you, Mollie. Your dad talked about you often. He was so proud of you."

My eyes burn, and my heart twists. Was Dad proud of me? He never showed it. Definitely never said it. But I'd like to think he'd be a little proud of how I turned out at least.

I paste on a smile. "Nice to meet you too."

"I'm so sorry for your loss. The community here has taken Garrett's death hard, but I can only imagine how tough it's been for y'all."

A piercing ache shoots through my heart and settles in the back of my throat. "The community" must've been a lot closer to Dad than I was. Then again, no one except Mom, Mom's parents, Wheeler, and I showed up to his funeral in Dallas three months ago, so who knows?

"I appreciate that."

"Well, we're glad you're here." Goody drops my hand. "Today should be relatively straightforward. As the executor of your father's will, I'll walk you through his estate and the distribution of his assets, along with his wishes for—"

Goody looks up at the jingle of the bell behind me. The creases at the edges of her eyes deepen.

"Hello, Cash! Always a pleasure seeing you."

Cash. Why is that name familiar?

"Ma'am. Good afternoon."

Something about the deep voice—its scraped-bare sound maybe, or the thick-as-molasses accent—has me glancing over my shoulder.

My heart takes a tumble at the *very* handsome man standing just inside the door. He looks to be in his late twenties, maybe early thirties. Tall—six three, I'd guess—with the kind of build you see on quarterbacks: broad shoulders, thick arms, long legs with thighs that strain against his fitted jeans. Wranglers, if I had to guess.

He's holding a cowboy hat to his chest, like he just swept it off his mass of messy brown hair, which curls out at the ends. Veins crisscross the back of his hand. He's sporting a scruffy beard that's longer along his top lip—I don't normally find mustaches attractive, but somehow, it's downright hot on this guy—and a white-and-blue-striped button-up that complements his cobalt eyes.

Eyes that are so blue, in fact, they seem to glow against his deeply tanned face.

Those eyes lock on mine. My pulse blares inside my ears. One beat. Two.

The intensity of the extended eye contact, the ballsiness of it, makes my stomach drop. His gaze flickers. Why do I get the feeling he's annoyed? Angry even?

The memory hits me: a pair of gangly blue-eyed boys in the bed of a pickup truck. One of them was punching another in the head, the blows increasing in frequency until a voice shouted at them from the cab to quit it.

The Rivers boys.

Despite the obvious prevalence of bodily injury in their family, I was so jealous of those kids. As an only child, all I wanted was a house full of siblings, and here were the Riverses with oodles of them. I distinctly remember seeing Mrs. Rivers in the passenger seat, her hand on her pregnant belly.

Their family owns the ranch next to Dad's property. I remember seeing the boys at the tractor supply store here in town and at the rodeo out in Lubbock once. Not often enough to be friends—their mom homeschooled them on their ranch, so they weren't around a lot—but often enough to know who they were.

Unable to withstand Cash's gaze another second, I look down at his boots. They're square-toed, dark brown. The leather is creased with age but obviously well cared for, the color gleaming from a recent coat of conditioner.

The whisper of vague recognition I felt earlier returns.

Thanks to my job, I know cowboy boots better than anyone. This is a pair of Lucchese: expertly made, expensive, and classic. They're the kind of cowboy boots you pass down from generation to generation.

Dad wore Lucchese. I don't know how I remember this, but the certainty of it sits in my gut like a brick.

"Mollie, allow me to introduce Cash Rivers." Goody extends her arm. "He's been the foreman at your family's ranch for, goodness, has it been—"

"Twelve years."

Cash's clipped reply makes me think he really is annoyed. With me? But why? And he's working on our property now? What happened to his family's ranch? I'm confused.

That does explain why he'd be at the reading of Dad's will, though. As the foreman, maybe he'll be giving me the literal lay of the land?

Not like it matters. The second Lucky Ranch is in my name, I'm putting it up for sale. I have absolutely no interest in running a Hill Country cattle ranch. I've always been more of an indoor girl, and my whole life is in Dallas anyway—my friends, my family. Bellamy Brooks, the cowboy boot company I started with Wheeler, is also based in the area. Business is finally taking off, and the inheritance I'm about to get will definitely bring us to the next level.

About the Author

Jessica Peterson writes romance with heat, humor, and heart. Heroes with hot accents are her specialty. When she's not writing, she can be found bellying up to a bar in the south's best restaurants with her husband, Ben, reading books with her adorable daughters, Gracie and Madeline, or snuggling up with her 70-pound lap dog, Martha.

A Carolina girl at heart, she fantasizes about splitting her time between Charleston and Asheville, but currently lives in Charlotte, NC.